THE WORLD'S CLASSICS

THE MIRROR OF THE SEA
and
A PERSONAL RECORD

JOSEPH CONRAD was born Józef Teodor Konrad Korzeniowski in the Russian part of Poland in 1857. His parents were punished by the Russians for their Polish patriotic activities and both died while Conrad was still a child. In 1874 he left Poland for France and in 1878 began a career with the British merchant navy. He spent nearly twenty years as a sailor and did not begin writing novels until he was approaching forty. He became a British citizen in 1886 and settled permanently in England after his marriage to Jessie George in 1896.

Conrad is a writer of extreme subtlety and sophistication; works such as *Heart of Darkness*, *Lord Jim*, and *Nostromo* display technical complexities which have established Conrad as one of the first English 'Modernists'. He is also noted for the unprecedented vividness with which he communicates a pessimist's view of man's personal and social destiny in such works as *The Secret Agent*, *Under Western Eyes*, and *Victory*. Despite the immediate critical recognition that they received in his lifetime Conrad's major novels did not sell, and he lived in relative poverty until the commercial success of *Chance* (1914) secured for him a wider public and an assured income. In 1923 he visited America, with great acclaim, and he was offered a knighthood (which he declined) shortly before his death in 1924. Since then his reputation has steadily grown and he is now seen as a writer who revolutionized the English novel and was arguably the most important single innovator of the twentieth century.

ZDZISŁAW NAJDER was active as a literary critic and editor in Poland until he became a political *émigré* in 1981. He was Director of the Polish Service of Radio Free Europe 1982-7, and has taught at several universities in the United States, including Columbia, Stanford, Yale, and Michigan.

THE WORLD'S CLASSICS

JOSEPH CONRAD

The Mirror of the Sea
and
A Personal Record

Edited with an Introduction by
ZDZISŁAW NAJDER

Oxford   New York
OXFORD UNIVERSITY PRESS

Oxford University Press, Walton Street, Oxford OX2 6DP

Oxford New York Toronto
Delhi Bombay Calcutta Madras Karachi
Petaling Jaya Singapore Hong Kong Tokyo
Nairobi Dar es Salaam Cape Town
Melbourne Auckland

and associated companies in
Berlin Ibadan

Oxford is a trade mark of Oxford University Press

Introduction, Note on the Text, and Explanatory Notes © Zdzisław Najder 1988

Select Bibliography, Chronology (revised by Zdzisław Najder) © John Batchelor 1983

First published as a World's Classics paperback 1988
Reprinted 1989

British Library Cataloguing in Publication Data
Conrad, Joseph, 1857–1924
The mirror of the sea; and, A personal
record.—(The World's classics)
1. Fiction in English. Conrad, Joseph,
1857–1924. Biographies
I. Title II. Najder, Zdzisław III. Conrad,
Joseph, 1857–1924. [Some reminiscences]. A
personal record
823'.912
ISBN 0-19-281729-9

Library of Congress Cataloging in Publication Data
Conrad, Joseph, 1857–1924.
The mirror of the sea; and, A personal record / Joseph Conrad;
edited with an introduction by Zdzisław Najder.
p.   cm.—(The World's classics)
Bibliography: p.
1. Conrad, Joseph, 1857–1924—Biography. 2. Novelists,
English—20th century—Biography. 3. Seafaring life. I. Najder,
Zdzisław. II. Conrad, Joseph, 1857–1924. Personal record. 1988.
III. Title.
PR6005.04Z467 1988 823'.912—dc19 88-4856
ISBN 0-19-281729-9

Printed in Great Britain by
Hazell Watson & Viney Ltd.
Aylesbury, Bucks.

CONTENTS

INTRODUCTION

The present volume groups together Joseph Conrad's two openly autobiographical books. They are different in both their genesis and their literary form. *The Mirror of the Sea* originated as a series of sketches, written for popular magazines and based not only on the author's personal memories but also on his specialist knowledge as a seaman. *A Personal Record* is a short volume of reminiscences, written originally for an ambitious literary periodical. However, accidentally or not, these two books supplement each other: the latter talks about Conrad's national background and about the beginnings of his two careers; as a sailor and as a writer; the former sums up, in a distilled and synthetic way, his seagoing experience.

They also supplement each other in their function as Conrad's messages to the reading public. The images of his own personality projected by these two books are complementary; taken together, they may be seen as presenting that vision of himself which Conrad wanted us to receive and accept.

But since they are so different, in their style, in the tone of the author's voice, and in artistic structure, they must be considered separately, before we try to sum them up.

THE MIRROR OF THE SEA

To appreciate it fully, it is best to read *The Mirror* not knowing, or else forgetting, how the volume originated and its parts got assembled: simply, to read the book as a whole.[1]

---

[1] The only comprehensive critical studies devoted especially to *The Mirror* are in Polish: Tadeusz Skutnik, 'O semantyce kompozycji *Zwierciadła morza*', in *O kompozycji tekstu Conradowskiego*, ed. A. Zgorzelski, Gdańsk, 1978 (of particular interest are Skutnik's remarks on the title, mottoes, and dedication), and in French: an extensive 'Notice' by Pierre Lefranc (especially valuable in the analysis of nautical aspects and in tracing the autobiographical counterparts, or more often lack of them, of the events described by Conrad), in the second volume of Conrad's *Œuvres*, ed. Sylvère Monod, Bibliothèque de la Pléiade (Paris, 1985). The best overall assessment is that by Morton Dauwen Zabel in his Introduction to *The Portable Conrad* (New York, 1947).

Ostensibly, this is a volume of 'memories and impressions', as its subtitle says, concerning the sea; and the first understanding of the title is probably that the author intends to hold to the sea the mirror of his prose. But, as often in Conrad's works, the title has another and more important meaning. The sea may be understood as being itself a mirror. The motto from Boethius' *On the Consolation of Philosophy*—a book in praise of philosophical thinking—seems to enforce this interpretation. The motto talks about a 'miracle or wonder' (there is here a hidden allusion to the title, as both 'mirror' and 'miracle' come from the same Latin 'miraculum') which 'greatly troubles' the author. But what is the sea a mirror of? Perhaps of Nature in general, of the Universe. Therefore, the book is a mirror of what is in itself a mirror. Such an interpretation is repeatedly confirmed by the text. As one instance of this, the other key word of the motto, 'wonder', returns in section XXXVI in a telling context. In what is in fact a biblical allusion to the Lord's 'wonders in the deep' (Ps. 107: 24), we read: 'the most amazing wonder of the deep is its unfathomable cruelty.'

Thus at the very beginning an alert reader is given a hint that the series of memories and impressions he is presented with contains also elements of a philosophical parable. Once we have registered that signal, we shall be less surprised to find in this book so many statements of the author's essential beliefs, sometimes springing up quite unexpectedly.

From the third sentence (with its gibe at 'a vain people of landsmen'), we also keep receiving signals that we are being addressed by a specialist, who relies not only on his knowledge but on his personal experience as well. We are made to feel privileged to have an expert—above the ordinary ranks of landlubber scribes—to introduce us to the world of seamen and ships. This stress on personal expertise seems at times overdone, but Conrad's insistence was possibly occasioned by the fact that most of the sketches appeared initially in popular magazines, and he wanted to accentuate their difference from the ordinary journalistic staple.

A look at the thematic range of the volume reveals that not so much the sea as the ship is the initial focus of attention. The ships leaving port and returning, their anchors, sails, and loads, their wreckings and their 'captivity' in docks are treated in six (out of fifteen) essays, and a seventh contains a eulogy to a particular ship, the balancelle *Tremolino*. Seamen take, as it were, the second place behind their vessels; and it is they, not the ships, who are apt to make mistakes and to fail. 'Ships are all right; it's the men in 'em' who are not always dependable. They are looked at from the vantage point of their work: of the duties they perform, the obstacles they must overcome, the weaknesses they have to master. There is little in *The Mirror* of the spirit of adventure for adventure's sake, and the thrills of pleasure-sailing are mentioned almost with condescension. Seamanship is regarded as an art of navigation—that is, of going from one place to another with a concrete, useful purpose; but still an art, which develops its special skills. Such attainment of skills forms 'the moral side' of any 'breadwinning industry'. And it 'is more than honesty; it is something wider, embracing honesty and grace and rule in an elevated and clear sentiment, not altogether utilitarian, which may be called the honour of labour' ('The Fine Art'). This non-utilitarian view of the moral aspects of work is characteristic of Conrad's ethics. And it is worth remembering that statement, thrown in by Conrad as if only in passing, because its underlying idea—that usefulness is not a sufficient ground of moral value—illuminates the hierarchy of values implicit in most of Conrad's fiction.

The work of a sailor is shown in *The Mirror of the Sea* to be distinguished by two other factors, which make it particularly 'art-like'. One is the special relationship between the man and the vessel he works in, 'loved in a disinterested way'; the other, even more important—and mostly gone with the disappearance of sailing ships—consists in the direct engagement of natural elements, water and wind, as adversaries. This engagement makes man not just an object of more or less accidental fate, but a protagonist, a fighter in the battles of his existence. Such an image of man participating in an agon with the elements is most visible in 'The Character of the Foe' and in 'Initiation'. The nostalgic idealization of past forms of seamanship serves in *The Mirror* a double purpose: it adds a romantic sheen to the author's reminiscences and strengthens his moral message.

In his guide to ships and seamanship, rich in technical detail and in anecdote, and ranging from a disquisition about the proper stowage of a cargo to glimpses of the history of naval warfare, Conrad uses two methods of presentation: one generalized, the other reminiscential. It is evident that he feels more at ease with the latter, but, since his objective is not only to recall his own memories but to give an overview of seamanship at the time of the great historical change from sail to steam, he has to draw synthetic pictures. They tend to be stiffish, and it is here that he resorts to easy anthropomorphism, most striking in his over-drawn images of the 'rulers' of East and West winds (amusingly tailored to fit Conrad's anti-Russian attitude).

That anthropomorphism is in conflict with one of the basic ideas of the book: namely, that Nature is quite indifferent to Man, that in fact these two have nothing in common.

The exposure of the sea's 'cynical indifference' to man's courage and endurance is the subject of the best piece in the volume, 'Initiation'; and the discovery that the sea—an enchanting sight as it may be—is essentially 'impenetrable and heartless', oblivious of 'good and evil', constitutes the philosophical point of arrival of *The Mirror of the Sea*. The sketches about 'The Nursery of the Craft' and 'The "Tremolino"', which follow 'Initiation', show the sea at its most attractive and enchanting—but we read them having been warned, and we perceive their raptures in the perspective of a sobering experience which has peeled off naïve illusions. The 'Tremolino' tale looks in this perspective for what it is: a romanticized story of a youthful and foolhardy adventure.

When we try to sum up the content of *The Mirror*—its 'message'—we arrive at a paradox. The book may seem to promise to be a collection of sketches about the glamour and romance of the sea; in fact it argues that 'the sea has never been friendly to man'. Sailing's ultimate aim is shown to be a safe landing; and the 'Emblems of Hope' in the title of the second sketch are anchors, which make a vessel stationary. This paradox is highlighted at the beginning of section XXXVIII: 'Happy he who, like Ulysses, has made an adventurous voyage'. One does not even have to remember Joachim Du Bellay's famous sonnet, from which the above is a quotation, to realize that Ulysses was happy not because he travelled (much against his wish), but because, after all his adventures, he finally returned home. Conrad does not carry the quotation to its original—and logical—conclusion, where Du Bellay states that he prefers the sweetness of his home village to sea air: that would have put him personally in a painful spot, as he himself, as a sailor, did not have a home to return to. This evasion is superbly characteristic of the author's personal presence in *The Mirror*. The book is not an autobiography in the sense of a factual report. When we try to pin down biographical data and connect the events described as Conrad's reminiscences with documented facts, an identification often turns out to be impossible. Many 'remembered' events simply do not have plausible counterparts in Conrad's life. Neither the risky berthing of a ship at the Circular Quay in Sydney, nor the putting another one off ground after an accidental stranding, nor many other events, including the rescue of the crew of a Danish brig in 'Initiation', can be traced down to facts in Conrad's life. He was, in spite of his protestations to the contrary, several times a passenger on a ship; and was master of only one seagoing vessel, although he uses the plural when mentioning his commands. Even 'The "Tremolino"', the most insistently autobiographical piece, verily bristles with details either outright unrealistic or at best lifted from some other time and place.

All that is, however, of interest mainly to Conrad's biographers. For the reader *The Mirror of the Sea* emanates a vision of its author and his life: not reconstructed, but re-imagined, re-created; a life emotionally and intellectually coherent and meaningful. It is a vision of a man attracted to the sea by its romantic glamour; who took his work in ships seriously both in the professional and in the moral sense; who views the sea as the testing ground of himself—and of man in general.

The sea of *The Mirror* is enchanting, cruel, and unlovable. Its fascination consists in the challenge it poses to man's courage and fidelity. And man's relation to it grows into a metaphor of the human condition in general: the sea mirrors nature, oblivious to human sacrifice, testing him coldly and mercilessly. It constitutes an immense stage for his achievement and failure, for his moral greatness and villainy—which are solely of his own making, not connected with any universal order of things.

The Mirror is an uneven book. There are fragments, as in the chapter 'Rulers of East and West', which may serve as a demonstration of Conrad's dangerous stylistic propensities: flight into sheer rhetoric, overdrawn metaphors, more pomp than substance. There is occasional padding, with words taking the lead of ideas and images rather than images and ideas dictating words. In addition, the composition of the volume looks—and is—partly accidental, with the last chapter evidently tagged on artificially. However, the degree of intellectual consistency indicates how representative of and integrated in Conrad's thought *The Mirror of the Sea* is, how deeply rooted in Conrad's philosophy is the basic imagery of the sea as a mirror of the Universe. There are three fine chapters ('Character of the Foe', 'Initiation', 'The Nursery of the Craft') and many fine fragments, which provide an excellent introduction to Conrad's typical motifs and ideas—like this remarkable sentence: 'Faithfulness is a great restraint, the strongest bond laid upon the self-will of men and ships on this globe of land and sea.'

*   *   *

Conrad's idea of a series of 'sea sketches' originated in late 1903; it seems most likely that it was suggested by Ford Madox Ford, with whom Conrad had collaborated on *The Inheritors* (1901) and *Romance* (1903). Writing to his literary agent, James B. Pinker, Conrad reeled off a list of planned titles: 'Gales of Wind', 'Up Anchor', 'Yards and Masts', 'The Cut of the Sails'; 'The Web of Ropes', 'Old Timbers', 'Round the Compass,' 'The Chance of Landfalls', 'The Run of the Seas'; most of them were later changed, some dropped altogether. Ford assisted Conrad in writing, or rather dictating, the first six sketches ('Landfalls and Departures', 'Emblems of Hope', 'The Fine Art', 'Weight of the Burden', 'Overdue and Missing', and 'The Grip of the Land'), which were begun in the first days of 1904 and ready by the beginning of March. The work was done in London, where both Conrad and Ford came to stay for three months. Conrad's attention and energy were at that time concentrated on ending *Nostromo*, which cost him an enormous effort.

In late March Conrad returned to his cottage in Kent; Ford's assistance ceased. By 18 April he had written three more 'papers' (as he now called the sketches): 'The Character of the Foe', 'Rulers of East and West', and 'In Captivity'. Then a longer break occurred. Although in May Conrad assured the patient Pinker that 'I am confident that from the word *go* I could get the Mirror of the Sea ready in six weeks', in summer and autumn 1904 only two more essays were written: 'The Faithful River' and 'Cobwebs and Gossamer'. Conrad returned to the series only in July 1905, adding 'Initiation', and in autumn that year the last three: 'The Nursery of the Craft', 'The "Tremolino" ' and 'The Heroic Age'.

The volume collecting the sketches—which appeared in various magazines, under different headings and in a sequence other than in the book—turned out to be not too easy to assemble. 'It is suprising how much time was taken up in putting it into some shape', complained Conrad to

Pinker on 6 March 1906. *The Mirror of the Sea* was published on 4 October 1906. It was well, sometimes even enthusiastically received by critics and Conrad's fellow-writers, notably John Galsworthy, Henry James, Rudyard Kipling, and H. G. Wells.

A PERSONAL RECORD

In 'A Familiar Preface', which Conrad wrote to *A Personal Record* in the summer of 1911, he says that 'this little book is the result of a friendly suggestion'. Even if true, this is certainly not the whole truth. It is quite possible that Ford Madox Ford encouraged Conrad to write his autobiography, but it is clear that Conrad had his own very strong reasons. And, ironically, what Ford wanted to publish in his *English Review*—the monthly he started in December 1908—was not 'this little book', but a text much longer.

We find the first mention of the project in Conrad's letter to James B. Pinker of 18 September 1908 (at that time the first section had already been written; it appeared in the opening issue of the *English Review*): 'There are to be intimate personal autobiographical things under the general title (for book form perhaps) of The Life and the Art.'

Five weeks before, on 10 August 1908, in The *Daily News*, Robert Lynd—a well-known critic—had published a review of Conrad's recent volume of short stories *A Set of Six*. He attacked Conrad for not writing in his native language: 'Mr Conrad, as everybody knows, is a Pole, who writes in English by choice, as it were, rather than by nature. . . . To some of us . . . it seems a very regrettable thing, even from the point of view of English literature. A writer who ceases to see the world coloured by his own language—for language gives colour to thoughts and things in a way that few people understand—is apt to lose the concentration and intensity of vision without which the greatest literature cannot be made. . . . Mr Conrad, without either country or language, may be thought to have found a new patriotism for himself in the sea. His vision of men, however, is the vision of a cosmopolitan, of a homeless person.'

Conrad reacted first with dejection. 'It is like abusing a tongue-tied man, for what one can say. The statement is simple and brutal; and any answer would involve too many feelings of one's inner life, stir too much secret bitterness and complex loyalty to be even attempted with any hopes of being understood', he complained in a letter (of 21 August) to his close friend, the literary critic Edward Garnett, the man who had accepted his first novel for publication fourteen years previously. But then he decided to do just that: to deal in print with his complex feelings and loyalties. *A Personal Record* became his considered reaction.

Privately and publicly, Conrad tried to play down the importance to himself of *Some Reminiscences* (the title under which *A Personal Record* originally appeared), and stressed Ford's role in prevailing upon him to take up the idea. He wrote to H. G. Wells:

Ford has persuaded me to give some personal stuff for the [*English*] R[*eview*]. . . . But I was thinking of doing something of that kind for the boys, yet fearing that I would never do it from mere horror of writing, and this seemed an unique opportunity to pull myself together for an effort in that direction. But I fear it is a silly enterprise besides (what with the stirring up of all these dead) being a somewhat ghoulish one. I explain to you so that you should not suspect me of incipient softening of the brain.' (3 Nov. 1908)

In his 'Author's Note', written in September 1919, Conrad even claimed—in sharp contrast to Lynd's criticism—that the comments on his not writing in his native language 'had been of the most flattering kind'. These were, however, attempts at covering up his tracks. The repeated insistence on both the painful subjects raised by Lynd—the choice of England 'over' Conrad's own home country and the writing in a foreign language—reveals the psychological impulse behind the series. The fact that an analogous accusation, expressed in the form of a charge of 'desertion', had been made earlier (in 1899) by a prestigious Polish novelist, Eliza Orzeszkowa, is an indication that Lynd expressed, in an aggressive way, thoughts and doubts which Conrad must have encountered many times before.

And he decided to reply, in the form not of a defence or explanation, but of an imaginative autobiographical statement. The result is a splendid piece of personal mythology.

A few weeks after the first announcement, quoted above, Conrad described his design to Pinker in greater detail:

To make Polish life enter English literature is no small ambition— to begin with. . . . To reveal a very particular state of society, bring forward individuals with very special traditions and touch in a personal way upon such events for instance as the liberation of the serfs . . . is a big enterprise. And yet it presents itself easily just because of the intimate nature of the task, and of the 2 vols. of my uncle's Memoirs which I have by me, to refresh my recollections and settle my ideas. . . . A mere casual suggestion has grown into a very absorbing plan. . . . I have even been thinking of a title something like 'The Art and the Life', or The Pages and the Years, Reminiscences. ([7?] Oct. 1908)

To his literary agent, with whom he was heavily in debt, Conrad presented the reminiscences as an easy piece, which would not distract him from the more demanding work (and paid in advance) on Under Western Eyes. But he was, as usual with him, deluding both himself and his creditor. Writing did not go all that easily, and did interfere with other work more wanted by his publishers, who evinced a marked lack of interest in the Reminiscences. 'Too much about life in Poland and about Mr Conrad's uncle, and very little about himself and about how he came to write', complained Pinker's American correspondent. (Such complaints probably influenced Conrad to abandon his original and more ambitious plans of painting a broader historical picture, as sketched in his letter to Pinker.)

By April 1909 Conrad had written seven chapters. He then fell ill, while at the same time his conflict with Ford, simmering for the last couple of months, boiled over, mostly because of Ford's irresponsibility and even arrogance. Conrad refused to contribute anything more to the *English Review*. The fate of *Some Reminiscences* hung for some time in the balance. Conrad sounded several prospective publishers about the advisability of continuing the work; he even outlined a plan of a follow-up 'under the general title of Some Portraits family and others—my uncle the conspirator, two marriages, episodes of the liberation of our peasants and of the '63 rising' (to Austin Harrison, [Mar. 1912]). But, finding no encouragement, he decided to publish the text as it stood, and even pretended that that had been his original intention.

The narrative structure of *A Personal Record* has evoked expressions of puzzlement; and it is true that the literary convention Conrad uses has been more common in Polish than in English literature. However, its origins are undoubtedly English: in Lawrence Sterne's *Sentimental Journey* (1768). That finely fanciful little book had been greatly admired in Conrad's native country and inspired many highly accomplished successors, which developed Sterne's artfully loose associative construction. In his youth, Conrad certainly read some of these books, and the Sternian parentage of his technique is at times fairly obvious, as at the beginning of chapter IV. In fact, there is in *A Personal Record*, in spite of its casually conversational air, little of randomness (with the one exception of the story about the greedy 'X' in chapter III, told for no discernible reason). Changes of subject-matter and of points of view, sometimes playfully flaunted, serve specific artistic and emotional purposes.

The tone of narration is seemingly debonair, with here and there harder glitters of dry wit and sarcasm (which Arnold Bennett particularly praised). This tone forms a screen, tinged with self-irony, through which the reader perceives subjects personal, intimate, puzzling, even embarrassing, sometimes intensely emotional: Conrad's memories of his parents, his leaving Poland with her demanding patriotic heritage; his writing in an alien language; his wish to become a seaman; his turning into a professional writer. But there is little of direct intimacy, with the exception of a few sentences about Conrad's mother and father. When one of his friends criticized the conversational reserve of *A Personal Record*, Conrad defended himself by saying: '. . . this defect saves the pangs of my shyness.' It was pride, rather—as he himself suggested in 'A Familiar Preface', when professing his 'repugnance' of open displays of emotions. Conrad specifically scorned the 'confessional' form of reminiscences and taunted its most eminent practitioner, Jean-Jacques Rousseau. His own principles of restraint and sober self-possession, as laid out in the same 'Preface', were grounded in a distrust of unbridled emotionalism, which may 'enchant' others but carries with itself the danger of falsehood: 'the effort to bring into play the extremities of emotions' is tainted with a 'debasing touch of insincerity'. This justification of the way in which his reminiscences are written contains a salient element of Conrad's artistic credo: he placed himself firmly on the opposite pole to not only Rousseau but also Dostoevsky.

The associative mode of his reminiscences allows Conrad to pass easily from a particular subject in hand to the general problem it poses. Events of his life are shown in sudden flashes of reflection, sometimes beguilingly playful, more often serious and definitive. Several memorable passages express his beliefs: that the 'aim of creation cannot be ethical at all' (and thus all human values are of man's own making); that 'the temporal world rests on a few simple ideas . . . among others, on the idea of Fidelity'; that art's true source is 'imagination, not invention'. His views on the role of imagination (which is for Conrad basically reconstructive, re-imagination in fact) in art and on the 'prose art of fiction', which 'is but truth often dragged out of a well and clothed in the painted robe of imaged phrases', are a continuation of thoughts expressed in his celebrated 'Preface' to *The Nigger of the 'Narcissus'*, written in 1897. And the words about 'that spirit of piety towards all things human which

sanctions the conceptions of a writer of tales' can be regarded as developing Conrad's old idea of human solidarity
which binds the writer of fiction to his readers, and as a
variation of his statement about art 'rendering the highest
kind of justice to the visible universe'.

The most vividly evocative fragment of *A Personal Record*
is Conrad's description of his meeting with Almayer; and
appropriately so, because it serves the double purpose of
illustrating the author's artistic principle of 'imaginative
and exact rendering of authentic memories' and of providing an additional justification for his becoming a writer.

The feeling of distance which Conrad keeps between
himself and his subject, and thus also between himself and
his readers, is intensified by the fact that so many of the
stories told in *A Personal Record* are reported after another
source, namely his uncle's Tadeusz Bobrowski's memoirs.
Indeed, several fragments of the book are recapitulations or
direct translations of Bobrowski's text. Thus—to give only
the more important instances—the characteristics of Conrad's mother and her sister, the story of Mr Nicholas B. (the
heroic dog-eater), the sordid tale of Conrad's paternal
grandmother and her second husband, the description of the
rampage of Mr Nicholas B.'s house, and of Conrad's sick
mother being compelled to return to exile, are all taken, in
various degrees of exactness, from Bobrowski's memoirs,
published eight years earlier.

Professing that 'in these personal notes' there was no
'drapery of fiction' such as the 'veil' which separates the
novelist from his reader, Conrad wove a different fabric, less
obviously conventional but not less artful, protective and
decorative at the same time. It exhibits the unity of artistic
and psychological principles on which the book is built, and
it enables Conrad to create his private mythology—an
artefact of his life, as it were—without blatant distortion of
facts.

And there are many distortions, but blunted and obfus-
cated by the way of telling, to be exposed only by an

inquisitive researcher. They are of scant importance for the appreciation of *A Personal Record*, but they are significant in pointing at the book's fundamental idea. This idea was formulated by Conrad himself: to give the vision of 'a coherent, justifiable personality both in its origin and in its action'. All departures from factual truth are explainable by reference to that basic idea, to that underlying need: to impress coherence on his life, with all its anomalous passages, unusual decisions, and sudden changes, with all its uncertainties, typical for a man prone to depression, the most severe bout of which, which confined him to bed for weeks, occurred only a few months after the writing of *A Personal Record*. This search for consistency, the real need of it, is shown not only in various omissions of events which would put it in question, and by adducement of events imagined, but, most visibly, in the avoidance of any suggestion, so typical in the autobiographies of writers close to Romanticism, of internal tensions within his mind, of the Faustian 'two souls in one breast', of hesitancy, conflicting desires and aspirations. Conrad wants to and does present himself as being of one piece.

To call this fictional, 'created' Conrad 'public' as opposed to 'private' (i.e. real) is, I think, misleading. It is not privacy and publicness that are in question here, but rather the actual Conrad and Conrad as he wished himself to be. Writing about himself was for Conrad a way of dealing not only with his readers, but first with himself. He wanted to be, not only to be seen like that.

When he looked back at his life, there loomed in it a few especially sensitive and painful issues. Leaving Poland had evidently impressed itself on his conscience as an act to be explained and somehow justified, especially in the light of his parents' sacrifice for their country. He declares his own 'fidelity to a special tradition', and even 'love' for Poland's memory, and shows Poles in a nimbus of romantic heroism, but repeatedly stresses the tragic hopelessness of Polish national aspirations: 'It has been the fate of that credulous nation to starve for upwards of a hundred years on a diet of false hopes.' He could thus, while preserving his natural pride, portray his departure as combined with a tragic awareness of the futility of continuing his ancestors' exertions. And the images of his native land are like memories of a long-submerged Atlantis, as if his own departure meant that it ceased to exist at all.

His resolve of going to sea presents Conrad as unswerving, wilful, and absurdly unusual; in fact it was neither. His joining the British merchant marine was a matter of accident, not of primary design. Conrad is quite right in claiming that he did not consciously 'choose' English as the language of his works; yet writing in English was for him pre-eminently not a consequence of some inherent determinism, but a result of the force of events. Similarly, Conrad adjusts many other, less essential elements and aspects of his life.

In conclusion, *A Personal Record* is a captivating and moving book, which tells us something about Joseph Conrad's real past, about his family and national background, and much about his persistent quest to impose on his life a meaning—a meaning consistent with the exacting demands of the moral principles he had formulated and in which he believed.

NOTE ON THE TEXT

THE MIRROR OF THE SEA

No full manuscript of the volume exists; most segments were apparently dictated.

The individual sections of *The Mirror* were initially published in the following order:

'Overdue and Missing', as 'Missing', *Daily Mail*, 8 Mar. 1904, and 'Overdue', *Daily Mail*, 16 Mar. 1904.

'The Grip of the Land', as 'Stranded', *Daily Mail*, 2 Dec. 1904.

'The Faithful River', as 'London River: the Great Artery of England', *The World's Work and Play*, Dec. 1904.

'Landfalls and Departures', *Pall Mall Magazine*, Jan. 1905.

'Emblems of Hope', as ' "Up Anchor" ', *Pall Mall Magazine*, Feb. 1905.

'The Character of the Foe', as 'Gales of Wind', *Pall Mall Magazine*, Mar. 1905.

'The Fine Art', as 'Fine Art', *Pall Mall Magazine*, Apr. 1905.

'Rulers of East and West', *Pall Mall Magazine*, May and June 1905.

'Cobwebs and Gossamer', as 'Tallness of the Spars', *Harper's Weekly*, 10 June 1905.

'The Weight of the Burden', as 'Weight of Her Burden', *Harper's Weekly*, 17 June 1905.

'In Captivity', as 'Her Captivity', *Blackwood's Magazine*, Sept. 1905.

'The Heroic Age', as '*Palmam qui meruit ferat*, 1805–1905', *Standard*, 21 Oct. 1905.

'Initiation', as 'Initiation. A Discourse concerning the "Name" of Ships and the Character of the Sea', *Blackwood's Magazine*, Jan. 1906.

'The Nursery of the Craft' and 'The "Tremolino" ' appeared for the first time in the book edition of *The Mirror of the Sea*.

For the book publication (4 Oct. 1906) this sequence, which differed from the chronological order of writing the pieces (from January 1904 to October 1905), was altered, as was the internal subdivision of sections. Conrad revised the texts, made many changes in style and choice of words, and deleted several fragments, as for instance at the beginning of 'The Character of the Foe'. He also excised a few more of his sallies against ignorant journalists.

Dent's Collected Edition, generally accepted as the textual basis of Conrad's works in the Oxford World's Classics series, follows the second, completely reset (although with layout changes only) Methuen edition of 1913. The Heinemann 1921 edition, the last one to be corrected by Conrad, introduced more changes, but not consistently. Punctuation is heavier, with many commas added—but only at the beginning of the volume. There are numerous changes in the spelling of combined words ('black-and-white' in place of 'black and white', 'arm-chair' instead of 'armchair', etc.); all these have been accepted only if they follow standard *OED* spelling. A few errors are corrected ('Kerguelen Island' instead of the non-existent 'Land'; 'Dead Sea' instead of 'dead sea' fruit, etc.). There is one editorial correction (in 'Overdue and Missing'): instead of 'of this paper' Conrad put 'presently used'. This text of *The Mirror* is, then, based on the Dent Collected Edition, but with numerous indisputable corrections adopted from the Heinemann 1921 edition.

A PERSONAL RECORD

No manuscript of the main text survives. The manuscript of the 'Author's Note' is at Princeton, that of the 'Familiar Preface' at Yale. All editions follow quite closely the text of the original serialization in the *English Review* (Dec.

1908–June 1909). The remarks made above about punctuation and spelling in the Dent Collected Edition and in the Heinemann 1921 edition of *The Mirror of the Sea* apply by and large also to *A Personal Record*. In this case as well, there are in the Heinemann edition several minor but noteworthy corrections which are accepted here; moreover, that last edition is often closer to the first than is the Dent Collected Edition.

Thus 'A Familiar Preface' is signed in the *English Review* and the first book edition (Nash, 1912) 'J. C. K.' the 'K' stands, of course, for 'Korzeniowski', Conrad's family name, and it is obviously significant that he reminds the reader of it in an introduction to an autobiographical text. The Dent Collected Edition drops the 'K', Heinemann has it. A few other corrections deserve mentioning: 'Slavonism' instead of 'Sclavonism', 'not yet thirty' instead 'not thirty yet' (The 'Author's Note'); the punctuation of the paragraph about resignation is made clearer (in 'A Familiar Preface'); the battle of 'Leipzig' rather than 'Leipsic'.

This text of *A Personal Record* is, therefore, the text of the Dent Collected Edition but with several corrections taken over from the Heinemann edition.

SELECT BIBLIOGRAPHY

Dent's Collected Edition (1946–55) contains almost all Conrad's works except the fragment called *The Sisters*, the dramatizations, and a tale written in collaboration with Ford Madox Hueffer (who later became Ford Madox Ford), *The Nature of a Crime. Congo Diary and Other Uncollected Pieces* (ed. Zdzisław Najder, 1978) contains Conrad's Congo notebooks, *The Sisters*, *The Nature of a Crime* and other minor pieces. Cambridge University Press is preparing a scholarly edition of the canon.

Important editions of Conrad's letters are as follows: G. Jean-Aubry: *Joseph Conrad: Life and Letters* (two volumes, 1927); *Letters from Conrad, 1895 to 1924* (ed. Edward Garnett, 1928); *Letters of Joseph Conrad to Marguerite Poradowska* (tr. and ed. J. A. Gee and P. J. Sturm, 1940); and *Conrad's Polish Background* (ed. Z. Najder, 1964). There are further collections by Richard Curle (1928), G. Jean-Aubry (1930), William Blackburn (1958); D. B. J. Randall (1968) and Cedric Watts (1969). In 1983 volume I (ed. F. R. Karl and Laurence Davies) of *The Collected Letters of Joseph Conrad* appeared; further volumes have been prepared.

Informative memoirs of Conrad include those by Ford Madox Ford (1924), Jessie Conrad (1926 and 1935), Richard Curle (1928), Bertrand Russell (1967), Borys Conrad (1970), and John Conrad (1981). Notable critical biographies have been written by Jocelyn Baines (1960), Bernard Meyer (a 'psychoanalytic' biography, 1967), Frederick Karl (1979) and Ian Watt (*Conrad in the Nineteenth Century*, 1980), and there is a biography by Roger Tennant (1981). An important scholarly account is Zdzisław Najder's *Joseph Conrad: A Chronicle* (1983).

Probably the most influential of the biographically related studies which make substantial use of documentary material are: J. D. Gordan, *Joseph Conrad: The Making of a Novelist* (1940), and Norman Sherry, *Conrad's Eastern World* (1966) and *Conrad's Western World* (1971). There are further relevant studies by Richard Curle (1914), Edward Crankshaw (1936), Gustav Morf (1930 and 1976), R. L. Mégroz (1931), J. H. Retinger (1941), Jerry Allen (1965), and Norman Sherry (1972).

Of the numerous critical books on Conrad, the following may

be found fruitful: Douglas Hewitt, *Conrad: A Reassessment* (1952), Thomas Moser, *Joseph Conrad: Achievement and Decline* (1957), Albert Guerard, *Conrad the Novelist* (1958), Eloise Knapp Hay, *The Political Novels of Joseph Conrad* (1963), Avrom Fleishman, *Conrad's Politics* (1967), and Jacques Berthoud, *Joseph Conrad: The Major Phase* (1978). Other studies of interest are by Paul Kirschner (1968), Bruce Johnson (1971), and Jan Verleun (1978 and 1979). There are important essays on Conrad in F. R. Leavis, *The Great Tradition* (1948) and *'Anna Karenina' and Other Essays* (1967), J. Hillis Miller, *Poets of Reality* (1966), and Norman Sherry, ed., *Joseph Conrad: A Commemoration* (1976). Fredric Jameson, *The Political Unconscious* (1981), has an important chapter on Conrad.

A CHRONOLOGY OF
JOSEPH CONRAD

1857   3 December: born Józef Teodor Konrad Korzeniowski, of Polish parents in the Ukraine.

1861   His father, the poet and translator Apollo Korzeniowski, arrested in Warsaw by the Russian authorities for patriotic conspiracy.

1862   Conrad's parents sentenced to exile in Vologda, Russia; their son accompanies them.

1865   Death of his mother.

1869   Death of Apollo Korzeniowski in Kraków (Cracow); Conrad's uncle, Tadeusz Bobrowski, becomes his guardian.

1874   Leaves Poland for Marseilles to become a trainee seaman in the French merchant marine.

1878   March: shoots himself in the chest in Marseilles but is not seriously wounded. His uncle comes and pays his debts. April: the Russian consul refuses to extend his passport, as Conrad is liable for Russian military service. Unable to remain in France, in July he joins his first British ship, the *Skimmer of the Sea*.

1886   Becomes a British subject and passes the examination for Ordinary Master of the British merchant marine.

1888   Master of the barque *Otago*, his only command.

1889   Resigns from the *Otago*. Begins to write *Almayer's Folly*.

1890   Works in the Belgian Congo.

1892   As first mate on board the *Torrens*, a passenger clipper, meets John Galsworthy, who becomes his loyal friend.

1894   January: leaves his last position as a seaman. February: death of Tadeusz Bobrowski. April: finishes the draft of *Almayer's Folly*. October: *Almayer's Folly* accepted by Unwin. Meets Edward Garnett, a literary critic; beginning of a lifetime friendship.

1895   *Almayer's Folly* published; adopts 'Joseph Conrad' as his pen-name.

in book form. *'Twixt Land and Sea* ('A Smile of Fortune', 'The Secret Sharer', 'Freya of the Seven Islands') published.

1913 *Chance* published.

1914 *Chance* is a great success; also Conrad's earlier work now finds a larger public. The Conrads visit Poland and are trapped there for a few weeks by the outbreak of war.

1915 *Within the Tides* ('The Planter of Malata', 'The Partner', 'The Inn of The Two Witches') and *Victory* published.

1917 *The Shadow-Line* published.

1919 *The Arrow of Gold* published. The Conrads move to Oswalds, Bishopsbourne, near Canterbury.

1920 *The Rescue* published, 24 years after it was begun.

1921 *Notes on Life and Letters* published.

1923 Conrad visits the United States and is lionized. *The Rover* published.

1924 May: declines the offer of a knighthood. 3 August: dies of a heart attack at Oswalds. *The Nature of a Crime* (collaboration with Ford) published.

1925 *Tales of Hearsay* ('The Warrior's Soul', 'Prince Roman', 'The Tale', 'The Black Mate') and *Suspense* (unfinished novel) published.

1926 *Last Essays* published.

1928 *The Sisters* (beginning of a novel) published.

THE MIRROR OF THE SEA

To
*Mrs. Katherine Sanderson**
whose warm welcome and gracious
hospitality extended to the friend
of her son cheered the first
dark days of my parting
with the sea
these pages are affectionately inscribed

AUTHOR'S NOTE

LESS perhaps than any other book written by me, or anybody else, does this volume require a preface. Yet since all the others including even the "Personal Record," which is but a fragment of biography, are to have their Author's Notes I cannot possibly leave this one without, lest a false impression of indifference or weariness should be created. I can see only too well that it is not going to be an easy task. Necessity— the mother of invention—being even unthinkable in this case, I do not know what to invent in the way of discourse; and necessity being also the greatest possible incentive to exertion I don't even know how to begin to exert myself. Here, too, the natural inclination comes in. I have been all my life averse from exertion.

Under these discouraging circumstances I am, however, bound to proceed from a sense of duty. This Note is a thing promised. In less than a minute's time, by a few incautious words I entered into a bond which has lain on my heart heavily ever since.

For, this book is a very intimate revelation; and what that is revealing can a few more pages add to some three hundred others of most sincere disclosures? I have attempted here to lay bare with the unreserve of a last hour's confession the terms of my relation with the sea, which beginning mysteriously, like any great passion the inscrutable Gods send to mortals, went on unreasoning and invincible, surviving the test of disillusion, defying the disenchantment that lurks in every day of a strenuous life; went on full of love's delight and love's anguish, facing them in open-eyed exultation, without bitterness and without repining, from the first hour to the last.

Subjugated but never unmanned I surrendered my being to that passion which various and great like life itself had also its periods of wonderful serenity which even a fickle mistress can give sometimes on her soothed breast, full of wiles, full of fury, and yet capable of an enchanting sweetness. And if anybody suggests that this must be the lyric illusion of an old, romantic heart, I can answer that for twenty years* I had lived like a hermit with my passion! Beyond the line of the sea horizon the world for me did not exist, as assuredly as it does not exist for the mystics who take refuge on the tops of high mountains. I am speaking now of that innermost life, containing the best and the worst that can happen to us in the temperamental depths of our being, where a man indeed must live alone but need not give up all hope of holding converse with his kind.

This perhaps is enough for me to say on this particular occasion about these, my parting words, about this, my last mood in my great passion for the sea. I call it great because it was great to me. Others may call it a foolish infatuation. Those words have been applied to every love story. But whatever it may be the fact remains that it was something too great for words.

This is what I always felt vaguely; and therefore the following pages rest like a true confession on matters of fact which to a friendly and charitable person may convey the inner truth of almost a lifetime. From sixteen to thirty-six cannot be called an age, yet it is a pretty long stretch of that sort of experience which teaches a man slowly to see and feel. It is for me a distinct period; and when I emerged from it into another air, as it were, and said to myself: "Now I must speak of these things or remain unknown to the end of my days," it was with the ineradicable hope, that accompanies one through solitude as well as through a crowd, of ultimately, some day, at some moment, making myself understood.

And I have been! I have been understood as completely as it is possible to be understood in this, our world, which seems to be mostly composed of riddles. There have been things said about this book which have moved me profoundly; the more profoundly because they were uttered by men whose occupation was avowedly to understand, and analyze, and expound—in a word, by literary critics. They spoke out according to their conscience, and some of them said things that made me feel both glad and sorry of ever having entered upon my confession. Dimly or clearly, they perceived the character of my intention and ended by judging me worthy to have made the attempt. They saw it was of a revealing character, but in some cases they thought that the revelation was not complete.

One of them said: "In reading these chapters one is always hoping for the revelation; but the personality is never quite revealed. We can only say that this thing happened to Mr. Conrad, that he knew such a man and that thus life passed him leaving those memories. They are the records of the events of his life, not in every instance striking or decisive events but rather those haphazard events which for no definite reason impress themselves upon the mind and recur in memory long afterward as symbols of one knows not what sacred ritual taking place behind the veil."*

To this I can only say that this book written in perfect sincerity holds back nothing—unless the mere bodily presence of the writer. Within these pages I make a full confession not of my sins but of my emotions. It is the best tribute my piety can offer to the ultimate shapers of my character, convictions, and, in a sense, destiny—to the imperishable sea, to the ships that are no more, and to the simple men who have had their day.

J. C.

1919.

CONTENTS

THE MIRROR OF THE SEA
Memories and Impressions

"... FOR THIS MIRACLE OR THIS WONDER
TROUBLETH ME RIGHT GRETLY"

Boethius, *De Con. Phil.*
B. IV. Prose vi.*

THE MIRROR OF THE SEA

> "And shippes by the brinke comen and gon,
> And in swich forme endure a day or two."
>
> *The Frankeleyn's Tale.**

I

LANDFALL and Departure mark the rhythmical swing of a seaman's life and of a ship's career. From land to land is the most concise definition of a ship's earthly fate.

A "Departure" is not what a vain people of landsmen may think. The term "Landfall" is more easily understood; you fall in with the land, and it is a matter of a quick eye and of a clear atmosphere. The Departure is not the ship's going away from her port any more than the Landfall can be looked upon as the synonym of arrival. But there is this difference in the Departure: that the term does not imply so much a sea event as a definite act entailing a process—the precise observation of certain landmarks by means of the compass card.

Your Landfall, be it a peculiarly shaped mountain, a rocky headland, or a stretch of sand-dunes, you meet at first with a single glance. Further recognition will follow in due course; but essentially a Landfall, good or bad, is made and done with at the first cry of "Land ho!" The departure is distinctly a ceremony of navigation. A ship may have left her port some time before; she may have been at sea, in the fullest sense of the phrase, for days; but, for all that, as long as the coast she was about to leave remained in sight, a southern-going ship of yesterday had not in the sailor's sense begun the enterprise of a passage.

The taking of Departure, if not the last sight of the land, is, perhaps, the last professional recognition of the land on the part of a sailor. It is the technical, as distinguished from the sentimental, "good-bye." Henceforth he has done with the coast astern of his ship. It is a matter personal to the man. It is not the ship that takes her Departure; the seaman takes his Departure by means of cross-bearings which fix the place of the first tiny pencil-cross on the white expanse of the track-chart, where the ship's position at noon shall be marked by just such another tiny pencil-cross for every day of her passage. And there may be sixty, eighty, any number of these crosses on the ship's track from land to land. The greatest number in my experience was a hundred and thirty of such crosses from the pilot station at the Sand Heads in the Bay of Bengal to the Scilly's light.* A bad passage. . . .

A Departure, the last professional sight of land, is always good, or at least good enough. For, even if the weather be thick, it does not matter much to a ship having all the open sea before her bows. A Landfall may be good or bad. You encompass the earth with one particular spot of it in your eye. In all the devious tracings the course of a sailing-ship leaves upon the white paper of a chart she is always aiming for that one little spot—maybe a small island in the ocean, a single headland upon the long coast of a continent, a lighthouse on a bluff, or simply the peaked form of a mountain like an ant heap afloat upon the waters. But if you have sighted it on the expected bearing, then that Landfall is

good. Fogs, snowstorms, gales thick with clouds and
rain—those are the enemies of good Landfalls.

II

Some commanders of ships take their Departure from
the home coast sadly, in a spirit of grief and discontent.
They have a wife, children perhaps, some affection at
any rate, or perhaps only some pet vice, that must be
left behind for a year or more. I remember only one
man who walked his deck with a springy step, and gave
the first course of the passage in an elated voice. But
he, as I learned afterwards, was leaving nothing behind
him, except a welter of debts and threats of legal pro-
ceedings.

On the other hand, I have known many captains who,
directly their ship had left the narrow waters of the
Channel, would disappear from the sight of their
ship's company altogether for some three days or more.
They would take a long dive, as it were, into their
state-room, only to emerge a few days afterwards with
a more or less serene brow. Those were the men easy to
get on with. Besides, such a complete retirement
seemed to imply a satisfactory amount of trust in their
officers, and to be trusted displeases no seaman worthy
of the name.

On my first voyage as chief mate with good Captain
MacW——* I remember that I felt quite flattered, and
went blithely about my duties, myself a commander for
all practical purposes. Still, whatever the greatness of
my illusion, the fact remained that the real commander
was there, backing up my self-confidence, though
invisible to my eyes behind a maplewood veneered
cabin-door with a white china handle.

That is the time, after your Departure is taken, when

the spirit of your commander communes with you in a muffled voice, as if from the sanctum sanctorum* of a temple; because, call her a temple or a "hell afloat"—as some ships have been called—the captain's state-room is surely the august place in every vessel.

The good MacW—— would not even come out to his meals, and fed solitarily in his holy of holies from a tray covered with a white napkin. Our steward used to bend an ironic glance at the perfectly empty plates he was bringing out from there. This grief for his home, which overcomes so many married seamen, did not deprive Captain MacW—— of his legitimate appetite. In fact, the steward would almost invariably come up to me, sitting in the captain's chair at the head of the table, to say in a grave murmur, "The captain asks for one more slice of meat and two potatoes." We, his officers, could hear him moving about in his berth, or lightly snoring, or fetching deep sighs, or splashing and blowing in his bath-room; and we made our reports to him through the keyhole, as it were. It was the crowning achievement of his ·amiable character that the answers we got were given in a quite mild and friendly tone. Some commanders in their periods of seclusion are constantly grumpy, and seem to resent the mere sound of your voice as an injury and an insult.

But a grumpy recluse cannot worry his subordinates, whereas the man in whom the sense of duty is strong (or, perhaps, only the sense of self-importance), and who persists in airing on deck his moroseness all day—and perhaps half the night—becomes a grievous infliction. He walks the poop darting gloomy glances, as though he wished to poison the sea, and snaps your head off savagely whenever you happen to blunder within ear-shot. And these vagaries are the harder to bear patiently, as becomes a man and an officer, because no sailor is really good-tempered during the first few days of a voyage. There are regrets, memories, the instinctive longing for the departed idleness, the instinctive hate of all work. Besides, things have a knack of going wrong at the start, especially in the matter of irritating trifles. And there is the abiding thought of a whole year of more or less hard life before one, because there was hardly a southern-going voyage in the yesterday of the sea which meant anything less than a twelvemonth. Yes; it needed a few days after the taking of your Departure for a ship's company to shake down into their places, and for the soothing deep-water ship routine to establish its beneficent sway.

It is a great doctor for sore hearts and sore heads, too, your ship's routine, which I have seen soothe—at least for a time—the most turbulent of spirits. There is health in it, and peace, and satisfaction of the accomplished round; for each day of the ship's life seems to close a circle within the wide ring of the sea horizon. It borrows a certain dignity of sameness from the majestic monotony of the sea. He who loves the sea loves also the ship's routine.

Nowhere else than upon the sea do the days, weeks, and months fall away quicker into the past. They seem to be left astern as easily as the light air-bubbles in the swirls of the ship's wake, and vanish into a great silence in which your ship moves on with a sort of magical effect. They pass away, the days, the weeks, the months. Nothing but a gale can disturb the orderly life of the ship; and the spell of unshaken monotony that seems to have fallen upon the very voices of her men is broken only by the near prospect of a Landfall.

Then is the spirit of the ship's commander stirred

strongly again. But it is not moved to seek seclusion
and to remain, hidden and inert, shut up in a small
cabin with the solace of a good bodily appetite. When
about to make the land, the spirit of the ship's commander is tormented by an unconquerable restlessness.
It seems unable to abide for many seconds together in
the holy of holies of the captain's state-room; it will go
out on deck and gaze ahead, through straining eyes, as
the appointed moment comes nearer. It is kept
vigorously upon the stretch of excessive vigilance.
Meantime, the body of the ship's commander is being
enfeebled by want of appetite; at least, such is my
experience, though "enfeebled" is perhaps not exactly
the word. I might say, rather, that it is spiritualized by
a disregard for food, sleep, and all the ordinary comforts,
such as they are, of sea life. In one or two cases I have
known that detachment from the grosser needs of
existence remain regrettably incomplete in the matter
of drink.

But these two cases were, properly speaking, patho-
logical cases, and the only two in all my sea experience.
In one of these two instances of a craving for stimulants,
developed from sheer anxiety, I cannot assert that the
man's seaman-like qualities were impaired in the least.
It was a very anxious case, too, the land being made
suddenly, close-to, on a wrong bearing, in thick weather,
and during a fresh on-shore gale. Going below to speak
to him soon after, I was unlucky enough to catch my
captain in the very act of hasty cork-drawing. The
sight, I may say, gave me an awful scare. I was well
aware of the morbidly sensitive nature of the man.
Fortunately, I managed to draw back unseen, and
taking care to stamp heavily with my sea-boots at the
foot of the cabin stairs, I made my second entry. But
for this unexpected glimpse, no act of his during the

next twenty-four hours could have given me the slightest suspicion that all was not well with his nerve.

III

Quite another case, and having nothing to do with drink, was that of poor Captain B——.* He used to suffer from sick headaches, in his young days, every time he was approaching a coast. Well over fifty years of age when I knew him, short, stout, dignified, perhaps a little pompous, he was a man of a singularly well-informed mind, the least sailor-like in outward aspect, but certainly one of the best seamen whom it has been my good luck to serve under. He was a Plymouth man, I think, the son of a country doctor, and both his elder boys were studying medicine. He commanded a big London ship, fairly well known in her day. I thought no end of him, and that is why I remember with a peculiar satisfaction the last words he spoke to me on board his ship after an eighteen months' voyage. It was in the dock in Dundee, where we had brought a full cargo of jute from Calcutta. We had been paid off that morning, and I had come on board to take my sea-chest away and to say good-bye. In his slightly lofty but courteous way he inquired what were my plans. I replied that I intended leaving for London by the afternoon train, and thought of going up for examination to get my master's certificate. I had just enough service for that.* He commended me for not wasting my time, with such an evident interest in my case that I was quite surprised; then, rising from his chair, he said:

"Have you a ship in view after you have passed?"

I answered that I had nothing whatever in view.

He shook hands with me, and pronounced the memorable words:

"If you happen to be in want of employment, remember that as long as I have a ship you have a ship, too."

In the way of compliment there is nothing to beat this from a ship's captain to his second mate at the end of a voyage, when the work is over and the subordinate is done with. And there is a pathos in that memory, for the poor fellow never went to sea again after all. He was already ailing when we passed St. Helena; was laid up for a time when we were off the Western Islands,* but got out of bed to make his Landfall. He managed to keep up on deck as far as the Downs,* where, giving his orders in an exhausted voice, he anchored for a few hours to send a wire to his wife and take aboard a North Sea pilot to help him sail the ship up the east coast. He had not felt equal to the task by himself, for it is the sort of thing that keeps a deep-water man on his feet pretty well night and day.

When we arrived in Dundee, Mrs. B—— was already there, waiting to take him home. We travelled up to London by the same train; but by the time I had managed to get through with my examination the ship had sailed on her next voyage without him, and, instead of joining her again, I went by request to see my old commander in his home. This is the only one of my captains I have ever visited in that way. He was out of bed by then, "quite convalescent," as he declared, making a few tottering steps to meet me at the sitting-room door. Evidently he was reluctant to take his final cross-bearings* of this earth for a Departure on the only voyage to an unknown destination a sailor ever undertakes. And it was all very nice—the large, sunny room; his deep easy-chair in a bow window, with pillows and a footstool; the quiet, watchful care of the elderly, gentle woman who had borne him five children, and had

not, perhaps, lived with him more than five full years
out of the thirty or so of their married life. There was
also another woman there in a plain black dress, quite
grey-haired, sitting very erect on her chair with some
sewing, from which she snatched side-glances in his
direction, and uttering not a single word during all the
time of my call. Even when, in due course, I carried
over to her a cup of tea, she only nodded at me silently,
with the faintest ghost of a smile on her tight-set lips.
I imagine she must have been a maiden sister of Mrs.
B—— come to help nurse her brother-in-law. His
youngest boy, a late-comer, a great cricketer it seemed,
twelve years old or thereabouts, chattered enthusiastically of the exploits of W. G. Grace.* And I remember
his eldest son, too, a newly-fledged doctor, who took me
out to smoke in the garden, and, shaking his head with
professional gravity, but with genuine concern, muttered: "Yes, but he doesn't get back his appetite. I
don't like that—I don't like that at all." The last
sight of Captain B—— I had was as he nodded his head
to me out of the bow window when I turned round to
close the front gate.

It was a distinct and complete impression, something that I don't know whether to call a Landfall or a
Departure. Certainly he had gazed at times very
fixedly before him with the Landfall's vigilant look, this
sea-captain seated incongruously in a deep-backed
chair. He had not then talked to me of employment, of
ships, of being ready to take another command; but
he had discoursed of his early days, in the abundant but
thin flow of a wilful invalid's talk. The women looked
worried, but sat still, and I learned more of him in that
interview than in the whole eighteen months we had
sailed together. It appeared he had "served his time"
in the copper-ore trade, the famous copper-ore trade of

old days between Swansea and the Chilian coast, coal
out and ore in, deep-loaded both ways, as if in wanton
defiance of the great Cape Horn seas—a work, this, for
staunch ships, and a great school of staunchness for
West-Country seamen. A whole fleet of copper-
bottomed barques, as strong in rib* and planking, as
well-found in gear, as ever was sent upon the seas,
manned by hardy crews and commanded by young
masters, was engaged in that now long-defunct trade.
"That was the school I was trained in," he said to me
almost boastfully, lying back amongst his pillows with a
rug over his legs. And it was in that trade that he
obtained his first command at a very early age. It was
then that he mentioned to me how, as a young commander, he was always ill for a few days before making
land after a long passage. But this sort of sickness
used to pass off with the first sight of a familiar land-
mark. Afterwards, he added, as he grew older, all that
nervousness wore off completely; and I observed his
weary eyes gaze steadily ahead, as if there had been
nothing between him and the straight line of sea and
sky, where whatever a seaman is looking for is first
bound to appear. But I have also seen his eyes rest
fondly upon the faces in the room, upon the pictures on
the wall, upon all the familiar objects of that home,
whose abiding and clear image must have flashed often
on his memory in times of stress and anxiety at sea.
Was he looking out for a strange Landfall, or taking
with an untroubled mind the bearings for his last
Departure?

It is hard to say; for in that voyage from which no
man returns Landfall and Departure are instantaneous,
merging together into one moment of supreme and
final attention. Certainly I do not remember observing
any sign of faltering in the set expression of his wasted

face, no hint of the nervous anxiety of a young commander about to make land on an uncharted shore. He had had too much experience of Departures and Landfalls! And had he not "served his time" in the famous copper-ore trade out of the Bristol Channel, the work of the staunchest ships afloat, and the school of staunch seamen?

IV

BEFORE an anchor can ever be raised, it must be let go; and this perfectly obvious truism brings me at once to the subject of the degradation of the sea language in the daily press of this country.

Your journalist, whether he takes charge of a ship or a fleet, almost invariably "casts" his anchor. Now, an anchor is never cast, and to take a liberty with technical language is a crime against the clearness, precision, and beauty of perfected speech.

An anchor is a forged piece of iron, admirably adapted to its end, and technical language is an instrument wrought into perfection by ages of experience, a flawless thing for its purpose. An anchor of yesterday (because nowadays there are contrivances like mushrooms and things like claws, of no particular expression or shape—just hooks)—an anchor of yesterday was in its way a most efficient instrument. To its perfection its size bears witness, for there is no other appliance so small for the great work it has to do. Look at the anchors hanging from the cat-heads*of a big ship! How tiny they are in proportion to the great size of the hull! Were they made of gold they would look like trinkets, like ornamental toys, no bigger in proportion than a jewelled drop in a woman's ear. And yet upon them will depend, more than once, the very life of the ship.

An anchor is forged and fashioned for faithfulness; give it ground that it can bite, and it will hold till the cable parts, and then, whatever may afterwards befall its ship, that anchor is "lost." The honest, rough piece of iron, so simple in appearance, has more parts than the human body has limbs: the ring, the stock, the crown, the flukes, the palms, the shank.* All this, according to the journalist, is "cast" when a ship arriving at an anchorage is brought up.

This insistence in using the odious word arises from the fact that a particularly benighted landsman must imagine the act of anchoring as a process of throwing something overboard, whereas the anchor ready for its work is already overboard, and is not thrown over, but simply allowed to fall. It hangs from the ship's side at the end of a heavy, projecting timber called the cat-head, in the bight of a short, thick chain whose end link is suddenly released by a blow from a top-maul or the pull of a lever when the order is given. And the order is not "Heave over!" as the paragraphist seems to imagine, but "Let go!"

As a matter of fact, nothing is ever cast in that sense on board ship but the lead, of which a cast is taken to search the depth of water on which she floats. A lashed boat, a spare spar, a cask, or what not secured about the decks, is "cast adrift" when it is untied. Also the ship herself is "cast to port or starboard" when getting under way. She, however, never "casts" her anchor.

To speak with severe technicality, a ship or a fleet is "brought up"—the complementary words unpronounced and unwritten being, of course, "to an anchor." Less technically, but not less correctly, the word "anchored," with its characteristic appearance and resolute sound, ought to be good enough for the newspapers of the greatest maritime country in the world. "The fleet anchored at Spithead"*: can any one want a better sentence for brevity and seamanlike ring? But the "cast-anchor" trick, with its affectation of being a sea-phrase—for why not write just as well "threw anchor," "flung anchor," or "shied anchor"?—is intolerably odious to a sailor's ear. I remember a coasting pilot of my early acquaintance (he used to read the papers assiduously) who, to define the utmost degree of lubber-liness in a landsman, used to say, "He's one of them poor, miserable 'cast-anchor' devils."

V

From first to last the seaman's thoughts are very much concerned with his anchors. It is not so much that the anchor is a symbol of hope as that it is the heaviest object that he has to handle on board his ship at sea in the usual routine of his duties. The beginning and the end of every passage are marked distinctly by work about the ship's anchors. A vessel in the Channel has her anchors always ready, her cables shackled on, and the land almost always in sight. The anchor and the land are indissolubly connected in a sailor's thoughts. But directly she is clear of the narrow seas, heading out into the world with nothing solid to speak of between her and the South Pole, the anchors are got in and the cables disappear from the deck. But the an-chors do not disappear. Technically speaking, they are "secured inboard"; and, on the forecastle head, lashed down to ring-bolts with ropes and chains, under the straining sheets of the head-sails, they look very idle and as if asleep. Thus bound, but carefully looked after, inert and powerful, those emblems of hope make company for the look-out man in the night watches; and so the days glide by, with a long rest for those character-istically shaped pieces of iron, reposing forward, visible from almost every part of the ship's deck, wait-ing for their work on the other side of the world some-where, while the ship carries them on with a great rush and splutter of foam underneath, and the sprays of the open sea rust their heavy limbs.

The first approach to the land, as yet invisible to the crew's eyes, is announced by the brisk order of the chief mate to the boatswain: "We will get the anchors over this afternoon" or "first thing to-morrow morn-ing," as the case may be. For the chief mate is the keeper of the ship's anchors and the guardian of her cable. There are good ships and bad ships, com-fortable ships and ships where, from first day to last of the voyage, there is no rest for a chief mate's body and soul. And ships are what men make them: this is a pronouncement of sailor wisdom, and, no doubt, in the main it is true.

However, there are ships where, as an old grizzled mate once told me, "nothing ever seems to go right!" And, looking from the poop where we both stood (I had paid him a neighbourly call in dock), he added: "She's one of them." He glanced up at my face, which ex-pressed a proper professional sympathy, and set me right in my natural surmise: "Oh, no; the old man's right enough. He never interferes. Anything that's done in a seamanlike way is good enough for him. And yet, somehow, nothing ever seems to go right in this ship. I tell you what: she is naturally unhandy."

The "old man," of course, was his captain, who just then came on deck in a silk hat and brown overcoat, and, with a civil nod to us, went ashore. He was cer-tainly not more than thirty, and the elderly mate, with a murmur to me of "That's my old man," proceeded to give instances of the natural unhandiness of the ship in a sort of deprecatory tone, as if to say, "You mustn't think I bear a grudge against her for that."

The instances do not matter. The point is that there are ships where things *do* go wrong; but whatever the ship—good or bad, lucky or unlucky—it is in the fore-part of her that her chief mate feels most at home. It is emphatically *his* end of the ship, though, of course, he is the executive supervisor of the whole. There are *his* anchors, *his* headgear,* his foremast, his station for manœuvring when the captain is in charge. And there, too, live the men, the ship's hands, whom it is his duty to keep employed, fair weather or foul, for the ship's welfare. It is the chief mate, the only figure of the ship's afterguard, who comes bustling forward at the cry of "All hands on deck!" He is the satrap of that province in the autocratic realm of the ship, and more personally responsible for anything that may happen there.

There, too, on the approach to the land, assisted by the boatswain and the carpenter, he "gets the anchors over" with the men of his own watch, whom he knows better than the others. There he sees the cable ranged, the windlass disconnected, the compressors* opened; and there, after giving his own last order, "Stand clear of the cable!" he waits attentive, in a silent ship that forges slowly ahead towards her picked-out berth, for the sharp shout from aft, "Let go!" Instantly bending over, he sees the trusty iron fall with a heavy plunge under his eyes, which watch and note whether it has gone clear.

For the anchor "to go clear" means to go clear of its own chain. Your anchor must drop from the bow of your ship with no turn of cable on any of its limbs, else you would be riding to a foul anchor. Unless the pull of the cable is fair on the ring, no anchor can be trusted even on the best of holding ground. In time of stress it is bound to drag, for implements and men must be treated fairly to give you the "virtue" which is in them. The anchor is an emblem of hope, but a foul anchor is worse than the most fallacious of false hopes that ever lured men or nations into a sense of security. And the sense of security, even the most warranted, is a bad counsellor. It is the sense which, like that exaggerated feeling of well-being ominous of the coming on of madness, precedes the swift fall of disaster. A seaman labouring under an undue sense of security becomes at once worth hardly half his salt. Therefore, of all my chief officers, the one I trusted most was a man called B——.* He had a red moustache, a lean face, also red, and an uneasy eye. He was worth all his salt.

On examining now, after many years, the residue of the feeling which was the outcome of the contact of our personalities, I discover, without much surprise, a certain flavour of dislike. Upon the whole, I think he was one of the most uncomfortable shipmates possible for a young commander. If it is permissible to criticise the absent, I should say he had a little too much of the sense of insecurity which is so invaluable in a seaman. He had an extremely disturbing air of being everlastingly ready (even when seated at table at my right hand before a plate of salt beef) to grapple with some impending calamity. I must hasten to add that he had also the other qualification necessary to make a trustworthy seaman—that of an absolute confidence in himself. What was really wrong with him was that he had these qualities in an unrestful degree. His eternally watchful demeanour, his jerky, nervous talk, even his, as it were, determined silences, seemed to imply—

and, I believe, they did imply—that to his mind the ship was never safe in my hands. Such was the man who looked after the anchors of a less than five-hundred-ton barque,* my first command, now gone from the face of the earth, but sure of a tenderly remembered existence as long as I live. No anchor could have gone down foul under Mr. B——'s piercing eye. It was good for one to be sure of that when, in an open roadstead, one heard in the cabin the wind pipe up; but still, there were moments when I detested Mr. B—— exceedingly. From the way he used to glare sometimes, I fancy that more than once he paid me back with interest. It so happened that we both loved the little barque very much. And it was just the defect of Mr. B——'s inestimable qualities that he would never persuade himself to believe that the ship was safe in my hands. To begin with, he was more than five years older than myself at a time of life when five years really do count, I being twenty-nine and he thirty-four; then, on our first leaving port (I don't see why I should make a secret of the fact that it was Bangkok), a bit of manœuvring of mine amongst the islands of the Gulf of Siam had given him an unforgettable scare. Ever since then he had nursed in secret a bitter idea of my utter recklessness. But upon the whole, and unless the grip of a man's hand at parting means nothing whatever, I conclude that we did like each other at the end of two years and three months well enough.

The bond between us was the ship; and therein a ship, though she has female attributes and is loved very unreasonably, is different from a woman. That I should have been tremendously smitten with my first command is nothing to wonder at, but I suppose I must admit that Mr. B——'s sentiment was of a higher order. Each of us, of course, was extremely anxious about

the good appearance of the beloved object; and, though
I was the one to glean compliments ashore, B—— had
the more intimate pride of feeling, resembling that of a
devoted handmaiden. And that sort of faithful and
proud devotion went so far as to make him go about
flicking the dust off the varnished teak-wood rail of the
little craft with a silk pocket-handkerchief—a present
from Mrs. B——, I believe.

That was the effect of his love for the barque. The
effect of his admirable lack of the sense of security once
went so far as to make him remark to me; "Well, sir,
you *are* a lucky man!"

It was said in a tone full of significance, but not
exactly offensive, and it was, I suppose, my innate tact
that prevented my asking, "What on earth do you
mean by that?"

Later on his meaning was illustrated more fully on a
dark night in a tight corner during a dead on-shore gale.
I had called him up on deck to help me consider our
extremely unpleasant situation. There was not much
time for deep thinking, and his summing-up was: "It
looks pretty bad, whichever we try, but, then, sir, you
always do get out of a mess somehow."

VI

It is difficult to disconnect the idea of ships' anchors
from the idea of the ship's chief mate—the man who
sees them go down clear and come up sometimes foul;
because not even the most unremitting care can always
prevent a ship swinging to winds and tide, from taking
an awkward turn of the cable round stock or fluke.
Then the business of "getting the anchor" and securing
it afterwards is unduly prolonged, and made a weariness
to the chief mate. He is the man who watches the

growth of the cable—a sailor's phrase which has all the force, precision, and imagery of technical language that, created by simple men with keen eyes for the real aspect of the things they see in their trade, achieves the just expression seizing upon the essential, which is the ambition of the artist in words. Therefore the sailor will never say, "cast anchor," and the shipmaster aft will hail his chief mate on the forecastle in impressionistic phrase: "How does the cable grow?" Because "grow" is the right word for the long drift of a cable emerging aslant under the strain, taut as a bow-string above the water. And it is the voice of the keeper of the ship's anchors that will answer: "Grows right ahead, sir," or "Broad on the bow," or whatever concise and deferential shout will fit the case.

There is no order more noisily given or taken up with lustier shouts on board a homeward-bound merchant ship than the command, "Man the windlass!" The rush of expectant men out of the forecastle, the snatching of hand-spikes,* the tramp of feet, the clink of the pawls,* make a stirring accompaniment to a plaintive up-anchor song with a roaring chorus; and this burst of noisy activity from a whole ship's crew seems like a voiceful awakening of the ship herself, till then, in the picturesque phrase of Dutch seaman, "lying asleep upon her iron."

For a ship with her sails furled on her squared yards,* and reflected from truck to water-line in the smooth gleaming sheet of a landlocked harbour, seems, indeed, to a seaman's eye the most perfect picture of slumbering repose. The getting of your anchor was a noisy operation on board a merchant ship of yesterday—an inspiring, joyous noise, as if, with the emblem of hope, the ship's company expected to drag up out of the depths, each man all his personal hopes into the reach of a securing hand—the hope of home, the hope of rest, of liberty, of dissipation, of hard pleasure, following the hard endurance of many days between sky and water. And this noisiness, this exultation at the moment of the ship's departure, make a tremendous contrast to the silent moments of her arrival in a foreign roadstead—the silent moments when, stripped of her sails, she forges ahead to her chosen berth, the loose canvas fluttering softly in the gear above the heads of the men standing still upon her decks, the master gazing intently forward from the break of the poop. Gradually she loses her way, hardly moving, with the three figures on her forecastle waiting attentively about the cat-head for the last order of, perhaps, full ninety days at sea: "Let go!"

This is the final word of a ship's ended journey, the closing word of her toil and of her achievement. In a life whose worth is told out in passages from port to port, the splash of the anchor's fall and the thunderous rumbling of the chain are like the closing of a distant period, of which she seems conscious with a slight deep shudder of all her frame. By so much is she nearer to her appointed death, for neither years nor voyages can go on for ever. It is to her like the striking of a clock, and in the pause which follows she seems to take count of the passing time.

This is the last important order; the others are mere routine directions. Once more the master is heard: "Give her forty-five fathom to the water's edge," and then he, too, is done for a time. For days he leaves all the harbour work to his chief mate, the keeper of the ship's anchor and of the ship's routine. For days his voice will not be heard raised about the decks, with that curt, austere accent of the man in charge, till, again, when the hatches are on, and in a silent and expectant ship, he shall speak up from aft in commanding tones: "Man the windlass!"

VII

THE other year, looking through a newspaper of sound principles, but whose staff *will* persist in "casting" anchors and going to sea "on" a ship (ough!), I came across an article upon the season's yachting. And, behold! it was a good article. To a man who had but little to do with pleasure sailing (though all sailing is a pleasure), and certainly nothing whatever with racing in open waters, the writer's strictures upon the handicapping of yachts were just intelligible and no more. And I do not pretend to any interest in the enumeration of the great races of that year. As to the 52-foot linear raters,* praised so much by the writer, I am warmed up by his approval of their performances; but, as far as any clear conception goes, the descriptive phrase, so precise to the comprehension of a yachtsman, evokes no definite image in my mind.

The writer praises that class of pleasure vessels, and I am willing to endorse his words, as any man who loves every craft afloat would be ready to do. I am disposed to admire and respect the 52-foot linear raters on the word of a man who regrets in such a sympathetic and understanding spirit the threatened decay of yachting seamanship.

Of course, yacht racing is an organized pastime, a function of social idleness ministering to the vanity of certain wealthy inhabitants of these isles nearly as much as to their inborn love of the sea. But the writer of the article in question goes on to point out, with insight and justice, that for a great number of people (20,000, I think he says) it is a means of livelihood—that it is, in his own words, an industry. Now, the moral side of an industry, productive or unproductive, the redeeming and ideal aspect of this bread-winning, is the attainment and preservation of the highest possible skill on the part of the craftsmen. Such skill, the skill of technique, is more than honesty; it is something wider, embracing honesty and grace and rule in an elevated and clear sentiment, not altogether utilitarian, which may be called the honour of labour. It is made up of accumulated tradition, kept alive by individual pride, rendered exact by professional opinion, and, like the higher arts, it is spurred on and sustained by discriminating praise.

This is why the attainment of proficiency, the pushing of your skill with attention to the most delicate shades of excellence, is a matter of vital concern. Efficiency of a practically flawless kind may be reached naturally in the struggle for bread. But there is something beyond—a higher point, a subtle and unmistakable touch of love and pride beyond mere skill; almost an inspiration which gives to all work that finish which is almost art—which *is* art.

As men of scrupulous honour set up a high standard of public conscience above the dead-level of an honest community, so men of that skill which passes into art by ceaseless striving raise the dead-level of correct practice in the crafts of land and sea. The conditions fostering the growth of that supreme, alive excellence, as well in work as in play, ought to be preserved with a most careful regard lest the industry or the game should perish of an insidious and inward decay. Therefore I have read with profound regret, in that article upon the yachting season of a certain year, that the seamanship on board racing yachts is not now what it used to be only a few, very few, years ago.

For that was the gist of that article, written evidently by a man who not only knows but *understands*—a thing (let me remark in passing) much rarer than one would expect, because the sort of understanding I mean is inspired by love; and love, though in a sense it may be admitted to be stronger than death, is by no means so universal and so sure. In fact, love is rare—the love of men, of things, of ideas, the love of perfected skill. For love is the enemy of haste; it takes count of passing days, of men who pass away, of a fine art matured slowly in the course of years and doomed in a short time to pass away, too, and be no more. Love and regret go hand in hand in this world of changes swifter than the shifting of the clouds reflected in the mirror of the sea.

To penalize a yacht in proportion to the fineness of her performances is unfair to the craft and to her men. It is unfair to the perfection of her form and to the skill of her servants. For we men are, in fact, the servants of our creations. We remain in everlasting bondage to the productions of our brain and to the work of our hands. A man is born to serve his time on this earth, and there is something fine in the service being given on other grounds than that of utility. The bondage of art is very exacting. And, as the writer of the article which started this train of thought says with lovable warmth, the sailing of yachts is a fine art.

His contention is that racing, without time allowances for anything else but tonnage—that is, for size— has fostered the fine art of sailing to the pitch of perfection. Every sort of demand is made upon the master of a sailing-yacht, and to be penalized in proportion to your success may be of advantage to the sport itself, but it has an obviously deteriorating effect upon the seamanship. The fine art is being lost.

VIII

The sailing and racing of yachts has developed a class of fore-and-aft*sailors, men born and bred to the sea, fishing in winter and yachting in summer; men to whom the handling of that particular rig presents no mystery. It is their striving for victory that has elevated the sailing of pleasure craft to the dignity of a fine art in that special sense. As I have said, I know nothing of racing and but little of fore-and-aft rig; but the advantages of such a rig are obvious, especially for purposes of pleasure, whether in cruising or racing. It requires less effort in handling; the trimming of the sail-planes to the wind can be done with speed and accuracy; the unbroken spread of the sail-area is of infinite advantage; and the greatest possible amount of canvas can be displayed upon the least possible quantity of spars. Lightness and concentrated power are the great qualities of fore-and-aft rig.

A fleet of fore-and-afters at anchor has its own slender graciousness. The setting of their sails resembles more than anything else the unfolding of a bird's wings; the facility of their evolutions is a pleasure to the eye. They are birds of the sea, whose swimming is like flying, and resembles more a natural function than the handling of man-invented appliances. The fore-and-aft rig in its simplicity and the beauty of its aspect under every angle of vision is, I believe, unapproachable. A schooner, yawl, or cutter in charge of a capable man seems to handle herself as if endowed with the power of reasoning and the gift of swift execution. One laughs with sheer pleasure at a smart piece of manœuvring, as at a manifestation of a living creature's quick wit and graceful precision.

Of those three varieties of fore-and-aft rig, the cutter—the racing rig *par excellence*—is of an appearance the most imposing, from the fact that practically all her canvas is in one piece. The enormous mainsail of a cutter, as she draws slowly past a point of land or the end of a jetty under your admiring gaze, invests her with an air of lofty and silent majesty. At anchor a schooner looks better; she has an aspect of greater efficiency and a better balance to the eye, with her two masts distributed over the hull with a swaggering rake*aft. The yawl rig one comes in time to love. It is, I should think, the easiest of all to manage.

For racing, a cutter; for a long pleasure voyage, a schooner; for cruising in home waters, the yawl; and the handling of them all is indeed a fine art. It requires not only the knowledge of the general principles of sailing, but a particular acquaintance with the character of the craft. All vessels are handled in the same way as far as theory goes, just as you may deal with all men on broad and rigid principles. But if you want that success in life which comes from the affection and confidence of your fellows, then with no two men, however similar they may appear in their nature, will you deal in the same way. There may be a rule of conduct; there is no rule of human fellowship. To deal with men is as fine an art as it is to deal with ships. Both men and ships live in an unstable element, are subject to subtle and powerful influences, and want to have their merits understood rather than their faults found out.

It is not what your ship will *not* do that you want to know to get on terms of successful partnership with her; it is, rather, that you ought to have a precise

knowledge of what she will do for you when called upon
to put forth what is in her by a sympathetic touch. At
first sight the difference does not seem great in either
line of dealing with the difficult problem of limitations.
But the difference is great. The difference lies in the
spirit in which the problem is approached. After all,
the art of handling ships is finer, perhaps, than the art
of handling men.

And, like all fine arts, it must be based upon a broad,
solid sincerity, which, like a law of Nature, rules an in-
finity of different phenomena. Your endeavour must
be single-minded. You would talk differently to a
coal-heaver and to a professor. But is this duplicity?
I deny it. The truth consists in the genuineness of the
feeling, in the genuine recognition of the two men, so
similar and so different, as your two partners in the
hazard of life. Obviously, a humbug, thinking only of
winning his little race, would stand a chance of profiting
by his artifices. Men, professors or coal-heavers, are
easily deceived; they even have an extraordinary knack
of lending themselves to deception, a sort of curious and
inexplicable propensity to allow themselves to be led by
the nose with their eyes open. But a ship is a creature
which we have brought into the world, as it were on
purpose to keep us up to the mark. In her handling a
ship will not put up with a mere pretender, as, for
instance, the public will do with Mr. X, the popular
statesman, Mr. Y, the popular scientist, or Mr. Z, the
popular—what shall we say?—anything from a teacher
of high morality to a bagman—who have won their
little race. But I would like (though not accustomed to
betting) to wager a large sum that not one of the few
first-rate skippers of racing yachts has ever been a
humbug. It would have been too difficult. The
difficulty arises from the fact that one does not deal with

ships in a mob, but with a ship as an individual. So we may have to do with men. But in each of us there lurks some particle of the mob spirit, of the mob temperament. No matter how earnestly we strive against each other, we remain brothers on the lowest side of our intellect and in the instability of our feelings. With ships it is not so. Much as they are to us they are nothing to each other. Those sensitive creatures have no ears for our blandishments. It takes something more than words to cajole them to do our will, to cover us with glory. Luckily, too, or else there would have been more shoddy reputations for first-rate seamanship. Ships have no ears, I repeat, though, indeed, I think I have known ships who really seemed to have had eyes, or else I cannot understand on what ground a certain 1000-ton barque of my acquaintance on one particular occasion refused to answer her helm, thereby saving a frightful smash to two ships and to a very good man's reputation. I knew her intimately for two years, and in no other instance either before or since have I known her to do that thing. The man she had served so well (guessing, perhaps, at the depths of his affection for her) I have known much longer, and in bare justice to him I must say that this confidence-shattering experience (though so fortunate) only augmented his trust in her. Yes, our ships have no ears, and thus they cannot be deceived. I would illustrate my idea of fidelity as between man and ship, between the master and his art, by a statement which, though it might appear shockingly sophisticated, is really very simple. I would say that a racing-yacht skipper who thought of nothing else but the glory of winning the race would never attain to any eminence of reputation. The genuine masters of their craft—I say this confidently from my experience of ships—have thought of nothing but of doing their very best by the vessel under their charge. To forget one's self, to surrender all personal feeling in the service of that fine art, is the only way for a seaman to the faithful discharge of his trust.

Such is the service of a fine art and of ships that sail the sea. And therein I think I can lay my finger upon the difference between the seamen of yesterday, who are still with us, and the seamen of to-morrow, already entered upon the possession of their inheritance. History repeats itself, but the special call of an art which has passed away is never reproduced. It is as utterly gone out of the world as the song of a destroyed wild bird. Nothing will awaken the same response of pleasurable emotion or conscientious endeavour. And the sailing of any vessel afloat is an art whose fine form seems already receding from us on its way to the over-shadowed Valley of Oblivion. The taking of a modern steamship about the world (though one would not minimize its responsibilities) has not the same quality of intimacy with nature, which, after all, is an in-dispensable condition to the building up of an art. It is less personal and a more exact calling; less arduous, but also less gratifying in the lack of close communion between the artist and the medium of his art. It is, in short, less a matter of love. Its effects are measured exactly in time and space as no effect of an art can be. It is an occupation which a man not desperately subject to sea-sickness can be imagined to follow with content, without enthusiasm, with industry, without affection. Punctuality is its watchword. The incertitude which attends closely every artistic endeavour is absent from its regulated enterprise. It has no great moments of self-confidence, or moments not less great of doubt and heart-searching. It is an industry which, like other industries, has its romance, its honour, and its rewards, its bitter anxieties and its hours of ease. But such sea-going has not the artistic quality of a single-handed struggle with something much greater than yourself; it is not the laborious, absorbing practice of an art whose ultimate result remains on the knees of the gods. It is not an individual, temperamental achievement, but simply the skilled use of a captured force, merely another step forward upon the way of universal conquest.

IX

Every passage of a ship of yesterday, whose yards were braced round eagerly the very moment the pilot, with his pockets full of letters, had got over the side, was like a race—a race against time, against an ideal standard of achievement outstripping the expectations of common men. Like all true art, the general conduct of a ship and her handling in particular cases had a technique which could be discussed with delight and pleasure by men who found in their work, not bread alone, but an outlet for the peculiarities of their temperament. To get the best and truest effect from the infinitely varying moods of sky and sea, not pictorially, but in the spirit of their calling, was their vocation, one and all; and they recognized this with as much sincerity, and drew as much inspiration from this reality, as any man who ever put brush to canvas. The diversity of temperaments was immense amongst those masters of the fine art.

Some of them were like Royal Academicians* of a certain kind. They never startled you by a touch of originality, by a fresh audacity of inspiration. They were safe, very safe. They went about solemnly in the assurance of their consecrated and empty reputation.

Names are odious, but I remember one of them who might have been their very president, the P.R.A. of the sea-craft. His weather-beaten and handsome face, his portly presence, his shirt-fronts and broad cuffs and gold links, his air of bluff distinction, impressed the humble beholders (stevedores, tally clerks, tide-waiters) as he walked ashore over the gangway of his ship lying at the Circular Quay in Sydney. His voice was deep, hearty, and authoritative—the voice of a very prince amongst sailors. He did everything with an air which put your attention on the alert and raised your expectations, but the result somehow was always on stereotyped lines, unsuggestive, empty of any lesson that one could lay to heart. He kept his ship in apple-pie order, which would have been seamanlike enough but for a finicking touch in its details. His officers affected a superiority over the rest of us, but the boredom of their souls appeared in their manner of dreary submission to the fads of their commander. It was only his apprenticed boys whose irrepressible spirits were not affected by the solemn and respectable mediocrity of that artist. There were four of these youngsters: one the son of a doctor, another of a colonel, the third of a jeweller; the name of the fourth was Twentyman,* and this is all I remember of his parentage. But not one of them seemed to possess the smallest spark of gratitude in his composition. Though their commander was a kind man in his way, and had made a point of introducing them to the best people in the town in order that they should not fall into the bad company of boys belonging to other ships, I regret to say that they made faces at him behind his back, and imitated the dignified carriage of his head without any concealment whatever.

This master of the fine art was a personage and nothing more; but, as I have said, there was an infinite diversity of temperament amongst the masters of the fine art I have known. Some were great impressionists. They impressed upon you the fear of God and Immensity—or, in other words, the fear of being drowned with every circumstance of terrific grandeur. One may think that the locality of your passing away by means of suffocation in water does not really matter very much. I am not so sure of that. I am, perhaps, unduly sensitive, but I confess that the idea of being suddenly spilt into an infuriated ocean in the midst of darkness and uproar affected me always with a sensation of shrinking distaste. To be drowned in a pond, though it might be called an ignominious fate by the ignorant, is yet a bright and peaceful ending in comparison with some other endings to one's earthly career which I have mentally quaked at in the intervals or even in the midst of violent exertions.

But let that pass. Some of the masters whose influence left a trace upon my character to this very day, combined a fierceness of conception with a certitude of execution upon the basis of just appreciation of means and ends which is the highest quality of the man of action. And an artist is a man of action, whether he creates a personality, invents an expedient, or finds the issue of a complicated situation.

There were masters, too, I have known, whose very art consisted in avoiding every conceivable situation. It is needless to say that they never did great things in their craft; but they were not to be despised for that. They were modest; they understood their limitations. Their own masters had not handed the sacred fire into the keeping of their cold and skilful hands. One of those last I remember specially, now gone to his rest from that sea which his temperament must have made a scene of little more than a peaceful pursuit. Once only did he attempt a stroke of audacity, one early morning, with a steady breeze, entering a crowded roadstead. But he was not genuine in this display which might have been art. He was thinking of his own self; he hankered after the meretricious glory of a showy performance.

As, rounding a dark, wooded point, bathed in fresh air and sunshine, we opened to view a crowd of shipping at anchor lying half a mile ahead of us perhaps, he called me aft from my station on the forecastle head, and, turning over and over his binoculars in his brown hands, said: "Do you see that big, heavy ship with white lower masts? I am going to take up a berth between her and the shore. Now do you see to it that the men jump smartly at the first order."

I answered, "Ay, ay, sir," and verily believed that this would be a fine performance. We dashed on through the fleet in magnificent style. There must have been many open mouths and following eyes on board those ships—Dutch, English, with a sprinkling of Americans and a German or two—who had all hoisted their flags at eight o'clock as if in honour of our arrival. It would have been a fine performance if it had come off, but it did not. Through a touch of self-seeking that modest artist of solid merit became untrue to his temperament. It was not with him art for art's sake: it was art for his own sake; and a dismal failure was the penalty he paid for that greatest of sins. It might have been even heavier, but, as it happened, we did not run our ship ashore, nor did we knock a large hole in the big ship whose lower masts were painted white. But it is a wonder that we did not carry away the cables of both our anchors, for, as may be imagined, I did not stand upon the order to "Let go!" that came to me in a quavering, quite unknown voice from his trembling lips. I let them both go with a celerity which to this day astonishes my memory. No average merchantman's anchors have ever been let go with such miraculous smartness. And they both held. I could have kissed their rough, cold iron palms in gratitude if they had not been buried in slimy mud under ten fathoms of water. Ultimately they brought us up with the jib-boom*of a Dutch brig poking through our spanker*—nothing worse. And a miss is as good as a mile.

But not in art. Afterwards the master said to me in a shy mumble, "She wouldn't luff up*in time, somehow. What's the matter with her?" And I made no answer.

Yet the answer was clear. The ship had found out the momentary weakness of her man. Of all the living creatures upon land and sea, it is ships alone that cannot be taken in by barren pretences, that will not put up with bad art from their masters.

X

FROM the main truck*of the average tall ship the horizon describes a circle of many miles, in which you can see another ship right down to her water-line; and these very eyes which follow this writing have counted in their time over a hundred sail becalmed, as if within a magic ring, not very far from the Azores—ships more or less tall. There were hardly two of them heading exactly the same way, as if each had meditated breaking out of the enchanted circle at a different point of the compass. But the spell of the calm is a strong magic. The following day still saw them scattered within sight of each other and heading different ways; but when, at last, the breeze came with the darkling ripple that ran very blue on a pale sea, they all went in the same direction together. For this was the homeward-bound fleet from the far-off ends of the earth, and a Falmouth fruit-schooner, the smallest of them all, was heading the flight. One could have imagined her very fair, if not divinely tall, leaving a scent of lemons and oranges in her wake.

The next day there were very few ships in sight from our mast-heads—seven at most, perhaps, with a few more distant specks, hull down, beyond the magic ring of the horizon. The spell of the fair wind has a subtle power to scatter a white-winged company of ships looking all the same way, each with its white fillet of tumbling foam under the bow. It is the calm that brings ships mysteriously together; it is your wind that is the great separator.

The taller the ship, the farther she can be seen; and her white tallness breathed upon by the wind first proclaims her size. The tall masts holding aloft the white canvas, spread out like a snare for catching the invisible power of the air, emerge gradually from the water, sail after sail, yard after yard, growing big, till, under the towering structure of her machinery, you perceive the insignificant, tiny speck of her hull.

The tall masts are the pillars supporting the balanced planes that, motionless and silent, catch from the air the ship's motive power, as it were a gift from Heaven vouchsafed to the audacity of man; and it is the ship's tall spars, stripped and shorn of their white glory, that incline themselves before the anger of the clouded heaven.

When they yield to a squall in a gaunt and naked submission, their tallness is brought best home even to the mind of a seaman. The man who has looked upon his ship going over too far is made aware of the preposterous tallness of a ship's spars. It seems impossible but that those gilt trucks which one had to tilt one's head back to see, now falling into the lower plane of vision, must perforce hit the very edge of the horizon. Such an experience gives you a better impression of the loftiness of your spars than any amount of running aloft could do. And yet in my time the royal yards*of an average profitable ship were a good way up above her decks.

No doubt a fair amount of climbing up iron ladders can be achieved by an active man in a ship's engine-room, but I remember moments when even to my supple limbs and pride of nimbleness the sailing-ship's machinery seemed to reach up to the very stars.

For machinery it is, doing its work in perfect silence and with a motionless grace, that seems to hide a capricious and not always governable power, taking nothing away from the material stores of the earth. Not for it the unerring precision of steel moved by white steam and living by red fire and fed with black coal. The other seems to draw its strength from the very soul of the world, its formidable ally, held to obedience by the frailest bonds, like a fierce ghost captured in a snare of something even finer than spun silk. For what is the array of the strongest ropes, the tallest spars, and the stoutest canvas against the mighty breath of the Infinite, but thistle stalks, cobwebs, and gossamer?

XI

Indeed, it is less than nothing, and I have seen, when the great soul of the world turned over with a heavy sigh, a perfectly new, extra-stout foresail vanish like a bit of some airy stuff much lighter than gossamer. Then was the time for the tall spars to stand fast in the great uproar. The machinery must do its work even if the soul of the world has gone mad.

The modern steamship advances upon a still and overshadowed sea with a pulsating tremor of her frame, an occasional clang in her depths, as if she had an iron heart in her iron body; with a thudding rhythm in her progress and the regular beat of her propeller, heard afar in the night with an august and plodding sound as of the march of an inevitable future. But in a gale, the silent machinery of a sailing-ship would catch not only the power, but the wild and exulting voice of the world's soul. Whether she ran with her tall spars swinging, or breasted it with her tall spars lying over, there was always that wild song, deep like a chant, for a bass to the shrill pipe of the wind played on the sea-tops, with a punctuating crash, now and then, of a breaking wave. At times the weird effects of that invisible orchestra would get upon a man's nerves till he wished himself deaf.

And this recollection of a personal wish, experienced upon several oceans, where the soul of the world has plenty of room to turn over with a mighty sigh, brings me to the remark that in order to take a proper care of a ship's spars it is just as well for a seaman to have nothing the matter with his ears. Such is the intimacy with which a seaman had to live with his ship of yesterday that his senses were like her senses, that the stress upon his body made him judge of the strain upon the ship's masts.

I had been some time at sea before I became aware of the fact that hearing plays a perceptible part in gauging the force of the wind. It was at night. The ship was one of those iron wool-clippers that the Clyde had floated out in swarms upon the world during the seventh decade of the last century. It was a fine period in ship-building, and also, I might say, a period of over-masting. The spars rigged up on the narrow hulls were indeed tall then, and the ship of which I think, with her coloured-glass skylight ends bearing the motto, "Let Glasgow Flourish," was certainly one of the most heavily-sparred specimens. She was built for hard driving, and unquestionably she got all the driving she could stand. Our captain* was a man famous for the quick passages he had been used to make in the old *Tweed*, a ship famous the world over for her speed. The *Tweed* had been a wooden vessel, and he brought the tradition of quick passages with him into the iron clipper. I was the junior in her, a third mate, keeping watch with the chief officer; and it was just during one of the night watches in a strong, freshening breeze*that I overheard two men in a sheltered nook of the main deck exchanging these informing remarks. Said one:

"Should think 'twas time some of them light sails were coming off her."

And the other, an older man, uttered grumpily:

"No fear! not while the chief mate's on deck. He's that deaf he can't tell how much wind there is."

And, indeed, poor P——,* quite young, and a smart seaman, was very hard of hearing. At the same time, he had the name of being the very devil of a fellow for carrying on sail on a ship. He was wonderfully clever at concealing his deafness, and, as to carrying on heavily, though he was a fearless man, I don't think that he ever meant to take undue risks. I can never forget his naïve sort of astonishment when remonstrated with for what appeared a most dare-devil performance. The only person, of course, that could remonstrate with telling effect was our captain, himself a man of dare-devil tradition; and really, for me, who knew under whom I was serving, those were impressive scenes.

Captain S—— had a great name for sailorlike qualities —the sort of name that compelled my youthful admiration. To this day I preserve his memory, for, indeed, it was he in a sense who completed my training. It was often a stormy process, but let that pass. I am sure he meant well, and I am certain that never, not even at the time, could I bear him malice for his extraordinary gift of incisive criticism. And to hear *him* make a fuss about too much sail on the ship seemed one of those incredible experiences that take place only in one's dreams.

It generally happened in this way: Night clouds racing overhead, wind howling, royals set, and the ship rushing on in the dark, an immense white sheet of foam level with the lee rail. Mr. P——, in charge of the deck, hooked on to the windward mizzen rigging in a state of perfect serenity; myself, the third mate, also hooked on somewhere to windward of the slanting poop, in a state of the utmost preparedness to jump at the very first hint of some sort of order, but otherwise in a perfectly acquiescent state of mind. Suddenly, out of the companion would appear a tall, dark figure, bareheaded, with a short white beard of a perpendicular cut, very visible in the dark—Captain S——, disturbed in his reading down below by the frightful bounding and lurching of the ship. Leaning very much against the precipitous incline of the deck, he would take a turn or two, perfectly silent, hang on by the compass for a while, take another couple of turns, and suddenly burst out:

"What are you trying to do with the ship?"

And Mr. P——, who was not good at catching what was shouted in the wind, would say interrogatively:

"Yes, sir?"

Then in the increasing gale*of the sea there would be

a little private ship's storm going on in which you could detect strong language, pronounced in a tone of passion, and exculpatory protestations uttered with every possible inflection of injured innocence.

"By Heavens, Mr. P——! I used to carry on sail in my time, but——"

And the rest would be lost to me in a stormy gust of wind.

Then, in a lull, P——'s protesting innocence would become audible:

"She seems to stand it very well."

And then another burst of an indignant voice:

"Any fool can carry sail on a ship——"

And so on and so on, the ship meanwhile rushing on her way with a heavier list, a noisier splutter, a more threatening hiss of the white, almost blinding, sheet of foam to leeward. For the best of it was that Captain S—— seemed constitutionally incapable of giving his officers a definite order to shorten sail; and so that extraordinarily vague row would go on till at last it dawned upon them both, in some particularly alarming gust, that it was time to do something. There is nothing like the fearful inclination of your tall spars overloaded with canvas to bring a deaf man and an angry one to their senses.

XII

So sail did get shortened more or less in time even in that ship, and her tall spars never went overboard while I served in her. However, all the time I was with them, Captain S—— and Mr. P—— did not get on very well together. If P—— carried on "like the very devil" because he was too deaf to know how much wind there was, Captain S—— (who, as I have said, seemed

constitutionally incapable of ordering one of his officers
to shorten sail) resented the necessity forced upon him
by Mr. P——'s desperate goings on. It was in Captain S——'s tradition rather to reprove his officers for
not carrying on quite enough—in his phrase "for not
taking every ounce of advantage of a fair wind." But
there was also a psychological motive that made him
extremely difficult to deal with on board that iron
clipper. He had just come out of the marvellous
Tweed,[*] a ship, I have heard, heavy to look at but of
phenomenal speed. In the middle sixties she had
beaten by a day and a half the steam mail-boat from
Hong-Kong to Singapore. There was something peculiarly lucky, perhaps, in the placing of her masts—who
knows? Officers of men-of-war used to come on board
to take the exact dimensions of her sail-plan. Perhaps
there had been a touch of genius or the finger of good
fortune in the fashioning of her lines at bow and stern.
It is impossible to say. She was built in the East
Indies somewhere, of teak-wood throughout, except the
deck. She had a great sheer,[*]high bows, and a clumsy
stern. The men who had seen her described her to me
as "nothing much to look at." But in the great Indian
famine of the 'seventies[*] that ship, already old then, made
some wonderful dashes across the Gulf of Bengal with
cargoes of rice from Rangoon to Madras.

She took the secret of her speed with her, and, un-
sightly as she was, her image surely has its glorious
place in the mirror of the old sea.

The point, however, is that Captain S——, who used
to say frequently, "She never made a decent passage
after I left her," seemed to think that the secret of her
speed lay in her famous commander. No doubt the
secret of many a ship's excellence does lie with the man
on board, but it was hopeless for Captain S—— to try

to make his new iron clipper equal the feats which made the old *Tweed* a name of praise upon the lips of English-speaking seamen. There was something pathetic in it, as in the endeavour of an artist in his old age to equal the masterpieces of his youth—for the *Tweed's* famous passages were Captain S——'s masterpieces. It was pathetic, and perhaps just the least bit dangerous. At any rate, I am glad that, what between Captain S——'s yearning for old triumphs and 'Mr. P——'s deafness, I have seen some memorable carrying on to make a passage. And I have carried on myself upon the tall spars of that Clyde ship-builder's masterpiece as I have never carried on in a ship before or since.

The second mate falling ill during the passage, I was promoted to officer of the watch, alone in charge of the deck. Thus the immense leverage of the ship's tall masts became a matter very near my own heart. I suppose it was something of a compliment for a young fellow to be trusted, apparently without any supervision, by such a commander as Captain S——; though as far as I can remember, neither the tone, nor the manner, nor yet the drift of Captain S——'s remarks addressed to myself did ever, by the most strained interpretation, imply a favourable opinion of my abilities. And he was, I must say, a most uncomfortable commander to get your orders from at night. If I had the watch from eight till midnight, he would leave the deck about nine with the words, "Don't take any sail off her." Then, on the point of disappearing down the companion-way, he would add curtly: "Don't carry anything away." I am glad to say that I never c'd; one night, however, I was caught, not quite prepared, by a sudden shift of wind.

There was, of course, a good deal of noise—running about, the shouts of the sailors, the thrashing of the

sails—enough, in fact, to wake the dead. But S——
never came on deck. When I was relieved by the chief
mate an hour afterwards, he sent for me. I went into
his state-room; he was lying on his couch wrapped up in
a rug, with a pillow under his head.

"What was the matter with you up there just now?"
he asked.

"Wind flew round on the lee quarter,* sir." I said.

"Couldn't you see the shift coming?"

"Yes, sir, I thought it wasn't very far off."

"Why didn't you have your courses* hauled up at
once, then?" he asked in a tone that ought to have
made my blood run cold.

But this was my chance and I did not let it slip.

"Well, sir," I said in an apologetic tone, "she was
going eleven knots very nicely, and I thought she would
do for another half-hour or so."

He gazed at me darkly out of his head, lying very
still on the white pillow, for a time.

"Ah, yes, another half-hour. That's the way ships
get dismasted."

And that was all I got in the way of a wigging. I
waited a little while and then went out, shutting carefully the door of the state-room after me.

Well, I have loved, lived with, and left the sea without ever seeing a ship's tall fabric of sticks, cobwebs, and
gossamer go by the board. Sheer good luck, no doubt.
But as to poor P——, I am sure that he would not have
got off scot-free like this but for the god of gales, who
called him away early from this earth, which is three
parts ocean, and therefore a fit abode for sailors. A
few years afterwards I met in an Indian port a man who
had served in the ships of the same company. Names
came up in our talk, names of our colleagues in the same
employ, and, naturally enough, I asked after P——.

Had he got a command yet? And the other man answered carelessly:

"No; but he's provided for, anyhow. A heavy sea took him off the poop in the run between New Zealand and the Horn."

Thus P—— passed away from amongst the tall spars of ships that he had tried to their utmost in many a spell of boisterous weather. He had shown me what carrying on meant, but he was not a man to learn discretion from. He could not help his deafness. One can only remember his cheery temper, his admiration for the jokes in *Punch*, his little oddities—like his strange passion for borrowing looking-glasses, for instance. Each of our cabins had its own looking-glass screwed to the bulkhead, and what he wanted with more of them we never could fathom. He asked for the loan in confidential tones. Why? Mystery. We made various surmises. No one will ever know now. At any rate, it was a harmless eccentricity, and may the god of gales, who took him away so abruptly between New Zealand and the Horn, let his soul rest in some Paradise of true seamen, where no amount of carrying on will ever dismast a ship!

XIII

THERE has been a time when a ship's chief mate, pocket-book in hand and pencil behind his ear, kept one eye aloft upon his riggers and the other down the hatchway on the stevedores, and watched the disposition of his ship's cargo, knowing that even before she started he was already doing his best to secure for her an easy and quick passage.

The hurry of the times, the loading and discharging organization of the docks, the use of hoisting machinery which works quickly and will not wait, the cry for prompt dispatch, the very size of his ship, stand nowadays between the modern seaman and the thorough knowledge of his craft.

There are profitable ships and unprofitable ships. The profitable ship will carry a large load through all the hazards of the weather, and, when at rest, will stand up in dock and shift from berth to berth without ballast. There is a point of perfection in a ship as a worker when she is spoken of as being able to *sail* without ballast. I have never met that sort of paragon myself, but I have seen these paragons advertised amongst ships for sale. Such excess of virtue and good-nature on the part of a ship always provoked my mistrust. It is open to any man to say that his ship will sail without ballast; and he will say it, too, with every mark of profound conviction, especially if he is not going to sail in her himself. The risk of advertising her as able to sail without ballast is not great, since the statement does not imply a warranty of her arriving anywhere. Moreover, it is strictly true that most ships will sail without ballast for some little time before they turn turtle upon the crew.

A shipowner loves a profitable ship; the seaman is proud of her; a doubt of her good looks seldom exists in his mind; but if he can boast of her more useful qualities it is an added satisfaction for his self-love.

The loading of ships was once a matter of skill, judgment, and knowledge. Thick books have been written about it. "Stevens on Stowage"* is a portly volume with the renown and weight (in its own world) of Coke on Littleton.* Stevens is an agreeable writer, and, as is the case with men of talent, his gifts adorn his sterling soundness. He gives you the official teaching on the whole subject, is precise as to rules, mentions illustra-

tive events, quotes law cases where verdicts turned
upon a point of stowage. He is never pedantic, and,
for all his close adherence to broad principles, he is
ready to admit that no two ships can be treated exactly
alike.

Stevedoring, which had been a skilled labour, is fast
becoming a labour without the skill. The modern
steamship with her many holds is not loaded within the
sailorlike meaning of the word. She is filled up. Her
cargo is not stowed in any sense; it is simply dumped
into her through six hatchways, more or less, by twelve
winches or so, with clatter and hurry and racket and
heat, in a cloud of steam and a mess of coal-dust. As
long as you keep her propeller underwater and take
care, say, not to fling down barrels of oil on top of bales
of silk, or deposit an iron bridge-girder of five ton or so
upon a bed of coffee-bags, you have done about all in
the way of duty that the cry for prompt dispatch will
allow you to do.

XIV

The sailing-ship, when I knew her in her days of
perfection, was a sensible creature. When I say her
days of perfection, I mean perfection of build, gear,
seaworthy qualities, and ease of handling, not the perfection of speed. That quality has departed with the
change of building material. No iron ship of yesterday
ever attained the marvels of speed which the seamanship of men famous in their time had obtained from
their wooden, copper-sheeted predecessors. Everything had been done to make the iron ship perfect, but
no wit of man had managed to devise an efficient coat-
ing composition to keep her bottom clean with the
smooth cleanness of yellow metal sheeting. After a

spell of a few weeks at sea, an iron ship begins to lag as if she had grown tired too soon. It is only her bottom that is getting foul. A very little affects the speed of an iron ship which is not driven on by a merciless propeller. Often it is impossible to tell what inconsiderate trifle puts her off her stride. A certain mysteriousness hangs around the quality of speed as it was displayed by the old sailing-ships commanded by a competent seaman. In those days the speed depended upon the seaman; therefore, apart from the laws, rules, and regulations for the good preservation of his cargo, he was careful of his loading, or what is technically called the trim of his ship. Some ships sailed fast on an even keel, others had to be trimmed quite one foot by the stern, and I have heard of a ship that gave her best speed on a wind when so loaded as to float a couple of inches by the head.*

I call to mind a winter landscape in Amsterdam —a flat foreground of waste land, with here and there stacks of timber, like the huts of a camp of some very miserable tribe; the long stretch of the Handelskade; cold, stone-faced quays, with the snow-sprinkled ground and the hard, frozen water of the canal, in which were set ships one behind another with their frosty mooring-ropes hanging slack and their decks idle and deserted, because, as the master stevedore (a gentle, pale person, with a few golden hairs on his chin and a reddened nose) informed me, their cargoes were frozen-in up-country on barges and schuyts.* In the distance, beyond the waste ground, and running parallel with the line of ships, a line of brown, warm-toned houses seemed bowed under snow-laden roofs. From afar at the end of Tsar Peter Straat, issued in the frosty air the tinkle of bells of the horse tramcars, appearing and disappearing in the opening between the buildings, like little toy carriages harnessed with toy horses and played with by people that appeared no bigger than children.

I was, as the French say, biting my fists with impatience for that cargo frozen up-country; with rage at that canal set fast, at the wintry and deserted aspect of all those ships that seemed to decay in grim depression for want of the open water. I was chief mate,* and very much alone. Directly I had joined I received from my owners* instructions to send all the ship's apprentices away on leave together, because in such weather there was nothing for anybody to do, unless to keep up a fire in the cabin stove. That was attended to by a snuffy and mop-headed, inconceivably dirty, and weirdly toothless Dutch ship-keeper, who could hardly speak three words of English, but who must have had some considerable knowledge of the language, since he managed invariably to interpret in the contrary sense everything that was said to him.

Notwithstanding the little iron stove, the ink froze on the swing-table in the cabin, and I found it more convenient to go ashore stumbling over the Arctic waste land and shivering in glazed tramcars in order to write my evening letter to my owners in a gorgeous café* in the centre of the town. It was an immense place, lofty and gilt, upholstered in red plush, full of electric lights, and so thoroughly warmed that even the marble tables felt tepid to the touch. The waiter who brought me my cup of coffee bore, by comparison with my utter isolation, the dear aspect of an intimate friend. There, alone in a noisy crowd, I would write slowly a letter addressed to Glasgow, of which the gist would be: There is no cargo, and no prospect of any coming till late spring apparently. And all the time I sat there the necessity of getting back to the ship bore heavily on my already half-congealed spirits—the

shivering in glazed tramcars, the stumbling over the
snow-sprinkled waste ground, the visions of ships
frozen in a row, appearing vaguely like corpses of black
vessels in a white world, so silent, so lifeless, so soulless
they seemed to be.

With precaution I would go up the side of my own
particular corpse, and would feel her as cold as ice itself
and as slippery under my feet. My cold berth would
swallow up like a chilly burial niche my bodily shivers
and my mental excitement. It was a cruel winter.
The very air seemed as hard and trenchant as steel;
but it would have taken much more than this to ex-
tinguish my sacred fire for the exercise of my craft. No
young man of twenty-four appointed chief mate for the
first time in his life would have let that Dutch tenacious
winter penetrate into his heart. I think that in those
days I never forgot the fact of my elevation for five
consecutive minutes. I fancy it kept me warm, even
in my slumbers, better than the high pile of blankets,
which positively crackled with frost as I threw them
off in the morning. And I would get up early for no
reason whatever except that I was in sole charge. The
new captain had not been appointed yet.

Almost each morning a letter from my owners would
arrive, directing me to go to the charterers and clamour
for the ship's cargo; to threaten them with the heaviest
penalties of demurrage; to demand that this assortment
of varied merchandise, set fast in a landscape of ice and
windmills somewhere up-country, should be put on rail
instantly, and fed up to the ship in regular quantities
every day. After drinking some hot coffee, like an
Arctic explorer setting off on a sledge journey towards
the North Pole, I would go ashore and roll shivering in
a tramcar into the very heart of the town, past clean-
faced houses, past thousands of brass knockers upon a

thousand painted doors glimmering behind rows of
trees of the pavement species, leafless, gaunt, seemingly
dead for ever.

That part of the expedition was easy enough, though
the horses were painfully glistening with icicles, and
the aspect of the tram-conductors' faces presented a
repulsive blending of crimson and purple. But as to
frightening or bullying, or even wheedling some sort
of answer out of Mr. Hudig, that was another matter
altogether. He was a big, swarthy Netherlander, with
black moustaches and a bold glance. He always began by shoving me into a chair before I had time to open
my mouth, gave me cordially a large cigar, and in
excellent English would start to talk everlastingly about
the phenomenal severity of the weather. It was impossible to threaten a man who, though he possessed
the language perfectly, seemed incapable of understanding any phrase pronounced in a tone of remonstrance or discontent. As to quarrelling with him, it
would have been stupid. The weather was too bitter
for that. His office was so warm, his fire so bright, his
sides shook so heartily with laughter, that I experienced
always a great difficulty in making up my mind to reach
for my hat.

At last the cargo did come. At first it came dribbling
in by rails in trucks, till the thaw set in; and then fast, in
a multitude of barges, with a great rush of unbound
waters. The gentle master stevedore had his hands
very full at last; and the chief mate became worried in
his mind as to the proper distribution of the weight of
his first cargo in a ship he did not personally know before.

Ships do want humouring. They want humouring
in handling; and if you mean to handle them well, they
must have been humoured in the distribution of the

weight which you ask them to carry through the good and evil fortune of a passage. Your ship is a tender creature, whose idiosyncrasies must be attended to if you mean her to come with credit to herself and you through the rough-and-tumble of her life.

XV

So seemed to think the new captain, who arrived the day after we had finished loading, on the very eve of the day of sailing. I first beheld him on the quay, a complete stranger to me, obviously not a Hollander, in a black bowler and a short drab overcoat, ridiculously out of tone with the winter aspect of the waste lands, bordered by the brown fronts of houses with their roofs dripping with melting snow.

This stranger was walking up and down absorbed in the marked contemplation of the ship's fore and aft trim; but when I saw him squat on his heels in the slush at the very edge of the quay to peer at the draught of water under her counter,* I said to myself, "this is the captain." And presently I descried his luggage coming along—a real sailor's chest, carried by means of rope-beckets between two men, with a couple of leather portmanteaus and a roll of charts sheeted in canvas piled upon the lid. The sudden, spontaneous agility with which he bounded aboard right off the rail afforded me the first glimpse of his real character. Without further preliminaries than a friendly nod, he addressed me: "You have got her pretty well in her fore and aft trim.* Now, what about your weights?"

I told him I had managed to keep the weight sufficiently well up, as I thought, one third of the whole being in the upper part "above the beams," as the technical expression has it. He whistled "Phew!"

scrutinizing me from head to foot. A sort of smiling vexation was visible on his ruddy face.

"Well, we shall have a lively time of it this passage, I bet," he said.

He knew. It turned out he had been chief mate of her for the two preceding voyages; and I was already familiar with his handwriting in the old log-books I had been perusing in my cabin with a natural curiosity, looking up the records of my new ship's luck, of her behaviour, of the good times she had had, and of the troubles she had escaped.

He was right in his prophecy. On our passage from Amsterdam to Samarang*with a general cargo, of which, alas! only one third in weight was stowed "above the beams," we had a lively time of it. It was lively, but not joyful. There was not even a single moment of comfort in it, because no seaman can feel comfortable in body or mind when he has made his ship uneasy.

To travel along with a cranky ship for ninety days or so is no doubt a nerve-trying experience; but in this case what was wrong with our craft was this: that by my system of loading she had been made much too stable.

Neither before nor since have I felt a ship roll so abruptly, so violently, so heavily. Once she began, you felt that she would never stop, and this hopeless sensation, characterizing the motion of ships whose centre of gravity is brought down too low in loading, made everyone on board weary of keeping on his feet. I remember once overhearing one of the hands say: "By Heavens, Jack!   I feel as if I didn't mind how soon I let myself go, and let the blamed hooker knock my brains out if she likes." The captain used to remark frequently: "Ah, yes; I dare say one third weight above beams would have been quite enough for most ships. But then, you see, there's no two of them alike on the seas, and she's an uncommonly ticklish jade to load."

Down south, running before the gales of high latitudes, she made our life a burden to us. There were days when nothing would keep even on the swing-tables, when there was no position where you could fix yourself so as not to feel a constant strain upon all the muscles of your body. She rolled and rolled with an awful dislodging jerk and that dizzily fast sweep of her masts on every swing. It was a wonder that the men sent aloft were not flung off the yards, the yards not flung off the masts, the masts not flung overboard. The captain in his arm-chair, holding on grimly at the head of the table, with the soup-tureen rolling on one side of the cabin and the steward sprawling on the other, would observe, looking at me: "That's your one-third above the beams. The only thing that surprises me is that the sticks have stuck to her all this time."

Ultimately some of the minor spars did go—nothing important: spanker-booms* and such-like—because at times the frightful impetus of her rolling would part a fourfold tackle of new three-inch Manilla line as if it were weaker than pack-thread.

It was only poetic justice that the chief mate who had made a mistake—perhaps a half-excusable one—about the distribution of his ship's cargo should pay the penalty. A piece of one of the minor spars that did carry away flew against the chief mate's back, and sent him sliding on his face for quite a considerable distance along the main deck. Thereupon followed various and unpleasant consequences of a physical order—"queer symptoms," as the captain, who treated them, used to say; inexplicable periods of powerlessness, sudden accesses of mysterious pain; and the patient agreed fully with the regretful mutters of his very attentive captain wishing that it had been a straightforward broken leg. Even the Dutch doctor who took the case up in Samarang offered no scientific explanation. All he said was: "Ah, friend, you are young yet; it may be very serious for your whole life. You must leave your ship; you must quite silent be for three months—quite silent."

Of course, he meant the chief mate to keep quiet— to lay up, as a matter of fact. His manner was impressive enough, if his English was childishly imperfect when compared with the fluency of Mr. Hudig, the figure at the other end of that passage, and memorable enough in its way. In a great airy ward of a Far Eastern hospital,* lying on my back, I had plenty of leisure to remember the dreadful cold and snow of Amsterdam, while looking at the fronds of the palmtrees tossing and rustling at the height of the window. I could remember the elated feeling and the soulgripping cold of those tramway journeys taken into town to put what in diplomatic language is called pressure upon the good Hudig, with his warm fire, his armchair, his big cigar, and the never-failing suggestion in his good-natured voice: "I suppose in the end it is you they will appoint captain before the ship sails?" It may have been his extreme good-nature, the serious, unsmiling good-nature of a fat, swarthy man with coalblack moustache and steady eyes; but he might have been a bit of a diplomatist, too. His enticing suggestions I used to repel modestly by the assurance that it was extremely unlikely, as I had not enough experience. "You know very well how to go about business matters," he used to say, with a sort of affected moodiness clouding his serene round face. I wonder whether he ever laughed to himself after I had left the office. I dare say he never did, because I understand that diplomatists, in and out of the career,* take themselves and their tricks with an exemplary seriousness.

But he had nearly persuaded me that I was fit in every way to be trusted with a command. There came three months of mental worry, hard rolling, remorse, and physical pain to drive home the lesson of insufficient experience.

Yes, your ship wants to be humoured with knowledge. You must treat with an understanding consideration the mysteries of her feminine nature, and then she will stand by you faithfully in the unceasing struggle with forces wherein defeat is no shame. It is a serious relation, that in which a man stands to his ship. She has her rights as though she could breathe and speak; and, indeed, there are ships that, for the right man, will do anything but speak, as the saying goes.

A ship is not a slave. You must make her easy in a seaway, you must never forget that you owe her the fullest share of your thought, of your skill, of your self-love. If you remember that obligation, naturally and without effort, as if it were an instinctive feeling of your inner life, she will sail, stay, run for you as long as she is able, or, like a sea-bird going to rest upon the angry waves, she will lay out the heaviest gale that ever made you doubt living long enough to see another sunrise.

XVI

OFTEN I turn with melancholy eagerness to the space reserved in the newspapers under the general heading of "Shipping Intelligence." I meet there the names of ships I have known. Every year some of these names disappear—the names of old friends. "Tempi passati!"*

The different divisions of that kind of news are set down in their order, which varies but slightly in its arrangement of concise headlines. And first comes "Speakings"—reports of ships met and signalled at sea, name, port, where from, where bound for, so many days out, ending frequently with the words "All well." Then come "Wrecks and Casualties"—a longish array of paragraphs, unless the weather has been fair and clear, and friendly to ships all over the world.

On some days there appears the heading "Overdue" —an ominous threat of loss and sorrow trembling yet in the balance of fate. There is something sinister to a seaman in the very grouping of the letters which form this word, clear in its meaning, and seldom threatening in vain.

Only a very few days more—appallingly few to the hearts which had set themselves bravely to hope against hope—three weeks, a month later, perhaps, the name of ships under the blight of the "Overdue" heading shall appear again in the column of "Shipping Intelligence," but under the final declaration of "Missing."

"The ship, or barque, or brig So-and-so, bound from such a port, with such and such cargo, for such another port, having left at such and such a date, last spoken at sea on such a day, and never having been heard of since, was posted to-day as missing." Such in its strictly official eloquence is the form of funeral orations on ships that, perhaps wearied with a long struggle, or in some unguarded moment that may come to the readiest of us, had let themselves be overwhelmed by a sudden blow from the enemy.

Who can say? Perhaps the men she carried had asked her to do too much, had stretched beyond breaking-point the enduring faithfulness which seems wrought and hammered into that assemblage of iron ribs and plating, of wood and steel and canvas and wire, which goes to the making of a ship—a complete creation endowed with character, individuality, qualities and defects, by men whose hands launch her upon the water, and that other men shall learn to know with an intimacy surpassing the intimacy of man with man, to love with a love nearly as great as that of man for woman, and often as blind in its infatuated disregard of defects.

There are ships which bear a bad name but I have yet to meet one whose crew for the time being failed to stand up angrily for her against every criticism. One ship which I call to mind now had the reputation of killing somebody every voyage she made. This was no calumny, and yet I remember well, somewhere far back in the late 'seventies, that the crew of that ship were, if anything, rather proud of her evil fame, as if they had been an utterly corrupt lot of desperadoes glorying in their association with an atrocious creature. We, belonging to other vessels moored all about the Circular Quay in Sydney, used to shake our heads at her with a great sense of the unblemished virtue of our own well-loved ships.

I shall not pronounce her name. She is "missing" now, after a sinister but, from the point of view of her owners, a useful career extending over many years, and, I should say, across every ocean of our globe. Having killed a man for every voyage, and perhaps rendered more misanthropic by the infirmities that come with years upon a ship, she had made up her mind to kill all hands at once before leaving the scene of her exploits. A fitting end, this, to a life of usefulness and crime—in a last outburst of an evil passion supremely satisfied on some wild night, perhaps, to the applauding clamour of wind and wave.

How did she do it? In the word "missing" there is a horrible depth of doubt and speculation. Did she go quickly from under the men's feet, or did she resist to the end, letting the sea batter her to pieces, start her butts, wrench her frame, load her with an increasing weight of salt water, and, dismasted, unmanageable, rolling heavily, her boats gone, her decks swept, had she wearied her men half to death with the unceasing labour at the pumps before she sank with them like a stone?

However, such a case must be rare. I imagine a raft of some sort could always be contrived; and, even if it saved no one, it would float on and be picked up, perhaps conveying some hint of the vanished name. Then that ship would not be, properly speaking, missing. She would be "lost with all hands," and in that distinction there is a subtle difference—less horror and a less appalling darkness.

XVII

The unholy fascination of dread dwells in the thought of the last moments of a ship reported as "missing" in the columns of the *Shipping Gazette.* Nothing of her ever comes to light—no grating, no lifebuoy, no piece of boat or branded oar—to give a hint of the place and date of her sudden end. The *Shipping Gazette* does not even call her "lost with all hands." She remains simply "missing"; she has disappeared enigmatically into a mystery of fate as big as the world, where your imagination of a brother-sailor, of a fellow-servant and lover of ships, may range unchecked.

And yet sometimes one gets a hint of what the last

scene may be like in the life of a ship and her crew, which resembles a drama in its struggle against a great force bearing it up, formless, ungraspable, chaotic and mysterious, as fate.

It was on a grey afternoon in the lull of a three days' gale that had left the Southern Ocean tumbling heavily upon our ship, under a sky hung with rags of clouds that seemed to have been cut and hacked by the keen edge of a sou'-west gale.

Our craft, a Clyde-built barque* of 1,000 tons, rolled so heavily that something aloft had carried away. No matter what the damage was, but it was serious enough to induce me to go aloft myself with a couple of hands and the carpenter to see the temporary repairs properly done.

Sometimes we had to drop everything and cling with both hands to the swaying spars, holding our breath in fear of a terribly heavy roll. And, wallowing as if she meant to turn over with us, the barque, her decks full of water, her gear flying in bights, ran at some ten knots an hour.* We had been driven far south—much farther that way than we had meant to go; and suddenly, up there in the slings* of the foreyard, in the midst of our work, I felt my shoulder gripped with such force in the carpenter's powerful paw that I positively yelled with unexpected pain. The man's eyes stared close in my face, and he shouted, "Look, sir! look! What's this?" pointing ahead with his other hand.

At first I saw nothing. The sea was one empty wilderness of black and white hills. Suddenly, half-concealed in the tumult of the foaming rollers I made out awash, something enormous, rising and falling—something spread out like a burst of foam, but with a more bluish, more solid look.

It was a piece of an ice-floe melted down to a fragment, but still big enough to sink a ship, and floating lower than any raft, right in our way, as if ambushed among the waves with murderous intent. There was no time to get down on deck. I shouted from aloft till my head was ready to split. I was heard aft, and we managed to clear the sunken floe which had come all the way from the Southern ice-cap to have a try at our unsuspecting lives. Had it been an hour later, nothing could have saved the ship, for no eye could have made out in the dusk that pale piece of ice swept over by the white-crested waves.

And as we stood near the taffrail side by side, my captain and I, looking at it, hardly discernible already, but still quite close-to on our quarter, he remarked in a meditative tone:

"But for the turn of that wheel just in time, there would have been another case of a 'missing' ship."

Nobody ever comes back from a "missing" ship to tell how hard was the death of the craft, and how sudden and overwhelming the last anguish of her men. Nobody can say with what thoughts, with what regrets, with what words on their lips they died. But there is something fine in the sudden passing away of these hearts from the extremity of struggle and stress and tremendous uproar—from the vast, unrestful rage of the surface to the profound peace of the depths, sleeping untroubled since the beginning of ages.

XVIII

But if the word "missing" brings all hope to an end and settles the loss of the underwriters, the word "overdue" confirms the fears already born in many homes ashore, and opens the door of speculation in the market of risks.

Maritime risks, be it understood. There is a class of optimists ready to reinsure an "overdue" ship at a heavy premium. But nothing can insure the hearts on shore against the bitterness of waiting for the worst.

For if a "missing" ship has never turned up within the memory of seamen of my generation, the name of an "overdue" ship, trembling as it were on the edge of the fatal heading, has been known to appear as "arrived."

It must blaze up, indeed, with a great brilliance the dull printer's ink expended on the assemblage of the few letters that form the ship's name to the anxious eyes scanning the page in fear and trembling.* It is like the message of reprieve from the sentence of sorrow suspended over many a home, even if some of the men in her have been the most homeless mortals that you may find among the wanderers of the sea.

The reinsurer, the optimist of ill-luck and disaster, slaps his pocket with satisfaction. The underwriter, who had been trying to minimize the amount of impending loss, regrets his premature pessimism. The ship has been stauncher, the skies more merciful, the seas less angry, or perhaps the men on board of a finer temper than he has been willing to take for granted.

"The ship So-and-so, bound to such a port, and posted as 'overdue,' has been reported yesterday as having arrived safely at her destination."

Thus run the official words of the reprieve addressed to the hearts ashore lying under a heavy sentence. And they come swiftly from the other side of the earth, over wires and cables, for your electric telegraph is a great alleviator of anxiety. Details, of course, shall follow. And they may unfold a tale of narrow escape, of steady ill-luck, of high winds and heavy weather, of ice, of interminable calms or endless head-gales; a tale of difficulties overcome, of adversity defied by a small knot of men upon the great loneliness of the sea; a tale of resource, of courage—of helplessness, perhaps.

Of all ships disabled at sea, a steamer who has lost her propeller is the most helpless. And if she drifts into an unpopulated part of the ocean she may soon become overdue. The menace of the "overdue" and the finality of "missing" come very quickly to steamers whose life, fed on coals and breathing the black breath of smoke into the air, goes on in disregard of wind and wave. Such a one, a big steamship, too, whose working life had been a record of faithful keeping time from land to land, in disregard of wind and sea, once lost her propeller down south, on her passage out to New Zealand.*

It was the wintry, murky time of cold gales and heavy seas. With the snapping of her tail-shaft her life seemed suddenly to depart from her big body, and from a stubborn, arrogant existence she passed all at once into the passive state of a drifting log. A ship sick with her own weakness has not the pathos of a ship vanquished in a battle with the elements, wherein consists the inner drama of her life. No seaman can look without compassion upon a disabled ship, but to look at a sailing-vessel with her lofty spars gone is to look upon a defeated but indomitable warrior. There is defiance in the remaining stumps of her masts, raised up like maimed limbs against the menacing scowl of a stormy sky; there is high courage in the upward sweep of her lines towards the bow; and as soon as, on a hastily rigged spar, a strip of canvas is shown to the wind to keep her head to sea, she faces the waves again with an unsubdued courage.

XIX

The efficiency of a steamship consists not so much in her courage as in the power she carries within herself.

It beats and throbs like a pulsating heart within her iron ribs, and when it stops, the steamer, whose life is not so much a contest as the disdainful ignoring of the sea, sickens and dies upon the waves. The sailing-ship, with her unthrobbing body, seemed to lead mysteriously a sort of unearthly existence, bordering upon the magic of the invisible forces, sustained by the inspiration of life-giving and death-dealing winds.

So that big steamer, dying by a sudden stroke, drifted an unwieldy corpse, away from the track of other ships. And she would have been posted really as "overdue," or maybe as "missing," had she not been sighted in a snowstorm, vaguely, like a strange rolling island, by a whaler going north from her Polar cruising ground. There was plenty of food on board, and I don't know whether the nerves of her passengers were at all affected by anything else than the sense of interminable boredom or the vague fear of that unusual situation. Does a passenger ever feel the life of the ship in which he is being carried like a sort of honoured bale of highly sensitive goods? For a man who has never been a passenger it is impossible to say. But I know that there is no harder trial for a seaman than to feel a dead ship under his feet.

There is no mistaking that sensation, so dismal, so tormenting, and so subtle, so full of unhappiness and unrest. I could imagine no worse eternal punishment for evil seamen who die unrepentant upon the earthly sea than that their souls should be condemned to man the ghosts of disabled ships, drifting for ever across a ghostly and tempestuous ocean.

She must have looked ghostly enough, that broken-down steamer rolling in that snowstorm—a dark apparition in a world of white snowflakes—to the staring eyes of that whaler's crew. Evidently they didn't believe in ghosts, for on arrival into port her captain unromantically reported having sighted a disabled steamer in latitude somewhere about 50° S. and a longitude still more uncertain. Other steamers came out to look for her, and ultimately towed her away from the cold edge of the world into a harbour with docks and workshops, where, with many blows of hammers, her pulsating heart of steel was set going again to go forth presently in the renewed pride of its strength, fed on fire and water, breathing black smoke into the air, pulsating, throbbing, shouldering its arrogant way against the great rollers in blind disdain of winds and sea.

The track she had made when drifting while her heart stood still within her iron ribs looked like a tangled thread on the white paper of the chart. It was shown to me by a friend, her second officer. In that surprising tangle there were words in minute letters—"gales," "thick fog," "ice"—written by him here and there as memoranda of the weather. She had interminably turned upon her tracks, she had crossed and recrossed her haphazard path till it resembled nothing so much as a puzzling maze of pencilled lines without a meaning. But in that maze there lurked all the romance of the "overdue" and a menacing hint of "missing."

"We had three weeks of it," said my friend. "Just think of that!"

"How did you feel about it?" I asked.

He waved his hand as much as to say: It's all in the day's work. But then, abruptly, as if making up his mind:

"I'll tell you. Towards the last I used to shut myself up in my berth and cry."

"Cry?"

"Shed tears," he explained, briefly, and rolled up the chart.

I can answer for it, he was a good man—as good as ever stepped upon a ship's deck—but he could not bear the feeling of a dead ship under his feet: the sickly, disheartening feeling which the men of some "overdue" ships that come into harbour at last under a jury-rig must have felt, combated, and overcome in the faithful discharge of their duty.

XX

IT IS difficult for a seaman to believe that his stranded ship does not feel as unhappy at the unnatural predicament of having no water under her keel as he is himself at feeling her stranded.

Stranding is, indeed, the reverse of sinking. The sea does not close upon the water-logged hull with a sunny ripple, or maybe with the angry rush of a curling wave, erasing her name from the roll of living ships. No. It is as if an invisible hand had been stealthily uplifted from the bottom to catch hold of her keel as it glides through the water.

More than any other event does "stranding" bring to the sailor a sense of utter and dismal failure. There are strandings and strandings, but I am safe to say that 90 per cent. of them are occasions in which a sailor, without dishonour, may well wish himself dead; and I have no doubt that of those who had the experience of their ship taking the ground, 90 per cent. did actually for five seconds or so wish themselves dead

"Taking the ground" is the professional expression for a ship that is stranded in gentle circumstances. But the feeling is more as if the ground had taken hold of her. It is for those on her deck a surprising sensa-

tion. It is as if your feet had been caught in an im-
ponderable snare; you feel the balance of your body
threatened, and the steady poise of your mind is destroyed at once. This sensation lasts only a second,
for even while you stagger something seems to turn
over in your head, bringing uppermost the mental
exclamation, full of astonishment and dismay, "By
Jove! she's on the ground!"

And that is very terrible. After all, the only mission of a seaman's calling is to keep ships' keels off the
ground. Thus the moment of her stranding takes
away from him every excuse for his continued existence.
To keep ships afloat is his business; it is his trust; it is
the effective formula at the bottom of all these vague
impulses, dreams, and illusions that go to the making
up of a boy's vocation. The grip of the land upon
the keel of your ship, even if nothing worse comes
of it than the wear and tear of tackle and the loss of
time, remains in a seaman's memory an indelibly fixed
taste of disaster.

"Stranded" within the meaning presently used stands
for a more or less excusable mistake. A ship may be
"driven ashore" by stress of weather. It is a catastrophe, a defeat. To be "run ashore" has the littleness,
poignancy, and bitterness of human error.

XXI

That is why your "strandings" are for the most
part so unexpected. In fact, they are all unexpected,
except those heralded by some short glimpse of the
danger, full of agitation and excitement, like an awakening from a dream of incredible folly.

The land suddenly at night looms up right over
your bows, or perhaps the cry of "Broken water ahead!"

is raised, and some long mistake, some complicated
edifice of self-delusion, over-confidence, and wrong
reasoning is brought down in a fatal shock, and the
heart-searing experience of your ship's keel scraping
and scrunching over, say, a coral reef. It is a sound,
for its size, far more terrific to your soul than that of a
world coming violently to an end. But out of that
chaos your belief in your own prudence and sagacity
reasserts itself. You ask yourself, Where on earth
did I get to? How on earth did I get there? with a
conviction that it could not be your own act, that there
has been at work some mysterious conspiracy of accident; that the charts are all wrong, and if the charts
are not wrong, that land and sea have changed their
places; that your misfortune shall for ever remain inexplicable, since you have lived always with the sense
of your trust, the last thing on closing your eyes, the
first on opening them as if your mind had kept firm
hold of your responsibility during the hours of sleep.

You contemplate mentally your mischance, till little
by little your mood changes, cold doubt steals into the
very marrow of your bones, you see the inexplicable
fact in another light. That is the time when you ask
yourself, How on earth could I have been fool enough
to get there? And you are ready to renounce all belief in your good sense, in your knowledge, in your
fidelity, in what you thought till then was the best in
you, giving you the daily bread of life and the moral
support of other men's confidence.

The ship is lost or not lost. Once stranded, you have
to do your best by her. She may be saved by your
efforts, by your resource and fortitude bearing up
against the heavy weight of guilt and failure. And
there are justifiable strandings in fogs, on uncharted
seas, on dangerous shores, through treacherous tides.

But, saved or not saved, there remains with her commander a distinct sense of loss, a flavour in the mouth of the real, abiding danger that lurks in all the forms of human existence. It is an acquisition, too, that feeling. A man may be the better for it, but he will not be the same. Damocles* has seen the sword suspended by a hair over his head, and though a good man need not be made less valuable by such a knowledge, the feast shall not henceforth have the same flavour.

Years ago I was concerned as chief mate in a case of stranding which was not fatal to the ship.* We went to work for ten hours on end, laying out anchors in readiness to heave off at high water. While I was still busy about the decks forward I heard the steward at my elbow saying: "The captain asks whether you mean to come in, sir, and have something to eat to-day."

I went into the cuddy. My captain sat at the head of the table like a statue. There was a strange motionlessness of everything in that pretty little cabin. The swing-table which for seventy odd days had been always on the move, if ever so little, hung quite still above the soup-tureen. Nothing could have altered the rich colour of my commander's complexion, laid on generously by wind and sea; but between the two tufts of fair hair above his ears, his skull, generally suffused with the hue of blood, shone dead white, like a dome of ivory. And he looked strangely untidy. I perceived he had not shaved himself that day; and yet the wildest motion of the ship in the most stormy latitudes we had passed through never made him miss one single morning ever since we left the Channel. The fact must be that a commander cannot possibly shave himself when his ship is aground. I have commanded ships myself, but I don't know; I have never tried to shave in my life.

He did not offer to help me or himself till I had coughed markedly several times. I talked to him professionally in a cheery tone, and ended with the confident assertion:

"We shall get her off before midnight, sir."

He smiled faintly without looking up, and muttered as if to himself:

"Yes, yes; the captain put the ship ashore and we got her off."

Then, raising his head, he attacked grumpily the steward, a lanky, anxious youth with a long, pale face and two big front teeth.

"What makes this soup so bitter? I am surprised the mate can swallow the beastly stuff. I'm sure the cook's ladled some salt water into it by mistake."

The charge was so outrageous that the steward for all answer only dropped his eyelids bashfully.

There was nothing the matter with the soup. I had a second helping. My heart was warm with hours of hard work at the head of a willing crew. I was elated with having handled heavy anchors, cables, boats without the slightest hitch;* pleased with having laid out scientifically bower, stream, and kedge* exactly where I believed they would do most good. On that occasion the bitter taste of a stranding was not for my mouth. That experience came later, and it was only then that I understood the loneliness of the man in charge.

It's the captain who puts the ship ashore; it's *we* who get her off.

XXII

I T SEEMS to me that no man born and truthful to himself could declare that he ever saw the sea looking young as the earth looks young in spring. But some of us, regarding the ocean with understanding and affection, have seen it looking old, as if the immemorial ages had been stirred up from the undisturbed bottom of ooze. For it is a gale of wind that makes the sea look old.

From a distance of years, looking at the remembered aspects of the storms lived through, it is that impression which disengages itself clearly from the great body of impressions left by many years of intimate contact.

If you would know the age of the earth, look upon the sea in a storm. The greyness of the whole immense surface, the wind furrows upon the faces of the waves, the great masses of foam, tossed about and waving, like matted white locks, give to the sea in a gale an appearance of hoary age, lustreless, dull, without gleams, as though it had been created before light itself.

Looking back after much love and much trouble, the instinct of primitive man, who seeks to personify the forces of Nature for his affection and for his fear, is awakened again in the breast of one civilized beyond that stage even in his infancy. One seems to have known gales as enemies, and even as enemies one embraces them in that affectionate regret which clings to the past.

Gales have their personalities, and, after all, perhaps it is not strange; for, when all is said and done, they are adversaries whose wiles you must defeat, whose violence you must resist, and yet with whom you must live in the intimacies of nights and days.

Here speaks the man of the masts and sails, to whom the sea is not a navigable element, but an intimate companion. The length of passages, the growing sense of solitude, the close dependence upon the very forces that, friendly to-day, without changing their nature, by the mere putting forth of their might, become dangerous to-morrow, make for that sense of fellowship which modern seamen, good men as they are, cannot hope to know. And, besides, your modern ship which is a steamship makes her passages on other principles than yielding to the weather and humouring the sea. She receives smashing blows, but she advances; it is a slogging fight, and not a scientific campaign. The machinery, the steel, the fire, the steam have stepped in between the man and the sea. A modern fleet of ships does not so much make use of the sea as exploit a highway. The modern ship is not the sport of the waves. Let us say that each of her voyages is a triumphant progress; and yet it is a question whether it is not a more subtle and more human triumph to be the sport of the waves and yet survive, achieving your end.

In his own time a man is always very modern. Whether the seamen of three hundred years hence will have the faculty of sympathy it is impossible to say. An incorrigible mankind hardens its heart in the progress of its own perfectability. How will they feel on seeing the illustrations to the sea novels of our day, or of our yesterday? It is impossible to guess. But the seaman of the last generation, brought into sympathy with the caravels of ancient time by his sailing-ship, their lineal descendant, cannot look upon those lumbering forms navigating the naïve seas of ancient woodcuts without a feeling of surprise, of affectionate derision, envy, and admiration. For those things, whose unmanageableness, even when represented on paper makes one gasp with a sort of amused horror, were manned by men who are his direct professional ancestors.

No; the seamen of three hundred years hence will probably be neither touched nor moved to derision, affection, or admiration. They will glance at the photogravures of our nearly defunct sailing-ships with a cold, inquisitive, and indifferent eye. Our ships of yesterday will stand to their ships as no lineal ancestors, but as mere predecessors whose course will have been run and the race extinct. Whatever craft he handles with skill, the seaman of the future shall be not our descendant, but only our successor.

XXIII

And so much depends upon the craft which, made by man, is one with man, that the sea shall wear for him another aspect. I remember once seeing the commander—officially the master, by courtesy the captain—of a fine iron ship of the old wool fleet shaking his head at a very pretty brigantine. She was bound the other way. She was a taut, trim, neat little craft, extremely well kept; and on that serene evening when we passed her close she looked the embodiment of coquettish comfort on the sea. It was somewhere near the Cape— *The* Cape being, of course, the Cape of Good Hope, the Cape of Storms of its Portuguese discoverer.* And whether it is that the word "storm" should not be pronounced upon the sea where the storms dwell thickly, or because men are shy of confessing their good hopes, it has become the nameless cape—the Cape *tout court.** The other great cape of the world, strangely enough, is seldom if ever called a cape. We say, "a voyage round the Horn"; "we rounded the horn"; "we got a frightful battering off the Horn"; but rarely "Cape Horn," and, indeed, with some reason, for Cape Horn is as much an island as a cape. The third stormy cape of the world, which is the Leeuwin,* receives generally its full name, as if to console its second-rate dignity. These are the capes that look upon the gales.

The little brigantine, then, had doubled the Cape. Perhaps she was coming from Port Elizabeth,* from East London*—who knows? It was many years ago, but I remember well the captain of the wool-clipper nodding at her with the words, "Fancy having to go about the sea in a thing like that!"

He was a man brought up in big deep-water ships, and the size of the craft under his feet was a part of his conception of the sea. His own ship was certainly big as ships went then. He may have thought of the size of his cabin, or unconsciously, perhaps—have conjured up a vision of a vessel so small tossing amongst the great seas. I didn't inquire, and to a young second mate the captain of the little pretty brigantine, sitting astride a camp stool with his chin resting on his hands that were crossed upon the rail, might have appeared a minor king amongst men. We passed her within earshot, without a hail, reading each other's names with the naked eye.

Some years later, the second mate, the recipient of that almost involuntary mutter, could have told his captain that a man brought up in big ships may yet take a peculiar delight in what we should both then have called a small craft. Probably the captain of the big ship would not have understood very well. His answer would have been a gruff, "Give me size," as I heard another man reply to a remark praising the handiness of a small vessel. It was not a love of the grandiose or the prestige attached to the command of great tonnage, for he continued, with an air of disgust and contempt, "Why, you get flung out of your bunk as likely as not in any sort of heavy weather."

I don't know. I remember a few nights in my life-time, and in a big ship, too (as big as they made them then), when one did not get flung out of one's bed simply because one never even attempted to get in; one had been made too weary, too hopeless, to try. The expedient of turning your bedding out on a damp floor and lying on it there was no earthly good, since you could not keep your place or get a second's rest in that or any other position. But of the delight of seeing a small craft run bravely amongst the great seas there can be no question to him whose soul does not dwell ashore. Thus I well remember a three days' run got out of a little barque* of 400 tons somewhere between the islands of St. Paul and Amsterdam and Cape Otway on the Australian coast. It was a hard, long gale, grey clouds and green sea, heavy weather undoubtedly, but still what a sailor would call manageable. Under two lower topsails and a reefed foresail the barque seemed to race with a long, steady sea that did not becalm her in the troughs. The solemn thundering combers caught her up from astern, passed her with a fierce boiling up of foam level with the bulwarks,*swept on ahead with a swish and a roar: and the little vessel, dipping her jib-boom into the tumbling froth, would go on running in a smooth, glassy hollow, a deep valley between two ridges of the sea, hiding the horizon ahead and astern. There was such fascination in her pluck, nimbleness, the continual exhibition of unfailing sea-worthiness, in the semblance of courage and endurance, that I could not give up the delight of watching her run through the three unforgettable days of that gale which my mate also delighted to extol as "a famous shove."

And this is one of those gales whose memory in after-years returns, welcome in dignified austerity,

as you would remember with pleasure the noble features of a stranger with whom you crossed swords
once in knightly encounter and are never to see again.
In this way gales have their physiognomy. You remember them by your own feelings, and no two gales
stamp themselves in the same way upon your emotions.
Some cling to you in woe-begone misery; others come
back fiercely and weirdly, like ghouls bent upon sucking
your strength away; others, again, have a catastrophic
splendour; some are unvenerated recollections, as of
spiteful wild-cats clawing at your agonized vitals; others
are severe like a visitation; and one or two rise up
draped and mysterious with an aspect of ominous menace. In each of them there is a characteristic point at
which the whole feeling seems contained in one single
moment. Thus there is a certain four o'clock in the
morning in the confused roar of a black-and-white world
when coming on deck to take charge of my watch
I received the instantaneous impression that the ship
could not live for another hour in such a raging
sea.

I wonder what became of the men who silently
(you couldn't hear yourself speak) must have shared
that conviction with me. To be left to write about it is
not, perhaps, the most enviable fate; but the point
is that this impression resumes in its intensity the whole
recollection of days and days of desperately dangerous
weather. We were then, for reasons which it is not
worth while to specify, in the close neighbourhood of
Kerguelen Island;*and now, when I open an atlas and
look at the tiny dots on the map of the Southern Ocean,
I see as if engraved upon the paper the enraged physiognomy of that gale.

Another, strangely, recalls a silent man. And yet
it was not din that was wanting; in fact, it was terrific.

That one was a gale that came upon the ship swiftly, like a pampero,* which last is a very sudden wind indeed. Before we knew very well what was coming all the sails we had set had burst; the furled ones were blowing loose, ropes flying, sea hissing—it hissed tremendously —wind howling, and the ship lying on her side, so that half of the crew were swimming and the other half clawing desperately at whatever came to hand, according to the side of the deck each man had been caught on by the catastrophe, either to leeward or to windward. The shouting I need not mention—it was the merest drop in an ocean of noise—and yet the character of the gale seems contained in the recollection of one small, not particularly impressive, sallow man without a cap and with a very still face. Captain Jones—let us call him Jones—had been caught unawares. Two orders he had given at the first sign of an utterly unforeseen onset; after that the magnitude of his mistake seemed to have overwhelmed him. We were doing what was needed and feasible. The ship behaved well. Of course, it was some time before we could pause in our fierce and laborious exertions; but all through the work, the excitement, the uproar, and some dismay, we were aware of this silent little man at the break of the poop, perfectly motionless, soundless, and often hidden from us by the drift of sprays.

When we officers clambered at last upon the poop, he seemed to come out of that numbed composure, and shouted to us down wind: "Try the pumps." Afterwards he disappeared. As to the ship, I need not say that, although she was presently swallowed up in one of the blackest nights I can remember, she did not disappear. In truth, I don't fancy that there had ever been much danger of that, but certainly the experience was noisy and particularly distracting—and yet it is the memory of a very quiet silence that survives.

XXIV

For after all, a gale of wind, the thing of mighty sound, is inarticulate. It is a man who, in chance phrase, interprets the elemental passion of his enemy. Thus there is another gale in my memory, a thing of endless, deep, humming roar, moonlight, and a spoken sentence.

It was off that other cape which is always deprived of its title as the Cape of Good Hope is robbed of its name. It was off the Horn. For a true expression of dishevelled wildness there is nothing like a gale in the bright moonlight of a high latitude.

The ship,* brought-to* and bowing to enormous flashing seas, glistened wet from deck to trucks; her one set sail stood out a coal-black shape upon the gloomy blueness of the air. I was a youngster then, and suffering from weariness, cold, and imperfect oilskins which let water in at every seam. I craved human companionship, and, coming off the poop, took my place by the side of the boatswain (a man whom I did not like) in a comparatively dry spot where at worst we had water only up to our knees. Above our heads the explosive booming gusts of wind passed continuously, justifying the sailor's saying "It blows great guns." And just from that need of human companionship, being very close to the man, I said, or rather shouted:

"Blows very hard, boatswain."

His answer was:

"Ay, and if it blows only a little harder things will begin to go. I don't mind as long as everything holds, but when things begin to go it's bad."

The note of dread in the shouting voice, the practical truth of these words, heard years ago from a man I did not like, have stamped its peculiar character on that gale.

A look in the eyes of a shipmate, a low murmur in the most sheltered spot where the watch on duty are huddled together, a meaning moan from one to the other with a glance at the windward sky, a sigh of weariness, a gesture of disgust passing into the keeping of the great wind, become part and parcel of the gale. The olive hue of hurricane clouds presents an aspect peculiarly appalling. The inky ragged wrack, flying before a nor'-west wind, makes you dizzy with its headlong speed that depicts the rush of the invisible air. A hard sou'-wester startles you with its close horizon and its low grey sky, as if the world were a dungeon wherein there is no rest for body or soul. And there are black squalls,* white squalls, thunder squalls, and unexpected gusts that come without a single sign in the sky; and of each kind no one of them resembles another.

There is infinite variety in the gales of wind at sea, and except for the peculiar, terrible, and mysterious moaning that may be heard sometimes passing through the roar of a hurricane—except for that unforgettable sound, as if the soul of the universe had been goaded into a mournful groan—it is, after all, the human voice that stamps the mark of human consciousness upon the character of a gale.

XXV

THERE is no part of the world of coasts, continents, oceans, seas, straits, capes, and islands which is not under the sway of a reigning wind, the sovereign of its typical weather. The wind rules the aspects of the sky and the action of the sea. But no wind rules unchallenged his realm of land and water. As with the kingdoms of the earth, there are regions more turbulent than others. In the middle belt of the earth the Trade Winds* reign supreme, undisputed, like monarchs of long-settled kingdoms, whose traditional power, checking all undue ambitions, is not so much an exercise of personal might as the working of long-established institutions. The intertropical kingdoms of the Trade Winds are favourable to the ordinary life of a merchantman. The trumpet-call of strife is seldom borne on their wings to the watchful ears of men on the decks of ships. The regions ruled by the north-east and south-east Trade Winds are serene. In a southern-going ship, bound out for a long voyage, the passage through their dominions is characterized by a relaxation of strain and vigilance on the part of the seamen. Those citizens of the ocean feel sheltered under the ægis of an uncontested law, of an undisputed dynasty. There, indeed, if anywhere on earth, the weather may be trusted.

Yet not too implicitly. Even in the constitutional realm of Trade Winds, north and south of the Equator ships are overtaken by strange disturbances. Still, the easterly winds, and, generally speaking, the easterly weather all the world over, is characterized by regularity and persistence.

As a ruler, the East Wind has a remarkable stability; as an invader of the high latitudes lying under the tumultuous sway of his great brother, the Wind of the West, he is extremely difficult to dislodge, by the reason of his cold craftiness and profound duplicity.

The narrow seas around these isles, where British admirals keep watch and ward upon the marches of the Atlantic Ocean, are subject to the turbulent sway of the West Wind. Call it north-west or south-west it is all

one—a different phase of the same character, a changed
expression on the same face. In the orientation of the
winds that rule the seas, the north and south directions
are of no importance. There are no North and South
Winds of any account upon this earth. The North
and South Winds are but small princes in the dynasties
that make peace and war upon the sea. They never
assert themselves upon a vast stage. They depend
upon local causes—the configuration of coasts, the
shapes of straits, the accidents of bold promontories
round which they play their little part. In the polity
of winds, as amongst the tribes of the earth, the real
struggle lies between East and West.

XXVI

The West Wind reigns over the seas surrounding
the coasts of these kingdoms; and from the gateways
of the channels, from promontories as if from watch-
towers, from estuaries of rivers as if from postern gates,
from passage-ways, inlets, straits, firths, the garrison
of the Isle and the crews of the ships going and returning
look to the westward to judge by the varied splendours
of his sunset mantle the mood of that arbitrary ruler.
The end of the day is the time to gaze at the kingly
face of the Westerly Weather, who is the arbiter
of ships' destinies. Benignant and splendid, or splendid
and sinister, the western sky reflects the hidden purposes of the royal mind. Clothed in a mantle of dazzling gold or·draped in rags of black clouds like a beggar,
the might of the Westerly Wind sits enthroned upon
the western horizon with the whole North Atlantic as a
footstool for his feet and the first twinkling stars making
a diadem for his brow. Then the seamen, attentive
courtiers of the weather, think of regulating the conduct

of their ships by the mood of the master. The West
Wind is too great a king to be a dissembler: he is no
calculator plotting deep schemes in a sombre heart;
he is too strong for small artifices; there is passion in
all his moods, even in the soft mood of his serene days,
in the grace of his blue sky whose immense and unfathomable tenderness reflected in the mirror of the sea
embraces, possesses, lulls to sleep the ships with white
sails. He is all things to all oceans; he is like a poet
seated upon a throne—magnificent, simple, barbarous,
pensive, generous, impulsive, changeable, unfathomable
—but when you understand him, always the same.
Some of his sunsets are like pageants devised for the
delight of the multitude, when all the gems of the royal
treasure-house are displayed above the sea. Others
are like the opening of his royal confidence, tinged with
thoughts of sadness and compassion in a melancholy
splendour meditating upon the short-lived peace of the
waters. And I have seen him put the pent-up anger
of his heart into the aspect of the inaccessible sun, and
cause it to glare fiercely like the eye of an implacable
autocrat out of a pale and frightened sky.

He is the war-lord who sends his battalions of
Atlantic rollers to the assault of our seaboard. The
compelling voice of the West Wind musters up to his
service all the might of the ocean. At the bidding of
the West Wind there arises a great commotion in the
sky above these Islands, and a great rush of waters
falls upon our shores. The sky of the Westerly Weather
is full of flying clouds, of great big white clouds coming
thicker and thicker till they seem to stand welded into
a solid canopy, upon whose grey face the lower wrack of
the gale, thin, black, and angry-looking, flies past with
vertiginous speed. Denser and denser grows this dome
of vapours, descending lower and lower upon the sea,

narrowing the horizon around the ship. And the characteristic aspect of Westerly Weather, the thick, grey, smoky, and sinister tone sets in, circumscribing the view of the men, drenching their bodies, oppressing their souls, taking their breath away with booming gusts, deafening, blinding, driving, rushing them onwards in a swaying ship towards our coasts lost in mists and rain.

The caprice of the winds, like the wilfulness of men, is fraught with the disastrous consequences of self-indulgence. Long anger, the sense of his uncontrolled power, spoils the frank and generous nature of the West Wind. It is as if his heart were corrupted by a malevolent and brooding rancour. He devastates his own kingdom in the wantonness of his force. South-west is the quarter of the heavens where he presents his darkened brow. He breathes his rage in terrific squalls, and overwhelms his realm with an inexhaustible welter of clouds. He strews the seeds of anxiety upon the decks of scudding ships, makes the foam-stripped ocean look old, and sprinkles with grey hairs the heads of ship masters in the homeward-bound ships running for the Channel. The Westerly Wind asserting his sway from the south-west quarter is often like a monarch gone mad, driving forth with wild imprecations the most faithful of his courtiers to shipwreck, disaster, and death.

The South-Westerly Weather is the thick weather *par excellence.** It is not the thickness of the fog; it is rather a contraction of the horizon, a mysterious veiling of the shores with clouds that seem to make a low vaulted dungeon around the running ship. It is not blindness; it is a shortening of the sight. The West Wind does not say to the seaman, "You shall be blind"; it restricts merely the range of his vision and raises the dread of land within his breast. It makes of him a man robbed of half his force, of half his efficiency. Many times in my life, standing in long sea-boots and streaming oilskins at the elbow of my commander on the poop of a homeward-bound ship making for the Channel, and gazing ahead into the grey and tormented waste, I have heard a weary sigh shape itself into a studiously casual comment:

"Can't see very far in this weather."

And have made answer in the same low, perfunctory tone:

"No, sir."

It would be merely the instinctive voicing of an ever-present thought associated closely with the consciousness of the land somewhere ahead and of the great speed of the ship. Fair wind, fair wind! Who would dare to grumble at a fair wind? It was a favour of the Western King, who rules masterfully the North Atlantic from the latitude of the Azores to the latitude of Cape Farewell.* A famous shove this to end a good passage with; and yet, somehow, one could not muster upon one's lips the smile of a courtier's gratitude. This favour was dispensed to you from under an overbearing scowl, which is the true expression of the great autocrat when he has made up his mind to give a battering to some ships and to hunt certain others home in one breath of cruelty and benevolence, equally distracting.

"No, sir. Can't see very far."

Thus would the mate's voice repeat the thought of the master, both gazing ahead, while under their feet the ship rushes at some twelve knots in the direction of the lee shore; and only a couple of miles in front of her swinging and dripping jib-boom, carried naked with an upward slant like a spear, a grey horizon closes the view with a multitude of waves surging upwards violently as if to strike at the stooping clouds.

Awful and threatening scowls darken the face of the West Wind in his clouded, south-west mood; and from the King's throne-hall in the western board stronger gusts reach you, like the fierce shouts of raving fury to which only the gloomy grandeur of the scene imparts a saving dignity. A shower pelts the deck and the sails of the ship as if flung with a scream by an angry hand, and when the night closes in, the night of a south-westerly gale, it seems more hopeless than the shades of Hades. The south-westerly mood of the great West Wind is a lightless mood, without sun, moon, or stars, with no gleam of light but the phosphorescent flashes of the great sheets of foam that, boiling up on each side of the ship, fling bluish gleams upon her dark and narrow hull, rolling as she runs, chased by enormous seas, distracted in the tumult.

There are some bad nights in the kingdom of the West Wind for homeward-bound ships making for the Channel; and the days of wrath dawn upon them colourless and vague like the timid turning up of invisible lights upon the scene of a tyrannical and passionate outbreak, awful in the monotony of its method and the increasing strength of its violence. It is the same wind, the same clouds, the same wildly racing seas, the same thick horizon around the ship. Only the wind is stronger, the clouds seem denser and more overwhelming, the waves appear to have grown bigger and more threatening during the night. The hours, whose minutes are marked by the crash of the breaking seas, slip by with the screaming, pelting squalls overtaking the ship as she runs on and on with darkened canvas, with streaming spars and dripping ropes. The downpours thicken. Preceding each shower a mysterious gloom, like the passage of a shadow above the firmament of grey clouds, filters down upon the ship. Now and then the rain pours upon your head in streams as if from spouts. It seems as if your ship were going to be drowned before she sank, as if all atmosphere had turned to water. You gasp, you splutter, you are blinded and deafened, you are submerged, obliterated, dissolved, annihilated, streaming all over as if your limbs, too, had turned to water. And every nerve on the alert you watch for the clearing-up mood of the Western King, that shall come with a shift of wind as like as not to whip all the three masts out of your ship in the twinkling of an eye.

XXVII

Heralded by the increasing fierceness of the squalls, sometimes by a faint flash of lightning like the signal of a lighted torch waved far away behind the clouds, the shift of wind comes at last, the crucial moment of the change from the brooding and veiled violence of the south-west gale to the sparkling, flashing, cutting, clear-eyed anger of the King's north-westerly mood. You behold another phase of his passion, a fury bejewelled with stars, mayhap*bearing the crescent of the moon on its brow, shaking the last vestiges of its torn cloud-mantle in inky-black squalls, with hail and sleet descending like showers of crystals and pearls, bounding off the spars, drumming on the sails, pattering on the oilskin coats, whitening the decks of homeward-bound ships. Faint, ruddy flashes of lightning flicker in the starlight upon her mast-heads. A chilly blast hums in the taut rigging, causing the ship to tremble to her very keel, and the soaked men on her decks to shiver in their wet clothes to the very marrow of their bones. Before one squall has flown over to sink in the eastern board, the edge of another peeps up already above the western horizon, racing up swift, shapeless, like a black bag full of frozen water ready to burst over your devoted head. The temper of the ruler of the ocean has changed. Each gust of the clouded mood that seemed warmed by the heat of a heart flaming with anger has its counterpart in the chilly blasts that seem blown from a breast turned to ice with a sudden revulsion of feeling. Instead of blinding your eyes and crushing your soul with a terrible apparatus of cloud and mists and seas and rain, the King of the West turns his power to contemptuous pelting of your back with icicles, to making your weary eyes water as if in grief and your worn-out carcass quake pitifully. But each mood of the great autocrat has its own greatness, and each is hard to bear. Only the north-west phase of that mighty display is not demoralizing to the same extent, because between the hail and sleet squalls of a north-westerly gale one can see a long way ahead.

To see! to see!—this is the craving of the sailor, as of the rest of blind humanity. To have his path made clear for him is the aspiration of every human being in our beclouded and tempestuous existence. I have heard a reserved, silent man, with no nerves to speak of, after three days of hard running in thick south-westerly weather, burst out passionately: "I wish to God we could get sight of something!"

We*had just gone down below for a moment to commune in a battened-down cabin, with a large white chart lying limp and damp upon a cold and clammy table under the light of a smoky lamp. Sprawling over that seaman's silent and trusted adviser, with one elbow upon the coast of Africa and the other planted in the neighbourhood of Cape Hatteras*(it was a general track-chart of the North Atlantic), my skipper lifted his rugged, hairy face, and glared at me in a half-exasperated, half-appealing way. We have seen no sun, moon, or stars for something like seven days. By the effect of the West Wind's wrath the celestial bodies had gone into hiding for a week or more, and the last three days had seen the force of a south-west gale grow from fresh, through strong, to heavy,* as the entries in my log-book could testify. Then we separated, he to go on deck again, in obedience to that mysterious call that seems to sound for ever in a shipmaster's ears, I to stagger into my cabin with some vague notion of putting down the words "Very heavy weather" in a log-book not quite written up-to-date. But I gave it up, and crawled into my bunk instead, boots and hat on, all standing (it did not matter; everything was soaking wet, a heavy sea having burst the poop skylights the night before), to remain in a nightmarish state between waking and sleeping for a couple of hours of so-called rest.

The south-westerly mood of the West Wind is an enemy of sleep, and even of a recumbent position, in the responsible officers of a ship. After two hours of futile, light-headed, inconsequent thinking upon all things under heaven in that dark, dank, wet, and devastated cabin, I arose suddenly and staggered up on deck. The autocrat of the North Atlantic was still oppressing his kingdom and its outlying dependencies, even as far as the Bay of Biscay, in the dismal secrecy of thick, very thick, weather. The force of the wind, though we were running before it at the rate of some ten knots an hour, was so great that it drove me with a steady push to the front of the poop, where my commander was holding on.

"What do you think of it?" he addressed me in an interrogative yell.

What I really thought was that we both had had just

about enough of it. The manner in which the great West Wind chooses at times to administer his possessions does not commend itself to a person of peaceful and law-abiding disposition, inclined to draw distinctions between right and wrong in the face of natural forces, whose standard, naturally, is that of might alone. But, of course, I said nothing. For a man caught, as it were, between his skipper and the great West Wind silence is the safest sort of diplomacy. Moreover, I knew my skipper. He did not want to know what I thought. Shipmasters hanging on a breath before the thrones of the winds ruling the seas have their psychology whose workings are as important to the ship and those on board of her as the changing moods of the weather. The man, as a matter of fact, under no circumstances, ever cared a brass farthing for what I or anybody else in his ship thought. He had had just about enough of it, I guessed, and what he was at really was a process of fishing for a suggestion. It was the pride of his life that he had never wasted a chance, no matter how boisterous, threatening, and dangerous, of a fair wind. Like men racing blindfold for a gap in a hedge, we were finishing a splendidly quick passage from the Antipodes, with a tremendous rush for the Channel in as thick a weather as any I can remember, but his psychology did not permit him to bring the ship to with a fair wind blowing—at least not on his own initiative. And yet he felt that very soon indeed something would have to be done. He wanted the suggestion to come from me, so that later on, when the trouble was over, he could argue this point with his own uncompromising spirit, laying the blame upon my shoulders. I must render him the justice that this sort of pride was his only weakness.

But he got no suggestion from me. I understood his psychology. Besides, I had my own stock of weaknesses at the time (it is a different one now), and amongst them was the conceit of being remarkably well up in the psychology of the Westerly Weather. I believed—not to mince matters—that I had a genius for reading the mind of the great ruler of high latitudes. I fancied I could discern already the coming of a change in his royal mood. And all I said was:

"The weather's bound to clear up with the shift of wind."

"Anybody knows that much!" he snapped at me, at the highest pitch of his voice.

"I mean before dark!" I cried.

This was all the opening he ever got from me. The eagerness with which he seized upon it gave me the measure of the anxiety he had been labouring under.

"Very well," he shouted, with an affectation of impatience, as if giving way to long entreaties. "All right. If we don't get a shift by then we'll take that foresail off her and put her head under her wing for the night."

I was struck by the picturesque character of the phrase as applied to a ship brought-to in order to ride out a gale with wave after wave passing under her breast. I could see her resting in the tumult of the elements like a sea-bird sleeping in wild weather upon the raging waters with its head tucked under its wing. In imaginative precision, in true feeling, this is one of the most expressive sentences I have ever heard on human lips. But as to taking the fore-sail off that ship before we put her head under her wing, I had my grave doubts. They were justified. That long-enduring piece of canvas was confiscated by the arbitrary decree of the West Wind, to whom belong the lives of men and the contrivances of their hands within the limits of his kingdom. With the sound of a faint explosion it vanished into the thick weather bodily, leaving behind

of its stout substance not so much as one solitary strip
big enough to be picked into a handful of lint for, say, a
wounded elephant. Torn out of its bolt-ropes,* it faded
like a whiff of smoke in the smoky drift of clouds
shattered and torn by the shift of wind. For the shift
of wind had come. The unveiled, low sun glared
angrily from a chaotic sky upon a confused and tremendous sea dashing itself upon a coast. We recognized
the headland, and looked at each other in the silence of
dumb wonder. Without knowing it in the least, we
had run up alongside the Isle of Wight, and that tower,
tinged a faint evening red in the salt wind-haze, was the
lighthouse of St. Catherine's Point.*

My skipper recovered first from his astonishment.
His bulging eyes sank back gradually into their orbits.
His psychology, taking it all round, was really very
creditable for an average sailor. He had been spared
the humiliation of laying his ship to with a fair wind;
and at once that man, of an open and truthful nature,
spoke up in perfect good faith, rubbing together his
brown, hairy hands—the hands of a master-craftsman
upon the sea.

"Humph! that's just about where I reckoned we had
got to."

The transparency and ingenuousness, in a way, of
that delusion, the airy tone, the hint of already growing
pride, were perfectly delicious. But, in truth, this was
one of the greatest surprises ever sprung by the clearing-
up mood of the West Wind upon one of the most accomplished of his courtiers.

XXVIII

The winds of North and South are, as I have said,
but small princes amongst the powers of the sea.   They

have no territory of their own; they are not reigning winds anywhere. Yet it is from their houses that the reigning dynasties which have shared between them the waters of the earth are sprung. All the weather of the world is based upon the contest of the Polar and Equatorial strains of that tyrannous race. The West Wind is the greatest king. The East rules between the Tropics. They have shared each ocean between them. Each has his genius of supreme rule. The King of the West never intrudes upon the recognized dominion of his kingly brother. He is a barbarian, of a northern type. Violent without craftiness, and furious without malice, one may imagine him seated masterfully with a double-edged sword on his knees upon the painted and gilt clouds of the sunset, bowing his shock head of golden locks, a flaming beard over his breast, imposing, colossal, mighty-limbed, with a thundering voice, distended cheeks, and fierce blue eyes, urging the speed of his gales. The other, the East King, the king of blood-red sunrises, I represent to myself as a spare Southerner with clear-cut features, black-browed and dark-eyed, grey-robed, upright in sunshine, resting a smooth-shaven cheek in the palm of his hand, impenetrable, secret, full of wiles, fine-drawn, keen—meditating aggressions.

The West Wind keeps faith with his brother the King of the Easterly Weather. "What we have divided we have divided," he seems to say in his gruff voice, this ruler without guile, who hurls as if in sport enormous masses of cloud across the sky, and flings the great waves of the Atlantic clear across from the shores of the New World upon the hoary headlands of Old Europe, which harbours more kings and rulers upon its seamed and furrowed body than all the oceans of the world together. "What we have divided we have divided; and if no rest and peace in this world have fallen to my share, leave me alone. Let me play at quoits with cyclonic gales, flinging the discs of spinning cloud and whirling air from one end of my dismal kingdom to the other: over the Great Banks*or along the edges of pack-ice—this one with true aim right into the bight of the Bay of Biscay, that other upon the fiords of Norway, across the North Sea where the fishermen of many nations look watchfully into my angry eye. This is the time of kingly sport."

And the royal master of high latitudes sighs mightily, with the sinking sun upon his breast and the double-edged sword upon his knees, as if wearied by the innumerable centuries of a strenuous rule and saddened by the unchangeable aspect of the ocean under his feet— by the endless vista of future ages where the work of sowing the wind and reaping the whirlwind* shall go on and on till his realm of living waters becomes a frozen and motionless ocean. But the other, crafty and unmoved, nursing his shaven chin between the thumb and forefinger of his slim and treacherous hand, thinks deep within his heart full of guile: "Aha! our brother of the West has fallen into the mood of kingly melancholy. He is tired of playing with circular gales, and blowing great guns, and unrolling thick streamers of fog in wanton sport at the cost of his own poor, miserable subjects. Their fate is most pitiful. Let us make a foray upon the dominions of that noisy barbarian, a great raid from Finisterre* to Hatteras, catching his fishermen unawares, baffling the fleets that trust to his power, and shooting sly arrows into the livers of men who court his good graces. He is, indeed, a worthless fellow." And forthwith, while the West Wind meditates upon the vanity of his irresistible might, the thing is done, and the Easterly Weather sets in upon the North Atlantic.

The prevailing weather of the North Atlantic is typical of the way in which the West Wind rules his realm on which the sun never sets. North Atlantic is the heart of a great empire. It is the part of the West Wind's dominions most thickly populated with generations of fine ships and hardy men. Heroic deeds and adventurous exploits have been performed there, within the very stronghold of his sway. The best sailors in the world have been born and bred under the shadow of his sceptre, learning to manage their ships with skill and audacity before the steps of his stormy throne. Reckless adventurers, toiling fishermen, admirals as wise and brave as the world has ever known have waited upon the signs of his Westerly sky. Fleets of victorious ships have hung upon his breath. He has tossed in his hand squadrons of war-scarred three-deckers, and shredded out in mere sport the bunting of flags hallowed in the traditions of honour and glory. He is a good friend and a dangerous enemy, without mercy to unseaworthy ships and faint-hearted seamen. In his kingly way he has taken but little account of lives sacrificed to his impulsive policy; he is a king with a double-edged sword bared in his right hand. The East Wind, an interloper in the dominions of Westerly Weather, is an impassive-faced tyrant with a sharp poniard held behind his back for a treacherous stab.

In his forays into the North Atlantic the East Wind behaves like a subtle and cruel adventurer without a notion of honour or fair play. Veiling his clear-cut lean face in a thin layer of a hard, high cloud, I have seen him, like a wizened robber sheik of the sea, hold up large caravans of ships to the number of three hundred or more at the very gates of the English Channel. And the worst of it was that there was no ransom that we could pay to satisfy his avidity; for whatever evil is wrought by the raiding East Wind, it is done only to spite his kingly brother of the West. We gazed helplessly at the systematic, cold, grey-eyed obstinacy of the Easterly Weather, while short rations became the order of the day, and the pinch of hunger under the breast-bone grew familiar to every sailor in that held-up fleet. Every day added to our numbers. In knots and groups and straggling parties we flung to and fro before the closed gate. And meantime the outward-bound ships passed, running through our humiliated ranks under all the canvas they could show. It is my idea that the Easterly Wind helps the ships away from home in the wicked hope that they shall all come to an untimely end and be heard of no more. For six weeks did the robber sheik hold the trade route of the earth, while our liege lord, the West Wind, slept profoundly like a tired Titan, or else remained lost in a mood of idle sadness known only to frank natures. All was still to the westward; we looked in vain towards his stronghold: the King slumbered on so deeply that he let his foraging brother steal the very mantle of gold-lined purple clouds from his bowed shoulders. What had become of the dazzling hoard of royal jewels exhibited at every close of day? Gone, disappeared, extinguished, carried off without leaving a single gold band or the flash of a single sunbeam in the evening sky! Day after day through a cold streak of heavens as bare and poor as the inside of a rifled safe a rayless and despoiled sun would slink shamefacedly, without pomp or show, to hide in haste under the waters. And still the King slept on, or mourned the vanity of his might and his power, while the thin-lipped intruder put the impress of his cold and implacable spirit upon the sky and sea. With every daybreak the rising sun had to wade through a crimson stream, luminous and sinister, like the spilt blood of celestial bodies murdered during the night.

In this particular instance the mean interloper held the road for some six weeks on end, establishing his particular administrative methods over the best part of the North Atlantic. It looked as if the Easterly Weather had come to stay for ever, or, at least, till we had all starved to death in the held-up fleet—starved within sight, as it were, of plenty, within touch, almost, of the bountiful heart of the Empire. There we were, dotting with our white dry sails the hard blueness of the deep sea. There we were, a growing company of ships, each with her burden of grain, of timber, of wool, of hides, and even of oranges, for we had one or two belated fruit schooners in company. There we were, in that memorable spring of a certain year in the late seventies, dodging to and fro, baffled on every tack, and with our stores running down to sweepings of bread-lockers and scrapings of sugar-casks. It was just like the East Wind's nature to inflict starvation upon the bodies of unoffending sailors, while he corrupted their simple souls by an exasperation leading to outbursts of profanity as lurid as his blood-red sunrises. They were followed by grey days under the cover of high, motionless clouds that looked as if carved in a slab of ash-coloured marble. And each mean starved sunset left us calling with imprecations upon the West Wind even in its most veiled misty mood to wake up and give us our liberty, if only to rush on and dash the heads of our ships against the very walls of our unapproachable home.

XXIX

In the atmosphere of the Easterly Weather, as pellucid as a piece of crystal and refracting like a prism, we could see the appalling numbers of our help-less company, even to those who in more normal conditions would have remained invisible, sails down under the horizon. It is the malicious pleasure of the East Wind to augment the power of your eyesight, in order, perhaps, that you should see better the perfect humiliation, the hopeless character of your captivity. Easterly Weather is generally clear, and that is all that can be said for it—almost supernaturally clear when it likes; but whatever its mood, there is something un-canny in its nature. Its duplicity is such that it will deceive a scientific instrument. No barometer will give warning of an Easterly gale, were it ever so wet. It would be an unjust and ungrateful thing to say that a barometer is a stupid contrivance. It is simply that the wiles of the East Wind are too much for its funda-mental honesty. After years and years of experience the most trusty instrument of the sort that ever went to sea screwed on to a ship's cabin bulkhead will, almost invariably, be induced to rise by the diabolic ingenuity of the Easterly Weather, just at the moment when the Easterly Weather, discarding its methods of hard, dry, impassive cruelty, contemplates drowning what is left of your spirit in torrents of a peculiarly cold and horrid rain. The sleet-and-hail squalls following the lightning at the end of a Westerly gale are cold and benumbing and stinging and cruel enough. But the dry, Easterly Weather, when it turns to wet, seems to rain poisoned showers upon your head. It is a sort of steady, per-sistent, overwhelming, endlessly driving downpour, which makes your heart sick, and opens it to dismal forebodings. And the stormy mood of the Easterly Weather looms black upon the sky with a peculiar and amazing blackness. The West Wind hangs heavy grey curtains of mist and spray before your gaze, but the

Eastern interloper of the narrow seas, when he has mustered his courage and cruelty to the point of a gale, puts your eyes out, puts them out completely, makes you feel blind for life upon a lee-shore. It is the wind, also, that brings snow.

Out of his black and merciless heart he flings a white blinding sheet upon the ships of the sea. He has more manners of villainy, and no more conscience than an Italian prince of the seventeenth century. His weapon is a dagger carried under a black cloak when he goes out on his unlawful enterprises. The mere hint of his approach fills with dread every craft that swims the sea, from fishing-smacks to four-masted ships that recognize the sway of the West Wind. Even in his most accommodating mood he inspires a dread of treachery. I have heard upwards of ten score of wind-lasses spring like one into clanking life in the dead of night, filling the Downs with a panic-struck sound of anchors being torn hurriedly out of the ground at the first breath of his approach. Fortunately, his heart often fails him: he does not always blow home upon our exposed coast; he has not the fearless temper of his Westerly brother.

The natures of those two winds that share the dominions of the great oceans are fundamentally different. It is strange that the winds which men are prone to style capricious remain true to their character in all the various regions of the earth. To us here, for instance, the East Wind comes across a great continent, sweeping over the greatest body of solid land upon this earth. For the Australian east coast the East Wind is the wind of the ocean, coming across the greatest body of water upon the globe; and yet here and there its characteristics remain the same with a strange consistency in everything that is vile and base. The mem-

bers of the West Wind's dynasty are modified in a way
by the regions they rule, as a Hohenzollern,* without
ceasing to be himself, becomes a Roumanian by virtue
of his throne, or a Saxe-Coburg*learns to put the dress of
Bulgarian phrases upon his particular thoughts, whatever they are.

The autocratic sway of the West Wind, whether
forty north or forty south of the Equator, is characterized by an open, generous, frank, barbarous recklessness. For he is a great autocrat, and to be a great autocrat you must be a great barbarian. I have been too
much moulded to his sway to nurse now any idea of
rebellion in my heart. Moreover, what is a rebellion
within the four walls of a room against the tempestuous
rule of the West Wind? I remain faithful to the memory of the mighty King with a double-edged sword in
one hand, and in the other holding out rewards of great
daily runs and famously quick passages to those of his
courtiers who knew how to wait watchfully for every
sign of his secret mood. As we deep-water men always
reckoned, he made one year in three fairly lively for
anybody having business upon the Atlantic or down
there along the "forties"*of the Southern Ocean.* You
had to take the bitter with the sweet; and it cannot be
denied he played carelessly with our lives and fortunes.
But, then, he was always a great king, fit to rule over the
great waters where, strictly speaking, a man would have
no business whatever but for his audacity.

The audacious should not complain. A mere trader
ought not to grumble at the tolls levied by a mighty
king. His mightiness was sometimes very overwhelming; but even when you had to defy him openly, as on
the banks of the Agulhas*homeward bound from the
East Indies, or on the outward passage round the Horn,
he struck at you fairly his stinging blows (full in the

face, too), and it was your business not to get too much staggered. And, after all, if you showed anything of a countenance, the good-natured barbarian would let you fight your way past the very steps of his throne. It was only now and then that the sword descended and a head fell; but if you fell you were sure of impressive obsequies and of a roomy, generous grave.

Such is the king to whom Viking chieftains bowed their heads, and whom the modern and palatial steamship defies with impunity seven times a week. And yet it is but defiance, not victory. The magnificent barbarian sits enthroned in a mantle of gold-lined clouds looking from on high on great ships gliding like mechanical toys upon his sea and on men who, armed with fire and iron, no longer need to watch anxiously for the slightest sign of his royal mood. He is disregarded; but he has kept all his strength, all his splendour, and a great part of his power. Time itself, that shakes all the thrones, is on the side of that king. The sword in his hand remains as sharp as ever upon both its edges; and he may well go on playing his royal game of quoits with hurricanes, tossing them over from the continent of republics to the continent of kingdoms, in the assurance that both the new republics and the old kingdoms, the heat of fire and the strength of iron, with the untold generations of audacious men, shall crumble to dust at the steps of his throne, and pass away, and be forgotten before his own rule comes to an end.

XXX

THE estuaries of rivers appeal strongly to an adventurous imagination. This appeal is not always a charm, for there are estuaries of a particularly dispiriting ugliness: lowlands, mudflats, or perhaps barren sandhills without beauty of form or amenity of aspect, covered with a shabby and scanty vegetation conveying the impression of poverty and uselessness. Sometimes such an ugliness is merely a repulsive mask. A river whose estuary resembles a breach in a sand rampart may flow through a most fertile country. But all the estuaries of great rivers have their fascination, the attractiveness of an open portal. Water is friendly to man. The ocean, a part of Nature farthest removed in the unchangeableness and majesty of its might from the spirit of mankind, has ever been a friend to the enterprising nations of the earth. And of all the elements this is the one to which men have always been prone to trust themselves, as if its immensity held a reward as vast as itself.

From the offing the open estuary promises every possible fruition to adventurous hopes. That road open to enterprise and courage invites the explorer of coasts to new efforts towards the fulfilment of great expectations. The commander of the first Roman galley* must have looked with an intense absorption upon the estuary of the Thames as he turned the beaked prow of his ship to the westward under the brow of the North Foreland.* The estuary of the Thames is not beautiful; it has no noble features, no romantic grandeur of aspect, no smiling geniality; but it is wide open, spacious, inviting, hospitable at the first glance, with a strange air of mysteriousness which lingers about it to this very day. The navigation of his craft must have engrossed all the Roman's attention in the calm of a summer's day (he would choose his weather), when the single row of long sweeps (the galley would be a light one, not a trireme)*could fall in easy cadence upon a sheet of water like plate-glass, reflecting faithfully the classic form of his vessel and the contour of the lonely shores close on his left hand. I assume he followed the land and passed through what is at present known as Margate Roads, groping his careful way along the hidden sandbanks, whose every tail and spit has its beacon or buoy nowadays. He must have been anxious, though no doubt he had collected beforehand on the shores of the Gauls a store of information from the talk of traders, adventurers, fishermen, slave-dealers, pirates—all sorts of unofficial men connected with the sea in a more or less reputable way. He would have heard of channels and sandbanks, of natural features of the land useful for sea-marks, of villages and tribes and modes of barter and precautions to take: with the instructive tales about native chiefs dyed*more or less blue, whose character for greediness, ferocity, or amiability must have been expounded to him with that capacity for vivid language which seems joined naturally to the shadiness of moral character and recklessness of disposition. With that sort of spiced food provided for his anxious thought, watchful for strange men, strange beasts, strange turns of the tide, he would make the best of his way up, a military seaman with a short sword on thigh and a bronze helmet on his head, the pioneer post-captain of an imperial fleet. Was the tribe inhabiting the Isle of Thanet*of a ferocious disposition, I wonder, and ready to fall, with stone-studded clubs and wooden lances hardened in the fire, upon the backs of unwary mariners?

Amongst the great commercial streams of these islands, the Thames is the only one I think open to romantic feeling, from the fact that the sight of human labour and the sounds of human industry do not come down its shores to the very sea, destroying the suggestion of mysterious vastness caused by the configuration

of the shore. The broad inlet of the shallow North
Sea passes gradually into the contracted shape of the
river; but for a long time the feeling of the open water
remains with the ship steering to the westward through
one of the lighted and buoyed passage-ways of the
Thames, such as Queen's Channel, Prince's Channel,
Four-Fathom Channel; or else coming down the Swin
from the north. The rush of the yellow flood-tide
hurries her up as if into the unknown between the two
fading lines of the coast. There are no features to this
land, no conspicuous, far-famed landmarks for the
eye; there is nothing so far down to tell you of the
greatest agglomeration of mankind on earth dwelling
no more than five-and-twenty miles away, where the
sun sets in a blaze of colour flaming on a gold background, and the dark, low shores trend towards each
other. And in the great silence the deep, faint booming
of the big guns being tested at Shoeburyness* hangs
about the Nore*—a historical spot in the keeping of
one of England's appointed guardians.

XXXI

The Nore sand remains covered at low-water, and
never seen by human eye; but the Nore is a name to con-
jure with visions of historical events, of battles, of
fleets, of mutinies, of watch and ward kept upon the
great throbbing heart of the State. This ideal point
of the estuary, this centre of memories, is marked upon
the steely grey expanse of the waters by a lightship
painted red that, from a couple of miles off, looks like a
cheap and bizarre little toy. I remember how, on
coming up the river for the first time,* I was surprised
at the smallness of that vivid object—a tiny warm
speck of crimson lost in an immensity of grey tones. I

was startled, as if of necessity the principal beacon
in the waterway of the greatest town on earth should
have presented imposing proportions. And, behold!
the brown sprit-sail of a barge hid it entirely from my
view.

Coming in from the eastward, the bright colouring
of the lightship marking the part of the river committed
to the charge of an Admiral (the Commander-in-Chief at
the Nore) accentuates the dreariness and the great
breadth of the Thames Estuary. But soon the course
of the ship opens the entrance of the Medway, with its
men-of-war moored in line, and the long wooden jetty
of Port Victoria, with its few low buildings like the
beginning of a hasty settlement upon a wild and unexplored shore. The famous Thames barges sit in
brown clusters upon the water with an effect of birds
floating upon a pond. On the imposing expanse of the
great estuary the traffic of the port where so much of
the world's work and the world's thinking is being done
becomes insignificant, scattered, streaming away in thin
lines of ships stringing themselves out into the eastern
quarter through the various navigable channels of which
the Nore lightship marks the divergence. The coasting
traffic inclines to the north; the deep-water ships steer
east with a southern inclination, on through the Downs,
to the most remote ends of the world. In the widening
of the shores sinking low in the grey, smoky distances
the greatness of the sea receives the mercantile fleet
of good ships that London sends out upon the turn of
every tide. They follow each other, going very close by
the Essex shore. Such as the beads of a rosary told
by businesslike shipowners for the greater profit of
the world they slip one by one into the open: while in
the offing the inward-bound ships come up singly and in
bunches from under the sea horizon closing the mouth

of the river between Orfordness*and North Foreland.
They all converge upon the Nore, the warm speck of
red upon the tones of drab and grey, with the distant
shores running together towards the west, low and
flat, like the sides of an enormous canal. The sea-reach
of the Thames is straight, and, once Sheerness is left
behind, its banks seem very uninhabited, except for the
cluster of houses which is Southend, or here and there
a lonely wooden jetty where petroleum ships discharge
their dangerous cargoes, and the oil-storage tanks, low
and round with slightly domed roofs, peep over the
edge of the foreshore, as it were a village of Central
African huts imitated in iron. Bordered by the black
and shining mudflats, the level marsh extends for
miles. Away in the far background the land rises,
closing the view with a continuous wooded slope, forming in the distance an interminable rampart overgrown
with bushes.

Then, on the slight turn of the Lower Hope Reach,
clusters of factory chimneys come distinctly into view,
tall and slender above the squat ranges of cement works
in Grays and Greenhithe. Smoking quietly at the top
against the great blaze of a magnificent sunset, they
give an industrial character to the scene, speak of work,
manufactures, and trade as palm-groves on the coral
strands of distant islands speak of the luxuriant grace,
beauty, and vigour of tropical nature. The houses
of Gravesend crowd upon the shore with an effect of
confusion as if they had tumbled down haphazard
from the top of the hill at the back. The flatness of
the Kentish shore ends there. A fleet of steam-tugs
lies at anchor in front of the various piers. A conspicuous
church spire, the first seen distinctly coming from the
sea, has a thoughtful grace, the serenity of a fine form
above the chaotic disorder of men's houses. But on

the other side, on the flat Essex side, a shapeless and
desolate red edifice, a vast pile of bricks with many
windows and a slate roof more inaccessible than an
Alpine slope, towers over the bend in monstrous ugliness, the tallest, heaviest building for miles around, a
thing like an hotel, like a mansion of flats (all to let),
exiled into these fields out of a street in West Kensing-
ton. Just round the corner, as it were, on a pier defined
with stone blocks and wooden piles, a white mast,
slender like a stalk of straw and crossed by a yard like
a knitting-needle, flying the signals of flag and balloon,
watches over a set of heavy dock-gates. Mast-heads
and funnel-tops of ships peep above the ranges of cor-
rugated iron roofs. This is the entrance to Tilbury
Dock, the most recent of all London docks, the nearest
to the sea.

Between the crowded houses of Gravesend and the
monstrous red-brick pile on the Essex shore the ship
is surrendered fairly to the grasp of the river. That
hint of loneliness, that soul of the sea which had accompanied her as far as the Lower Hope Reach, abandons
her at the turn of the first bend above. The salt, acrid
flavour is gone out of the air, together with a sense of
unlimited space opening free beyond the threshold of
sandbanks below the Nore. The waters of the sea
rush on past Gravesend, tumbling the big mooring
buoys laid along the face of the town; but the sea-
freedom stops short there, surrendering the salt tide
to the needs, the artifices, the contrivances of toiling
men. Wharves, landing-places, dock-gates, waterside
stairs, follow each other continuously right up to London Bridge, and the hum of men's work fills the river
with a menacing, muttering note as of a breathless,
ever-driving gale. The waterway, so fair above and
wide below, flows oppressed by bricks and mortar

and stone, by blackened timber and grimed glass and
rusty iron, covered with black barges, whipped up
by paddles and screws, overburdened with craft, overhung with chains, overshadowed by walls making a
steep gorge for its bed, filled with a haze of smoke and
dust.

This stretch of the Thames from London Bridge
to the Albert Docks is to other watersides of river ports
what a virgin forest would be to a garden. It is a
thing grown up, not made. It recalls a jungle by the
confused, varied, and impenetrable aspect of the buildings that line the shore, not according to a planned
purpose, but as if sprung up by accident from scattered
seeds. Like the matted growth of bushes and creepers
veiling the silent depths of an unexplored wilderness,
they hide the depths of London's infinitely varied,
vigorous, seething life. In other river ports it is not so.
They lie open to their stream, with quays like broad
clearings, with streets like avenues cut through thick
timber for the convenience of trade. I am thinking
now of river ports I have seen—of Antwerp, for instance; of Nantes or Bordeaux, or even old Rouen,
where the night-watchmen of ships, elbows on rail,
gaze at shop-windows and brilliant cafês, and see the
audience go in and come out of the opera-house. But
London, the oldest and greatest of river ports, does not
possess as much as a hundred yards of open quays upon
its river front. Dark and impenetrable at night, like
the face of a forest, is the London waterside. It is the
waterside of watersides, where only one aspect of the
world's life can be seen, and only one kind of men toils
on the edge of the stream. The lightless walls seem to
spring from the very mud upon which the stranded
barges lie; and the narrow lanes coming down to the
foreshore resemble the paths of smashed bushes and

crumbled earth where big game comes to drink on the banks of tropical streams.

Behind the growth of the London waterside the docks of London spread out unsuspected, smooth, and placid, lost amongst the buildings like dark lagoons hidden in a thick forest. They lie concealed in the intricate growth of houses with a few stalks of mast-heads here and there overtopping the roof of some four-story warehouse.

It is a strange conjunction this of roofs and mast-heads, of walls and yard-arms. I remember once having the incongruity of the relation brought home to me in a practical way. I was the chief officer of a fine ship, just docked with a cargo of wool from Sydney, after a ninety days' passage.* In fact, we had not been in more than half an hour and I was still busy making her fast to the stone posts of a very narrow quay in front of a lofty warehouse. An old man, with a grey whisker under the chin and brass buttons on his pilot-cloth jacket, hurried up along the quay hailing my ship by name. He was one of those officials called berthing-masters—not the one who had berthed us, but another who, apparently, had been busy securing a steamer at the other end of the dock. I could see from afar his hard blue eyes staring at us, as if fascinated, with a queer sort of absorption. I wondered what that worthy sea-dog had found to criticise in my ships' rigging. And I, too, glanced aloft anxiously. I could see nothing wrong there. But perhaps that superannuated fellow-craftsman was simply admiring the ship's perfect order aloft, I thought, with some secret pride; for the chief officer is responsible for his ship's appearance, and as to her outward condition, he is the man to praise or blame. Meantime the old salt ("ex-coasting skipper" was writ large all over his person) had hobbled up alongside in his bumpy, shiny boots, and, waving an arm, short and thick like the flipper of a seal, terminated by a paw, red as an uncooked beefsteak, addressed the poop in a muffled, faint roaring voice, as if a sample of every North-Sea fog of his life had been permanently lodged in his throat: "Haul 'em round, Mr. Mate!" were his words. "If you don't look sharp, you'll have your topgallant yards through the windows of that 'ere warehouse presently!" This was the only cause of his interest in the ship's beautiful spars. I own that for a time I was struck dumb by the bizarre associations of yard-arms and windowpanes. To break windows is the last thing one would think of in connection with a ship's topgallant yard, unless, indeed, one were an experienced berthing-master in one of the London docks. This old chap was doing his little share of the world's work with proper efficiency. His little blue eyes had made out the danger many hundred yards off. His rheumaticky feet, tired with balancing that squat body for many years upon the decks of small coasters, and made sore by miles of tramping upon the flagstones of the dock side, had hurried up in time to avert a ridiculous catastrophe. I answered him pettishly, I fear, and as if I had known all about it before.

"All right, all right! can't do everything at once."

He remained near by, muttering to himself till the yards had been hauled round at my order, and then raised again his foggy, thick voice:

"None too soon," he observed, with a critical glance up at the towering side of the warehouse. "That's a half-sovereign in your pocket, Mr. Mate. You should always look first how you are for them windows before you begin to breast in your ship to the quay."

It was good advice. But one cannot think of every-thing or foresee contacts of things apparently as remote as stars and hop-poles.

XXXII

The view of ships lying moored in some of the older docks of London has always suggested to my mind the image of a flock of swans kept in the flooded backyard of grim tenement houses. The flatness of the walls surrounding the dark pool on which they float brings out wonderfully the flowing grace of the lines on which a ship's hull is built. The lightness of these forms, devised to meet the winds and the seas, makes, by contrast with the great piles of bricks, the chains and cables of their moorings appear very necessary, as if nothing less could prevent them from soaring upwards and over the roofs. The least puff of wind stealing round the corners of the dock buildings stirs these cap-tives fettered to rigid shores. It is as if the soul of a ship were impatient of confinement. Those masted hulls, relieved of their cargo, become restless at the slightest hint of the wind's freedom. However tightly moored, they range a little at their berths, swaying imperceptibly the spirelike assemblages of cordage and spars. You can detect their impatience by watching the sway of the mast-heads against the motionless, the soulless gravity of mortar and stones. As you pass alongside each hopeless prisoner chained to the quay, the slight grinding noise of the wooden fenders makes a sound of angry muttering. But, after all, it may be good for ships to go through a period of restraint and repose, as the restraint and self-communion of inactiv-ity may be good for an unruly soul—not, indeed, that I mean to say that ships are unruly: on the contrary,

they are faithful creatures, as so many men can testify.
And faithfulness is a great restraint, the strongest bond
laid upon the self-will of men and ships on this globe
of land and sea.

This interval of bondage in the docks rounds each
period of a ship's life with the sense of accomplished
duty, of an effectively played part in the work of the
world. The dock is the scene of what the world would
think the most serious part in the light, bounding,
swaying life of a ship. But there are docks and docks.
The ugliness of some docks is appalling. Wild horses
would not drag from me the name of a certain river in
the north* whose narrow estuary is inhospitable and
dangerous, and whose docks are like a nightmare of
dreariness and misery. Their dismal shores are stud-
ded thickly with scaffoldlike, enormous timber struc-
tures, whose lofty heads are veiled periodically by the
infernal gritty night of a cloud of coal-dust. The most
important ingredient for getting the world's work along
is distributed there under the circumstances of the
greatest cruelty meted out to helpless ships. Shut up
in the desolate circuit of these basins you would think
a free ship would droop and die like a wild bird put
into a dirty cage. But a ship, perhaps because of her
faithfulness to men, will endure an extraordinary lot
of ill-usage. Still, I have seen ships issue from certain
docks like half-dead prisoners from a dungeon, bedraggled, overcome, wholly disguised in dirt, and with
their men rolling white eyeballs in black and worried
faces raised to a heaven which, in its smoky and soiled
aspect, seemed to reflect the sordidness of the earth
below. One thing, however, may be said for the docks
of the Port of London on both sides of the river: for
all the complaints of their insufficient equipment, of
their obsolete rules, of failure (they say) in the matter

of quick dispatch, no ship need ever issue from their gates in a half-fainting condition. London is a general cargo port, as is only proper for the greatest capital of the world to be. General cargo ports belong to the aristocracy of the earth's trading places, and in that aristocracy London, as it is its way, has a unique physiognomy.

The absence of picturesqueness cannot be laid to the charge of the docks opening into the Thames. For all my unkind comparisons to swans and backyards, it cannot be denied that each dock or group of docks along the north side of the river has its own individual attractiveness. Beginning with the cosy little St. Katherine's Dock, lying overshadowed and black like a quiet pool amongst rocky crags, through the venerable and sympathetic London Docks, with not a single line of rails in the whole of their area and the aroma of spices lingering between its warehouses, with their far-famed wine-cellars—down through the interesting group of West India Docks, the fine docks at Blackwall, on past the Galleons Reach entrance of the Victoria and Albert Docks, right down to the vast gloom of the great basins in Tilbury, each of those places of restraint for ships has its own peculiar physiognomy, its own expression. And what makes them unique and attractive is their common trait of being romantic in their usefulness.

In their way they are as romantic as the river they serve is unlike all the other commercial streams of the world. The cosiness of the St. Katherine's Dock, the old-world air of the London Docks, remain impressed upon the memory. The docks down the river, abreast of Woolwich, are imposing by their proportions and the vast scale of the ugliness that forms their surroundings—ugliness so picturesque as to become a delight to the eye. When one talks of the Thames docks, "beauty" is a vain word, but romance has lived too long upon this river not to have thrown a mantle of glamour upon its banks.

The antiquity of the port appeals to the imagination by the long chain of adventurous enterprises that had their inception in the town and floated out into the world on the waters of the river. Even the newest of the docks, the Tilbury Dock, shares in the glamour conferred by historical associations. Queen Elizabeth has made one of her progresses down there, not one of her journeys of pomp and ceremony, but an anxious business progress at a crisis of national history.* The menace of that time has passed away, and now Tilbury is known by its docks. These are very modern, but their remoteness and isolation upon the Essex marsh, the days of failure attending their creation,* invested them with a romantic air. Nothing in those days could have been more striking than the vast, empty basins, surrounded by miles of bare quays and the ranges of cargo-sheds, where two or three ships seemed lost like bewitched children in a forest of gaunt, hydraulic cranes. One received a wonderful impression of utter abandonment, of wasted efficiency. From the first the Tilbury Docks were very efficient and ready for their task, but they had come, perhaps, too soon into the field. A great future lies before Tilbury Docks. They will never fill a long-felt want (in the sacramental phrase that is applied to railways, tunnels, newspapers, and new editions of books). They were too early in the field. The want will never be felt because, free of the trammels of the tide, easy of access, magnificent and desolate, they are already there, prepared to take and keep the biggest ships that float upon the sea. They are worthy of the oldest river port in the world.

And truth to say, for all the criticisms flung upon

the heads of the dock companies, the other docks of the Thames are no disgrace to the town with a population greater than that of some commonwealths. The growth of London as a well-equipped port has been slow, while not unworthy of a great centre of distribution. It must not be forgotten that London has not the backing of great industrial districts or great fields of natural exploitation. In this it differs from Liverpool, from Cardiff, from Newcastle, from Glasgow; and therein the Thames differs from the Mersey, from the Tyne, from the Clyde. It is an historical river; it is a romantic stream flowing through the centre of great affairs, and for all the criticism of the river's administration, my contention is that its development has been worthy of its dignity. For a long time the stream itself could accommodate quite easily the oversea and coasting traffic. That was in the days when, in the part called the Pool, just below London Bridge, the vessels moored stem and stern in the very strength of the tide formed one solid mass like an island covered with a forest of gaunt, leafless trees; and when the trade had grown too big for the river there came the St. Katherine's Docks and the London Docks, magnificent undertakings answering to the need of their time. The same may be said of the other artificial lakes full of ships that go in and out upon this high road to all parts of the world. The labour of the imperial waterway goes on from generation to generation, goes on day and night. Nothing ever arrests its sleepless industry but the coming of a heavy fog, which clothes the teeming stream in a mantle of impenetrable stillness.

After the gradual cessation of all sound and movement on the faithful river, only the ringing of ships' bells is heard, mysterious and muffled in the white vapour from London Bridge right down to the Nore, for miles and miles in a decrescendo tinkling, to where the estuary broadens out into the North Sea, and the anchored ships lie scattered thinly in the shrouded channels between the sandbanks of the Thames' mouth. Through the long and glorious tale of years of the river's strenuous service to its people these are its only breathing times.

XXXIII

A SHIP in dock, surrounded by quays and the walls of warehouses, has the appearance of a prisoner meditating upon freedom in the sadness of a free spirit put under restraint. Chain cables and stout ropes keep her bound to stone posts at the edge of a paved shore, and a berthing-master, with brass buttons on his coat, walks about like a weather-beaten and ruddy gaoler, casting jealous, watchful glances upon the moorings that fetter a ship lying passive and still and safe, as if lost in deep regrets of her days of liberty and danger on the sea.

The swarm of renegades—dock-masters, berthing-masters, gatemen, and such like—appear to nurse an immense distrust of the captive ship's resignation. There never seem chains and ropes enough to satisfy their minds concerned with the safe binding of free ships to the strong, muddy, enslaved earth. "You had better put another bight of a hawser astern, Mr. Mate," is the usual phrase in their mouth. I brand them for renegades, because most of them have been sailors in their time. As if the infirmities of old age—the grey hair, the wrinkles at the corners of the eyes, and the knotted veins of the hands—were the symptoms of moral poison, they prowl about the quays with an underhand air of gloating over the broken spirit of noble captives. They want more fenders, more breasting-ropes; they want more springs, more shackles, more fetters; they want to make ships with volatile souls as motionless as square blocks of stone. They stand on the mud of pavements, these degraded sea-dogs, with long lines of railway-trucks clanking their couplings behind their backs, and run malevolent glances over your ship from headgear to taffrail, only wishing to tryannize over the poor creature under the hypocritical cloak of benevolence and care. Here and there cargo cranes looking like instruments of torture for ships swing cruel hooks at the end of long chains. Gangs of dock-labourers swarm with muddy feet over the gangways. It is a moving sight this, of so many men of the earth, earthy, who never cared anything for a ship, trampling, unconcerned, brutal, and hobnailed upon her helpless body.

Fortunately, nothing can deface the beauty of a ship. That sense of a dungeon, that sense of a horrible and degrading misfortune overtaking a creature fair to see and safe to trust, attaches only to ships moored in the docks of great European ports. You feel that they are dishonestly locked up, to be hunted about from wharf to wharf on a dark, greasy, square pool of black water as a brutal reward at the end of a faithful voyage.

A ship anchored in an open roadstead, with cargo-lighters alongside and her own tackle* swinging the burden over the rail, is accomplishing in freedom a function of her life. There is no restraint; there is space: clear water around her, and a clear sky above her mast-heads, with a landscape of green hills and charming bays opening around her anchorage. She is not abandoned by her own men to the tender mercies of shore people. She still shelters, and is looked after by her own little devoted band, and you feel that presently she will glide between the headlands and disappear. It is only at home, in dock, that she lies abandoned, shut off from freedom by all the artifices of men that think of quick dispatch and profitable freights. It is only then that the odious, rectangular shadows of walls and roofs fall upon her decks, with showers of soot.

To a man who has never seen the extraordinary nobility, strength, and grace that the devoted generations of ship-builders have evolved from some pure nooks of their simple souls, the sight that could be seen five-and-twenty years ago of a large fleet of clippers moored along the north side of the New South Dock was an inspiring spectacle. Then there was a quarter of a mile of them, from the iron dockyard-gates guarded by policemen, in a long, forest-like perspective of masts, moored two and two to many stout wooden jetties. Their spars dwarfed with their loftiness the corrugated-iron sheds, their jib-booms extended far over the shore, their white-and-gold figure-heads, almost dazzling in their purity, overhung the straight long quay above the mud and dirt of the wharfside, with the busy figures of groups of single men moving to and fro, restless and grimy under their soaring immobility.

At tide-time you would see one of the loaded ships with battened-down hatches drop out of the ranks and float in the clear space of the dock, held by lines dark and slender, like the first threads of a spider's web, extending from her bows and her quarters to the mooring-posts on shore. There, graceful and still, like a bird ready to spread its wings, she waited till, at the opening of the gates, a tug or two would hurry in noisily, hovering round her with an air of fuss and solicitude, and take her out into the river, tending, shepherding her through open bridges, through dam-like gates between the flat pier-heads, with a bit of green lawn surrounded by gravel and a white signal-mast with yard and gaff, flying a couple of dingy blue, red, or white flags.

This New South Dock (it was its official name), round which my earlier professional memories are centred, belongs to the group of West India Docks, together with two smaller and much older basins called Import and Export respectively, both with the greatness of their trade departed from them already. Picturesque and clean as docks go, these twin basins spread side by side the dark. lustre of their glassy water sparsely peopled by a few ships laid up on buoys or tucked far away from each other at the end of sheds in the corners of empty quays, where they seemed to slumber quietly remote, untouched by the bustle of men's affairs—in retreat rather than in activity. They were quaint and sympathetic, those two homely basins, unfurnished and silent, with no aggressive display of cranes, no apparatus of hurry and work on their narrow shores. No railway-lines cumbered them. The knots of labourers trooping in clumsily round the corners of cargo-sheds to eat their food in peace out of red cotton handkerchiefs had the air of picknicking by the side of a lonely mountain pool. They were restful (and I should say very unprofitable), those basins, where the chief officer of one of the ships involved in the harassing, strenuous, noisy activity of the New South Dock only a few yards away could escape in the dinner-hour to stroll, unhampered by men and affairs, meditating (if he chose) on the vanity of all things human. At one time they must have been full of good old slow West Indiamen of the square-stern type, that took their captivity, one imagines, as stolidly as they had

faced the buffeting of the waves with their blunt, honest
bows, and disgorged sugar, rum, molasses, coffee, or
logwood sedately with their own winch and tackle.
But when I knew them, of exports there was never a
sign that one could detect; and all the imports I have
ever seen were some rare cargoes of tropical timber,
enormous baulks roughed out of iron trunks grown in
the woods about the Gulf of Mexico. They lay piled
up in stacks of mighty boles, and it was hard to believe that all this mass of dead and stripped trees had
come out of the flanks of a slender, innocent-looking
little barque with, as likely as not, a homely woman's
name—Ellen this or Annie that—upon her fine bows.
But this is generally the case with a discharged cargo.
Once spread at large over the quay, it looks the most
impossible bulk to have all come there out of that ship
alongside.

They were quiet, serene nooks in the busy world of
docks, these basins where it has never been my good
luck to get a berth after some more or less arduous
passage. But one could see at a glance that men and
ships were never hustled there. They were so quiet
that, remembering them well, one comes to doubt that
they ever existed—places of repose for tired ships to
dream in, places of meditation rather than work, where
wicked ships—the cranky, the lazy, the wet, the bad
sea boats, the wild steerers, the capricious, the pig-
headed, the generally ungovernable—would have full
leisure to take count and repent of their sins, sorrowful
and naked, with their rent garments of sailcloth stripped
off them, and with the dust and ashes of the London
atmosphere upon their mast-heads. For that the worst
of ships would repent if she were ever given time I
make no doubt. I have known too many of them. No
ship is wholly bad; and now that their bodies that had

braved so many tempests have been blown off the
face of the sea by a puff of steam, the evil and
the good together into the limbo of things that
have served their time, there can be no harm in
affirming that in these vanished generations of willing
servants there never has been one utterly unredeem-
able soul.

In the New South Dock there was certainly no time
for remorse, introspection, repentance, or any phenomena of inner life either for the captive ships or for
their officers.   From six in the morning till six at night
the hard labour of the prison-house, which rewards the
valiance of ships that win the harbour, went on steadily,
great slings of general cargo swinging over the rail, to
drop plump into the hatchways at the sign of the gang-
way-tender's hand.   The New South Dock was especially a loading dock for the Colonies in those great
(and last) days of smart wool-clippers, good to look at
and—well—exciting to handle.   Some of them were
more fair to see than the others; many were (to put it
mildly) somewhat overmasted; all were expected to
make good passages; and of all that line of ships, whose
rigging made a thick, enormous network against the
sky, whose brasses flashed almost as far as the eye of
the policeman at the gates could reach, there was hardly
one that knew of any other port amongst all the ports on
the wide earth but London and Sydney, or London and
Melbourne, or London and Adelaide, perhaps with
Hobart Town*added for those of smaller tonnage.   One
could almost have believed, as her grey-whiskered
second mate*used to say of the old *Duke of S*——, that
they knew the road to the Antipodes better than their
own skippers, who, year in, year out, took them from
London—the place of captivity—to some Australian port*
where, twenty-five years ago, though moored well and

tight enough to the wooden wharves, they felt themselves no captives, but honoured guests.

XXXIV

These towns of the Antipodes, not so great then as they are now, took an interest in the shipping, the running links with "home," whose numbers confirmed the sense of their growing importance. They made it part and parcel of their daily interests. This was especially the case in Sydney, where, from the heart of the fair city, down the vista of important streets, could be seen the wool-clippers lying at the Circular Quay— no walled prison-house of a dock that, but the integral part of one of the finest, most beautiful, vast, and safe bays the sun ever shone upon. Now great steam-liners lie at these berths, always reserved for the sea-aristocracy—grand and imposing enough ships, but here to-day and gone next week; whereas the general cargo, emigrant, and passenger clippers of my time, rigged with heavy spars, and built on fine lines, used to remain for months together waiting for their load of wool. Their names attained the dignity of household words. On Sundays and holidays the citizens trooped down, on visiting bent, and the lonely officer on duty solaced himself by playing the cicerone—especially to the citizenesses with engaging manners and a well-developed sense of the fun that may be got out of the inspection of a ship's cabins and state-rooms. The tinkle of more or less untuned cottage pianos floated out of open stern-ports till the gas lamps began to twinkle in the streets, and the ship's night-watchman, coming sleepily on duty after his unsatisfactory day slumbers, hauled down the flags and fastened a lighted lantern at the break of the gangway. The night closed rapidly

upon the silent ships with their crews on shore. Up a
short, steep ascent by the King's Head pub., patronized
by the cooks and stewards of the fleet, the voice of a
man crying "Hot saveloys!"* at the end of George
Street, where the cheap eating-houses (sixpence a meal)
were kept by Chinamen (Sun-kum-on's was not bad),
is heard at regular intervals. I have listened for hours
to this most pertinacious pedlar (I wonder whether he is
dead or has made a fortune) while sitting on the rail of
the old *Duke of S*—— (she's dead, poor thing! a violent
death* on the coast of New Zealand), fascinated by the
monotony, the regularity, the abruptness of the re-
curring cry, and so exasperated at the absurd spell, that
I wished the fellow would choke himself to death with a
mouthful of his own infamous wares.

A stupid job, and fit only for an old man, my com-
rades used to tell me, to be the night-watchman of a
captive (though honoured) ship. And generally the
oldest of the able seamen in a ship's crew does get it.
But sometimes neither the oldest nor any other fairly
steady seaman is forthcoming. Ships' crews had the
trick of melting away swiftly in those days. So, probably on account of my youth, innocence, and pensive
habits (which made me sometimes dilatory in my work
about the rigging), I was suddenly nominated, in our
chief mate Mr. B——'s* most sardonic tones, to that
enviable situation. I do not regret the experience.
The night humours of the town descended from the
street to the waterside in the still watches of the night:
larrikins rushing down in bands to settle some quarrel
by a stand-up fight, away from the police, in an in-
distinct ring half hidden by piles of cargo, with the
sounds of blows, a groan now and then, the stamping of
feet, and the cry of "Time!" rising suddenly above the
sinister and excited murmurs; night-prowlers, pursued

or pursuing, with a stifled shriek followed by a profound silence, or slinking stealthily alongside like ghosts, and addressing me from the quay below in mysterious tones with incomprehensible propositions. The cabmen, too, who twice a week, on the night when the A.S.N. Company's* passenger-boat was due to arrive, used to range a battalion of blazing lamps opposite the ship, were very amusing in their way. They got down from their perches and told each other impolite stories in racy language, every word of which reached me distinctly over the bulwarks as I sat smoking on the main-hatch. On one occasion I had an hour or so of a most intellectual conversation with a person whom I could not see distinctly, a gentleman from England, he said, with a cultivated voice, I on deck and he on the quay sitting on the case of a piano (landed out of our hold that very afternoon), and smoking a cigar which smelt very good. We touched, in our discourse, upon science, politics, natural history, and operatic singers. Then, after remarking abruptly, "You seem to be rather intelligent, my man," he informed me pointedly that his name was Mr. Senior, and walked off—to his hotel, I suppose. Shadows! Shadows! I think I saw a white whisker as he turned under the lamp-post. It is a shock to think that in the natural course of nature he must be dead by now. There was nothing to object to in his intelligence but a little dogmatism maybe. And his name was Senior! Mr. Senior!

The position had its drawbacks, however. One wintry, blustering, dark night in July, as I stood sleepily out of the rain under the break of the poop something resembling an ostrich dashed up the gangway. I say ostrich because the creature, though it ran on two legs, appeared to help its progress by working a pair of short wings; it was a man, however, only his coat, ripped up the back and flapping in two halves above his shoulders, gave him that weird and fowl-like appearance. At least, I suppose it was his coat, for it was impossible to make him out distinctly. How he managed to come so straight upon me, at speed and without a stumble over a strange deck, I cannot imagine. He must have been able to see in the dark better than any cat. He overwhelmed me with panting entreaties to let him take shelter till morning in our forecastle. Following my strict orders, I refused his request, mildly at first, in a sterner tone as he insisted with growing impudence.

"For God's sake let me, matey! Some of 'em are after me—and I've got hold of a ticker here."

"You clear out of this!" I said.

"Don't be hard on a chap, old man!" he whined, pitifully.

"Now, then, get ashore at once. Do you hear?"

Silence. He appeared to cringe, mute, as if words had failed him through grief; then—bang! came a concussion and a great flash of light in which he vanished, leaving me prone on my back with the most abominable black eye that anybody ever got in the faithful discharge of duty. Shadows! Shadows! I hope he escaped the enemies he was fleeing from to live and flourish to this day. But his fist was uncommonly hard and his aim miraculously true in the dark.

There were other experiences, less painful and more funny for the most part, with one amongst them of a dramatic complexion; but the greatest experience of them all was Mr. B——, our chief mate himself.

He used to go ashore every night to forgather in some hotel's parlour with his crony, the mate of the barque *Cicero*, lying on the other side of the Circular Quay. Late at night I would hear from afar their stumbling footsteps and their voices raised in endless argument. The mate of the *Cicero* was seeing his friend on board. They would continue their senseless and muddled discourse in tones of profound friendship for half an hour or so at the shore end of our gangway, and then I would hear Mr. B—— insisting that he must see the other on board his ship. And away they would go, their voices, still conversing with excessive amity, being heard moving all round the harbour. It happened more than once that they would thus perambulate three or four times the distance, each seeing the other on board his ship out of pure and disinterested affection. Then, through sheer weariness, or perhaps in a moment of forgetfulness, they would manage to part from each other somehow, and by and by the planks of our long gangway would bend and creak under the weight of Mr. B—— coming on board for good at last.

On the rail his burly form would stop and stand swaying.

"Watchman!"

"Sir."

A pause.

He waited for a moment of steadiness before negotiating the three steps of the inside ladder from rail to deck; and the watchman, taught by experience, would forbear offering help which would be received as an insult at that particular stage of the mate's return. But many times I trembled for his neck. He was a heavy man.

Then with a rush and a thump it would be done. He never had to pick himself up; but it took him a minute or so to pull himself together after the descent.

"Watchman!"

"Sir."

"Captain aboard?"

"Yes, sir."

Pause.

"Dog aboard?"

"Yes, sir."

Pause.

Our dog was a gaunt and unpleasant beast, more like a wolf in poor health than a dog, and I never noticed Mr. B—— at any other time show the slightest interest in the doings of the animal. But that question never failed.

"Let's have your arm to steady me along."

I was always prepared for that request. He leaned on me heavily till near enough the cabin-door to catch hold of the handle. Then he would let go my arm at once.

"That'll do. I can manage now."

And he could manage. He could manage to find his way into his berth, light his lamp, get into his bed—ay, and get out of it when I called him at half-past five, the first man on deck, lifting the cup of morning coffee to his lips with a steady hand, ready for duty as though he had virtuously slept ten solid hours—a better chief officer than many a man who had never tasted grog in his life. He could manage all that, but could never manage to get on in life.

Only once he failed to seize the cabin-door handle at the first grab. He waited a little, tried again, and again failed. His weight was growing heavier on my arm. He sighed slowly.

"D——n that handle!"

Without letting go his hold of me he turned about, his face lit up bright as day by the full moon.

"I wish she were out at sea," he growled, savagely.

"Yes, sir."

I felt the need to say something, because he hung on to me as if lost, breathing heavily.

"Ports are no good—ships rot, men go to the devil!"

I kept still, and after a while he repeated with a sigh:

"I wish she were at sea out of this."

"So do I, sir," I ventured.

Holding my shoulder, he turned upon me.

"You! What's that to you where she is? You don't—drink."

And even on that night he "managed it" at last. He got hold of the handle. But he did not manage to light his lamp (I don't think he even tried), though in the morning as usual he was the first on deck, bull-necked, curly-headed, watching the hands turn-to with his sardonic expression and unflinching gaze.

I met him ten years afterwards, casually, unexpectedly, in the street, on coming out of my consignee office. I was not likely to have forgotten him with his "I can manage now." He recognized me at once, remembered my name, and in what ship I had served under his orders. He looked me over from head to foot.

"What are you doing here?" he asked.

"I am commanding a little barque," I said, "loading here for Mauritius."* Then, thoughtlessly, I added: "And what are you doing, Mr. B——?"

"I," he said, looking at me unflinchingly, with his old sardonic grin—"I am looking for something to do."

I felt I would rather have bitten out my tongue. His jet-black, curly hair had turned iron-grey; he was scrupulously neat as ever, but frightfully threadbare. His shiny boots were worn down at heel. But he forgave me, and we drove off together in a hansom to dine on board my ship. He went over her conscientiously, praised her heartily, congratulated me on my command with absolute sincerity. At dinner, as I offered

him wine and beer he shook his head, and as I sat looking at him interrogatively, muttered in an undertone:
"I've given up all that."

After dinner we came again on deck. It seemed as
though he could not tear himself away from the ship.
We were fitting some new lower rigging, and he hung
about, approving, suggesting, giving me advice in his
old manner. Twice he addressed me as "My boy,"
and corrected himself quickly to "Captain." My
mate was about to leave me (to get married), but I concealed the fact from Mr. B——. I was afraid he would
ask me to give him the berth in some ghastly jocular
hint that I could not refuse to take. I was afraid. It
would have been impossible. I could not have given
orders to Mr. B——, and I am sure he would not have
taken them from me very long. He could not have
managed *that*, though he had managed to break himself
from drink—too late.

He said good-bye at last. As I watched his burly,
bull-necked figure walk away up the street, I wondered
with a sinking heart whether he had much more than
the price of a night's lodging in his pocket. And I
understood that if that very minute I were to call out
after him, he would not even turn his head. He, too, is
no more than a shadow, but I seem to hear his words
spoken on the moonlit deck of the old *Duke*——:

"Ports are no good—ships rot, men go to the devil!"

XXXV

"SHIPS!" exclaimed an elderly seaman in clean shore
togs. "Ships"—and his keen glance, turning away
from my face, ran along the vista of magnificent figure-
heads that in the late seventies used to overhang in a
serried rank the muddy pavement by the side of the

New South Dock—"ships are all right; it's the men in 'em. . . ."

Fifty hulls, at least, moulded on lines of beauty and speed—hulls of wood, of iron, expressing in their forms the highest achievement of modern ship-building—lay moored all in a row, stem to quay, as if assembled there for an exhibition, not of a great industry, but of a great art. Their colours were grey, black, dark green, with a narrow strip of yellow moulding defining their sheer, or with a row of painted ports decking in warlike decoration their robust flanks of cargo-carriers that would know no triumph but of speed in carrying a burden, no glory other than of a long service, no victory but that of an endless, obscure contest with the sea. The great empty hulls with swept holds, just out of dry-dock with their paint glistening freshly, sat high-sided with ponderous dignity alongside the wooden jetties, looking more like unmovable buildings than things meant to go afloat; others, half loaded, far on the way to recover the true sea-physiognomy of a ship brought down to her load-line,* looked more accessible. Their less steeply slanting gangways seemed to invite the strolling sailors in search of a berth to walk on board and try "for a chance" with the chief mate, the guardian of a ship's efficiency. As if anxious to remain unperceived amongst their overtopping sisters, two or three "finished" ships floated low, with an air of straining at the leash of their level headfasts, exposing to view their cleared decks and covered hatches, prepared to drop stern first out of the labouring ranks, displaying the true comeliness of form which only her proper sea-trim gives to a ship. And for a good quarter of a mile, from the dockyard-gate to the farthest corner, where the old housed-in hulk, the *President* (drill-ship, then, of the Naval Reserve), used to lie with her frigate side* rubbing against the stone of the quay, above all these hulls, ready and unready, a hundred and fifty lofty masts, more or less, held out the web of their rigging like an immense net, in whose close mesh, black against the sky, the heavy yards seemed to be entangled and suspended.

It was a sight. The humblest craft that floats makes its appeal to a seaman by the faithfulness of her life; and this was the place where one beheld the aristocracy of ships. It was a noble gathering of the fairest and swiftest, each bearing at the bow the carved emblem of her name as in a gallery of plaster-casts, figures of women with mural crowns,* women with flowing robes, with gold fillets on their hair or blue scarves round their waists, stretching out rounded arms as if to point the way; heads of men helmeted or bare; full lengths of warriors, of kings, of statesmen, of lords and princesses, all white from top to toe; with here and there a dusky turbaned figure, bedizened in many colours of some Eastern sultan or hero, all inclined forward under the slant of mighty bowsprits as if eager to begin another run of 11,000 miles*in their leaning attitudes. These were the fine figure-heads of the finest ships afloat. But why, unless for the love of the life those effigies shared with us in their wandering impassivity, should one try to reproduce in words an impression of whose fidelity there can be no critic and no judge, since such an exhibition* of the art of shipbuilding and the art of figure-head carving as was seen from year's end to year's end in the open-air gallery of the New South Dock no man's eye shall behold again? All that patient pale company of queens and princesses, of kings and warriors, of allegorical women, of heroines and statesmen and heathen gods, crowned, helmeted, bareheaded, has run for good off the sea stretching to the last

above the tumbling foam their fair, rounded arms; holding out their spears, swords, shields, tridents in the
same unwearied, striving forward pose. And nothing
remains but lingering perhaps in the memory of a few
men, the sound of their names, vanished a long time
ago from the first page of the great London dailies;
from big posters in railway-stations and the doors of
shipping offices; from the minds of sailors, dock-masters,
pilots, and tugmen; from the hail of gruff voices and the
flutter of signal flags exchanged between ships closing
upon each other and drawing apart in the open immensity of the sea.

The elderly, respectable seaman, withdrawing his
gaze from that multitude of spars, gave me a glance to
make sure of our fellowship in the craft and mystery
of the sea. We had met casually, and had got into
contact as I had stopped near him, my attention
being caught by the same peculiarity he was looking
at in the rigging of an obviously new ship, a ship with
her reputation all to make yet in the talk of the seamen
who were to share their life with her. Her name was
already on their lips. I had heard it uttered between
two thick, red-necked fellows of the semi-nautical type
at the Fenchurch Street railway station,*where, in those
days, the everyday male crowd was attired in jerseys
and pilot-cloth mostly, and had the air of being more
conversant with the times of high-water than with the
times of the trains. I had noticed that new ship's
name on the first page of my morning paper. I had
stared at the unfamiliar grouping of its letters, blue
on white ground, on the advertisement-boards, whenever the train came to a standstill alongside one of the
shabby, wooden, wharf-like platforms of the dock
railway-line. She had been named, with proper ob-
servances, on the day she came off the stocks, no doubt,

but she was very far yet from "having a name." Untried, ignorant of the ways of the sea, she had been thrust amongst that renowned company of ships to load for her maiden voyage. There was nothing to vouch for her soundness and the worth of her character, but the reputation of the building-yard whence she was launched headlong into the world of waters. She looked modest to me. I imagined her diffident, lying very quiet, with her side nestling shyly against the wharf to which she was made fast with very new lines, intimidated by the company of her tried and experienced sisters already familiar with all the violences of the ocean and the exacting love of men. They had had more long voyages to make their names in than she had known weeks of carefully tended life, for a new ship receives as much attention as if she were a young bride. Even crabbed old dock-masters look at her with benevolent eyes. In her shyness at the threshold of a laborious and uncertain life, where so much is expected of a ship, she could not have been better heartened and comforted, had she only been able to hear and understand, than by the tone of deep conviction in which my elderly, respectable seaman repeated the first part of his saying, "Ships are all right . . ."

His civility prevented him from repeating the other, the bitter part. It had occurred to him that it was perhaps indelicate to insist. He had recognized in me a ship's officer, very possibly looking for a berth like himself, and so far a comrade, but still a man belonging to that sparsely peopled after-end of a ship, where a great part of her reputation as a "good ship," in seaman's parlance, is made or marred.

"Can you say that of all ships without exception?" I asked, being in an idle mood, because, if an obvious ship's officer, I was not, as a matter of fact, down at the docks to "look for a berth," an occupation as engrossing as gambling, and as little favourable to the free exchange of ideas, besides being destructive of the kindly temper needed for casual intercourse with one's fellow-creatures.

"You can always put up with 'em," opined the respectable seaman, judicially.

He was not averse from talking, either. If he had come down to the dock to look for a berth, he did not seem oppressed by anxiety as to his chances. He had the serenity of a man whose estimable character is fortunately expressed by his personal appearance in an unobtrusive, yet convincing, manner which no chief officer in want of hands could resist. And, true enough, I learned presently that the mate of the *Hyperion* had "taken down" his name for quartermaster. "We sign on Friday, and join next day for the morning tide," he remarked, in a deliberate, careless tone, which contrasted strongly with his evident readiness to stand there yarning for an hour or so with an utter stranger.

"*Hyperion*," I said. "I don't remember ever seeing that ship anywhere. What sort of a name has she got?"

It appeared from his discursive answer that she had not much of a name one way or another. She was not very fast. It took no fool, though, to steer her straight, he believed. Some years ago he had seen her in Calcutta, and he remembered being told by somebody then that on her passage up the river* she had carried away both her hawse-pipes.* But that might have been the pilot's fault. Just now, yarning with the apprentices on board, he had heard that this very voyage, brought up in the Downs, outward bound, she broke her sheer, struck adrift, and lost an anchor and chain. But that might have occurred through want of careful tending in a tideway. All the same, this looked as

though she were pretty hard on her ground-tackle.*
Didn't it? She seemed a heavy ship to handle, anyway.
For the rest, as she had a new captain and a new mate
this voyage, he understood, one couldn't say how she
would turn out. . . .

In such marine shore-talk as this is the name of a
ship slowly established, her fame made for her, the tale
of her qualities and of her defects kept, her idiosyncrasies commented upon with the zest of personal gossip, her achievements made much of, her faults glossed
over as things that, being without remedy in our
imperfect world, should not be dwelt upon too much by
men who, with the help of ships, wrest out a bitter
living from the rough grasp of the sea. All that talk
makes up her "name," which is handed over from one
crew to another without bitterness, without animosity,
with the indulgence of mutual dependence, and with
the feeling of close association in the exercise of her perfections and in the danger of her defects.

This feeling explains men's pride in ships. "Ships
are all right," as my middle-aged, respectable quartermaster said with much conviction and some irony;
but they are not exactly what men make them. They
have their own nature; they can of themselves minister
to our self-esteem by the demand their qualities make
upon our skill and their shortcomings upon our hardi-
ness and endurance. Which is the more flattering
exaction it is hard to say; but there is the fact that in
listening for upwards of twenty years to the sea-talk
that goes on afloat and ashore I have never detected
the true note of animosity. I won't deny that at sea,
sometimes, the note of profanity was audible enough
in those chiding interpellations a wet, cold, weary
seaman addresses to his ship, and in moments of exasperation is disposed to extend to all ships that ever were

launched—to the whole everlastingly exacting brood that swims in deep waters. And I have heard curses launched at the unstable element itself, whose fascination, outlasting the accumulated experience of ages, had captured him as it had captured the generations of his forbears.

For all that has been said of the love that certain natures (on shore) have professed to feel for it, for all the celebrations it had been the object of in prose and song, the sea has never been friendly to man. At most it has been the accomplice of human restlessness, and playing the part of dangerous abettor of world-wide ambitions. Faithful to no race after the manner of the kindly earth, receiving no impress from valour and toil and self-sacrifice, recognizing no finality of dominion, the sea has never adopted the cause of its masters like those lands where the victorious nations of mankind have taken root, rocking their cradles and setting up their gravestones. He—man or people —who, putting his trust in the friendship of the sea, neglects the strength and cunning of his right hand, is a fool! As if it were too great, too mighty for common virtues, the ocean has no compassion, no faith, no law, no memory. Its fickleness is to be held true to men's purposes only by an undaunted resolution and by a sleepless, armed, jealous vigilance, in which, perhaps, there has always been more hate than love. *Odi et amo**
may well be the confession of those who consciously or blindly have surrendered their existence to the fascination of the sea. All the tempestuous passions of mankind's young days, the love of loot and the love of glory, the love of adventure and the love of danger, with the great love of the unknown and vast dreams of dominion and power, have passed like images reflected from a mirror, leaving no record upon the

mysterious face of the sea. Impenetrable and heartless, the sea has given nothing of itself to the suitors for its precarious favours. Unlike the earth, it cannot be subjugated at any cost of patience and toil. For all its fascination that has lured so many to a violent death, its immensity has never been loved as the mountains, the plains, the desert itself, have been loved. Indeed, I suspect that, leaving aside the protestations and tributes of writers who, one is safe in saying, care for little else in the world than the rhythm of their lines and the cadence of their phrase, the love of the sea, to which some men and nations confess so readily, is a complex sentiment wherein pride enters for much, necessity for not a little, and the love of ships—the untiring servants of our hopes and our self-esteem—for the best and most genuine part. For the hundreds who have reviled the sea, beginning with Shakespeare in the line—

"More fell than hunger, anguish, or the sea."*

down to the last obscure sea-dog of the "old model," having but few words and still fewer thoughts, there could not be found, I believe, one sailor who has ever coupled a curse with the good or bad name of a ship. If ever his profanity, provoked by the hardships of the sea, went so far as to touch his ship, it would be lightly, as a hand may, without sin, be laid in the way of kindness on a woman.

XXXVI

The love that is given to ships is profoundly different from the love men feel for every other work of their hands—the love they bear to their houses, for instance —because it is untainted by the pride of possession.

The pride of skill, the pride of responsibility, the pride of endurance there may be, but otherwise it is a disinterested sentiment. No seaman ever cherished a ship, even if she belonged to him, merely because of the profit she put in his pocket. No one, I think, ever did; for a ship-owner, even of the best, has always been outside the pale of that sentiment embracing in a feeling of intimate, equal fellowship the ship and the man, backing each other against the implacable, if sometimes dissembled, hostility of their world of waters. The sea—this truth must be confessed—has no generosity. No display of manly qualities—courage, hardihood, endurance, faithfulness—has ever been known to touch its irresponsible consciousness of power. The ocean has the conscienceless temper of a savage autocrat spoiled by much adulation. He cannot brook the slightest appearance of defiance, and has remained the irreconcilable enemy of ships and men ever since ships and men had the unheard-of audacity to go afloat together in the face of his frown. From that day he has gone on swallowing up fleets and men without his resentment being glutted by the number of victims— by so many wrecked ships and wrecked lives. To-day, as ever, he is ready to beguile and betray, to smash and to drown the incorrigible optimism of men who, backed by the fidelity of ships, are trying to wrest from him the fortune of their house, the dominion of their world, or only a dole of food for their hunger. If not always in the hot mood to smash, he is always stealthily ready for a drowning. The most amazing wonder of the deep*is its unfathomable cruelty.

I felt its dread for the first time in mid-Atlantic one day, many years ago, when we took off the crew of a Danish brig*homeward bound from the West Indies. A thin, silvery mist softened the calm and majestic splendour of light without shadows—seemed to render the sky less remote and the ocean less immense. It was one of the days, when the might of the sea appears indeed lovable, like the nature of a strong man in moments of quiet intimacy. At sunrise we had made out a black speck to the westward, apparently suspended high up in the void behind a stirring, shimmering veil of silvery blue gauze that seemed at times to stir and float in the breeze which fanned us slowly along. The peace of that enchanting forenoon was so profound, so untroubled, that it seemed that every word pronounced loudly on our deck would penetrate to the very heart of that infinite mystery born from the conjunction of water and sky. We did not raise our voices. "A water-logged derelict, I think, sir," said the second officer, quietly, coming down from aloft with the binoculars in their case slung across his shoulders; and our captain, without a word, signed to the helmsman to steer for the black speck. Presently we made out a low, jagged stump sticking up forward—all that remained of her departed masts.

The captain was expatiating in a low conversational tone to the chief mate upon the danger of these derelicts, and upon his dread of coming upon them at night, when suddenly a man forward screamed out, "There's people on board of her, sir! I see them!" in a most extraordinary voice—a voice never heard before in our ship; the amazing voice of a stranger. It gave the signal for a sudden tumult of shouts. The watch below ran up the forecastle head in a body, the cook dashed out of the galley. Everybody saw the poor fellows now. They were there! And all at once our ship, which had the well-earned name of being without a rival for speed in light winds, seemed to us to have lost the power of motion, as if the sea, becoming viscous, had clung to her sides. And yet she moved. Immensity, the inseparable companion of a ship's life, chose that day to breathe upon her as gently as a sleeping child. The clamour of our excitement had died out, and our living ship, famous for never losing steerage way as long as there was air enough to float a feather, stole, without a ripple, silent and white as a ghost, towards her mutilated and wounded sister, come upon at the point of death in the sunlit haze of a calm day at sea.

With the binoculars glued to his eyes, the captain said in a quavering tone: "They are waving to us with something aft there." He put down the glasses on the skylight brusquely, and began to walk about the poop. "A shirt or a flag," he ejaculated, irritably. "Can't make it out. . . . Some damn rag or other!" He took a few more turns on the poop, glancing down over the rail now and then to see how fast we were moving. His nervous footsteps rang sharply in the quiet of the ship, where the other men, all looking the same way, had forgotten themselves in a staring immobility. "This will never do!" he cried out, suddenly. "Lower the boats at once! Down with them!"

Before I jumped into mine he took me aside, as being an experienced junior, for a word of warning:

"You look out as you come alongside that she doesn't take you down with her. You understand?"

He murmured this confidentially, so that none of the men at the falls*should overhear, and I was shocked. "Heavens! as if in such an emergency one stopped to think of danger!" I exclaimed to myself mentally, in scorn of such cold-blooded caution.

It takes many lessons to make a real seaman, and I got my rebuke at once. My experienced commander seemed in one searching glance to read my thoughts on my ingenuous face.

"What you're going for is to save life, not to drown your boat's crew for nothing," he growled, severely, in my ear. But as we shoved off he leaned over and cried out: "It all rests on the power of your arms, men. Give way for life!"

We made a race of it, and I would never have believed that a common boat's crew of a merchantman could keep up so much determined fierceness in the regular swing of their stroke. What our captain had clearly perceived before we left had become plain to all of us since. The issue of our enterprise hung on a hair above that abyss of waters which will not give up its dead till the Day of Judgment. It was a race of two ship's boats matched against Death for a prize of nine men's lives, and Death had a long start. We saw the crew of the brig from afar working at the pumps—still pumping on that wreck, which already had settled so far down that the gentle, low swell, over which our boats rose and fell easily without a check to their speed, welling up almost level with her head-rails,* plucked at the ends of broken gear swinging desolately under her naked bowsprit.

We could not, in all conscience, have picked out a better day for our regatta had we had the free choice of all the days that ever dawned upon the lonely struggles and solitary agonies of ships since the Norse rovers first steered to the westward against the run of Atlantic waves. It was a very good race. At the finish there was not an oar's length between the first and second boat, with Death coming in a good third on the top of the very next smooth swell, for all one knew to the contrary. The scuppers* of the brig gurgled softly all together when the water rising against her sides subsided sleepily with a low wash, as if playing about an immovable rock. Her bulwarks were gone fore and aft, and one saw her bare deck low-lying like a raft and swept clean of boats, spars, houses—of everything except the ringbolts and the heads of the pumps. I had one dismal glimpse of it as I braced myself up to receive upon my breast the last man to leave her, the captain, who literally let himself fall into my arms.

It had been a weirdly silent rescue—a rescue without a hail, without a single uttered word, without a gesture or a sign, without a conscious exchange of glances. Up to the very last moment those on board stuck to their pumps, which spouted two clear streams of water upon their bare feet. Their brown skin showed through the rents of their shirts; and the two small bunches of half-naked, tattered men went on bowing from the waist to each other in their back-breaking labour, up and down, absorbed, with no time for a glance over the shoulder at the help that was coming to them. As we dashed, unregarded, alongside a voice let out one, only one hoarse howl of command, and then, just as they stood, without caps, with the salt drying grey in the wrinkles and folds of their hairy, haggard faces, blinking stupidly at us their red eyelids, they made a bolt away from the handles, tottering and jostling against each other, and positively flung themselves over upon our very heads. The clatter they made tumbling into the boats had an extraordinarily destructive effect upon the illusion of tragic dignity our self-esteem had thrown over the contests of mankind with the sea. On that exquisite day of gentle breathing peace and veiled sunshine perished my romantic love to what men's imagination had proclaimed the most august aspect of Nature. The cynical indifference of the sea to the merits of human suffering and courage, laid bare in this ridiculous, panic-tainted performance extorted from the dire extremity of nine good and honourable seamen, revolted me. I saw the duplicity of the sea's most tender mood. It was so because it could not help itself, but the awed respect of the early days was gone. I felt ready to smile bitterly at its enchanting charm and glare viciously at its furies. In a moment, before we shoved off, I had looked coolly at the life of my choice. Its illusions were gone, but its fascination remained. I had become a seaman at last.

We pulled hard for a quarter of an hour, then laid on our oars waiting for our ship. She was coming down on us with swelling sails, looking delicately tall and exquisitely noble through the mist. The captain of the brig, who sat in the stern sheets by my side with his face in his hands, raised his head and began to speak with a sort of sombre volubility. They had lost their masts and sprung a leak in a hurricane; drifted for weeks, always at the pumps, met more bad weather; the ships they sighted failed to make them out, the leak gained upon them slowly, and the seas had left them nothing to make a raft of. It was very hard to see ship after ship pass by at a distance, "as if everybody had agreed that we must be left to drown," he added. But they went on trying to keep the brig afloat as long as possible, and working the pumps constantly on insufficient food, mostly raw, till "yesterday evening," he continued, monotonously, "just as the sun went down, the men's hearts broke."

He made an almost imperceptible pause here, and went on again with exactly the same intonation:

"They told me the brig could not be saved, and they thought they had done enough for themselves. I said nothing to that. It was true. It was no mutiny. I had nothing to say to them. They lay about aft all night, as still as so many dead men. I did not lie down.

I kept a look-out. When the first light came I saw your ship at once. I waited for more light; the breeze began to fail on my face. Then I shouted out as loud as I was able, 'Look at that ship!' but only two men got up very slowly and came to me. At first only we three stood alone, for a long time, watching you coming down to us, and feeling the breeze drop to a calm almost; but afterwards others, too, rose, one after another, and by and by I had all my crew behind me. I turned round and said to them that they could see the ship was coming our way, but in this small breeze she might come too late after all, unless we turned to and tried to keep the brig afloat long enough to give you time to save us all. I spoke like that to them, and then I gave the command to man the pumps."

He gave the command, and gave the example, too, by going himself to the handles, but it seems that these men did actually hang back for a moment, looking at each other dubiously before they followed him. "He! he! he!" He broke out into a most unexpected, imbecile, pathetic, nervous little giggle. "Their hearts were broken so! They had been played with too long," he explained, apologetically, lowering his eyes, and became silent.

Twenty-five years is a long time—a quarter of a century is a dim and distant past; but to this day I remember the dark-brown feet, hands, and faces of two of these men whose hearts had been broken by the sea. They were lying very still on their sides on the bottom boards between the thwarts, curled up like dogs. My boat's crew, leaning over the looms of their oars, stared and listened as if at the play. The master of the brig looked up suddenly to ask me what day it was.

They had lost the date. When I told him it was Sunday, the 22nd, he frowned, making some mental calculation, then nodded twice sadly to himself, staring at nothing.

His aspect was miserably unkempt and wildly sorrowful. Had it not been for the unquenchable candour of his blue eyes, whose unhappy, tired glance every moment sought his abandoned, sinking brig, as if it could find rest nowhere else, he would have appeared mad. But he was too simple to go mad, too simple with that manly simplicity which alone can bear men unscathed in mind and body through an encounter with the deadly playfulness of the sea or with its less abominable fury.

Neither angry, nor playful, nor smiling, it enveloped our distant ship growing bigger as she neared us, our boats with the rescued men and the dismantled hull of the brig we were leaving behind, in the large and placid embrace of its quietness, half lost in the fair haze, as if in a dream of infinite and tender clemency. There was no frown, no wrinkle on its face, not a ripple. And the run of the slight swell was so smooth that it resembled the graceful undulation of a piece of shimmering grey silk shot with gleams of green. We pulled an easy stroke; but when the master of the brig, after a glance over his shoulder, stood up with a low exclamation, my men feathered their oars instinctively, without an order, and the boat lost her way.

He was steadying himself on my shoulder with a strong grip, while his other arm, flung up rigidly, pointed a denunciatory finger at the immense tranquillity of the ocean. After his first exclamation, which stopped the swing of our oars, he made no sound, but his whole attitude seemed to cry out an indignant "Behold!" . . . I could not imagine what vision of evil had come to him. I was startled, and the amazing energy of his immobilized gesture made my heart beat faster with the anticipation of something monstrous and unsuspected. The stillness around us became crushing.

For a moment the succession of silky undulations ran on innocently. I saw each of them swell up the misty line of the horizon, far, far away beyond the derelict brig, and the next moment, with a slight friendly toss of our boat, it had passed under us and was gone. The lulling cadence of the rise and fall, the invariable gentleness of this irresistible force, the great charm of the deep waters, warmed my breast deliciously, like the subtle poison of a love-potion. But all this lasted only a few soothing seconds before I jumped up, too, making the boat roll like the veriest land-lubber.

Something startling, mysterious, hastily confused was taking place. I watched it with incredulous and fascinated awe, as one watches the confused, swift movements of some deed of violence done in the dark. As if at a given signal, the run of the smooth undulations seemed checked suddenly around the brig. By a strange optical delusion the whole sea appeared to rise upon her in one overwhelming heave of its silky surface where in one spot a smother of foam broke out ferociously. And then the effort subsided. It was all over, and the smooth swell ran on as before from the horizon in uninterrupted cadence of motion, passing under us with a slight friendly toss of our boat. Far away, where the brig had been, an angry white stain undulating on the surface of steely-grey waters, shot with gleams of green, diminished swiftly without a hiss, like a patch of pure snow melting in the sun. And the great stillness after this initiation into the sea's implacable hate seemed full of dread thoughts and shadows of disaster.

"Gone!" ejaculated from the depths of his chest my

bowman* in a final tone. He spat in his hands, and took a better grip on his oar. The captain of the brig lowered his rigid arm slowly, and looked at our faces in a solemnly conscious silence, which called upon us to share in his simple-minded, marvelling awe. All at once he sat down by my side, and leaned forward earnestly at my boat's crew, who, swinging together in a long, easy stroke, kept their eyes fixed upon him faithfully.

"No ship could have done so well," he addressed them, firmly, after a moment of strained silence, during which he seemed with trembling lips to seek for words fit to bear such high testimony. "She was small, but she was good. I had no anxiety. She was strong. Last voyage I had my wife and two children in her. No other ship could have stood so long the weather she had to live through for days and days before we got dismasted a fortnight ago. She was fairly worn out, and that's all. You may believe me. She lasted under us for days and days, but she could not last for ever. It was long enough. I am glad it is over. No better ship was ever left to sink at sea on such a day as this."

He was competent to pronounce the funereal oration of a ship, this son of ancient sea-folk, whose national existence, so little stained by the excesses of manly virtues, had demanded nothing but the merest foothold from the earth. By the merits of his sea-wise forefathers and by the artlessness of his heart, he was made fit to deliver this excellent discourse. There was nothing wanting in its orderly arrangement—neither piety nor faith, nor the tribute of praise due to the worthy dead, with the edifying recital of their achievement. She had lived, he had loved her; she had suffered, and he was glad she was at rest. It was an excellent discourse. And it was orthodox, too, in its fidelity to the cardinal article of a seaman's faith, of which it was a single-minded confession. "Ships are all right." They are. They who live with the sea have got to hold by that creed first and last; and it came to me, as I glanced at him sideways, that some men were not altogether unworthy in honour and conscience to pronounce the funereal eulogium of a ship's constancy in life and death.

After this, sitting by my side with his loosely clasped hands hanging between his knees, he uttered no word, made no movement till the shadow of our ship's sails fell on the boat, when, at the loud cheer greeting the return of the victors with their prize, he lifted up his troubled face with a faint smile of pathetic indulgence. This smile of the worthy descendant of the most ancient sea-folk whose audacity and hardihood had left no trace of greatness and glory upon the waters, completed the cycle of my initiation. There was an infinite depth of hereditary wisdom in its pitying sadness. It made the hearty bursts of cheering sound like a childish noise of triumph. Our crew shouted with immense confidence—honest souls! As if anybody could ever make sure of having prevailed against the sea, which has betrayed so many ships of great "name," so many proud men, so many towering ambitions of fame, power, wealth, greatness!

As I brought the boat under the falls my captain, in high good-humour, leaned over, spreading his red and freckled elbows on the rail, and called down to me sarcastically out of the depths of his cynic philosopher's beard:

"So you have brought the boat back after all, have you?"

Sarcasm was "his way," and the most that can be said for it is that it was natural. This did not make it lovable. But it is decorous and expedient to fall in with one's commander's way. "Yes. I brought the boat back all right, sir," I answered. And the good man believed me. It was not for him to discern upon me the marks of my recent initiation. And yet I was not exactly the same youngster who had taken the boat away—all impatience for a race against Death, with the prize of nine men's lives at the end.

Already I looked with other eyes upon the sea. I knew it capable of betraying the generous ardour of youth as implacably as, indifferent to evil and good, it would have betrayed the basest greed or the noblest heroism. My conception of its magnanimous greatness was gone. And I looked upon the true sea—the sea that plays with men till their hearts are broken, and wears stout ships to death. Nothing can touch the brooding bitterness of its soul. Open to all and faithful to none, it exercises its fascination for the undoing of the best. To love it is not well. It knows no bond of plighted troth, no fidelity to misfortune, to long companionship, to long devotion. The promise it holds out perpetually is very great; but the only secret of its possession is strength, strength—the jealous, sleepless strength of a man guarding a coveted treasure within his gates.

XXXVII

THE cradle of oversea traffic and of the art of naval combats, the Mediterranean, apart from all the associations of adventure and glory, the common heritage of all mankind, makes a tender appeal to a seaman. It has sheltered the infancy of his craft. He looks upon it as a man may look at a vast nursery in an old, old mansion where innumerable generations of his own people have learned to walk. I say his own people because, in a sense, all sailors belong to one family: all are descended from that adventurous and shaggy ancestor who, bestriding a shapeless log and paddling with a crooked branch, accomplished the first coasting trip in a sheltered bay ringing with the admiring howls of his tribe.   It is a matter of regret that all those brothers in craft and feeling, whose generations have learned to walk a ship's deck in that nursery, have been also more than once fiercely engaged in cutting each other's throats there. But life, apparently, has such exigencies. Without human propensity to murder and other sorts of unrighteousness there would have been no historical heroism.   It is a consoling reflection.   And then, if one examines impartially the deeds of violence, they appear of but small consequence.   From Salamis* to Actium,* through Lepanto* and the Nile* to the naval massacre of Navarino,* not to mention other armed encounters of lesser interest, all the blood heroically spilt into the Mediterranean has not stained with a single trail of purple the deep azure of its classic waters.

Of course, it may be argued that battles have shaped the destiny of mankind. The question whether they have shaped it well would remain open, however. But it would be hardly worth discussing. It is very probable that, had the Battle of Salamis never been fought, the face of the world would have been much as we behold it now, fashioned by the mediocre inspiration and the short-sighted labours of men. From a long and miserable experience of suffering, injustice, disgrace, and aggression the nations of the earth are mostly swayed by fear—fear of the sort that a little cheap oratory turns easily to rage, hate, and violence. Innocent, guileless fear has been the cause of many wars. Not, of course, the fear of war itself, which, in the evolution of sentiments and ideas, has come to be regarded at last as a half-mystic and glorious ceremony

with certain fashionable rites and preliminary in-
cantations, wherein the conception of its true nature has
been lost. To apprehend the true aspect, force, and
morality of war as a natural function of mankind one
requires a feather in the hair and a ring in the nose, or,
better still, teeth filed to a point and a tattooed breast.
Unfortunately, a return to such simple ornamentation is
impossible. We are bound to the chariot of progress.
There is no going back; and, as bad luck would have it,
our civilization, which has done so much for the comfort
and adornment of our bodies and the elevation of our
minds, has made lawful killing frightfully and needlessly
expensive.

The whole question of improved armaments had been
approached by the governments of the earth in a spirit
of nervous and unreflecting haste, whereas the right way
was lying plainly before them, and had only to be pursued with calm determination. The learned vigils and
labours of a certain class of inventors should have been
rewarded with honourable liberality as justice demanded; and the bodies of the inventors should have
been blown to pieces by means of their own perfected
explosives and improved weapons with extreme publicity as the commonest prudence dictated. By this
method the ardour of research in that direction would
have been restrained without infringing the sacred
privileges of science. For the lack of a little cool thinking in our guides and masters this course has not been
followed, and a beautiful simplicity has been sacrificed
for no real advantage. A frugal mind cannot defend
itself from considerable bitterness when reflecting that
at the Battle of Actium (which was fought for no less
a stake than the dominion of the world) the fleet of
Octavianus Cæsar and the fleet of Antonius, including
the Egyptian division and Cleopatra's galley with

purple sails, probably cost less than two modern battleships, or, as the modern naval book-jargon has it, two capital units. But no amount of lubberly book-jargon can disguise a fact well calculated to afflict the soul of every sound economist. It is not likely that the Mediterranean will ever behold a battle with a greater issue; but when the time comes for another historical fight its bottom will be enriched as never before by a quantity of jagged scrap-iron, paid for at pretty nearly its weight of gold by the deluded populations inhabiting the isles and continents of this planet.

XXXVIII

Happy he who, like Ulysses, has made an adventurous voyage;* and there is no such sea for adventurous voyages as the Mediterranean—the inland sea which the ancients looked upon as so vast and so full of wonders. And, indeed, it was terrible and wonderful; for it is we alone who, swayed by the audacity of our minds and the tremors of our hearts, are the sole artisans of all the wonder and romance of the world.

It was for the Mediterranean sailors that fair-haired sirens sang among the black rocks seething in white foam and mysterious voices spoke in the darkness above the moving wave—voices menacing, seductive, or prophetic, like that voice heard at the beginning of the Christian era by the master of an African vessel in the Gulf of Syrta, whose calm nights are full of strange murmurs and flitting shadows. It called him by name, bidding him go and tell all men that the great god Pan was dead.* But the great legend of the Mediterranean, the legend of traditional song and grave history lives, fascinating and immortal, in our minds.

The dark and fearful sea of the subtle Ulysses'

wanderings, agitated by the wrath cf Olympian gods, harbouring on its isles the fury of strange monsters and the wiles of strange women; the highway of heroes and sages, of warriors, pirates, and saints; the workaday sea of Carthaginian merchants and the pleasure lake of the Roman Cæsars, claims the veneration of every seaman as the historical home of that spirit of open defiance against the great waters of the earth which is the very soul of his calling. Issuing thence to the west and south as a youth leaves the shelter of his parental house, this spirit found the way to the Indies, discovered the coasts of a new continent, and traversed at last the immensity of the great Pacific, rich in groups of islands remote and mysterious like the constellations of the sky.

The first impulse of navigation took its visible form in that tideless basin freed from hidden shoals and treacherous currents, as if in tender regard for the infancy of the art. The steep shores of the Mediterranean favoured the beginners in one of humanity's most daring enterprises, and the enchanting inland sea of classic adventure has led mankind gently from headland to headland, from bay to bay, from island to island, out into the promise of world-wide oceans beyond the Pillars of Hercules.

XXXIX

The charm of the Mediterranean dwells in the unforgettable flavour of my early days, and to this hour this sea, upon which the Romans alone ruled without dispute, has kept for me the fascination of youthful romance. The very first Christmas night I ever spent away from land was employed in running before a Gulf of Lions gale, which made the old ship groan in every timber as she skipped before it over the short seas until we brought her to, battered and out of breath, under the lee of Majorca,* where the smooth water was torn by fierce cat's-paws under a very stormy sky.

We—or, rather, they, for I had hardly had two glimpses of salt water in my life till then—kept her standing off and on all that day, while I listened for the first time with the curiosity of my tender years to the song of the wind in a ship's rigging. The monotonous and vibrating note was destined to grow into the intimacy of the heart, pass into blood and bone, accompany the thoughts and acts of two full decades, remain to haunt like a reproach the peace of the quiet fireside, and enter into the very texture of respectable dreams dreamed safely under a roof of rafters and tiles. The wind was fair, but that day we ran no more.

The thing (I will not call her a ship twice in the same half-hour) leaked. She leaked fully, generously, overflowingly, all over—like a basket. I took an enthusiastic part in the excitement caused by that last infirmity of noble ships, without concerning myself much with the why or the wherefore. The surmise of my maturer years is that, bored by her interminable life, the venerable antiquity was simply yawning with ennui at every seam. But at the time I did not know; I knew generally very little, and least of all what I was doing in that *galère*.*

I remember that, exactly as in the comedy of Molière, my uncle*asked the precise question in the very words— not of my confidential valet, however, but across great distances of land, in a letter whose mocking but indulgent turn ill concealed his almost paternal anxiety. I fancy I tried to convey to him my (utterly unfounded) impression that the West Indies awaited my coming. I had to go there. It was a sort of mystic conviction— something in the nature of a call. But it was difficult to state intelligibly the grounds of this belief to that man of rigorous logic, if of infinite charity.

The truth must have been that, all unversed in the arts of the wily Greek, the deceiver of gods, the lover of strange women, the evoker of bloodthirsty shades, I yet longed for the beginning of my own obscure Odyssey, which, as was proper for a modern, should unroll its wonders and terrors beyond the Pillars of Hercules.* The disdainful ocean did not open wide to swallow up my audacity, though the ship, the ridiculous and ancient *galère* of my folly, the old, weary, disenchanted sugar-wagon, seemed extremely disposed to open out and swallow up as much salt water as she could hold. This, if less grandiose, would have been as final a catastrophe.

But no catastrophe occurred. I lived to watch on a strange shore* a black and youthful Nausicaa,* with a joyous train of attendant maidens, carrying baskets of linen to a clear stream overhung by the heads of slender palm-trees. The vivid colours of their draped raiment and the gold of their earrings invested with a barbaric and regal magnificence their figures, stepping out freely in a shower of broken sunshine. The whiteness of their teeth was still more dazzling than the splendour of jewels at their ears. The shaded side of the ravine gleamed with their smiles. They were as unabashed as so many princesses, but, alas! not one of them was the daughter of a jet-black sovereign. Such was my abominable luck in being born by the mere hair's breadth of twenty-five centuries too late into a world where kings have been growing scarce with scandalous rapidity, while the few who remain have adopted the uninteresting manners and customs of simple million-aires. Obviously it was a vain hope in 187—*to see the ladies of a royal household walk in chequered sunshine,

with baskets of linen on their heads, to the banks of a
clear stream overhung by the starry fronds of palm-
trees. It was a vain hope. If I did not ask myself
whether, limited by such discouraging impossibilities,
life were still worth living, it was only because I had
then before me several other pressing questions, some
of which have remained unanswered to this day. The
resonant, laughing voices of these gorgeous maidens
scared away the multitude of humming-birds, whose
delicate wings wreathed with the mist of their vibration
the tops of flowering bushes.

No, they were not princesses. Their unrestrained
laughter filling the hot, fern-clad ravine had a soulless
limpidity, as of wild, inhuman dwellers in tropical
woodlands. Following the example of certain prudent
travellers, I withdrew unseen—and returned, not much
wiser, to the Mediterranean, the sea of classic adventures.

XL

IT WAS written that there, in the nursery of our
navigating ancestors, I should learn to walk in the
ways of my craft and grow in the love of the sea, blind
as young love often is, but absorbing and unselfish as all
true love must be. I demanded nothing from it—not
even adventure. In this I showed, perhaps, more
intuitive wisdom than high self-denial. No adventure
ever came to one for the asking. He who starts on a
deliberate quest of adventure goes forth but to gather
Dead-Sea fruit,* unless, indeed, he be beloved of the gods
and great amongst heroes, like that most excellent
cavalier Don Quixote de la Mancha.* By us ordinary
mortals of a mediocre animus that is only too anxious to
pass by wicked giants for so many honest windmills,

adventures are entertained like visiting angels. They come upon our complacency unawares. As unbidden guests are apt to do, they often come at inconvenient times. And we are glad to let them go unrecognized, without any acknowledgment of so high a favour. After many years, on looking back from the middle turn of life's way* at the events of the past, which, like a friendly crowd, seem to gaze sadly after us hastening towards the Cimmerian shore,* we may see here and there, in the grey throng, some figure glowing with a faint radiance, as though it had caught all the light of our already crepuscular sky. And by this glow we may recognize the faces of our true adventures, of the once unbidden guests entertained unawares in our young days.

If the Mediterranean, the venerable (and sometimes atrociously ill-tempered) nurse of all navigators, was to rock my youth, the providing of the cradle necessary for that operation was entrusted by Fate to the most casual assemblage of irresponsible young men (all, however, older than myself) who, as if drunk with Provençal sunshine, frittered life away in joyous levity on the model of Balzac's *Histoire des Treize** qualified by a dash of romance *de cape et d'épée.**

She* who was my cradle in those years had been built on the River of Savona by a famous builder of boats, was rigged in Corsica by another good man, and was described on her papers as a "tartane" of sixty tons. In reality, she was a true balancelle, with two short masts raking forward and two curved yards, each as long as her hull; a true child of the Latin Lake,* with a spread of two enormous sails resembling the pointed wings on a sea-bird's slender body, and herself, like a bird indeed, skimming rather than sailing the seas.

Her name was the *Tremolino*. How is this to be

translated? The *Quiverer?* What a name to give the pluckiest little craft that ever dipped her sides in angry foam! I had felt her, it is true, trembling for nights and days together under my feet, but it was with the high-strung tenseness of her faithful courage. In her short, but brilliant, career she has taught me nothing, but she has given me everything. I owe to her the awakened love for the sea that, with the quivering of her swift little body and the humming of the wind under the foot of her lateen sails, stole into my heart with a sort of gentle violence, and brought my imagination under its despotic sway. The *Tremolino!* To this day I cannot utter or even write that name without a strange tightening of the breast and the gasp of mingled delight and dread of one's first passionate experience.

XLI

We four formed (to use a term well understood nowadays in every social sphere) a "syndicate" owning the *Tremolino:* an international and astonishing syndicate. And we were all ardent Royalists of the snow-white Legitimist complexion—Heaven only knows why! In all associations of men there is generally one who, by the authority of age and of a more experienced wisdom, imparts a collective character to the whole set. If I mention that the oldest of us was very old, extremely old—nearly thirty years old—and that he used to declare with gallant carelessness, "I live by my sword," I think I have given enough information on the score of our collective wisdom. He was a North Carolinian gentleman, J. M. K. B.*were the initials of his name, and he really did live by the sword, as far as I know. He died by it, too, later on, in a Balkanian squabble, in the cause of some Serbs or else Bulgarians,

who were neither Catholics nor gentlemen—at least, not
in the exalted but narrow sense he attached to that
last word.

Poor J. M. K. B., *Américain, Catholique, et gentilhomme,** as he was disposed to describe himself in moments of lofty expansion! Are there still to be found in
Europe gentlemen keen of face and elegantly slight
of body, of distinguished aspect, with a fascinating
drawing-room manner and with a dark, fatal glance,
who live by their swords, I wonder? His family had
been ruined in the Civil War, I fancy, and seems for a
decade or so to have led a wandering life in the Old
World. As to Henry C——, the next in age and wisdom of our band, he had broken loose from the un-
yielding rigidity of his family, solidly rooted, if I remember rightly, in a well-to-do London suburb. On
their respectable authority he introduced himself
meekly to strangers as a "black sheep." I have never
seen a more guileless specimen of an outcast. Never.

However, his people had the grace to send him a
little money now and then. Enamoured of the South,
of Provence, of its people, its life, its sunshine, and its
poetry, narrow-chested, tall and short-sighted, he
strode along the streets and the lanes, his long feet
projecting far in advance of his body, and his white
nose and gingery moustache buried in an open book:
for he had the habit of reading as he walked. How he
avoided falling into precipices, off the quays, or down
staircases is a great mystery. The sides of his overcoat
bulged out with pocket editions of various poets.
When not engaged in reading Virgil, Homer, or Mistral,*
in parks, restaurants, streets, and such-like public
places, he indited sonnets (in French) to the eyes, ears,
chin, hair, and other visible perfections of a nymph
called Thérèse, the daughter, honesty compels me to

state, of a certain Madame Leonore who kept a small café for sailors in one of the narrowest streets of the old town.

No more charming face, clear-cut like an antique gem, and delicate in colouring like the petal of a flower, had ever been set on, alas! a somewhat squat body. He read his verses aloud to her in the very café with the innocence of a little child and the vanity of a poet. We followed him there willingly enough, if only to watch the divine Thérèse laugh, under the vigilant black eyes of Madame Leonore, her mother. She laughed very prettily, not so much at the sonnets, which she could not but esteem, as at poor Henry's French accent, which was unique, resembling the warbling of birds, if birds ever warbled with a stuttering, nasal intonation.

Our third partner was Roger P. de la S——, the most Scandinavian-looking of Provençal squires, fair, and six feet high, as became a descendant of sea-roving Northmen, authoritative, incisive, wittily scornful, with a comedy in three acts in his pocket, and in his breast a heart blighted by a hopeless passion for his beautiful cousin, married to a wealthy hide and tallow merchant. He used to take us to lunch at their house without ceremony. I admired the good lady's sweet patience. The husband was a conciliatory soul, with a great fund of resignation, which he expended on "Roger's friends." I suspect he was secretly horrified at these invasions. But it was a Carlist* salon, and as such we were made welcome. The possibility of raising Catalonia in the interest of the *Rey netto*,* who had just then crossed the Pyrenees, was much discussed there.

Don Carlos, no doubt, must have had many queer friends (it is the common lot of all Pretenders), but amongst them none more extravagantly fantastic than the *Tremolino* Syndicate, which used to meet in a tavern on the quays of the old port. The antique city of Massilia* had surely never, since the days of the earliest Phœnicians, known an odder set of shipowners. We met to discuss and settle the plan of operations for each voyage of the *Tremolino*. In these operations a banking-house, too, was concerned—a very respectable banking-house. But I am afraid I shall end by saying too much. Ladies, too, were concerned (I am really afraid I am saying too much)—all sorts of ladies, some old enough to know better than to put their trust in princes, others young and full of illusions.

One of these last was extremely amusing in the imitations, she gave us in confidence, of various highly placed personages she was perpetually rushing off to Paris to interview in the interests of the cause—*Por el Rey !** For she* was a Carlist, and of Basque blood at that, with something of a lioness in the expression of her courageous face (especially when she let her hair down), and with the volatile little soul of a sparrow dressed in fine Parisian feathers, which had the trick of coming off disconcertingly at unexpected moments.

But her imitations of a Parisian personage, very highly placed indeed, as she represented him standing in the corner of a room with his face to the wall, rubbing the back of his head and moaning helplessly, ''Rita, you are the death of me!'' were enough to make one (if young and free from cares) split one's sides laughing. She had an uncle still living, a very effective Carlist, too, the priest of a little mountain parish in Guipuzcoa.* As the sea-going member of the syndicate (whose plans depended greatly on Doña Rita's information), I used to be charged with humbly affectionate messages for the old man. These messages I was supposed to deliver to the Arragonese muleteers (who were sure to await at certain times the *Tremolino* in the neighbour-

hood of the Gulf of Rosas),*for faithful transportation
inland, together with the various unlawful goods
landed secretly from under the *Tremolino's* hatches.

Well, now, I have really let out too much (as I feared
I should in the end) as to the usual contents of my sea-
cradle. But let it stand. And if anybody remarks
cynically that I must have been a promising infant in
those days, let that stand, too. I am concerned but for
the good name of the *Tremolino*, and I affirm that a ship
is ever guiltless of the sins, transgressions, and follies of
her men.

XLII

It was not *Tremolino's* fault that the syndicate depended so much on the wit and wisdom and the information of Doña Rita. She had taken a little
furnished house on the Prado for the good of the
cause—*Por el Rey!* She was always taking little
houses for somebody's good, for the sick or the sorry, for
broken-down artists, cleaned-out gamblers, temporarily
unlucky speculators—*vieux amis*—old friends, as she
used to explain apologetically, with a shrug of her fine
shoulders.

Whether Don Carlos was one of the "old friends,"
too, it's hard to say. More unlikely things have been
heard of in smoking-rooms. All I know is that one
evening, entering incautiously the salon of the little
house just after the news of a considerable Carlist success had reached the faithful, I was seized round the
neck and waist and whirled recklessly three times round
the room, to the crash of upsetting furniture and the
humming of a valse tune in a warm contralto voice.

When released from the dizzy embrace, I sat down on
the carpet—suddenly, without affectation. In this un-
pretentious attitude I became aware that J. M. K. B.

had followed me into the room, elegant, fatal, correct, and severe in a white tie and large shirt-front. In answer to his politely sinister, prolonged glance of inquiry, I overheard Doña Rita mumuring, with some confusion and annoyance, "*Vous êtes bête, mon cher Voyons! Ça n'a aucune conséquence.*"* Well content in this case to be of no particular consequence, I had already about me the elements of some worldly sense.

Rearranging my collar, which, truth to say, ought to have been a round one above a short jacket, but was not, I observed felicitously that I had come to say good-bye, being ready to go off to sea that very night with the *Tremolino*. Our hostess, slightly panting yet, and just a shade dishevelled, turned tartly upon J. M. K. B., desiring to know when *he* would be ready to go off by the *Tremolino*, or in any other way, in order to join the royal headquarters. Did he intend, she asked ironically, to wait for the very eve of the entry into Madrid? Thus by a judicious exercise of tact and asperity we re-established the atmospheric equilibrium of the room long before I left them a little before midnight, now tenderly reconciled, to walk down to the harbour and hail the *Tremolino* by the usual soft whistle from the edge of the quay. It was our signal, invariably heard by the ever-watchful Dominic,* the *padrone.*

He would raise a lantern silently to light my steps along the narrow, spring plank of our primitive gangway. "And so we are going off," he would murmur directly my foot touched the deck. I was the harbinger of sudden departures, but there was nothing in the world sudden enough to take Dominic unawares. His thick black moustaches, curled every morning with hot tongs by the barber at the corner of the quay, seemed to hide a perpetual smile. But nobody, I believe, had ever seen the true shape of his lips. From the slow, imperturbable gravity of that broad-chested man you would think he had never smiled in his life. In his eyes lurked a look of perfectly remorseless irony, as though he had been provided with an extremely experienced soul; and the slightest distension of his nostrils would give to his bronzed face a look of extraordinary boldness, This was the only play of feature of which he seemed capable, being a Southerner of a concentrated, deliberate type. His ebony hair curled slightly on the temples. He may have been forty years old, and he was a great voyager on the inland sea.

Astute and ruthless, he could have rivalled in resource the unfortunate son of Laertes and Anticlea.[*] If he did not pit his craft and audacity against the very gods, it is only because the Olympian gods are dead. Certainly no woman could frighten him. A one-eyed giant[*]would not have had the ghost of a chance against Dominic Cervoni, of Corsica, not Ithaca; and no king, son of kings, but of very respectable family—authentic Caporali, he affirmed. But that is as it may be. The Caporali families date back to the twelfth century.

For want of more exalted adversaries Dominic turned his audacity fertile in impious stratagems against the powers of the earth, as represented by the institution of Custom-houses and every mortal belonging thereto—scribes, officers, and guardacostas[*] afloat and ashore. He was the very man for us, this modern and unlawful wanderer with his own legend of loves, dangers, and bloodshed. He told us bits of it sometimes in measured, ironic tones. He spoke Catalonian, the Italian of Corsica and the French of Provence with the same easy naturalness. Dressed in shore-togs, a white starched shirt, black jacket, and round hat, as I took him once to see Doña Rita, he was extremely presentable. He could make himself interesting by a tactful and rugged reserve set off by a grim, almost imperceptible, playfulness of tone and manner.

He had the physical assurance of strong-hearted men. After half an hour's interview in the dining-room, during which they got in touch with each other in an amazing way, Rita told us in her best *grande dame* manner: "*Mais il est parfait, cet homme.*"* He was perfect. On board the *Tremolino*, wrapped up in a black *caban*,* the picturesque cloak of Mediterranean seamen, with those massive moustaches and his remorseless eyes set off by the shadow of the deep hood, he looked piratical and monkish and darkly initiated into the most awful mysteries of the sea.

XLIII

Anyway, he was perfect, as Doña Rita had declared. The only thing unsatisfactory (and even inexplicable) about our Dominic was his nephew, Cesar.* It was startling to see a desolate expression of shame veil the remorseless audacity in the eyes of that man superior to all scruples and terrors.

"I would never have dared to bring him on board your balancelle," he once apologized to me. "But what am I to do? His mother is dead, and my brother has gone into the bush."

In this way I learned that our Dominic had a brother. As to "going into the bush," this only means that a man has done his duty successfully in the pursuit of a hereditary vendetta. The feud which had existed for ages between the families of Cervoni and Brunaschi was so old that it seemed to have smouldered out at last. One evening Pietro Brunaschi, after a laborious day amongst his olive-trees, sat on a chair against the wall of his house with a bowl of broth on his knees and a piece of bread in his hand. Dominic's brother, going home with a gun on his shoulder, found a sudden offence in this picture of content and rest so obviously calculated to awaken the feelings of hatred and revenge. He and Pietro had never had any personal quarrel; but, as Dominic explained, "all our dead cried out to him." He shouted from behind a wall of stones, "O Pietro! Behold what is coming!" And as the other looked up innocently he took aim at the forehead and squared the old vendetta account so neatly that, according to Dominic, the dead man continued to sit with the bowl of broth on his knees and the piece of bread in his hand.

This is why—because in Corsica your dead will not leave you alone—Dominic's brother had to go into the *maquis*, into the bush on the wild mountain-side, to dodge the gendarmes for the insignificant remainder of his life, and Dominic had charge of his nephew with a mission to make a man of him.

No more unpromising undertaking could be imagined. The very material for the task seemed wanting. The Cervonis, if not handsome men, were good sturdy flesh and blood. But this extraordinarily lean and livid youth seemed to have no more blood in him than a snail.

"Some cursed witch must have stolen my brother's child from the cradle and put that spawn of a starved devil in its place," Dominic would say to me. "Look at him! Just look at him!"

To look at Cesar was not pleasant. His parchment skin, showing dead white on his cranium through the thin wisps of dirty brown hair, seemed to be glued directly and tightly upon his big bones. Without being in any way deformed, he was the nearest approach which I have ever seen or could imagine to what is commonly understood by the word "monster." That

the source of the effect produced was really moral I
have no dcubt. An utterly, hopelessly depraved
nature was expressed in physical terms, that taken
each separately had nothing positively startling. You
imagined him clammily cold to the touch, like a snake.
The slightest reproof, the most mild and justifiable
remonstrance, would be met by a resentful glare and
an evil shrinking of his thin dry upper lip, a snarl of hate
to which he generally added the agreeable sound of
grinding teeth.

It was for this venomous performance rather than
for his lies, impudence, and laziness that his uncle used
to knock him down. It must not be imagined that it
was anything in the nature of a brutal assault. Dominic's brawny arm would be seen describing deliberately
an ample horizontal gesture, a dignified sweep, and
Cesar would go over suddenly like a ninepin—which
was funny to see. But, once down, he would writhe on
the deck, gnashing his teeth in impotent rage—which
was pretty horrible to behold. And it also happened
more than once that he would disappear completely—
which was startling to observe. This is the exact truth.
Before some of these majestic cuffs Cesar would go down
and vanish. He would vanish heels overhead into open
hatchways, into scuttles, behind up-ended casks, according to the place where he happened to come into
contact with his uncle's mighty arm.

Once—it was in the old harbour, just before the
Tremolino's last voyage—he vanished thus overboard
to my infinite consternation. Dominic and I had been
talking business together aft, and Cesar had sneaked up
behind us to listen, for, amongst his other perfections,
he was a consummate eavesdropper and spy. At the
sound of the heavy plop alongside horror held me
rooted to the spot; but Dominic stepped quietly to

the rail and leaned over waiting for his nephew's miserable head to bob up for the first time.

"Ohé, Cesar!" he yelled, contemptuously, to the spluttering wretch. "Catch hold of that mooring hawser*—*charogne !*"*

He approached me to resume the interrupted conversation.

"What about Cesar?" I asked, anxiously.

"*Canallia !** Let him hang there," was his answer. And he went on talking over the business in hand calmly, while I tried vainly to dismiss from my mind the picture of Cesar steeped to the chin in the water of the old harbour, a decoction of centuries of marine refuse. I tried to dismiss it, because the mere notion of that liquid made me feel very sick. Presently Dominic, hailing an idle boatman, directed him to go and fish his nephew out; and by and by Cesar appeared walking on board from the quay, shivering, streaming with filthy water, with bits of rotten straws in his hair and a piece of dirty orange-peel stranded on his shoulder. His teeth chattered; his yellow eyes squinted balefully at us as he passed forward. I thought it my duty to remonstrate.

"Why are you always knocking him about, Dominic?" I asked. Indeed, I felt convinced it was no earthly good—a sheer waste of muscular force.

"I must try to make a man of him," Dominic answered, hopelessly.

I restrained the obvious retort that in this way he ran the risk of making, in the words of the immortal Mr. Mantalini,* "a demnition damp, unpleasant corpse of him."

"He wants to be a locksmith!" burst out Cervoni. "To learn how to pick locks, I suppose," he added with sardonic bitterness.

"Why not let him be a locksmith?" I ventured.

"Who would teach him?" he cried. "Where could I leave him?" he asked, with a drop in his voice; and I had my first glimpse of genuine despair. "He steals, you know, alas! *Par la Madonne !*[*] I believe he would put poison in your food and mine—the viper!"

He raised his face and both his clenched fists slowly to heaven. However, Cesar never dropped poison into our cups. One cannot be sure, but I fancy he went to work in another way.

This voyage,[*] of which the details need not be given, we had to range far afield for sufficient reasons. Coming up from the South to end it with the important and really dangerous part of the scheme in hand, we found it necessary to look into Barcelona for certain definite information. This appears like running one's head into the very jaws of the lion, but in reality it was not so. We had one or two high, influential friends there, and many others humble but valuable because bought for good hard cash. We were in no danger of being molested; indeed, the important information reached us promptly by the hands of a Custom-house officer, who came on board full of showy zeal to poke an iron rod into the layer of oranges which made the visible part of our cargo in the hatchway.

I forgot to mention before that the *Tremolino* was officially known as a fruit and cork-wood trader. The zealous officer managed to slip a useful piece of paper into Dominic's hand as he went ashore, and a few hours afterwards, being off duty, he returned on board again athirst for drinks and gratitude. He got both as a matter of course. While he sat sipping his liqueur in the tiny cabin Dominic plied him with questions as to the whereabouts of the guardacostas. The Preventive Service afloat was really the one for us to reckon with,

and it was material for our success and safety to know
the exact position of the patrol craft in the neighbourhood. The news could not have been more favourable.
The officer mentioned a small place on the coast some
twelve miles off, where, unsuspicious and unready, she
was lying at anchor, with her sails unbent, painting
yards and scraping spars. Then he left us after the
usual compliments, smirking reassuringly over his
shoulder.

I had kept below pretty close all day from excess of
prudence. The stake played on that trip was big.

"We are ready to go at once, but for Cesar, who has
been missing ever since breakfast," announced Dominic to me in his slow, grim way.

Where the fellow had gone, and why, we could not
imagine. The usual surmises in the case of a missing
seaman did not apply to Cesar's absence. He was too
odious for love, friendship, gambling, or even casual
intercourse. But once or twice he had wandered away
like this before.

Dominic went ashore to look for him, but returned at
the end of two hours alone and very angry, as I could
see by the token of the invisible smile under his moustache being intensified. We wondered what had become of the wretch, and made a hurried investigation
amongst our portable property. He had stolen nothing.

"He will be back before long," I said, confidently.

Ten minutes afterwards one of the men on deck
called out loudly:

"I can see him coming."

Cesar had only his shirt and trousers on. He had
sold his coat, apparently for pocket-money.

"You knave!" was all Dominic said, with a terrible
softness of voice. He restrained his choler for a time.

"Where have you been, vagabond?" he asked, menacingly.

Nothing would induce Cesar to answer that question. It was as if he even disdained to lie. He faced us, drawing back his lips and gnashing his teeth, and did not shrink an inch before the sweep of Dominic's arm. He went down as if shot, of course. But this time I noticed that, when picking himself up, he remained longer than usual on all fours, baring his big teeth over his shoulder and glaring upwards at his uncle with a new sort of hate in his round, yellow eyes. That permanent sentiment seemed pointed at that moment by especial malice and curiosity. I became quite interested. If he ever manages to put poison in the dishes, I thought to myself, this is how he will look at us as we sit at our meal. But I did not, of course, believe for a moment that he would ever put poison in our food. He ate the same things himself. Moreover, he had no poison. And I could not imagine a human being so blinded by cupidity as to sell poison to such an atrocious creature.

XLIV

We slipped out to sea quietly at dusk, and all through the night everything went well. The breeze was gusty; a southerly blow was making up. It was fair wind for our course. Now and then Dominic slowly and rhythmically struck his hands together a few times, as if applauding the performance of the *Tremolino*. The balancelle hummed and quivered as she flew along, dancing lightly under our feet.

At daybreak I pointed out to Dominic, amongst the several sail in view running before the gathering storm, one particular vessel. The press of canvas she carried made her loom up high, end on, like a grey column standing motionless directly in our wake.

"Look at this fellow, Dominic," I said. "He seems to be in a hurry."

The Padrone made no remark but wrapping his black cloak about him stood up to look. His weather-tanned face, framed in the hood, had an aspect of authority and challenging force, with the deep-set eyes gazing far away fixedly, without a wink, like the intent, merciless, steady eyes of a sea-bird.

"*Chi va piano va sano*,"*he remarked at last, with a derisive glance over the side, in ironic allusion to our own tremendous speed.

The *Tremolino* was doing her best, and seemed to hardly touch the great bursts of foam over which she darted. I crouched down again to get some shelter from the low bulwark. After more than half an hour of swaying immobility expressing a concentrated, breathless watchfulness, Dominic sank on the deck by my side. Within the monkish cowl his eyes gleamed with a fierce expression which surprised me. All he said was:

"He has come out here to wash the new paint off his yards, I suppose."

"What?" I shouted, getting up on my knees. "Is she the guardacosta?"

The perpetual suggestion of a smile under Dominic's piratical moustaches seemed to become more accentuated—quite real, grim, actually almost visible through the wet and uncurled hair. Judging by that symptom, he must have been in a towering rage. But I could also see that he was puzzled, and that discovery affected me disagreeably. Dominic puzzled! For a long time, leaning against the bulwark, I gazed over the stern at the grey column that seemed to stand swaying slightly in our wake always at the same distance.

Meanwhile Dominic, black and cowled, sat cross-legged on the deck, with his back to the wind, recalling vaguely an Arab chief in his *bournuss**sitting on the sand. Above his motionless figure the little cord and tassel on the stiff point of the hood swung about inanely in the gale. At last I gave up facing the wind and rain, and crouched down by his side. I was satisfied that the sail was a patrol craft. Her presence was not a thing to talk about, but soon, between two clouds charged with hail-showers, a gleam of sunshine fell upon her sails, and our men discovered her character for themselves. From that moment I noticed that they seemed to take no heed of each other or of anything else. They could spare no eyes and no thought but for the slight column-shape astern of us. Its swaying had become perceptible. For a moment she remained dazzlingly white, then faded away slowly to nothing in a squall, only to reappear again, nearly black, resembling a post stuck upright against the slaty background of solid cloud. Since first noticed she had not gained on us a foot.

"She will never catch the *Tremolino*," I said, exultingly.

Dominic did not look at me. He remarked absently, but justly, that the heavy weather was in our pursuer's favour. She was three times our size. What we had to do was to keep our distance till dark, which we could manage easily, and then haul off to seaward and consider the situation. But his thoughts seemed to stumble in the darkness of some not-solved enigma, and soon he fell silent. We ran steadily, wing-and-wing.* Cape San Sebastian*nearly ahead seemed to recede from us in the squalls of rain, and come out again to meet our rush, every time more distinct between the showers.

For my part I was by no means certain that this

*gabelou**(as our men alluded to her opprobriously) was after us at all. There were nautical difficulties in such a view which made me express the sanguine opinion that she was in all innocence simply changing her station. At this Dominic condescended to turn his head.

"I tell you she is in chase," he affirmed, moodily, after one short glance astern.

I never doubted his opinion. But with all the ardour of a neophyte and the pride of an apt learner I was at that time a great nautical casuist.

"What I can't understand," I insisted, subtly, "is how on earth, with this wind, she has managed to be just where she was when we first made her out. It is clear that she could not and did not gain twelve miles on us during the night. And there are other impossibilities. . . ."

Dominic had been sitting motionless, like an inanimate black cone posed on the stern deck, near the rudder-head, with a small tassel fluttering on its sharp point, and for a time he preserved the immobility of his meditation. Then, bending over with a short laugh, he gave my ear the bitter fruit of it. He understood everything now perfectly. She was where we had seen her first, not because she had caught us up, but because we had passed her during the night while she was already waiting for us, hove-to, most likely, on our very track.

"Do you understand—already?" Dominic muttered in a fierce undertone. "Already! You know we left a good eight hours before we were expected to leave, otherwise she would have been in time to lie in wait for us on the other side of the Cape,* and"—he snapped his teeth like a wolf close to my face—"and she would have had us like—that."

I saw it all plainly enough now. They had eyes in their heads and all their wits about them in that craft. We had passed them in the dark as they jogged on easily towards their ambush with the idea that we were yet far behind. At daylight, however, sighting a balancelle ahead under a press of canvas, they had made sail in chase. But if that was so, then——

Dominic seized my arm.

"Yes, yes! She came out on an information—do you see it?—on information. . . . We have been sold—betrayed. Why? How? What for? We always paid them all so well on shore. . . . No! But it is my head that is going to burst."

He seemed to choke, tugged at the throat button of the cloak, jumped up open-mouthed as if to hurl curses and denunciation, but instantly mastered himself, and, wrapping up the cloak closer about him, sat down on the deck again as quiet as ever.

"Yes, it must be the work of some scoundrel ashore," I observed.

He pulled the edge of the hood well forward over his brow before he muttered:

"A scoundrel . . . Yes. . . . It's evident."

"Well," I said, "they can't get us, that's clear."

"No," he assented, quietly, "they cannot."

We shaved the Cape very close to avoid an adverse current. On the other side, by the effect of the land, the wind failed us so completely for a moment that the *Tremolino's* two great lofty sails hung idle to the masts in the thundering uproar of the seas breaking upon the shore we had left behind. And when the returning gust filled them again, we saw with amazement half of the new mainsail, which we thought fit to drive the boat under before giving way, absolutely fly out of the bolt-ropes. We lowered the yard at once, and saved it all, but it was no longer a sail; it was only a heap of soaked strips of canvas cumbering the deck and weighting the craft. Dominic gave the order to throw the whole lot overboard.

"I would have had the yard thrown overboard, too," he said, leading me aft again, "if it had not been for the trouble. Let no sign escape you," he continued, lowering his voice, "but I am going to tell you something terrible. Listen: I have observed that the roping stitches on that sail have been cut! You hear? Cut with a knife in many places. And yet it stood all that time. Not enough cut. That flap did it at last. What matters it? But look! there's treachery seated on this very deck. By the horns of the devil! seated here at our very backs. Do not turn, signorino."*

We were facing aft then.

"What's to be done?" I asked, appalled.

"Nothing. Silence! Be a man, signorino."

"What else?" I said.

To show I could be a man, I resolved to utter no sound as long as Dominic himself had the force to keep his lips closed. Nothing but silence becomes certain situations. Moreover, the experience of treachery seemed to spread a hopeless drowsiness over my thoughts and senses. For an hour or more we watched our pursuer surging out nearer and nearer from amongst the squalls that sometimes hid her altogether. But even when not seen, we felt her there like a knife at our throats. She gained on us frightfully. And the *Tremolino*, in a fierce breeze and in much smoother water, swung on easily under her one sail, with something appallingly careless in the joyous freedom of her motion. Another half-hour went by. I could not stand it any longer.

"They will get the poor barky," I stammered out, suddenly, almost on the verge of tears.

Dominic stirred no more than a carving. A sense of catastrophic loneliness overcame my inexperienced soul. The vision of my companions passed before me. The whole Royalist gang was in Monte Carlo now, I reckoned. And they appeared to me clear-cut and very small, with affected voices and stiff gestures, like a procession of rigid marionettes upon a toy stage. I gave a start. What was this? A mysterious, remorseless whisper came from within the motionless black hood at my side.

"*Il faut la tuer*."*

I heard it very well.

"What do you say, Dominic?" I asked, moving nothing but my lips.

And the whisper within the hood repeated mysteriously. "She must be killed."

My heart began to beat violently.

"That's it," I faltered out. "But how?"

"You love her well?"

"I do."

"Then you must find the heart for that work, too. You must steer her yourself, and I shall see to it that she dies quickly, without leaving as much as a chip behind."

"Can you?" I murmured, fascinated by the black hood turned immovably over the stern, as if in unlawful communion with that old sea of magicians, slave-dealers, exiles, and warriors, the sea of legends and terrors, where the mariners of remote antiquity used to hear the restless shade of an old wanderer weep aloud in the dark.

"I know a rock," whispered the initiated voice within the hood secretly. "But—caution! It must be

done before our men perceive what we are about.
Whom can we trust now? A knife drawn across the
fore halyards* would bring the foresail down, and put
an end to our liberty in twenty minutes. And the best
of our men may be afraid of drowning. There is our
little boat, but in an affair like this no one can be sure
of being saved."

The voice ceased. We had started from Barcelona
with our dinghy in tow; afterwards it was too risky to
try to get her in, so we let her take her chance of the
seas at the end of a comfortable scope of rope. Many
times she had seemed to us completely overwhelmed,
but soon we would see her bob up again on a wave,
apparently as buoyant and whole as ever.

"I understand," I said, softly. "Very well, Dominic.
When?"

"Not yet. We must get a little more in first,"
answered the voice from the hood in a ghostly murmur.

XLV

It was settled. I had now the courage to turn about.
Our men crouched about the decks here and there with
anxious, crestfallen faces, all turned one way to watch
the chaser. For the first time that morning I perceived Cesar stretched out full length on the deck near
the foremast and wondered where he had been skulking
till then. But he might in truth have been at my elbow
all the time for all I knew. We had been too absorbed
in watching our fate to pay attention to each other.
Nobody had eaten anything that morning, but the men
had been coming constantly to drink at the water-butt.*

I ran down to the cabin. I had there, put away in a
locker, ten thousand francs in gold, of whose presence
on board, so far as I was aware, not a soul except

Dominic had the slightest inkling. When I emerged on deck again Dominic had turned about and was peering from under his cowl at the coast. Cape Creux* closed the view ahead. To the left a wide bay, its waters torn and swept by fierce squalls, seemed full of smoke. Astern the sky had a menacing look.

Directly he saw me, Dominic, in a placid tone, wanted to know what was the matter. I came close to him and, looking as unconcerned as I could, told him in an undertone that I had found the locker broken open and the money-belt gone. Last evening it was still there.

"What did you want to do with it?" he asked me, trembling violently.

"Put it round my waist, of course," I answered, amazed to hear his teeth chattering.

"Cursed gold!" he muttered. "The weight of the money might have cost you your life, perhaps." He shuddered. "There is no time to talk about that now."

"I am ready."

"Not yet. I am waiting for that squall to come over," he muttered. And a few leaden minutes passed.

The squall came over at last. Our pursuer, overtaken by a sort of murky whirlwind, disappeared from our sight. The *Tremolino* quivered and bounded forward. The land ahead vanished, too, and we seemed to be left alone in a world of water and wind.

"*Prenez la barre, monsieur*,"* Dominic broke the silence suddenly in an austere voice. "Take hold of the tiller." He bent his hood to my ear. "The balancelle is yours. Your own hands must deal the blow. I—I have yet another piece of work to do." He spoke up loudly to the man who steered. "Let the signorino take the tiller, and you with the others stand by to haul the boat alongside quickly at the word."

The man obeyed, surprised, but silent. The others stirred, and pricked up their ears at this. I heard their murmurs: "What now? Are we going to run in somewhere and take to our heels? The Padrone knows what he is doing."

Dominic went forward. He paused to look down at Cesar, who, as I have said before, was lying full length face down by the foremast, then stepped over him, and dived out of my sight under the foresail. I saw nothing ahead. It was impossible for me to see anything except the foresail open and still, like a great shadowy wing. But Dominic had his bearings. His voice came to me from forward, in a just audible cry:

"Now, signorino!"

I bore on the tiller, as instructed before. Again I heard him faintly, and then I had only to hold her straight. No ship ran so joyously to her death before. She rose and fell, as if floating in space, and darted forward, whizzing like an arrow. Dominic, stooping under the foot of the foresail, reappeared, and stood steadying himself against the mast, with a raised forefinger in an attitude of expectant attention. A second before the shock his arm fell down by his side. At that I set my teeth. And then——

Talk of splintered planks and smashed timbers! This shipwreck lies upon my soul with the dread and horror of a homicide, with the unforgettable remorse of having crushed a living, faithful heart at a single blow. At one moment the rush and the soaring swing of speed; the next a crash, and death, stillness—a moment of horrible immobility, with the song of the wind changed to a strident wail, and the heavy waters boiling up menacing and sluggish around the corpse. I saw in a distracting minute the foreyard fly fore and aft with a brutal swing, the men all in a heap, cursing with

fear, and hauling frantically at the line of the boat.
With a strange welcoming of the familiar I saw also
Cesar amongst them, and recognized Dominic's old,
well-known, effective gesture, the horizontal sweep
of his powerful arm. I recollect distinctly saying to
myself, "Cesar must go down, of course," and then, as
I was scrambling on all fours, the swinging tiller I had
let go caught me a crack under the ear, and knocked
me over senseless.

I don't think I was actually unconscious for more
than a few minutes, but when I came to myself the
dinghy was driving before the wind into a sheltered
cove, two men just keeping her straight with their oars.
Dominic, with his arm around my shoulders, supported
me in the stern sheets.

We landed in a familiar part of the country. Dominic
took one of the boat's oars with him. I suppose he
was thinking of the stream we would have presently
to cross, on which there was a miserable specimen of a
punt, often robbed of its pole. But first of all we had
to ascend the ridge of land at the back of the Cape.
He helped me up. I was dizzy. My head felt very
large and heavy. At the top of the ascent I clung to
him, and we stopped to rest.

To the right, below us, the wide, smoky bay was
empty. Dominic had kept his word. There was not
a chip to be seen around the black rock from which the
Tremolino, with her plucky heart crushed at one blow,
had slipped off into deep water to her eternal rest.
The vastness of the open sea was smothered in driving
mists, and in the centre of the thinning squall, phantom-
like, under a frightful press of canvas, the unconscious
guardacosta dashed on, still chasing to the northward. Our men were already descending the reverse
slope to look for that punt which we knew from

experience was not always to be found easily. I looked after them with dazed, misty eyes. One, two, three, four.

"Dominic, where's Cesar?" I cried.

As if repulsing the very sound of the name, the Padrone made that ample, sweeping, knocking-down gesture. I stepped back a pace and stared at him fearfully. His open shirt uncovered his muscular neck and the thick hair on his chest. He planted the oar upright in the soft soil, and rolling up slowly his right sleeve, extended the bare arm before my face.

"This," he began, with an extreme deliberation, whose superhuman restraint vibrated with the suppressed violence of his feelings, "is the arm which delivered the blow. I am afraid it is your own gold that did the rest. I forgot all about your money." He clasped his hands together in sudden distress. "I forgot, I forgot," he repeated, disconsolately.

"Cesar stole the belt?" I stammered out, bewildered.

"And who else? *Canallia!* He must have been spying on you for days. And he did the whole thing. Absent all day in Barcelona. *Traditore!** Sold his jacket—to hire a horse. Ha! ha! A good affair! I tell you it was he who set him at us. . . ."

Dominic pointed at the sea, where the guardacosta was a mere dark speck. His chin dropped on his breast.

". . . On information," he murmured, in a gloomy voice. "A Cervoni! Oh! my poor brother! . . ."

"And you drowned him," I said, feebly.

"I struck once, and the wretch went down like a stone —with the gold. Yes. But he had time to read in my eyes that nothing could save him while I was alive. And had I not the right—I, Dominic Cervoni, Padrone who brought him aboard your fellucca—my nephew, a traitor?"

He pulled the oar out of the ground and helped me

carefully down the slope. All the time he never once looked me in the face. He punted us over, then shouldered the oar again and waited till our men were at some distance before he offered me his arm. After we had gone a little way, the fishing hamlet we were making for came into view. Dominic stopped.

"Do you think you can make your way as far as the houses by yourself?" he asked me, quietly.

"Yes, I think so. But why? Where are you going, Dominic?"

"Anywhere. What a question! Signorino, you are but little more than a boy to ask such a question of a man having this tale in his family. Ah! *Traditore !* What made me ever own that spawn of a hungry devil for our own blood! Thief, cheat, coward, liar—other men can deal with that. But I was his uncle, and so . . . I wish he had poisoned me—*charogne !* But this: that I, a confidential man and a Corsican, should have to ask your pardon for bringing on board your vessel, of which I was Padrone, a Cervoni, who has betrayed you—a traitor!—that is too much. It is too much. Well, I beg your pardon; and you may spit in Dominic's face because a traitor of our blood taints us all. A theft may be made good between men, a lie may be set right, a death avenged, but what can one do to atone for a treachery like this? . . . Nothing."

He turned and walked away from me along the bank of the stream, flourishing a vengeful arm and repeating to himself slowly, with savage emphasis: "Ah! *Canaille Canaille ! Canaille ! . . .*" He left me there trembling with weakness and mute with awe. Unable to make a sound, I gazed after the strangely desolate figure of that seaman carrying an oar on his shoulder up a barren, rock-strewn ravine under the dreary leaden sky of *Tremolino's* last day. Thus, walking deliberately, with his back to the sea, Dominic vanished from my sight.

With the quality of our desires, thoughts, and wonder proportioned to our infinite littleness we measure even time itself by our own stature. Imprisoned in the house of personal illusions thirty centuries in mankind's history seem less to look back upon than thirty years of our own life. And Dominic Cervoni takes his place in my memory by the side of the legendary wanderer*on the sea of marvels and terrors, by the side of the fatal and impious adventurer, to whom the evoked shade of the soothsayer predicted a journey inland with an oar on his shoulder, till he met men who had never set eyes on ships and oars. It seems to me I can see them side by side in the twilight of an arid land, the unfortunate possessors of the secret lore of the sea, bearing the emblem of their hard calling on their shoulders, surrounded by silent and curious men: even as I, too, having turned my back upon the sea, am bearing those few pages in the twilight, with the hope of finding in an inland valley the silent welcome of some patient listener.

XLVI

"A FELLOW has now no chance of promotion unless he jumps into the muzzle of a gun and crawls out of the touchhole."*

He who, a hundred years ago, more or less, pronounced the above words in the uneasiness of his heart, thirsting for professional distinction, was a young naval officer. Of his life, career, achievements, and end nothing is preserved for the edification of his young successors in the fleet of to-day—nothing but this phrase, which, sailorlike in the simplicity of personal sentiment and strength of graphic expression, embodies the spirit of the epoch. This obscure but vigorous testimony has its price, its significance, and its lesson. It comes to us from a worthy ancestor. We do not know whether he lived long enough for a chance of that promotion whose way was so arduous. He belongs to the great array of the unknown—who are great, indeed, by the sum total of the devoted effort put out, and the colossal scale of success attained by their insatiable and steadfast ambition. We do not know his name; we only know of him what is material for us to know— that he was never backward on occasions of desperate service. We have this on the authority of a distinguished seaman of Nelson's time. Departing this life as Admiral of the Fleet on the eve of the Crimean War, Sir Thomas Byam Martin has recorded for us amongst his all too short autobiographical notes these few characteristic words uttered by one young man of the many who must have felt that particular inconvenience of a heroic age.

The distinguished Admiral had lived through it himself, and was a good judge of what was expected in those days from men and ships. A brilliant frigate captain, a man of sound judgment, of dashing bravery and of serene mind, scrupulously concerned for the welfare and honour of the navy, he missed a larger fame only by the chances of the service. We may well quote on this day the words written of Nelson, in the decline of a well-spent life, by Sir T. B. Martin, who died just fifty years ago on the very anniversary of Trafalgar.

"Nelson's nobleness of mind was a prominent and beautiful part of his character. His foibles—faults if you like—will never be dwelt upon in any memorandum of mine," he declares, and goes on—"he whose splendid and matchless achievements will be remembered with admiration while there is gratitude in the hearts of Britons, or while a ship floats upon the ocean; he whose example on the breaking out of the war gave so chivalrous an impulse to the younger men of the service that all rushed into rivalry of daring which disdained every warning of prudence and led to acts of heroic enterprise which tended greatly to exalt the glory of our nation.*"

These are his words, and they are true. The dashing young frigate captain, the man who in middle age was nothing loth to give chase single-handed in his seventy-four to a whole fleet, the man of enterprise and consummate judgment, the old Admiral of the Fleet, the good and trusted servant of his country under two kings and a queen,* had felt correctly Nelson's influence, and expressed himself with precision out of the fulness of his seaman's heart.

"Exalted," he wrote, not "augmented." And therein his feeling and his pen captured the very truth. Other men there were ready and able to add to the treasure of victories the British navy has given to the nation. It was the lot of Lord Nelson to exalt all this glory. Exalt! the word seems to be created for the man.

XLVII

The British navy may well have ceased to count its victories. It is rich beyond the wildest dreams of success and fame. It may well, rather, on a culminating day of its history, cast about for the memory of some reverses to appease the jealous fates which attend the prosperity and triumphs of a nation. It holds, indeed, the heaviest inheritance that has ever been entrusted to the courage and fidelity of armed men.

It is too great for mere pride. It should make the seamen of to-day humble in the secret of their hearts,

and indomitable in their unspoken resolution. In all
the records of history there has never been a time when
a victorious fortune has been so faithful to men making
war upon the sea. And it must be confessed that on
their part they knew how to be faithful to their victorious fortune. They were exalted. They were always
watching for her smile; night or day, fair weather or
foul, they waited for her slightest sign with the offering
of their stout hearts in their hands. And for the
inspiration of this high constancy they were indebted to
Lord Nelson alone. Whatever earthly affection he
abandoned or grasped, the great Admiral was always,
before all, beyond all, a lover of Fame. He loved her
jealously, with an inextinguishable ardour and an insatiable desire—he loved her with a masterful devotion
and an infinite trustfulness. In the plenitude of his
passion he was an exacting lover. And she never betrayed the greatness of his trust! She attended him to
the end of his life, and he died pressing her last gift
(nineteen prizes) to his heart. "Anchor, Hardy—
anchor!"*was as much the cry of an ardent lover as of a
consummate seaman. Thus he would hug to his breast
the last gift of Fame.

It was this ardour which made him great. He was a
flaming example to the wooers of glorious fortune.
There have been great officers before—Lord Hood,*
for instance, whom he himself regarded as the greatest
sea officer England ever had. A long succession of
great commanders opened the sea to the vast range of
Nelson's genius. His time had come; and, after the great
sea officers, the great naval tradition passed into the
keeping of a great man. Not the least glory of the navy
is that it understood Nelson. Lord Hood trusted him.
Admiral Keith* told him: "We can't spare you either
as Captain or Admiral." Earl St. Vincent* put into

his hands, untrammelled by orders, a division of his fleet, and Sir Hyde Parker*gave him two more ships at Copenhagen than he had asked for. So much for the chiefs; the rest of the navy surrendered to him their devoted affection, trust, and admiration. In return he gave them no less than his own exalted soul. He breathed into them his own ardour and his own ambition. In a few short years he revolutionized, not the strategy or tactics of sea-warfare, but the very conception of victory itself. And this is genius. In that alone through the fidelity of his fortune and the power of his inspiration, he stands unique amongst the leaders of fleets and sailors. He brought heroism into the line of duty. Verily he is a terrible ancestor.

And the men of his day loved him. They loved him not only as victorious armies have loved great commanders; they loved him with a more intimate feeling as one of themselves. In the words of a contemporary, he had "a most happy way of gaining the affectionate respect of all who had the felicity to serve under his command."*

To be so great and to remain so accessible to the affection of one's fellow-men is the mark of exceptional humanity. Lord Nelson's greatness was very human. It had a moral basis; it needed to feel itself surrounded by the warm devotion of a band of brothers.* He was vain and tender. The love and admiration which the navy gave him so unreservedly soothed the restlessness of his professional pride. He trusted them as much as they trusted him. He was a seaman of seamen. Sir T. B. Martin states that he never conversed with any officer who had served under Nelson "without hearing the heartiest expressions of attachment to his person and admiration of his frank and conciliatory manner to his subordinates."* And Sir Robert Stop-

ford, who commanded one of the ships with which
Nelson chased to the West Indies a fleet nearly double
in number, says in a letter: "We are half-starved and
otherwise inconvenienced by being so long out of port,
but our reward is that we are with Nelson."*

This heroic spirit of daring and endurance, in which
all public and private differences were sunk throughout
the whole fleet, is Lord Nelson's great legacy, triply
sealed by the victorious impress of the Nile, Copenhagen, and Trafalgar. This is a legacy whose value
the changes of time cannot affect. The men and the
ships he knew how to lead lovingly to the work of
courage and the reward of glory have passed away, but
Nelson's uplifting touch remains in the standard of
achievement he has set for all time. The principles
of strategy may be immutable. It is certain they have
been, and shall be again, disregarded from timidity,
from blindness, through infirmity of purpose. The
tactics of great captains on land and sea can be infinitely discussed. The first object of tactics is to close
with the adversary on terms of the greatest possible
advantage; yet no hard-and-fast rules can be drawn
from experience, for this capital reason, amongst others
—that the quality of the adversary is a variable element
in the problem. The tactics of Lord Nelson have been
amply discussed, with much pride and some profit.
And yet, truly, they are already of but archaic interest.
A very few years more, and the hazardous difficulties
of handling a fleet under canvas will have passed beyond the conception of seamen who hold in trust for
their country Lord Nelson's legacy of heroic spirit.
The change in the character of the ships is too great
and too radical. It is good and proper to study the
acts of great men with thoughtful reverence, but already
the precise intention of Lord Nelson's famous memoran-

dum* seems to lie under that veil which Time throws over the clearest conceptions of every great art. It must not be forgotten that this was the first time when Nelson, commanding in chief, had his opponents under way—the first time and the last. Had he lived, had there been other fleets left to oppose him, we would, perhaps, have learned something more of his greatness as a sea officer. Nothing could have been added to his greatness as a leader. All that can be affirmed is, that on no other day of his short and glorious career was Lord Nelson more splendidly true to his genius and to his country's fortune.

XLVIII

And yet the fact remains that, had the wind failed and the fleet lost steerage way,* or, worse still, had it been taken aback from the eastward, with its leaders within short range of the enemy's guns, nothing, it seems, could have saved the headmost ships from capture or destruction. No skill of a great sea officer would have availed in such a contingency. Lord Nelson was more than that, and his genius would have remained undiminished by defeat. But obviously tactics, which are so much at the mercy of irremediable accident, must seem to a modern seaman a poor matter of study. The Commander-in-Chief in the great fleet action that will take its place next to the Battle of Trafalgar in the history of the British navy will have no such anxiety, and will feel the weight of no such dependence. For a hundred years now no British fleet has engaged the enemy in line of battle. A hundred years is a long time, but the difference of modern conditions is enormous. The gulf is great. Had the last great fight of the English navy been that of the First of June,* for instance,

had there been no Nelson's victories, it would have been
well-nigh impassable. The great Admiral's slight and
passion-worn figure stands at the parting of the ways.
He had the audacity of genius, and a prophetic inspiration.

The modern naval man must feel that the time has
come for the tactical practice of the great sea officers
of the past to be laid by in the temple of august memories. The fleet tactics of the sailing days have been
governed by two points: the deadly nature of a raking
fire, and the dread, natural to a commander dependent
upon the winds, to find at some crucial moment part
of his fleet thrown hopelessly to leeward. These two
points were of the very essence of sailing tactics, and
these two points have been eliminated from the modern
tactical problem by the changes of propulsion and armament. Lord Nelson was the first to disregard them
with conviction and audacity sustained by an unbounded trust in the men he led. This conviction,
this audacity, and this trust stand out from amongst
the lines of the celebrated memorandum, which is but
a declaration of his faith in a crushing superiority of
fire as the only means of victory and the only aim of
sound tactics. Under the difficulties of the then existing conditions he strove for that, and for that alone,
putting his faith into practice against every risk. And
in that exclusive faith Lord Nelson appears to us as
the first of the moderns.

Against every risk I have said; and the men of to-day,
born and bred to the use of steam, can hardly realize
how much of that risk was in the weather. Except at
the Nile, where the conditions were ideal for engaging
a fleet moored in shallow water, Lord Nelson was not
lucky in his weather. Practically it was nothing but a
quite unusual failure of the wind which cost him his

arm during the Teneriffe expedition.* On Trafalgar
Day the weather was not so much unfavourable as
extremely dangerous.

It was one of those covered days of fitful sunshine,
of light, unsteady winds, with a swell from the westward
and hazy in general, but with the land about the Cape
at times distinctly visible. It has been my lot to look
with reverence upon the very spot more than once,
and for many hours together. All but thirty years
ago, certain exceptional circumstances made me very
familiar for a time with that bight in the Spanish coast
which would be enclosed within a straight line drawn
from Faro to Spartel.* My well-remembered experience
has convinced me that, in that corner of the ocean,
once the wind has got to the northward of west (as it
did on the 20th, taking the British fleet aback), appearances of westerly weather go for nothing, and that
it is infinitely more likely to veer right round to the
east than to shift back again. It was in those conditions
that, at seven on the morning of the 21st, the signal
for the fleet to bear up*and steer east was made. Holding a clear recollection of these languid easterly sighs
rippling unexpectedly against the run of the smooth
swell, with no other warning than a ten-minutes' calm
and a queer darkening of the coast-line, I cannot think,
without a gasp of professional awe, of that fateful moment. Perhaps personal experience, at a time of life
when responsibility had a special freshness and importance, has induced me to exaggerate to myself the
danger of the weather. The great Admiral and good
seaman could read aright the signs of sea and sky,
as his order to prepare to anchor at the end of the
day sufficiently proves; but, all the same, the mere idea
of these baffling easterly airs, coming on at any time
within half an hour or so, after the firing of the first shot,

is enough to take one's breath away, with the image
of the rearmost ships of both divisions falling off, unmanageable, broadside on to the westerly swell, and of
two British Admirals in desperate jeopardy. To this
day I cannot free myself from the impression that, for
some forty minutes, the fate of the great battle hung
upon a breath of wind such as I have felt stealing from
behind, as it were, upon my cheek while engaged in
looking to the westward for the signs of the true weather.

Never more shall British seamen going into action
have to trust the success of their valour to a breath of
wind. The God of gales and battles, favouring her
arms to the last, has let the sun of England's sailing-
fleet and of its greatest master set in unclouded glory.
And now the old ships and their men are gone; the new
ships and the new men, many of them bearing the old,
auspicious names, have taken up their watch on the
stern and impartial sea, which offers no opportunities
but to those who know how to grasp them with a ready
hand and undaunted heart.

XLIX

This the navy of the Twenty Years' War*knew well
how to do, and never better than when Lord Nelson
had breathed into its soul his own passion of honour
and fame. It was a fortunate navy. Its victories
were no mere smashing of helpless ships and massacres
of cowed men. It was spared that cruel favour, for
which no brave heart had ever prayed. It was fortunate in its adversaries. I say adversaries, for on
recalling such proud memories we should avoid the
word "enemies," whose hostile sound perpetuates
the antagonisms and strife of nations so irremediable
perhaps, so fateful—and also so vain. War is one of

the gifts of life; but, alas! no war appears so very necessary when time has laid its soothing hand upon the passionate misunderstandings and the passionate desires of great peoples. *"Le temps,"* as a distinguished Frenchman has said, *"est un galant homme."** He fosters the spirit of concord and justice, in whose work there is as much glory to be reaped as in the deeds of arms.

One of them disorganized by revolutionary changes, the other rusted in the neglect of a decayed monarchy, the two fleets* opposed to us entered the contest with odds against them from the first. By the merit of our daring and our faithfulness, and the genius of a great leader, we have in the course of the war augmented our advantage and kept it to the last. But in the exulting illusion of irresistible might a long series of military successes brings to a nation the less obvious aspect of such a fortune may perchance be lost to view. The old navy in its last days earned a fame that no belittling malevolence dare cavil at. And this supreme favour they owe to their adversaries alone.

Deprived by an ill-starred fortune of that self-confidence which strengthens the hands of an armed host, impaired in skill but not in courage, it may safely be said that our adversaries managed yet to make a better fight of it in 1797 than they did in 1793. Later still, the resistance offered at the Nile was all, and more than all, that could be demanded from seamen, who, unless blind or without understanding, must have seen their doom sealed from the moment that the *Goliath*, bearing up under the bows of the *Guerrier*, took up an inshore berth. The combined fleets of 1805, just come out of port, and attended by nothing but the disturbing memories of reverses, presented to our approach a determined front, on which Captain Blackwood,* in a knightly spirit, congratulated his Admiral. By the exertions of their valour our adversaries have but added a greater lustre to our arms. No friend could have done more, for even in war, which severs for a time all the sentiments of human fellowship, this subtle bond of association remains between brave men —that the final testimony to the value of victory must be received at the hands of the vanquished.

Those who from the heat of that battle sank together to their repose in the cool depths of the ocean would not understand the watchwords of our day, would gaze with amazed eyes at the engines of our strife. All passes, all changes: the animosity of peoples, the handling of fleets, the forms of ships; and even the sea itself seems to wear a different and diminished aspect from the sea of Lord Nelson's day. In this ceaseless rush of shadows and shades, that, like the fantastic forms of clouds cast darkly upon the waters on a windy day, fly past us to fall headlong below the hard edge of an implacable horizon, we must turn to the national spirit, which, superior in its force and continuity to good and evil fortune, can alone give us the feeling of an enduring existence and of an invincible power against the fates.

Like a subtle and mysterious elixir poured into the perishable clay of successive generations, it grows in truth, splendour, and potency with the march of ages. In its incorruptible flow all round the globe of the earth it preserves from the decay and forgetfulness of death the greatness of our great men, and amongst them the passionate and gentle greatness of Nelson, the nature of whose genius was, on the faith of a brave seaman and distinguished Admiral, such as to "exalt the glory of our nation."

THE END

A PERSONAL RECORD
Some Reminiscences

AUTHOR'S NOTE

THE re-issue of this book in a new form does not strictly speaking require another Preface. But since this is distinctly a place for personal remarks I take the opportunity to refer in this Author's Note to two points arising from certain statements about myself I have noticed of late in the press.

One of them bears upon the question of language.* I have always felt myself looked upon somewhat in the light of a phenomenon, a position which outside the circus world cannot be regarded as desirable. It needs a special temperament for one to derive much gratification from the fact of being able to do freakish things intentionally, and, as it were, from mere vanity.

The fact of my not writing in my native language has been of course commented upon frequently in reviews and notices of my various works and in the more extended critical articles. I suppose that was unavoidable; and indeed these comments were of the most flattering kind to one's vanity.* But in that matter I have no vanity that could be flattered. I could not have it. The first object of this note is to disclaim any merit there might have been in an act of deliberate volition.

The impression of my having exercised a choice between the two languages, French and English, both foreign to me, has got abroad somehow. That impression is erroneous. It originated, I believe, in an article written by Sir Hugh Clifford*and published in the year 98, I think, of the last century. Some time before,

Sir Hugh Clifford came to see me. He is, if not the first, then one of the first two friends I made for myself by my work, the other being Mr. Cunninghame Graham,* who, characteristically enough, had been captivated by my story, *An Outpost of Progress*. These friendships which have endured to this day I count amongst my precious possessions.

Mr. Hugh Clifford (he was not decorated then) had just published his first volume of Malay sketches.* I was naturally delighted to see him and infinitely gratified by the kind things he found to say about my first books and some of my early short stories, the action of which is placed in the Malay Archipelago. I remember that after saying many things which ought to have made me blush to the roots of my hair with outraged modesty, he ended by telling me with the uncompromising yet kindly firmness of a man accustomed to speak unpalatable truths even to Oriental potentates (for their own good of course) that as a matter of fact I didn't know anything about Malays. I was perfectly aware of this. I have never pretended to any such knowledge, and I was moved—I wonder to this day at my impertinence —to retort: "Of course I don't know anything about Malays. If I knew only one hundredth part of what you and Frank Swettenham* know of Malays I would make everybody sit up." He went on looking kindly (but firmly) at me and then we both burst out laughing. In the course of that most welcome visit twenty years ago, which I remember so well, we talked of many things; the characteristics of various languages was one of them, and it is on that day that my friend carried away with him the impression that I had exercised a deliberate choice between French and English. Later, when moved by his friendship (no empty word to him) to write a study* in the *North American Review* on

Joseph Conrad, he conveyed that impression to the public.

This misapprehension, for it is nothing else, was no doubt my fault. I must have expressed myself badly in the course of a friendly and intimate talk when one doesn't watch one's phrases carefully. My recollection of what I meant to say is: that *had I been under the necessity* of making a choice between the two, and though I knew French fairly well and was familiar with it from infancy, I would have been afraid to attempt expression in a language so perfectly "crystallized." This, I believe, was the word I used. And then we passed to other matters. I had to tell him a little about myself; and what he told me of his work in the East, his own particular East of which I had but the mistiest, short glimpse, was of the most absorbing interest. The present Governor of Nigeria may not remember that conversation as well as I do, but I am sure that he will not mind this, what in diplomatic language is called "rectification" of a statement made to him by an obscure writer his generous sympathy had prompted him to seek out and make his friend.

The truth of the matter is that my faculty to write in English is as natural as any other aptitude with which I might have been born. I have a strange and overpowering feeling that it had always been an inherent part of myself. English was for me neither a matter of choice nor adoption. The merest idea of choice had never entered my head. And as to adoption— well, yes, there was adoption; but it was I who was adopted by the genius of the language, which directly I came out of the stammering stage made me its own so completely that its very idioms I truly believe had a direct action on my temperament and fashioned my still plastic character.

It was a very intimate action and for that very reason it is too mysterious to explain. The task would be as impossible as trying to explain love at first sight. There was something in this conjunction of exulting, almost physical recognition, the same sort of emotional surrender and the same pride of possession, all united in the wonder of a great discovery; but there was on it none of that shadow of dreadful doubt that falls on the very flame of our perishable passions. One knew very well that this was for ever.

A matter of discovery and not of inheritance, that very inferiority of the title makes the faculty still more precious, lays the possessor under a lifelong obligation to remain worthy of his great fortune. But it seems to me that all this sounds as if I were trying to explain —a task which I have just pronounced to be impossible. If in action we may admit with awe that the Impossible recedes before men's indomitable spirit, the Impossible in matters of analysis will always make a stand at some point or other. All I can claim after all those years of devoted practice, with the accumulated anguish of its doubts, imperfections and falterings in my heart, is the right to be believed when I say that if I had not written in English I would not have written at all.

The other remark which I wish to make here is also a rectification but of a less direct kind. It has nothing to do with the medium of expression. It bears on the matter of my authorship in another way. It is not for me to criticise my judges, the more so because I always felt that I was receiving more than justice at their hands. But it seems to me that their unfailingly interested sympathy has ascribed to racial and historical influences much, of what, I believe, appertains simply to the individual. Nothing is more foreign than what in the literary world is called Slavonism, to the Polish temperament with its tradition of self-government, its chivalrous view of moral restraints and an exaggerated respect for individual rights: not to mention the important fact that the whole Polish mentality, Western in complexion, had received its training from Italy and France and, historically, had always remained, even in religious matters, in sympathy with the most liberal currents of European thought. An impartial view of humanity in all its degrees of splendour and misery together with a special regard for the rights of the unprivileged of this earth, not on any mystic ground but on the ground of simple fellowship and honourable reciprocity of services, was the dominant characteristic of the mental and moral atmosphere of the houses which sheltered my hazardous childhood:—matters of calm and deep conviction both lasting and consistent, and removed as far as possible from that humanitarianism that seems to be merely a matter of crazy nerves or a morbid conscience.

One of the most sympathetic of my critics tried to account for certain characteristics of my work by the fact of my being, in his own words, "the son of a Revolutionist."* No epithet could be more inapplicable to a man with such a strong sense of responsibility in the region of ideas and action and so indifferent to the promptings of personal ambition as my father. Why the description "revolutionary" should have been applied all through Europe to the Polish risings of 1831 and 1863* I really cannot understand. These risings were purely revolts against foreign domination. The Russians themselves called them "rebellions," which, from their point of view, was the exact truth. Amongst the men concerned in the preliminaries of the 1863 movement my father was no more revolutionary than the others,* in the sense of working for the subversion of any social or political scheme of existence. He was simply a patriot in the sense of a man who believing in the spirituality of a national existence could not bear to see that spirit enslaved.

Called out publicly in a kindly attempt to justify the work of the son, that figure of my past cannot be dismissed without a few more words. As a child of course I knew very little of my father's activities, for I was not quite twelve when he died. What I saw with my own eyes was the public funeral,* the cleared streets, the hushed crowds; but I understood perfectly well that this was a manifestation of the national spirit seizing a worthy occasion. That bareheaded mass of work people, youths of the University, women at the windows, school-boys on the pavement, could have known nothing positive about him except the fame of his fidelity to the one guiding emotion in their hearts. I had nothing but that knowledge myself; and this great silent demonstration seemed to me the most natural tribute in the world—not to the man but to the Idea.

What had impressed me much more intimately was the burning of his manuscripts a fortnight or so before his death. It was done under his own superintendence. I happened to go into his room a little earlier than usual that evening, and remaining unnoticed stayed to watch the nursing-sister feeding the blaze in the fireplace. My father sat in a deep arm-chair propped up with pillows. This is the last time I saw him out of bed. His aspect was to me not so much that of a man desperately ill, as mortally weary—a vanquished man. That act of destruction affected me profoundly by its air of surrender.* Not before death however. To a man of such strong faith death could not have been an enemy.

For many years I believed that every scrap of his

writings had been burnt, but in July of 1914 the Librarian of the University of Cracow calling on me during our short visit to Poland, mentioned the existence of a few manuscripts of my father and especially of a series of letters written before and during his exile to his most intimate friend who had sent them to the University for preservation.* I went to the Library at once, but had only time then for a mere glance. I intended to come back next day and arrange for copies being made of the whole correspondence. But next day there was war. So perhaps I shall never know now what he wrote to his most intimate friend in the time of his domestic happiness, of his new paternity, of his strong hopes—and later, in the hours of disillusion, bereavement and gloom.

I had also imagined him to be completely forgotten forty-five years after his death. But this was not the case. Some young men of letters had discovered him, mostly as a remarkable translator of Shakespeare, Victor Hugo and Alfred de Vigny,* to whose drama *Chatterton*, translated by himself, he had written an eloquent preface defending the poet's deep humanity and his ideal of noble stoicism. The political side of his life was being recalled too; for some men of his time, his co-workers in the task of keeping the national spirit firm in the hope of an independent future, had been in their old age publishing their memoirs, where the part he played was for the first time publicly disclosed to the world.* I learned then of things in his life I never knew before, things which outside the group of the initiated could have been known to no living being except my mother. It was thus that from a volume of posthumous memoirs dealing with those bitter years I learned the fact that the first inception of the secret National Committee* intended primarily to organize moral resistance

to the augmented pressure of Russianism arose on my
father's initiative, and that its first meetings were held
in our Warsaw house,* of which all I remember distinctly
is one room, white and crimson, probably the drawing-
room. In one of its walls there was the loftiest of all
archways. Where it led to remains a mystery; but to
this day I cannot get rid of the belief that all this was of
enormous proportions, and that the people appearing
and disappearing in that immense space were beyond
the usual stature of mankind as I got to know it in later
life. Amongst them I remember my mother, a more
familiar figure than the others, dressed in the black of
the national mourning worn in defiance of ferocious
police regulations. I have also preserved from that
particular time the awe of her mysterious gravity which,
indeed, was by no means smileless. For I remember
her smiles, too. Perhaps for me she could always find a
smile. She was young then, certainly not yet thirty.*
She died four years later in exile.

In the pages which follow I mention her visit to
her brother's house about a year before her death.* I
also speak a little of my father as I remember him in
the years following what was for him the deadly blow of
her loss. And now, having been again evoked in answer to the words of a friendly critic, these Shades may
be allowed to return to their place of rest where their
forms in life linger yet, dim but poignant, and awaiting
the moment when their haunting reality, their last trace
on earth, shall pass for ever with me out of the world.

1919.   J. C.

A FAMILIAR PREFACE

As a general rule we do not want much encouragement to talk about ourselves; yet this little book is the result of a friendly suggestion, and even of a little friendly pressure.* I defended myself with some spirit; but, with characteristic tenacity, the friendly voice insisted, "You know, you really must."

It was not an argument, but I submitted at once. If one must! . . .

You perceive the force of a word. He who wants to persuade should put his trust not in the right argument, but in the right word. The power of sound has always been greater than the power of sense. I don't say this by way of disparagement. It is better for mankind to be impressionable than reflective. Nothing humanely great—great, I mean, as affecting a whole mass of lives—has come from reflection. On the other hand, you cannot fail to see the power of mere words; such words as Glory, for instance, or Pity. I won't mention any more. They are not far to seek. Shouted with perseverance, with ardour, with conviction, these two by their sound alone have set whole nations in motion and upheaved the dry, hard ground on which rests our whole social fabric. There's "virtue" for you if you like! . . . Of course the accent must be attended to. The right accent. That's very important. The capacious lung, the thundering or the tender vocal chords. Don't talk to me of your Archimedes' lever. He was an absent-minded person with a mathematical imagination. Mathematics command all my respect, but I have no use for engines. Give me the right word and the right accent and I will move the world.

What a dream for a writer! Because written words have their accent, too. Yes! Let me only find the right word! Surely it must be lying somewhere among the wreckage of all the plaints and all the exultations poured out aloud since the first day when hope, the undying, came down on earth. It may be there, close by, disregarded, invisible, quite at hand. But it's no good. I believe there are men who can lay hold of a needle in a pottle of hay at the first try. For myself, I have never had such luck.

And then there is that accent. Another difficulty. For who is going to tell whether the accent is right or wrong till the word is shouted, and fails to be heard, perhaps, and goes down-wind, leaving the world unmoved? Once upon a time there lived an Emperor* who was a sage and something of a literary man. He jotted down on ivory tablets thoughts, maxims, reflections which chance has preserved for the edification of posterity. Among other sayings—I am quoting from memory—I remember this solemn admonition: "Let all thy words have the accent of heroic truth.*" The accent of heroic truth! This is very fine, but I am thinking that it is an easy matter for an austere Emperor to jot down grandiose advice. Most of the working truths on this earth are humble, not heroic; and there have been times in the history of mankind when the accents of heroic truth have moved it to nothing but derision.

Nobody will expect to find between the covers of this little book words of extraordinary potency or accents of irresistible heroism. However humiliating for my self-esteem, I must confess that the counsels of Marcus Aurelius are not for me. They are more fit for a moralist than for an artist. Truth of a modest sort I can promise you, and also sincerity. That complete, praiseworthy sincerity which, while it delivers one into the hands of one's enemies, is as likely as not to embroil one with one's friends.

"Embroil" is perhaps too strong an expression. I can't imagine among either my enemies or my friends a being so hard up for something to do as to quarrel with me. "To disappoint one's friends" would be nearer the mark. Most, almost all, friendships of the writing period of my life have come to me through my books; and I know that a novelist lives in his work. He stands there, the only reality in an invented world, among imaginary things, happenings, and people. Writing about them, he is only writing about himself. But the disclosure is not complete. He remains, to a certain extent, a figure behind the veil; a suspected rather than a seen presence—a movement and a voice behind the draperies of fiction. In these personal notes there is no such veil. And I cannot help thinking of a passage in the "Imitation of Christ"*where the ascetic author, who knew life so profoundly, says that "there are persons esteemed on their reputation who by showing themselves destroy the opinion one had of them." This is the danger incurred by an author of fiction who sets out to talk about himself without disguise.

While these reminiscent pages were appearing serially I was remonstrated with for bad economy; as if such writing were a form of self-indulgence wasting the substance of future volumes. It seems that I am not sufficiently literary. Indeed, a man who never wrote a line for print till he was thirty-six*cannot bring himself to look upon his existence and his experience, upon

the sum of his thoughts, sensations, and · emotions,
upon his memories and his regrets, and the whole possession of his past, as only so much material for his
hands. Once before, some three years ago, when I
published "The Mirror of the Sea," a volume of
impressions and memories, the same remarks were
made to me. Practical remarks. But, truth to say,
I have never understood the kind of thrift they recommend. I wanted to pay my tribute to the sea, its ships
and its men, to whom I remain indebted for so much
which has gone to make me what I am. That seemed
to me the only shape in which I could offer it to their
shades. There could not be a question in my mind of
anything else. It is quite possible that I am a bad
economist; but it is certain that I am incorrigible.

Having matured in the surroundings and under
the special conditions of sea-life, I have a special piety
toward that form of my past; for its impressions were
vivid, its appeal direct, its demands such as could be
responded to with the natural elation of youth and
strength equal to the call. There was nothing in them
to perplex a young conscience. Having broken away
from my origins under a storm of blame from every
quarter which had the merest shadow of right to voice
an opinion, removed by great distances from such
natural affections as were still left to me, and even
estranged, in a measure, from them by the totally un-
intelligible character of the life which had seduced me
so mysteriously from my allegiance, I may safely say
that through the blind force of circumstances the sea
was to be all my world and the merchant service my
only home for a long succession of years. No wonder,
then, that in my two exclusively sea books—"The
Nigger of the 'Narcissus,'" and "The Mirror of the Sea"
(and in the few short sea stories like "Youth" and

"Typhoon")—I have tried with an almost filial regard to render the vibration of life in the great world of waters, in the hearts of the simple men who have for ages traversed its solitudes, and also that something sentient which seems to dwell in ships—the creatures of their hands and the objects of their care.

One's literary life must turn frequently for sustenance to memories and seek discourse with the shades, unless one has made up one's mind to write only in order to reprove mankind for what it is, or praise it for what it is not, or—generally—to teach it how to behave. Being neither quarrelsome, nor a flatterer, nor a sage, I have done none of these things, and I am prepared to put up serenely with the insignificance which attaches to persons who are not meddlesome in some way or other. But resignation is not indifference. I would not like to be left standing as a mere spectator on the bank of the great stream carrying onward so many lives. I would fain claim for myself the faculty of so much insight as can be expressed in a voice of sympathy and compassion.

It seems to me that in one, at least, authoritative quarter of criticism I am suspected of a certain un-emotional, grim acceptance of facts—of what the French would call *sécheresse du cœur*.* Fifteen years of unbroken silence before praise or blame testify sufficiently to my respect for criticism, that fine flower of personal expression in the garden of letters. But this is more of a personal matter, reaching the man behind the work, and therefore it may be alluded to in a volume which is a personal note in the margin of the public page. Not that I feel hurt in the least. The charge—if it amounted to a charge at all—was made in the most considerate terms; in a tone of regret.

My answer is that if it be true that every novel

contains an element of autobiography—and this can hardly be denied, since the creator can only express himself in his creation—then there are some of us to whom an open display of sentiment is repugnant. I would not unduly praise the virtue of restraint. It is often merely temperamental. But it is not always a sign of coldness. It may be pride. There can be nothing more humiliating then to see the shaft of one's emotion miss the mark of either laughter or tears. Nothing more humiliating! And this for the reason that should the mark be missed, should the open display of emotion fail to move, then it must perish unavoidably in disgust or contempt. No artist can be reproached for shrinking from a risk which only fools run to meet and only genius dare confront with impunity. In a task which mainly consists in laying one's soul more or less bare to the world, a regard for decency, even at the cost of success, is but the regard for one's own dignity which is inseparably united with the dignity of one's work.

And then—it is very difficult to be wholly joyous or wholly sad on this earth. The comic, when it is human, soon takes upon itself a face of pain; and some of our griefs (some only, not all, for it is the capacity for suffering which makes man august in the eyes of men) have their source in weaknesses which must be recognized with smiling compassion as the common inheritance of us all. Joy and sorrow in this world pass into each other, mingling their forms and their murmurs in the twilight of life as mysterious as an overshadowed ocean, while the dazzling brightness of supreme hopes lies far off, fascinating and still, on the distant edge of the horizon.

Yes! I, too, would like to hold the magic wand giving that command over laughter and tears which is declared to be the highest achievement of imaginative literature. Only, to be a great magician one must surrender oneself to occult and irresponsible powers, either outside or within one's breast. We have all heard of simple men selling their souls for love or power to some grotesque devil. The most ordinary intelligence can perceive without much reflection that anything of the sort is bound to be a fool's bargain. I don't lay claim to particular wisdom because of my dislike and distrust of such transactions. It may be my sea training acting upon a natural disposition to keep good hold on the one thing really mine, but the fact is that I have a positive horror of losing even for one moving moment that full possession of myself which is the first condition of good service. And I have carried my notion of good service from my earlier into my later existence. I, who have never sought in the written word anything else but a form of the Beautiful—I have carried over that article of creed from the decks of ships to the more circumscribed space of my desk, and by that act, I suppose, I have become permanently imperfect in the eyes of the ineffable company of pure esthetes.

As in political so in literary action a man wins friends for himself mostly by the passion of his prejudices and by the consistent narrowness of his outlook. But I have never been able to love what was not lovable or hate what was not hateful out of deference for some general principle. Whether there be any courage in making this admission I know not. After the middle turn of life's way we consider dangers and joys with a tranquil mind. So I proceed in peace to declare that I have always suspected in the effort to bring into play the extremities of emotions the debasing touch of insincerity. In order to move others deeply we must deliberately allow ourselves to be carried away beyond the bounds of our normal sensibility—innocently enough, perhaps, and of necessity, like an actor who raises his voice on the stage above the pitch of natural conversation—but still we have to do that. And surely this is no great sin. But the danger lies in the writer becoming the victim of his own exaggeration, losing the exact notion of sincerity, and in the end coming to despise truth itself as something too cold, too blunt for his purpose—as, in fact, not good enough for his insistent emotion. From laughter and tears the descent is easy to snivelling and giggles.

These may seem selfish considerations; but you can't, in sound morals, condemn a man for taking care of his own integrity. It is his clear duty. And least of all can you condemn an artist pursuing, however humbly and imperfectly, a creative aim. In that interior world where his thought and his emotions go seeking for the experience of imagined adventures, there are no policemen, no law, no pressure of circumstance or dread of opinion to keep him within bounds. Who then is going to say Nay to his temptations if not his conscience?

And besides—this, remember, is the place and the moment of perfectly open talk—I think that all ambitions are lawful except those which climb upward on the miseries or credulities of mankind. All intellectual and artistic ambitions are permissible, up to and even beyond the limit of prudent sanity. They can hurt no one. If they are mad, then so much the worse for the artist. Indeed, as virtue is said to be, such ambitions are their own reward. Is it such a very mad presumption to believe in the sovereign power of one's art, to try for other means, for other ways of affirming this belief in the deeper appeal of one's work? To try to go deeper is not to be insensible. An historian of hearts is not an historian of emotions, yet he penetrates further, restrained as he may be, since his aim is to reach the very fount of laughter and tears. The sight of human affairs deserves admiration and pity. They are worthy of respect, too. And he is not insensible who pays them the undemonstrative tribute of a sigh which is not a sob, and of a smile which is not a grin. Resignation, not mystic, not detached, but resignation open-eyed, conscious, and informed by love, is the only one of our feelings for which it is impossible to become a sham.

Not that I think resignation the last word of wisdom. I am too much the creature of my time for that. But I think that the proper wisdom is to will what the gods will, without perhaps being certain what their will is— or even if they have a will of their own. And in this matter of life and art it is not the Why that matters so much to our happiness as the How. As the Frenchman said, "*Il y a toujours la manière.*"* Very true. Yes. There is the manner. The manner in laughter, in tears, in irony, in indignations and enthusiasms, in judgments—and even in love; the manner in which, as in the features and character of a human face, the inner truth is foreshadowed for those who know how to look at their kind.

Those who read me know my conviction that the world, the temporal world, rests on a few very simple ideas; so simple that they must be as old as the hills. It rests notably, among others, on the idea of Fidelity. At a time when nothing which is not revolutionary in some way or other can expect to attract much attention I have not been revolutionary in my writings. The revolutionary spirit is mighty convenient in this, that it frees one from all scruples as regards ideas. Its hard, absolute optimism is repulsive to my mind by the menace of fanaticism and intolerance it contains. No doubt one should smile at these things; but, imperfect Esthete, I am no better Philosopher. All claim to special righteousness awakens in me that scorn and anger from which a philosophical mind should be free. . . .

I fear that trying to be conversational I have only managed to be unduly discursive. I have never been very well acquainted with the art of conversation— that art which, I understand, is supposed to be lost now. My young days, the days when one's habits and character are formed, have been rather familiar with long silences. Such voices as broke into them were anything but conversational. No. I haven't got the habit. Yet this discursiveness is not so irrelevant to the handful of pages which follow. They, too, have been charged with discursiveness, with disregard of chronological order (which is in itself a crime) with unconventionality of form (which is an impropriety). I was told severely that the public would view with displeasure the informal character of my recollections. "Alas!" I protested, mildly. "Could I begin with the sacramental words, 'I was born on such a date in such a place?' The remoteness of the locality would have robbed the statement of all interest. I haven't lived through wonderful adventures to be related *seriatim.*[*] I haven't known distinguished men on whom I could pass fatuous remarks. I haven't been mixed up with great or scandalous affairs. This is but a bit of psychological document, and even so, I haven't written it with a view to put forward any conclusion of my own."

But my objector was not placated. These were good reasons for not writing at all—not a defence of what stood written already, he said.

I admit that almost anything, anything in the world, would serve as a good reason for not writing at all. But since I have written them, all I want to say in their defence is that these memories put down without any regard for established conventions have not been thrown off without system and purpose. They have their hope and their aim. The hope that from the reading of these pages there may emerge at last the vision of a personality; the man behind the books so fundamentally dissimilar as, for instance, "Almayer's Folly" and "The Secret Agent," and yet a coherent, justifiable personality both in its origin and in its action. This is the hope. The immediate aim, closely associated with the hope, is to give the record of personal memories by presenting faithfully the feelings and sensations connected with the writing of my first book and with my first contact with the sea.

In the purposely mingled resonance of this double strain a friend here and there will perhaps detect a subtle accord.

J. C. K.

A PERSONAL RECORD

A PERSONAL RECORD

I

Books may be written in all sorts of places. Verbal inspiration may enter the berth of a mariner on board a ship frozen fast in a river in the middle of a town;*and since saints are supposed to look benignantly on humble believers, I indulge in the pleasant fancy that the shade of old Flaubert*—who imagined himself to be (amongst other things) a descendant of Vikings—might have hovered with amused interest over the decks of a 2,000-ton steamer called the *Adowa*,* on board of which, gripped by the inclement winter alongside a quay in Rouen, the tenth chapter of "Almayer's Folly" was begun. With interest, I say, for was not the kind Norman giant with enormous moustaches and a thundering voice the last of the Romantics? Was he not, in his unworldly, almost ascetic, devotion to his art a sort of literary, saint-like hermit?

"'*It has set at last,*' *said Nina to her mother, pointing to the hills behind which the sun had sunk.*" . . . These words of Almayer's romantic daughter I remember tracing on the grey paper of a pad which rested on the blanket of my bed-place. They referred to a sunset in Malayan Isles, and shaped themselves in my mind, in a hallucinated vision of forests and rivers and seas, far removed from a commercial and yet romantic town of the northern hemisphere. But at that moment the mood of visions and words was cut short by the third

3

officer, a cheerful and casual youth, coming in with a bang of the door and the exclamation: "You've made it jolly warm in here."

It was warm. I had turned on the steam-heater after placing a tin under the leaky water-cock—for perhaps you do not know that water will leak where steam will not. I am not aware of what my young friend had been doing on deck all that morning, but the hands he rubbed together vigorously were very red and imparted to me a chilly feeling by their mere aspect. He has remained the only banjoist of my acquaintance, and being also a younger son of a retired colonel, the poem of Mr. Kipling,* by a strange aberration of associated ideas, always seems to me to have been written with an exclusive view to his person. When he did not play the banjo he loved to sit and look at it. He proceeded to this sentimental inspection, and after meditating a while over the strings under my silent scrutiny, inquired airily:

"What are you always scribbling there, if it's fair to ask?"

It was a fair enough question, but I did not answer him, and simply turned the pad over with a movement of instinctive secrecy: I could not have told him he had put to flight the psychology of Nina Almayer, her opening speech of the tenth chapter and the words of Mrs. Almayer's wisdom which were to follow in the ominous oncoming of a tropical night. I could not have told him that Nina had said: "It has set at last." He would have been extremely surprised and perhaps have dropped his precious banjo. Neither could I have told him that the sun of my sea-going was setting too, even as I wrote the words expressing the impatience of passionate youth bent on its desire. I did not know this myself, and it is safe to say he would not have cared, though he was an excellent young fellow and treated me with more deference than, in our relative positions, I was strictly entitled to.

He lowered a tender gaze on his banjo and I went on looking through the port-hole. The round opening framed in its brass rim a fragment of the quays, with a row of casks ranged on the frozen ground and the tail-end of a great cart. A red-nosed carter in a blouse and a woollen nightcap leaned against the wheel. An idle, strolling custom-house guard, belted over his blue *capote*, had the air of being depressed by exposure to the weather and the monotony of official existence. The background of grimy houses found a place in the picture framed by my port-hole, across a wide stretch of paved quay, brown with frozen mud. The colouring was sombre, and the most conspicuous feature was a little *café* with curtained windows and a shabby front of white woodwork, corresponding with the squalor of these poorer quarters bordering the river. We had been shifted down there from another berth in the neighbourhood of the Opera House, where that same port-hole gave me a view of quite another sort of *café*— the best in the town, I believe, and the very one where the worthy Bovary*and his wife, the romantic daughter of old Père Renault, had some refreshment after the memorable performance of an opera which was the tragic story of Lucia di Lammermoor*in a setting of light music.

I could recall no more the hallucination of the Eastern Archipelago which I certainly hoped to see again. The story of "Almayer's Folly" got put away under the pillow for that day. I do not know that I had any occupation to keep me away from it; the truth of the matter is, that on board that ship we were leading just then a contemplative life. I will not say anything of my privileged position. I was there "just to oblige," as an actor of standing may take a small part in the benefit performance of a friend.

As far as my feelings were concerned, I did not wish to be in that steamer at that time and in those circumstances. And perhaps I was not even wanted there in the usual sense in which a ship "wants" an officer. It was the first and last instance in my sea life when I served ship-owners who have remained completely shadowy to my apprehension. I do not mean this for the well-known firm of London ship-brokers which had chartered the ship to the, I will not say short-lived, but ephemeral Franco-Canadian Transport Company. A death leaves something behind, but there was never anything tangible left from the F.C.T.C. It flourished no longer than roses live,* and unlike the roses, it blossomed in the dead of winter, emitted a sort of faint perfume of adventure, and died before spring set in. But indubitably it was a company, it had even a house-flag, all white with the letters F.C.T.C. artfully tangled up in a complicated monogram. We flew it at our main-mast head, and now I have come to the conclusion that it was the only flag of its kind in existence. All the same, we on board, for many days, had the impression of being a unit of a large fleet with fortnightly departures for Montreal and Quebec as advertised in pamphlets and prospectuses which came aboard in a large package in Victoria Dock, London, just before we started for Rouen, France. And in the shadowy life of the F.C.T.C. lies the secret of that, my last employment in my calling, which in a remote sense interrupted the rhythmical development of Nina Almayer's story.

The then secretary of the London Shipmasters' Society, with its modest rooms in Fenchurch Street, was a man of indefatigable activity and the greatest devotion to his task. He is responsible for what was my last association with a ship. I call it that because it can hardly be called a sea-going experience. Dear Captain Froud*—it is impossible not to pay him the tribute of affectionate familiarity at this distance of years—had very sound views as to the advancement of knowledge and status for the whole body of the officers of the mercantile marine. He organised for us courses of professional lectures, St. John Ambulance classes, corresponded industriously with public bodies and members of Parliament on subjects touching the interests of the service; and as to the oncoming of some inquiry or commission relating to matters of the sea and to the work of seamen, it was a perfect godsend to his need of exerting himself on our corporate behalf. Together with this high sense of his official duties he had in him a vein of personal kindness, a strong disposition to do what good he could to the individual members of that craft of which in his time he had been a very excellent master. And what greater kindness can one do to a seaman than to put him in the way of employment? Captain Froud did not see why the Shipmasters' Society, besides its general guardianship of our interests, should not be unofficially an employment agency of the very highest class.

"I am trying to persuade all our great ship-owning firms to come to us for their men. There is nothing of a trade-union spirit about our society and I really don't see why they should not," he said once to me. "I am always telling the captains, too, that all things being equal they ought to give preference to the members of the society. In my position I can generally find for them what they want amongst our members or our associate members."

In my wanderings about London from West to East

and back again (I was very idle then), the two little rooms in Fenchurch Street were a sort of resting-place where my spirit, hankering after the sea, could feel itself nearer to the ships, the men, and the life of its choice—nearer there than any other spot of the solid earth. This resting-place used to be, at about five o'clock in the afternoon, full of men and tobacco smoke, but Captain Froud had the smaller room to himself, and there he granted private interviews, whose principal motive was to render service. Thus, one murky November afternoon, he beckoned me in with a crooked finger and that peculiar glance above his spectacles which is perhaps my strongest physical recollection of the man.

"I have had in here a shipmaster this morning," he said, getting back to his desk and motioning me to a chair, "who is in want of an officer. It's for a steamship. You know, nothing pleases me more than to be asked, but unfortunately I do not quite see my way. . . ."

As the outer room was full of men, I cast a wondering glance at the closed door, but he shook his head.

"Oh, yes, I should be only too glad to get that berth for one of them. But the fact of the matter is, the captain of that ship wants an officer who can speak French fluently, and that's not so easy to find. I do not know anybody myself but you. It's a second officer's berth, and, of course, you would not care . . . would you now? I know that it isn't what you are looking for."

It was not. I had given myself up to the idleness of a haunted man who looks for nothing but words wherein to capture his visions. But I admit that outwardly I resembled sufficiently a man who could make a second officer for a steamer chartered by a French company.

I showed no sign of being haunted by the fate of Nina and by the murmurs of tropical forests; and even my intimate intercourse with Almayer (a person of weak character) had not put a visible mark upon my features. For many years he and the world of his story had been the companions of my imagination without, I hope, impairing my ability to deal with the realities of sea life. I had had the man and his surroundings with me ever since my return from the eastern waters, some four years before the day of which I speak.

It was in the front sitting-room of furnished apartments in a Pimlico* square that they first began to live again with a vividness and poignancy quite foreign to our former real intercourse. I had been treating myself to a long stay on shore, and in the necessity of occupying my mornings, Almayer (that old acquaintance) came nobly to the rescue. Before long, as was only proper, his wife and daughter joined him round my table, and then the rest of that Pantai*band came full of words and gestures. Unknown to my respectable landlady, it was my practice directly after my breakfast to hold animated receptions of Malays, Arabs and half-castes. They did not clamour aloud for my attention. They came with silent and irresistible appeal—and the appeal, I affirm here, was not to my self-love or my vanity. It seems now to have had a moral character, for why should the memory of these beings, seen in their obscure sun-bathed existence, demand to express itself in the shape of a novel, except on the ground of that mysterious fellowship which unites in a community of hopes and fears all the dwellers on this earth?

I did not receive my visitors with boisterous rapture as the bearers of any gifts of profit or fame. There was no vision of a printed book before me as I sat writing

at that table, situated in a decayed part of Belgravia.*
After all these years, each leaving its evidence of slowly
blackened pages, I can honestly say that it is a sentiment akin to piety which prompted me to render in
words assembled with conscientious care the memory of
things far distant and of men who had lived.

But, coming back to Captain Froud and his fixed idea
of never disappointing ship-owners or ship-captains, it
was not likely that I should fail him in his ambition—
to satisfy at a few hours' notice the unusual demand for
a French-speaking officer. He explained to me that the
ship was chartered by a French company intending to
establish a regular monthly line of sailings from Rouen,
for the transport of French emigrants to Canada. But,
frankly, this sort of thing did not interest me very much.
I said gravely that if it were really a matter of keeping
up the reputation of the Shipmasters' Society, I would
consider it. But the consideration was just for form's
sake. The next day I interviewed the Captain, and I
believe we were impressed favourably with each other.
He explained that his chief mate was an excellent man
in every respect, and that he could not think of dis-
missing him so as to give me the higher position; but
that if I consented to come as second officer I would be
given certain special advantages—and so on.

I told him that if I came at all the rank really did not
matter.

"I am sure," he insisted, "you will get on first rate
with Mr. Paramor."

I promised faithfully to stay for two trips at least,
and it was in those circumstances that what was to be
my last connection with a ship began. And after all
there was not even one single trip. It may be that it
was simply the fulfilment of a fate, of that written
word on my forehead which apparently forbade me,

through all my sea wanderings, ever to achieve the crossing of the Western Ocean—using the words in that special sense in which sailors speak of Western Ocean trade, of Western Ocean packets, of Western Ocean hard cases. The new life attended closely upon the old, and the nine chapters of "Almayer's Folly" went with me to the Victoria Dock, whence in a few days we started for Rouen. I won't go so far as saying that the engaging of a man fated never to cross the Western Ocean was the absolute cause of the Franco-Canadian Transport Company's failure to achieve even a single passage. It might have been that, of course; but the obvious, gross obstacle was clearly the want of money. Four hundred and sixty bunks for emigrants were put together in the 'tween decks by industrious carpenters while we lay in the Victoria Dock, but never an emigrant turned up in Rouen—of which, being a humane person, I confess I was glad. Some gentlemen from Paris—I think there were three of them, and one was said to be the Chairman—turned up indeed and went from end to end of the ship, knocking their silk hats cruelly against the deck-beams. I attended them personally, and I can vouch for it that the interest they took in things was intelligent enough, though, obviously they had never seen anything of the sort before. Their faces as they went ashore wore a cheerfully inconclusive expression. Notwithstanding that this inspecting ceremony was supposed to be a preliminary to immediate sailing, it was then, as they filed down our gangway, that I received the inward monition that no sailing within the meaning of our charter-party would ever take place.

It must be said that in less than three weeks a move took place. When we first arrived we had been taken up with much ceremony well towards the centre of the town, and, all the street corners being placarded with the tricolour posters announcing the birth of our company, the *petit bourgeois** with his wife and family made a Sunday holiday from the inspection of the ship. I was always in evidence in my best uniform to give information as though I had been a Cook's tourists' interpreter, while our quarter-masters reaped a harvest of small change from personally conducted parties. But when the move was made—that move which carried us some mile and a half down the stream to be tied up to an altogether muddier and shabbier quay—then indeed the desolation of solitude became our lot. It was a complete and soundless stagnation; for, as we had the ship ready for sea to the smallest detail, as the frost was hard and the days short, we were absolutely idle— idle to the point of blushing with shame when the thought struck us that all the time our salaries went on. Young Cole was aggrieved because, as he said, we could not enjoy any sort of fun in the evening after loafing like this all day: even the banjo lost its charm since there was nothing to prevent his strumming on it all the time between the meals. The good Paramor—he was really a most excellent fellow—became unhappy as far as was possible to his cheery nature, till one dreary day I suggested out of sheer mischief, that he should employ the dormant energies of the crew in hauling both cables up on deck and turning them end for end.

For a moment Mr. Paramor was radiant. "Excellent idea!" but directly his face fell. "Why . . . Yes! But we can't make that job last more than three days," he muttered discontentedly. I don't know how long he expected us to be stuck on the river-side outskirts of Rouen, but I know that the cables got hauled up and turned end for end according to my satanic suggestion, put down again, and their very existence utterly forgotten, I believe, before a French river pilot came on board to take our ship down, empty as she came, into the Havre roads. You may think that this state of forced idleness favoured some advance in the fortunes of Almayer and his daughter. Yet it was not so. As if it were some sort of evil spell, my banjoist cabin-mate's interruption, as related above, had arrested them short at the point of that fateful sunset for many weeks together. It was always thus with this book, begun in '89 and finished in '94—with that shortest of all the novels which it was to be my lot to write. Between its opening exclamation calling Almayer to his dinner in his wife's voice and Abdullah's (his enemy) mental reference to the God of Islam—"The Merciful, the Compassionate"—which closes the book, there were to come several long sea passages, a visit (to use the elevated phraseology suitable to the occasion) to the scenes (some of them) of my childhood and the realization of childhood's vain words, expressing a light-hearted and romantic whim.

It was in 1868, when nine years old or thereabouts, that while looking at a map of Africa of the time and putting my finger on the blank space then representing the unsolved mystery of that continent, I said to myself with absolute assurance and an amazing audacity which are no longer in my character now:

"When I grow up I shall go *there*."

And of course I thought no more about it till after a quarter of a century or so an opportunity offered to go there—as if the sin of childish audacity was to be visited on my mature head. Yes. I did go there: *t'ere* being the region of Stanley Falls which in '68 was the blankest of blank spaces on the earth's figured surface. And the MS. of "Almayer's Folly," carried about me as if it were a talisman or a treasure, went *there* too.

That it ever came out of *there* seems a special dispensation of Providence; because a good many of my other properties, infinitely more valuable and useful to me, remained behind through unfortunate accidents of transportation. I call to mind, for instance, a specially awkward turn of the Congo* between Kinchassa and Leopoldsville—more particularly when one had to take it at night in a big canoe with only half the proper number of paddlers. I failed in being the second white man on record drowned at that interesting spot through the upsetting of a canoe. The first was a young Belgian officer, but the accident happened some months before my time, and he, too, I believe, was going home; not perhaps quite so ill as myself—but still he was going home. I got round the turn more or less alive, though I was too sick to care whether I did or not, and, always with "Almayer's Folly" amongst my diminishing baggage, I arrived at that delectable capital Boma,* where before the departure of the steamer which was to take me home I had the time to wish myself dead over and over again with perfect sincerity. At that date there were in existence only seven chapters of "Almayer's Folly," but the chapter in my history which followed was that of a long, long illness and very dismal convalescence. Geneva, or more precisely the hydropathic establishment of Champel,* is rendered for ever famous by the termination of the eighth chapter in the history of Almayer's decline and fall. The events of the ninth are inextricably mixed up with the details of the proper management of a waterside warehouse owned by a certain city firm whose name does not matter. But that work, undertaken to accustom myself again to the activities of a healthy existence, soon came to an end. The earth had nothing to hold me with for very long. And then that memorable story, like a cask of choice Madeira, got carried for three years to and fro upon the sea. Whether this treatment improved its flavour or not, of course I would not like to say. As far as appearance is concerned, it certainly did nothing of the kind. The whole MS. acquired a faded look and an ancient, yellowish complexion. It became at last unreasonable to suppose that anything in the world would ever happen to Almayer and Nina. And yet something most unlikely to happen on the high seas was to wake them up from their state of suspended animation.

What is it that Novalis* says? "It is certain my conviction gains infinitely the moment another soul will believe in it." And what is a novel if not a conviction of our fellow-men's existence strong enough to take upon itself a form of imagined life clearer than reality and whose accumulated verisimilitude of selected episodes puts to shame the pride of documentary history? Providence which saved my MS. from the Congo rapids brought it to the knowledge of a helpful soul far out on the open sea. It would be on my part the greatest ingratitude ever to forget the sallow, sunken face and the deep-set, dark eyes of the young Cambridge man* (he was a "passenger for his health" on board the good ship *Torrens**outward bound to Australia) who was the first reader of "Almayer's Folly"—the very first reader I ever had. "Would it bore you very much reading a MS. in a handwriting like mine?" I asked him one evening on a sudden impulse at the end of a longish conversation whose subject was Gibbon's History* Jacques (that was his name) was sitting in my cabin one stormy dog-watch*below, after bringing me a book to read from his own travelling store.

"Not at all," he answered with his courteous intonation and a faint smile. As I pulled a drawer open his suddenly aroused curiosity gave him a watchful expression. I wonder what he expected to see. A poem, maybe. All that's beyond guessing now. He was not a cold, but a calm man, still more subdued by disease—a man of few words and of an unassuming modesty in general intercourse, but with something uncommon in the whole of his person which set him apart from the undistinguished lot of our sixty passengers. His eyes had a thoughtful introspective look. In his attractive, reserved manner, and in a veiled, sympathetic voice, he asked:

"What is this?" "It is a sort of tale," I answered with an effort. "It is not even finished yet. Nevertheless, I would like to know what you think of it." He put the MS. in the breast-pocket of his jacket; I remember perfectly his thin brown fingers folding it lengthwise. "I will read it to-morrow," he remarked, seizing the door-handle, and then, watching the roll of the ship for a propitious moment, he opened the door and was gone. In the moment of his exit I heard the sustained booming of the wind, the swish of the water on the decks of the *Torrens*, and the subdued, as if distant, roar of the rising sea. I noted the growing disquiet in the great restlessness of the ocean, and responded professionally to it with the thought that at eight o'clock, in another half-hour or so at the furthest, the top-gallant sails would have to come off the ship.

Next day, but this time in the first dog-watch, Jacques entered my cabin. He had a thick, woollen muffler round his throat and the MS. was in his hand. He tendered it to me with a steady look but without a word. I took it in silence. He sat down on the couch and still said nothing. I opened and shut a drawer under my desk, on which a filled-up log-slate lay wide open in its wooden frame waiting to be copied neatly into the sort of book I was accustomed to write with care, the ship's log-book. I turned my back squarely on the desk. And even then Jacques never offered a word. "Well, what do you say?" I asked at last. "Is it worth finishing?" This question expressed exactly the whole of my thoughts.

"Distinctly," he answered in his sedate veiled voice, and then coughed a little.

"Were you interested?" I inquired further, almost in a whisper.

"Very much!"

In a pause I went on meeting instinctively the heavy rolling of the ship, and Jacques put his feet upon the couch. The curtain of my bed-place swung to and fro as it were a punkah, the bulkhead lamp circled in its gimbals, and now and then the cabin door rattled slightly in the gusts of wind. It was in latitude 40 south, and nearly in the longitude of Greenwich, as far as I can remember, that these quiet rites of Almayer's and Nina's resurrection were taking place. In the prolonged silence it occurred to me that there was a good deal of retrospective writing in the story as far as it went. Was it intelligible in its action, I asked myself, as if already the story-teller were being born into the body of a seaman. But I heard on deck the whistle of the officer of the watch and remained on the alert to catch the order that was to follow this call to attention. It reached me as a faint, fierce shout to "Square the yards." "Aha!" I thought to myself, "a westerly blow coming on." Then I turned to my very first reader, who, alas! was not to live long enough to know the end of the tale.

"Now let me ask you one more thing: Is the story quite clear to you as it stands?"

He raised his dark, gentle eyes to my face and seemed surprised.

"Yes! Perfectly."

This was all I was to hear from his lips concerning the merits of "Almayer's Folly." We never spoke together of the book again. A long period of bad weather set in and I had no thoughts left but for my duties, whilst poor Jacques caught a fatal cold and had to keep close in his cabin. When we arrived at Adelaide the first reader of my prose went at once up-country, and died rather suddenly in the end, either in Australia or it may be on the passage while going home through the Suez Canal. I am not sure which it was now, and I do not think I ever heard precisely; though I made inquiries about him from some of our return passengers who, wandering about to "see the country" during the ship's stay in port, had come upon him here and there. At last we sailed, homeward bound, and still not one line was added to the careless scrawl of the many pages which poor Jacques had had the patience to read with the very shadows of Eternity gathering already in the hollows of his kind, steadfast eyes.

The purpose instilled into me by his simple and final "Distinctly" remained dormant, yet alive to await its opportunity. I dare say I am compelled, unconsciously compelled, now to write volume after volume, as in past years I was compelled to go to sea, voyage after voyage. Leaves must follow upon each other as leagues used to follow in the days gone by, on and on to the appointed end, which, being Truth itself, is One—one for all men and for all occupations.

I do not know which of the two impulses has appeared more mysterious and more wonderful to me. Still, in writing, as in going to sea, I had to wait my opportunity. Let me confess here that I was never one

of those wonderful fellows that would go afloat in a
wash-tub for the sake of the fun, and if I may pride myself upon my consistency it was ever just the same with
my writing. Some men, I have heard, write in railway
carriages, and could do it, perhaps, sitting cross-legged
on a clothes-line; but I must confess that my sybaritic
disposition will not consent to write without something
at least resembling a chair. Line by line, rather than
page by page, was the growth of "Almayer's Folly."

And so it happened that I very nearly lost the MS.,
advanced now to the first words of the ninth chapter, in
the Friedrichstrasse railway station (that's in Berlin,
you know) on my way to Poland, or more precisely
Ukraine.* On an early, sleepy morning, changing trains
in a hurry, I left my Gladstone bag*in a refreshment-
room. A worthy and intelligent *Kofferträger** rescued
it. Yet in my anxiety I was not thinking of the MS. but
of all the other things that were packed in the bag.

In Warsaw, where I spent two days, those wandering
pages were never exposed to the light, except once, to
candle-light, while the bag lay open on a chair. I was
dressing hurriedly to dine at a sporting club. A friend
of my childhood (he had been in the Diplomatic Service,
but had turned to growing wheat on paternal acres,
and we had not seen each other for over twenty years)
was sitting on the hotel sofa waiting to carry me off
there.

"You might tell me something of your life while you
are dressing," he suggested kindly.

I do not think I told him much of my life-story either
then or later. The talk of the select little party with
which he made me dine was extremely animated and
embraced most subjects under heaven, from big-game
shooting in Africa to the last poem published in a very
modernist review, edited by the very young and

patronised by the highest society. But it never touched upon "Almayer's Folly," and next morning, in uninterrupted obscurity, this inseparable companion went on rolling with me in the south-east direction towards the Government of Kiev.

At that time there was an eight-hours' drive, if not more, from the railway station* to the country house* which was my destination.

"Dear boy" (these words were always written in English)—so ran the last letter from that house received in London—"Get yourself driven to the only inn in the place, dine as well as you can, and some time in the evening my own confidential servant, factotum* and major-domo, a Mr. V. S. (I warn you he is of noble extraction), will present himself before you, reporting the arrival of the small sledge which will take you here on the next day. I send with him my heaviest fur, which I suppose, with such overcoats as you may have with you, will keep you from freezing on the road."

Sure enough, as I was dining, served by a Hebrew waiter, in an enormous barn-like bedroom with a freshly painted floor, the door opened and, in a travelling costume of long boots, big sheep-skin cap and a short coat girt with a leather belt, the Mr. V. S. (of noble extraction), a man of about thirty-five, appeared with an air of perplexity on his open and moustachioed countenance. I got up from the table and greeted him in Polish, with, I hope, the right shade of consideration demanded by his noble blood and his confidential position. His face cleared up in a wonderful way. It appeared that, notwithstanding my uncle's* earnest assurances, the good fellow had remained in doubt of our understanding each other. He imagined I would talk to him in some foreign language. I was told that his last words on getting into the sledge to come to meet me shaped an anxious exclamation:

"Well! Well! Here I am going, but God only knows how I am to make myself understood to our master's nephew."

We understood each other very well from the first. He took charge of me as if I were not quite of age. I had a delightful boyish feeling of coming home from school when he muffled me up next morning in an enormous bear-skin travelling-coat and took his seat protectively by my side. The sledge was a very small one and it looked utterly insignificant, almost like a toy behind the four big bays harnessed two and two. We three, counting the coachman, filled it completely. He was a young fellow with clear blue eyes; the high collar of his livery fur coat framed his cheery countenance and stood all round level with the top of his head.

"Now, Joseph," my companion addressed him, "do you think we shall manage to get home before six?" His answer was that we would surely, with God's help, and providing there were no heavy drifts in the long stretch between certain villages whose names came with an extremely familiar sound to my ears. He turned out an excellent coachman with an instinct for keeping the road amongst the snow-covered fields and a natural gift of getting the best out of the horses.

"He is the son of that Joseph that I supposed the Captain remembers. He who used to drive the Captain's late grandmother of holy memory," remarked V. S. busy tucking fur rugs about my feet.

I remembered perfectly the trusty Joseph who used to drive my grandmother. Why! he it was who let me hold the reins for the first time in my life and allowed me to play with the great four-in-hand whip outside the doors of the coach-house.

"What became of him?" I asked. "He is no longer serving, I suppose."

"He served our master," was the reply. "But he died of cholera ten years ago now—that great epidemic we had. And his wife died at the same time—the whole houseful of them, and this is the only boy that was left."

The MS. of "Almayer's Folly" was reposing in the bag under our feet.

I saw again the sun setting on the plains as I saw it in the travels of my childhood. It set, clear and red, dipping into the snow in full view as if it were setting on the sea. It was twenty-three years since I had seen the sun set over that land; and we drove on in the darkness which fell swiftly upon the livid expanse of snows till, out of the waste of a white earth joining a be-starred sky, surged up black shapes, the clumps of trees about a village of the Ukrainian plain. A cottage or two glided by, a low interminable wall and then, glimmering and winking through a screen of fir-trees, the lights of the master's house.

That very evening the wandering MS. of "Almayer's Folly" was unpacked and unostentatiously laid on the writing-table in my room, the guest-room which had been, I was informed in an affectedly careless tone, awaiting me for some fifteen years or so. It attracted no attention from the affectionate presence hovering round the son of the favourite sister.

"You won't have many hours to yourself while you are staying with me, brother," he said—this form of address borrowed from the speech of our peasants being the usual expression of the highest good humour in a moment of affectionate elation. "I shall be always coming in for a chat."

As a matter of fact we had the whole house to chat in and were everlastingly intruding upon each other. I

invaded the retirement of his study, where the principal
feature was a colossal silver inkstand presented to him
on his fiftieth year by a subscription of all his wards
then living. He had been guardian of many orphans of
land-owning families from the three southern provinces
—ever since the year 1860. Some of them had been my
schoolfellows and playmates, but not one of them, girls
or boys, that I know of, has ever written a novel. One
or two were older than myself—considerably older, too.
One of them, a visitor I remember in my early years,
was the man who first put me on horseback, and his
four-horse bachelor turn-out, his perfect horsemanship
and general skill in manly exercises was one of my
earliest admirations. I seem to remember my mother
looking on from a colonnade in front of the dining-room
windows as I was lifted upon the pony, held, for all I
know, by the very Joseph—the groom attached specially
to my grandmother's service—who died of cholera. It
was certainly a young man in a dark blue, tail-less coat
and huge Cossack trousers, that being the livery of the
men about the stables. It must have been in 1864, but
reckoning by another mode of calculating time, it was
certainly in the year* in which my mother obtained
permission to travel south and visit her family, from the
exile into which she had followed my father. For that,
too, she had had to ask permission,*and I know that one
of the conditions of that favour was that she should be
treated exactly as a condemned exile herself. Yet a
couple of years later, in memory of her eldest brother*
who had served in the Guards and dying early left hosts
of friends and a loved memory in the great world of
St. Petersburg, some influential personages procured for
her this permission—it was officially called the "Highest
Grace"—of a three months' leave from exile.

This is also the year in which I first begin to remember

my mother with more distinctness than a mere loving, wide-browed, silent, protecting presence, whose eyes had a sort of commanding sweetness; and I also remember, the great gathering of all the relations from near and far, and the grey heads of the family friends paying her the homage of respect and love in the house of her favourite brother who, a few years later, was to take the place for me of both my parents.

I did not understand the tragic significance of it all at the time, though indeed I remember that doctors also came. There were no signs of invalidism about her—but I think that already they had pronounced her doom unless perhaps the change to a southern climate could re-establish her declining strength. For me it seems the very happiest period of my existence. There was my cousin, a delightful, quick-tempered little girl, some months younger than myself, whose life, lovingly watched over, as if she were a royal princess, came to an end with her fifteenth year. There were other children too, many of whom are dead now, and not a few whose very names I have forgotten. Over all this hung the oppressive shadow of the great Russian Empire—the shadow lowering with the darkness of a new-born national hatred fostered by the Moscow school of journalists*against the Poles after the ill-omened rising of 1863.

This is a far cry back from the MS. of "Almayer's Folly," but the public record of these formative impressions is not the whim of an uneasy egotism. These, too, are things human, already distant in their appeal. It is meet that something more should be left for the novelist's children than the colours and figures of his own hard-won creation. That which in their grown-up years may appear to the world about them as the most enigmatic side of their natures and perhaps must remain for ever obscure even to themselves, will be their unconscious response to the still voice of that inexorable past from which his work of fiction and their personalities are remotely derived.

Only in men's imagination does every truth find an effective and undeniable existence. Imagination, not invention, is the supreme master of art as of life. An imaginative and exact rendering of authentic memories may serve worthily that spirit of piety towards all things human which sanctions the conceptions of a writer of tales, and the emotions of the man reviewing his own experience.

II

As I have said, I was unpacking my luggage after a journey from London into Ukraine. The MS. of "Almayer's Folly"—my companion already for some three years or more, and then in the ninth chapter of its age—was deposited unostentatiously on the writing-table placed between two windows. It didn't occur to me to put it away in the drawer the table was fitted with, but my eye was attracted by the good form of the same drawer's brass handles. Two candelabra, with four candles each, lighted up festally the room which had waited so many years for the wandering nephew. The blinds were down.

Within five hundred yards of the chair on which I sat stood the first peasant hut of the village—part of my maternal grandfather's estate, the only part remaining in the possession of a member of the family; and beyond the village in the limitless blackness of a winter's night there lay the great unfenced fields—not a flat and severe plain, but a kindly, bread-giving land of low, rounded ridges, all white now, with the black patches of timber nestling in the hollows. The road by which I had come ran through a village with a turn just outside the gates closing the short drive. Somebody was abroad on the deep snow-track; a quick tinkle of bells stole gradually into the stillness of the room like a tuneful whisper.

My unpacking had been watched over by the servant who had come to help me, and, for the most part, had been standing attentive but unnecessary at the door of

the room. I did not want him in the least, but I did not
like to tell him to go away. He was a young fellow,
certainly more than ten years younger than myself; I
had not been—I won't say in that place but within
sixty miles of it, ever since the year '67; yet his guileless
physiognomy of the open peasant type seemed strangely
familiar. It was quite possible that he might have
been a descendant, a son or even a grandson, of the
servants whose friendly faces had been familiar to me
in my early childhood. As a matter of fact he had no
such claim on my consideration. He was the product of
some village near by and was there on his promotion,
having learned the service in one or two houses as
pantry-boy. I know this because I asked the worthy
V—— next day. I might well have spared the question. I discovered before long that all the faces about
the house and all the faces in the village: the grave faces
with long moustaches of the heads of families, the
downy faces of the young men, the faces of the little
fair-haired children, the handsome, tanned, wide-
browed faces of the mothers seen at the doors of the
huts, were as familiar to me as though I had known them
all from childhood, and my childhood were a matter of
the day before yesterday.

The tinkle of the traveller's bells, after growing
louder, had faded away quickly, and the tumult of
barking dogs in the village had calmed down at last.
My uncle, lounging in the corner of a small couch,
smoked his long Turkish *chibouk* in silence.

"This is an extremely nice writing-table you have
got for my room," I remarked.

"It is really your property," he said, keeping his eyes
on me, with an interested and wistful expression, as he
had done ever since I had entered the house. "Forty
years ago your mother used to write at this very table.

In our house in Oratow*it stood in the little sitting-room
which, by a tacit arrangement, was given up to the
girls—I mean to your mother and her sister who died
so young. It was a present to them jointly from our
uncle Nicholas B.*when your mother was seventeen and
your aunt* two years younger. She was a very dear,
delightful girl, that aunt of yours, of whom I suppose
you know nothing more than the name. She did not
shine so much by personal beauty and a cultivated
mind, in which your mother was far superior. It was
her good sense, the admirable sweetness of her nature,
her exceptional facility and ease in daily relations
that endeared her to everybody. Her death was a
terrible grief and a serious moral loss for us all. Had
she lived she would have brought the greatest blessings
to the house it would have been her lot to enter, as wife,
mother and mistress of a household. She would have
created round herself an atmosphere of peace and content which only those who can love unselfishly are able
to evoke. Your mother—of far greater beauty, ex-
ceptionally distinguished in person, manner and intellect—had a less easy disposition. Being more
brilliantly gifted, she also expected more from life. At
that trying time, especially, we were greatly concerned
about her state. Suffering in her health from the shock
of her father's*death (she was alone in the house with
him when he died suddenly), she was torn by the inward struggle between her love for the man*whom she
was to marry in the end and her knowledge of her dead
father's declared objection to that match. Unable to
bring herself to disregard that cherished memory and
that judgment she had always respected and trusted,
and, on the other hand, feeling the impossibility to resist a sentiment so deep and so true, she could not have
been expected to preserve her mental and moral bal-

ance. At war with herself, she could not give to others
that feeling of peace which was not her own. It was
only later, when united at last with the man of her
choice, that she developed those uncommon gifts of
mind and heart which compelled the respect and admiration even of our foes. Meeting with calm fortitude the cruel trials of a life reflecting all the national
and social misfortunes of the community, she realised
the highest conceptions of duty as a wife, a mother
and a patriot, sharing the exile of her husband and
representing nobly the ideal of Polish womanhood.*
Our Uncle Nicholas was not a man very accessible to
feelings of affection. Apart from his worship for
Napoleon the Great, he loved really, I believe, only
three people in the world: his mother—your great-
grandmother, whom you have seen but cannot possibly
remember; his brother, our father, in whose house he
lived for so many years; and of all of us, his nephews
and nieces grown up around him, your mother alone.
The modest, lovable qualities of the youngest sister he
did not seem able to see. It was I who felt most profoundly this unexpected stroke of death falling upon the
family less than a year after I had become its head. It
was terribly unexpected. Driving home one wintry
afternoon to keep me company in our empty house,
where I had to remain permanently administering the
estate and attending to the complicated affairs—the
girls took it in turn week and week about—driving, as
I said, from the house of the Countess Tekla Potocka,
where our invalid mother was staying then to be near a
doctor, they lost the road and got stuck in a snowdrift.
She was alone with the coachman and old Valery, the
personal servant of our late father. Impatient of delay while they were trying to dig themselves out, she
jumped out of the sledge and went to look for the road

herself. All this happened in '51, not ten miles from the house in which we are sitting now. The road was soon found, but snow had begun to fall thickly again, and they were four more hours getting home. Both the men took off their sheepskin-lined great-coats and used all their own rugs to wrap her up against the cold, notwithstanding her protests, positive orders and even struggles, as Valery afterwards related to me. 'How could I,' he remonstrated with her, 'go to meet the blessed soul of my late master if I let any harm come to you while there's a spark of life left in my body?' When they reached home, at last, the poor old man was stiff and speechless from exposure, and the coachman was in not much better plight, though he had the strength to drive round to the stables himself. To my reproaches for venturing out at all in such weather, she answered characteristically that she could not bear the thought of abandoning me to my cheerless solitude. It is incomprehensible how it was that she was allowed to start. I suppose it had to be! She made light of the cough which came on next day, but shortly afterwards inflammation of the lungs set in, and in three weeks she was no more! She was the first to be taken away of the young generation under my care. Behold the vanity of all hopes and fears! I was the most frail at birth of all the children. For years I remained so delicate that my parents had but little hope of bringing me up; and yet I have survived five brothers and two sisters, and many of my contemporaries; I have outlived my wife and daughter, too—and from all those who have had some knowledge at least of these old times, you alone are left. It has been my lot to lay in an early grave many honest hearts, many brilliant promises, many hopes full of life."

He got up brusquely, sighed, and left me, saying:

"We will dine in half an hour." Without moving, I listened to his quick steps resounding on the waxed floor of the next room, traversing the ante-room lined with bookshelves, where he paused to put his *chibouk* in the pipe-stand before passing into the drawing-room (these were all *en suite*),* where he became inaudible on the thick carpet. But I heard the door of his study-bedroom close. He was then sixty-two years old and had been for a quarter of a century the wisest, the firmest, the most indulgent of guardians, extending over me a paternal care and affection, a moral support which I seemed to feel always near me in the most distant parts of the earth.

As to Mr. Nicholas B., sub-lieutenant of 1808, lieutenant of 1813 in the French Army, and for a short time *Officier d'Ordonnance**of Marshal Marmont;*afterwards Captain in the 2nd Regiment of Mounted Rifles in the Polish Army—such as it existed up to 1830 in the reduced kingdom established by the Congress of Vienna —I must say that from all that more distant past, known to me traditionally and a little *de visu*,* and called out by the words of the man just gone away, he remains the most incomplete figure. It is obvious that I must have seen him in '64, for it is certain that he would not have missed the opportunity of seeking my mother for what he must have known would be the last time. From my early boyhood to this day, if I try to call up his image, a sort of mist rises before my eyes, a mist in which I perceive vaguely only a neatly brushed head of white hair (which is exceptional in the case of the B. family, where it is the rule for men to go bald in a becoming manner, before thirty) and a thin, curved, dignified nose, a feature in strict accordance with the physical tradition of the B. family. But it is not by these fragmentary remains of perishable mortality that he lives in my memory. I knew, at a very early age, that my grand-uncle Nicholas B. was a Knight of the Legion of Honour*and that he had also the Polish Cross for valour, *Virtuti Militari*.* The knowledge of these glorious facts inspired in me an admiring veneration; yet it is not that sentiment, strong as it was, which resumes for me the force and the significance of his personality. It is overborne by another and complex impression of awe, compassion and horror. Mr. Nicholas B. remains for me the unfortunate and miserable (but heroic) being who once upon a time had eaten a dog.

It is a good forty years since I heard the tale, and the effect has not worn off yet. I believe this is the very first, say, realistic, story I heard in my life; but all the same, I don't know why I should have been so frightfully impressed. Of course I know what our village dogs look like—but still . . . No! At this very day, recalling the horror and compassion of my childhood, I ask myself whether I am right in disclosing to a cold and fastidious world that awful episode in the family history. I ask myself—is it right?—especially as the B. family had always been honourably known in a wide country-side for the delicacy of their tastes in the matter of eating and drinking. But upon the whole, and considering that this gastronomical degradation overtaking a gallant young officer lies really at the door of the Great Napoleon, I think that to cover it up by silence would be an exaggeration of literary restraint. Let the truth stand here. The responsibility rests with the Man of St. Helena*in view of his deplorable levity in the conduct of the Russian campaign.* It was during the memorable retreat from Moscow that Mr. Nicholas B., in company of two brother officers—as to whose morality and natural refinement I know nothing—

bagged a dog on the outskirts of a village and subsequently devoured him. As far as I can remember, the weapon used was a cavalry sabre, and the issue of the sporting episode was rather more of a matter of life and death than if it had been an encounter with a tiger. A picket of Cossacks was sleeping in that village lost in the depths of the great Lithuanian forest. The three sportsmen had observed them from a hiding-place making themselves very much at home amongst the huts just before the early winter darkness set in at four o'clock. They had observed them with disgust and perhaps with despair. Late in the night the rash counsels of hunger overcame the dictates of prudence. Crawling through the snow, they crept up to the fence of dry branches which generally encloses a village in that part of Lithuania. What they expected to get, and in what manner, and whether this expectation was worth the risk, goodness only knows. However, these Cossack parties in most cases wandering without an officer, were known to guard themselves badly and often not at all. In addition, the village lying at a great distance from the line of French retreat, they could not suspect the presence of stragglers from the Grand Army. The three officers had strayed away in a blizzard from the main column and had been lost for days in the woods, which explains sufficiently the terrible straits to which they were reduced. Their plan was to try and attract the attention of the peasants in that one of the huts which was nearest to the enclosure; but as they were preparing to venture into the very jaws of the lion, so to speak, a dog (it is mighty strange that there was but one), a creature quite as formidable under the circumstances as a lion, began to bark on the other side of the fence . . . .

At this stage of the narrative, which I heard many

times (by request) from the lips of Captain Nicholas
B.'s sister-in-law, my grandmother,* I used to tremble
with excitement.

The dog barked. And if he had done no more than
bark, three officers of the Great Napoleon's army would
have perished honourably on the points of Cossacks'
lances, or perchance escaping the chase, would have
died decently of starvation. But before they had time
to think of running away, that fatal and revolting dog,
being carried away by the excess of his zeal, dashed
out through a gap in the fence. He dashed out and
died. His head, I understand, was severed at one
blow from his body. I understand also that, later on,
within the gloomy solitudes of the snow-laden woods,
when in a sheltering hollow, a fire had been lit by the
party, the condition of the quarry was discovered to be
distinctly unsatisfactory. It was not thin—on the
contrary, it seemed unhealthily obese; its skin showed
bare patches of an unpleasant character. However,
they had not killed that dog for the sake of the pelt.
He was large. . . . He was eaten. . . . The
rest is silence . . . A silence in which a small boy
shudders and says firmly:

"I could not have eaten that dog."

And his grandmother remarks with a smile:

"Perhaps you don't know what it is to be hungry."

I have learned something of it since. Not that I have
been reduced to eat dog. I have fed on the emble-
matical animal, which, in the language of the volatile
Gauls, is called *la vache enragée*,* I have lived on ancient
salt junk,* I know the taste of shark, of trepang,* of snake,
of nondescript dishes containing things without a
name—but of the Lithuanian village dog never! I
wish it to be distinctly understood that it is not I, but
my grand-uncle Nicholas, of the Polish landed gentry,

Chevalier de la Légion d'Honneur, etc. etc., who, in his young days, had eaten the Lithuanian dog.

I wish he had not. The childish horror of the deed clings absurdly to the grizzled man. I am perfectly helpless against it. Still, if he really had to, let us charitably remember that he had eaten him on active service, while bearing up bravely against the greatest military disaster of modern history, and, in a manner, for the sake of his country. He had eaten him to appease his hunger, no doubt, but also for the sake of an unappeasable and patriotic desire, in the glow of a great faith that lives still, and in the pursuit of a great illusion kindled like a false beacon by a great man to lead astray the effort of a brave nation.

*Pro patria !**

Looked at in that light it appears a sweet and decorous meal.

And looked at in the same light, my own diet of *la vache enragée* appears a fatuous and extravagant form of self-indulgence; for why should I, the son of a land which such men as these have turned up with their ploughshares and bedewed with their blood, undertake the pursuit of fantastic meals of salt junk and hard tack upon the wide seas? On the kindest view it seems an unanswerable question. Alas! I have the conviction that there are men of unstained rectitude who are ready to murmur scornfully the word desertion. Thus the taste of innocent adventure may be made bitter to the palate. The part of the inexplicable should be allowed for in appraising the conduct of men in a world where no explanation is final. No charge of faithlessness ought to be lightly uttered. The appearances of this perishable life are deceptive like everything that falls under the judgment of our imperfect senses. The inner voice may remain true enough in its secret counsel. The fidelity to a special tradition may last through the events of an unrelated existence, following faithfully, too, the traced way of an inexplicable impulse.

It would take too long to explain the intimate alliance of contradictions in human nature which makes love itself wear at times the desperate shape of betrayal. And perhaps there is no possible explanation. Indulgence—as somebody said—is the most intelligent of all the virtues. I venture to think that it is one of the least common, if not the most uncommon of all. I would not imply by this that men are foolish—or even most men. Far from it. The barber and the priest, backed by the whole opinion of the village, condemned justly the conduct of the ingenious hidalgo*who, sallying forth from his native place, broke the head of the muleteer, put to death a flock of inoffensive sheep, and went through very doleful experiences in a certain stable. God forbid that an unworthy churl should escape merited censure by hanging on to the stirrup-leather of the sublime *caballero*. His was a very noble, a very unselfish fantasy, fit for nothing except to raise the envy of baser mortals. But there is more than one aspect to the charm of that exalted and dangerous figure. He, too, had his frailties. After reading so many romances he desired naïvely to escape with his very body from the intolerable reality of things. He wished to meet eye to eye the valorous giant Brandabarbaran, Lord of Arabia, whose armour is made of the skin of a dragon, and whose shield, strapped to his arm, is the gate of a fortified city. O amiable and natural weakness! O blessed simplicity of a gentle heart without guile! Who would not succumb to such a consoling temptation? Nevertheless it was a form of self-indulgence, and the ingenious hidalgo of La Mancha was not a good citizen. The priest and the barber were not unreasonable in their strictures. Without going so far as the old King Louis-Philippe,* who used to say in his exile, "The people are never in fault"—one may admit that there must be some righteousness in the assent of a whole village. Mad!' Mad! He who kept in pious meditation the ritual vigil-of-arms by the well of an inn and knelt reverently to be knighted at daybreak by the fat, sly rogue of a landlord, has come very near perfection. He rides forth, his head encircled by a halo— the patron saint of all lives spoiled or saved by the irresistible grace of imagination. But he was not a good citizen.

Perhaps that and nothing else was meant by the well-remembered exclamation of my tutor.

It was in the jolly year 1873,* the very last year in which I have had a jolly holiday. There have been idle years afterwards, jolly enough in a way and not altogether without their lesson, but this year of which I speak was the year of my last schoolboy holiday. There are other reasons why I should remember that year, but they are too long to state formally in this place. Moreover they have nothing to do with that holiday. What has to do with the holiday is that before the day on which the remark was made we had seen Vienna, the Upper Danube, Munich, the Falls of the Rhine, the Lake of Constance—in fact it was a memorable holiday of travel. Of late we had been tramping slowly up the Valley of the Reuss. It was a delightful time. It was much more like a stroll than a tramp. Landing from a Lake of Lucerne steamer in Fluellen, we found ourselves at the end of the second day, with the dusk overtaking our leisurely footsteps, a little way beyond Hospenthal. This is not the day on which the remark was made: in the shadows of the deep valley and with the habitations of men left some way behind, our thoughts ran not upon the ethics of conduct but upon the simpler human problem of shelter and food. There did not seem anything of the kind in sight, and we were thinking of turning back when suddenly at a bend of the road we came upon a building, ghostly in the twilight.

At that time the work on the St. Gothard Tunnel was going on, and that magnificent enterprise of burrowing was directly responsible for the unexpected building standing all alone upon the very roots of the mountains. It was long, though not big at all; it was low; it was built of boards, without ornamentation, in barrack hut style, with the white window-frames quite flush with the yellow face of its plain front. And yet it was an hotel; it had even a name which I have forgotten. But there was no gold-laced door-keeper at its humble door. A plain but vigorous servant-girl answered our inquiries, then a man and woman who owned the place appeared. It was clear that no travellers were expected, or perhaps even desired, in this strange hostelry, which in its severe style resembled the house which surmounts the unseaworthy-looking hulls of the toy Noah's Arks, the universal possession of European childhood. However, its roof was not hinged and it was not full to the brim of slab-sided and painted animals of wood. Even the live tourist animal was nowhere in evidence. We had something to eat in a long, narrow room at one end of a long, narrow table, which, to my tired perception and to my sleepy eyes, seemed as if it would tilt up like a see-saw plank, since there was no one at the other end to balance it against our two dusty and travel-stained figures. Then we hastened upstairs to bed in a room smelling of pine planks, and I was fast asleep before my head touched the pillow.

In the morning my tutor*(he was a student of the Cracow University) woke me up early, and as we were dressing remarked: "There seems to be a lot of people staying in this hotel. I have heard a noise of talking up till eleven o'clock." This statement surprised me; I had heard no noise whatever, having slept like a top.

We went downstairs into the long and narrow dining-room with its long and narrow table. There were two rows of plates on it. At one of the many uncurtained windows stood a tall, bony man with a bald head set off by a bunch of black hair above each ear and with a long black beard. He glanced up from the paper he was reading and seemed genuinely astonished at our intrusion. By-and-by more men came in. Not one of them looked like a tourist. Not a single woman appeared. These men seemed to know each other with some intimacy, but I cannot say they were a very talkative lot. The bald-headed man sat down gravely at the head of the table. It all had the air of a family party. By-and-by, from one of the vigorous servant-girls in national costume, we discovered that the place was really a boarding-house for some English engineers engaged at the works of the St. Gothard Tunnel; and I could listen my fill to the sounds of the English language as far as it is used at a breakfast-table by men who do not believe in wasting many words on the mere amenities of life.

This was my first contact with British mankind apart from the tourist kind seen in the hotels of Zurich and Lucerne—the kind which has no real existence in a workaday world. I know now that the bald-headed man spoke with a strong Scotch accent. I have met many of his kind since, both ashore and afloat. The second engineer of the steamer *Mavis*,* for instance, ought to have been his twin brother. I cannot help

thinking that he really was, though for some reasons of
his own he assured me that he never had a twin brother.
Anyway, the deliberate, bald-headed Scot with the
coal-black beard appeared to my boyish eyes a very
romantic and mysterious person.

We slipped out unnoticed. Our mapped-out route
led over the Furca Pass towards the Rhône Glacier,
with the further intention of following down the trend
of the Häsli Valley. The sun was already declining
when we found ourselves on the top of the pass, and the
remark alluded to was presently uttered.

We sat down by the side of the road to continue the
argument begun half a mile or so before. I am certain
it was an argument because I remember perfectly how
my tutor argued and how without the power of reply
I listened with my eyes fixed obstinately on the ground.
A stir on the road made me look up—and then I saw
my unforgettable Englishman. There are acquaintances of later years, familiars, shipmates, whom I remember less clearly. He marched rapidly towards the
east (attended by a hang-dog Swiss guide) with the
mien of an ardent and fearless traveller. He was clad
in a knickerbocker suit, but as at the same time he wore
short socks under his laced boots, for reasons which,
whether hygienic or conscientious, were surely imaginative, his calves exposed to the public gaze and to the
tonic air of high altitudes, dazzled the beholder by the
splendour of their marble-like condition and their rich
tone of young ivory. He was the leader of a small
caravan. The light of a headlong, exalted satisfaction
with the world of men and the scenery of mountains
illumined his clean-cut, very red face, his short, silver-
white whiskers, his innocently eager and triumphant
eyes. In passing he cast a glance of kindly curiosity
and a friendly gleam of big, sound, shiny teeth towards

the man and the boy sitting like dusty tramps by the roadside, with a modest knapsack lying at their feet. His white calves twinkled sturdily, the uncouth Swiss guide with a surly mouth stalked like an unwilling bear at his elbow; a small train of three mules followed in single file the lead of this inspiring enthusiast. Two ladies rode past one behind the other, but from the way they sat I only saw their calm, uniform backs, and the long ends of blue veils hanging behind far down over their identical hat-brims. His two daughters, surely. An industrious luggage-mule, with unstarched ears and guarded by a slouching, sallow driver, brought up the rear. My tutor, after pausing for a look and a faint smile, resumed his earnest argument.

I tell you it was a memorable year! One does not meet such an Englishman twice in a lifetime. Was he in the mystic ordering of common events the ambassador of my future, sent out to turn the scale at a critical moment on the top of an Alpine pass, with the peaks of the Bernese Oberland for mute and solemn witnesses? His glance, his smile, the unextinguishable and comic ardour of his striving-forward appearance helped me to pull myself together. It must be stated that on that day and in the exhilarating atmosphere of that elevated spot I had been feeling utterly crushed. It was the year in which I had first spoken aloud of my desire to go to sea. At first, like those sounds that, ranging outside the scale to which men's ears are attuned, remain inaudible to our sense of hearing, this declaration passed unperceived. It was as if it had not been. Later on, by trying various tones, I managed to arouse here and there a surprised momentary attention—the "What was that funny noise?" sort of inquiry. Later on it was—"Did you hear what that boy said? What an extraordinary outbreak!" Presently a wave of scandalised astonishment (it could not have been greater if I had announced the intention of entering a Carthusian monastery) ebbing out of the educational and academical town of Cracow spread itself over several provinces. It spread itself shallow but far-reaching. It stirred up a mass of remonstrance, indignation, pitying wonder, bitter irony and downright chaff. I could hardly breathe under its weight, and certainly had no words for an answer. People wondered what Mr. T. B.* would do now with his worrying nephew and, I dare say, hoped kindly that he would make short work of my nonsense.

What he did was to come down all the way from Ukraine to have it out with me and to judge by himself, unprejudiced, impartial and just, taking his stand on the ground of wisdom and affection. As far as is possible for a boy whose power of expression is still unformed, I opened the secret of my thoughts to him and he in return allowed me a glimpse into his mind and heart; the first glimpse of an inexhaustible and noble treasure of clear thought and warm feeling, which through life was to be mine to draw upon with a never-deceived love and confidence. Practically, after several exhaustive conversations, he concluded that he would not have me later on reproach him for having spoiled my life by an unconditional opposition. But I must take time for serious reflection. And I must not only think of myself but of others; weigh the claims of affection and conscience against my own sincerity of purpose. "Think well what it all means in the larger issues, my boy," he exhorted me finally with special friendliness. "And meantime try to get the best place you can at the yearly examinations."

The scholastic year came to an end. I took a fairly good place at the exams, which for me (for certain

reasons)*happened to be a more difficult task than for
other boys. In that respect I could enter with a good
conscience upon that holiday which was like a long
visit *pour prendre congé**of the mainland of old Europe
I was to see so little of for the next four-and-twenty
years. Such, however, was not the avowed purpose of
that tour. It was rather, I suspect, planned in order
to distract and occupy my thoughts in other directions.
Nothing had been said for months of my going to sea.
But my attachment to my young tutor and his influence
over me were so well known that he must have received
a confidential mission to talk me out of my romantic
folly. It was an excellently appropriate arrangement, as
neither he nor I had ever had a single glimpse of the sea
in our lives. That was to come by-and-by for both
of us in Venice, from the outer shore of Lido. Meantime he had taken his mission to heart so well that I
began to feel crushed before we reached Zurich. He
argued in railway trains, in lake steamboats, he had
argued away for me the obligatory sunrise on the Righi,
by Jove! Of his devotion to his unworthy pupil there
can be no doubt. He had proved it already by two
years of unremitting and arduous care. I could not
hate him. But he had been crushing me slowly, and
when he started to argue on the top of the Furca Pass
he was perhaps nearer a success than either he or I
imagined. I listened to him in despairing silence, feeling that ghostly, unrealised and desired sea of my
dreams escape from the unnerved grip of my will.

The enthusiastic old Englishman had passed—and
the argument went on. What reward could I expect
from such a life at the end of my years, either in ambition, honour or conscience? An unanswerable question. But I felt no longer crushed. Then our eyes
met and a genuine emotion was visible in his as well as

in mine. The end came all at once. He picked up the knapsack suddenly and got on to his feet.

"You are an incorrigible, hopeless Don Quixote. That's what you are."

I was surprised. I was only fifteen and did not know what he meant exactly. But I felt vaguely flattered at the name of the immortal knight turning up in connection with my own folly, as some people would call it to my face. Alas! I don't think there was anything to be proud of. Mine was not the stuff the protectors of forlorn damsels, the redressers of this world's wrongs are made of; and my tutor was the man to know that best. Therein, in his indignation, he was superior to the barber and the priest when he flung at me an honoured name like a reproach.

I walked behind him for full five minutes; then without looking back he stopped. The shadows of distant peaks were lengthening over the Furca Pass. When I came up to him he turned to me and in full view of the Finster-Aarhorn, with his band of giant brothers rearing their monstrous heads against a brilliant sky, put his hand on my shoulder affectionately.

"Well! That's enough. We will have no more of it."

And indeed there was no more question of my mysterious vocation between us. There was to be no more question of it at all, nowhere or with any one. We began the descent of the Furca Pass conversing merrily. Eleven years later, month for month, I stood on Tower Hill on the steps of the St. Katherine's Dockhouse, a master*in the British Merchant Service. But the man who put his hand on my shoulder at the top of the Furca Pass was no longer living.

That very year of our travels he took his degree of the Philosophical Faculty—and only then his true vocation* declared itself. Obedient to the call, he entered at once upon the four-year course of the Medical Schools. A day*came when, on the deck of a ship moored in Calcutta, I opened a letter telling me of the end of an enviable existence. He had made for himself a practice in some obscure little town* of Austrian Galicia. And the letter went on to tell me how all the bereaved poor of the district, Christians and Jews alike, had mobbed the good doctor's coffin with sobs and lamentations at the very gate of the cemetery.

How short his years and how clear his vision! What greater reward in ambition, honour and conscience could he have hoped to win for himself when, on the top of the Furca Pass, he bade me look well to the end of my opening life.

III

THE devouring in a dismal forest of a luckless Lithuanian dog by my grand-uncle Nicholas B. in company of two other military and famished scarecrows, symbolised, to my childish imagination, the whole horror of the retreat from Moscow and the immorality of a conqueror's ambition. An extreme distaste for that objectionable episode has tinged the views I hold as to the character and achievements of Napoleon the Great. I need not say that these are unfavourable. It was morally reprehensible for that great captain to induce a simple-minded Polish gentleman to eat dog by raising in his breast a false hope of national independence. It has been the fate of that credulous nation to starve for upwards of a hundred years on a diet of false hopes and —well—dog. It is, when one thinks of it, a singularly poisonous regimen. Some pride in the national constitution which has survived a long course of such dishes is really excusable. But enough of generalising. Returning to particulars, Mr. Nicholas B. confided to his sister-in-law (my grandmother) in his misanthropically laconic manner that this supper in the woods had been nearly "the death of him." This is not surprising. What surprises me is that the story was ever heard of; for grand-uncle Nicholas differed in this from the generality of military men of Napoleon's time (and perhaps of all time), that he did not like to talk of his campaigns, which began at Friedland*and ended somewhere in the neighbourhood of Bar-le-Duc.* His admiration of the great Emperor was unreserved in

46

everything but expression. Like the religion of earnest men, it was too profound a sentiment to be displayed before a world of little faith. Apart from that he seemed as completely devoid of military anecdotes as though he had hardly ever seen a soldier in his life. Proud of his decorations, earned before he was twenty-five, he refused to wear the ribbons at the buttonhole in the manner practised to this day in Europe and even was unwilling to display the insignia on festive occasions, as though he wished to conceal them in the fear of appearing boastful. "It is enough that I have them," he used to mutter. In the course of thirty years they were seen on his breast only twice—at an auspicious marriage in the family and at the funeral of an old friend. That the wedding which was thus honoured was not the wedding of my mother, I learned only late in life, too late to bear a grudge against Mr. Nicholas B., who made amends at my birth by a long letter of congratulation containing the following prophecy: "He will see better times." Even in his embittered heart there lived a hope. But he was not a true prophet.

He was a man of strange contradictions. Living for many years in his brother's house, the home of many children, a house full of life, of animation, noisy with a constant coming and going of many guests, he kept his habits of solitude and silence. Considered as obstinately secretive in all his purposes, he was in reality the victim of a most painful irresolution in all matters of civil life. Under his taciturn, phlegmatic behaviour was hidden a faculty of short-lived, passionate anger. I suspect he had no talent for narrative; but it seemed to afford him sombre satisfaction to declare that he was the last man to ride over the bridge of the river Elster after the battle of Leipzig.* Lest some construction favourable to his valour should be put on the fact, he condescended to explain how it came to pass. It seems that shortly after the retreat began he was sent back to the town where some divisions of the French Army (and amongst them the Polish corps of Prince Joseph Poniatowski),* jammed hopelessly in the streets, were being simply exterminated by the troops of the Allied Powers. When asked what it was like in there, Mr. Nicholas B. muttered the only word "Shambles." Having delivered his message to the Prince he hastened away at once to render an account of his mission to the superior who had sent him. By that time the advance of the enemy had enveloped the town, and he was shot at from houses and chased all the way to the river bank by a disorderly mob of Austrian Dragoons and Prussian Hussars. The bridge had been mined early in the morning and his opinion was that the sight of the horsemen converging from many sides in the pursuit of his person alarmed the officer in command of the sappers and caused the premature firing of the charges. He had not gone more than 200 yards on the other side when he heard the sound of the fatal explosions. Mr. Nicholas B. concluded his bald narrative with the word "Imbecile," uttered with the utmost deliberation. It testified to his indignation at the loss of so many thousands of lives. But his phlegmatic physiognomy lighted up when he spoke of his only wound, with something resembling satisfaction. You will see that there was some reason for it when you learn that he was wounded in the heel. "Like his Majesty the Emperor Napoleon himself," he reminded his hearers with assumed indifference. There can be no doubt that the indifference was assumed if one thinks what a very distinguished sort of wound it was. In all the history of warfare there are, I believe, only three warriors

publicly known to have been wounded in the heel—
Achilles and Napoleon—demigods indeed—to whom the
familial piety of an unworthy descendant adds the
name of the simple mortal, Nicholas B.

The Hundred Days* found Mr. Nicholas B. staying
with a distant relative of ours, owner of a small estate in
Galicia. How he got there across the breadth of an
armed Europe and after what adventures I am afraid
will never be known now. All his papers were destroyed shortly before his death; but if there was
amongst them, as he affirmed, a concise record of his
life, then I am pretty sure it did not take up more than
a half-sheet of foolscap or so. This relative* of ours
happened to be an Austrian officer, who had left the
service after the battle of Austerlitz. Unlike Mr.
Nicholas B., who concealed his decorations, he liked to
display his honourable discharge in which he was
mentioned as *unschreckbar* (fearless) before the enemy.
No conjunction could seem more unpromising, yet it
stands in the family tradition that these two got on very
well together in their rural solitude.

When asked whether he had not been sorely tempted
during the Hundred Days to make his way again to
France and join the service of his beloved Emperor,
Mr. Nicholas B. used to mutter: "No money. No
horse. Too far to walk."

The fall of Napoleon and the ruin of national hopes
affected adversely the character of Mr. Nicholas B.
He shrank from returning to his province. But for that
there was also another reason. Mr. Nicholas B. and
his brother—my maternal grandfather—had lost their
father early, while they were quite children. Their
mother,* young still and left very well off, married again
a man* of great charm and of an amiable disposition but
without a penny. He turned out an affectionate and

careful stepfather; it was unfortunate though that while
directing the boys' education and forming their character by wise counsel he did his best to get hold of the
fortune by buying and selling land in his own name and
investing capital in such a manner as to cover up the
traces of the real ownership. It seems that such
practices can be successful if one is charming enough to
dazzle one's own wife permanently and brave enough to
defy the vain terrors of public opinion. The critical
time came when the elder of the boys on attaining his
majority in the year 1811 asked for the accounts and
some part at least of the inheritance to begin life upon.
It was then that the stepfather declared with calm
finality that there were no accounts to render and no
property to inherit. The whole fortune was his very
own. He was very good-natured about the young
man's misapprehension of the true state of affairs, but
of course felt obliged to maintain his position firmly.
Old friends came and went busily, voluntary mediators
appeared travelling on most horrible roads from the
most distant corners of the three provinces; and the
Marshal of the Nobility (*ex-officio* guardian of all well-
born orphans) called a meeting of landowners to
"ascertain in a friendly way how the misunderstanding
between X and his stepsons had arisen and devise
proper measures to remove the same." A deputation to
that effect visited X, who treated them to excellent
wines, but absolutely refused his ear to their remonstrances. As to the proposals for arbitration he simply
laughed at them; yet the whole province must have
been aware that fourteen years before, when he married
the widow, all his visible fortune consisted (apart from
his social qualities) in a smart four-horse turn-out with
two servants, with whom he went about visiting from
house to house; and as to any funds he might have pos-

sessed at that time their existence could only be inferred from the fact that he was very punctual in settling his modest losses at cards. But by the magic power of stubborn and constant assertion, there were found presently, here and there, people who mumbled that surely "there must be something in it." However, on his next nameday (which he used to celebrate by a great three-days' shooting-party), of all the invited crowd only two guests turned up, distant neighbours of no importance; one notoriously a fool, and the other a very pious and honest person but such a passionate lover of the gun that on his own confession he could not have refused an invitation to a shooting-party from the devil himself. X met this manifestation of public opinion with the serenity of an unstained conscience. He refused to be crushed. Yet he must have been a man of deep feeling, because, when his wife took openly the part of her children, he lost his beautiful tranquillity, proclaimed himself heart-broken and drove her out of the house, neglecting in his grief to give her enough time to pack her trunks.

This was the beginning of a lawsuit, an abominable marvel of chicane, which by the use of every legal subterfuge was made to last for many years. It was also the occasion for a display of much kindness and sympathy. All the neighbouring houses flew open for the reception of the homeless. Neither legal aid nor material assistance in the prosecution of the suit was ever wanting. X, on his side, went about shedding tears publicly over his stepchildren's ingratitude and his wife's blind infatuation; but as at the same time he displayed great cleverness in the art of concealing material documents (he was even suspected of having burnt a lot of historically interesting family papers), this scandalous litigation had to be ended by a compromise lest worse should befall. It was settled finally

by a surrender, out of the disputed estate, in full
satisfaction of all claims, of two villages with the names
of which I do not intend to trouble my readers. After
this lame and impotent conclusion neither the wife nor
the stepsons had anything to say to the man who had
presented the world with such a successful example
of self-help based on character, determination and
industry; and my great-grandmother, her health
completely broken down, died a couple of years later
in Carlsbad. Legally secured by a decree in the
possession of his plunder, X regained his wonted serenity
and went on living in the neighbourhood in a comfortable style and in apparent peace of mind. His big
shoots were fairly well attended again. He was never
tired of assuring people that he bore no grudge for what
was past; he protested loudly of his constant affection
for his wife and step-children. It was true, he said,
that they had tried their best to strip him as naked as a
Turkish saint in the decline of his days; and because he
had defended himself from spoliation, as anybody else
in his place would have done, they had abandoned him
now to the horrors of a solitary old age. Nevertheless,
his love for them survived these cruel blows. And there
might have been some truth in his protestations. Very
soon he began to make overtures of friendship to his
eldest stepson, my maternal grandfather; and when
these were peremptorily rejected, he went on renewing
them again and again with characteristic obstinacy.
For years he persisted in his efforts at reconciliation,
promising my grandfather to execute a will in his favour
if he only would be friends again to the extent of calling
now and then (it was fairly close neighbourhood for
these parts, forty miles or so), or even of putting in an
appearance for the great shoot on the name-day. My
grandfather was an ardent lover of every sport. His

temperament was as free from hardness and animosity as can be imagined. Pupil of the liberal-minded Benedictines who directed the only public school*of some standing then in the south, he had also read deeply the authors of the eighteenth century. In him Christian charity was joined to a philosophical indulgence for the failings of human nature. But the memory of these miserably anxious early years, his young man's years robbed of all generous illusions by the cynicism of the sordid lawsuit, stood in the way of forgiveness. He never succumbed to the fascination of the great shoot; and X, his heart set to the last on reconciliation with the draft of the will ready for signature kept by his bedside, died intestate. The fortune thus acquired and augmented by a wise and careful management passed to some distant relatives whom he had never seen and who even did not bear his name.

Meantime the blessing of general peace descended upon Europe. Mr. Nicholas B. bidding good-bye to his hospitable relative, the "fearless" Austrian officer, departed from Galicia, and without going near his native place, where the odious lawsuit was still going on, proceeded straight to Warsaw and entered the army of the newly constituted Polish kingdom under the sceptre of Alexander I.* Autocrat of all the Russias.

This Kingdom, created by the Vienna Congress as an acknowledgment to a nation of its former independent existence, included only the central provinces of the old Polish patrimony. A brother of the Emperor, the Grand Duke Constantine*(Pavlovitch), its Viceroy and Commander-in-Chief, married morganatically to a Polish lady to whom he was fiercely attached, extended this affection to what he called "My Poles" in a capricious and savage manner. Sallow in complexion, with a Tartar physiognomy and fierce little eyes, he

walked with his fists clenched, his body bent forward,
darting suspicious glances from under an enormous
cocked hat. His intelligence was limited and his sanity
itself was doubtful. The hereditary taint expressed
itself, in his case, not by mystic leanings as in his two
brothers, Alexander and Nicholas*(in their various ways,
for one was mystically liberal and the other mystically
autocratic), but by the fury of an uncontrollable temper
which generally broke out in disgusting abuse on the
parade ground. He was a passionate militarist and an
amazing drill-master. He treated his Polish Army as
a spoiled child treats a favourite toy, except that he did
not take it to bed with him at night. It was not small
enough for that. But he played with it all day and
every day, delighting in the variety of pretty uniforms
and in the fun of incessant drilling. This childish
passion, not for war but for mere militarism, achieved a
desirable result. The Polish Army, in its equipment, in
its armament and in its battlefield efficiency, as then
understood, became, by the end of the year 1830, a
first-rate tactical instrument. Polish peasantry (not
serfs)*served in the ranks by enlistment, and the officers
belonged mainly to the smaller nobility. Mr. Nicholas
B., with his Napoleonic record, had no difficulty in ob-
taining a lieutenancy, but the promotion in the Polish
Army was slow, because, being a separate organisation,
it took no part in the wars of the Russian Empire either
against Persia or Turkey. Its first campaign, against
Russia itself, was to be its last. In 1831,* on the outbreak of the Revolution, Mr. Nicholas B. was the
senior captain of his regiment. Some time before he
had been made head of the remount establishment
quartered outside the kingdom in our southern
provinces, whence almost all the horses for the Polish
cavalry were drawn. For the first time since he went

away from home at the age of eighteen to begin his
military life by the battle of Friedland, Mr. Nicholas
B. breathed the air of the "Border," his native air.
Unkind fate was lying in wait for him amongst the
scenes of his youth. At the first news of the rising in
Warsaw, all the remount establishment, officers, vets.,
and the very troopers, were put promptly under arrest
and hurried off in a body beyond the Dnieper to the
nearest town in Russia proper. From there they were
dispersed to the distant parts of the Empire. On this
occasion poor Mr. Nicholas B. penetrated into Russia
much farther than he ever did in the times of Napoleonic invasion, if much less willingly. Astrakhan was
his destination. He remained there three years, allowed to live at large in the town, but having to report
himself every day at noon to the military commandant,
who used to detain him frequently for a pipe and a chat.
It is difficult to form a just idea of what a chat
with Mr. Nicholas B. could have been like. There
must have been much compressed rage under his
taciturnity, for the commandant communicated to him
the news from the theatre of war, and this news was
such as it could be, that is, very bad for the Poles. Mr.
Nicholas B. received these communications with outward phlegm, but the Russian showed a warm sympathy
for his prisoner. "As a soldier myself I understand
your feelings. You, of course, would like to be in the
thick of it. By heavens! I am fond of you. If it
were not for the terms of the military oath I would let
you go on my own responsibility. What difference
could it make to us, one more or less of you?"

At other times he wondered with simplicity.

"Tell me, Nicholas Stepanovitch"—(my great-
grandfather's name was Stephen and the commandant
used the Russian form of polite address)—"tell me why

is it that you Poles are always looking for trouble? What else could you expect from running up against Russia?"

He was capable, too, of philosophical reflections.

"Look at your Napoleon now. A great man. There is no denying it that he was a great man as long as he was content to thrash those Germans and Austrians and all those nations. But no! He must go to Russia looking for trouble, and what's the consequence? Such as you see me, I have rattled this sabre of mine on the pavements of Paris."*

After his return to Poland Mr. Nicholas B. described him as a "worthy man but stupid," whenever he could be induced to speak of the conditions of his exile. Declining the option offered him to enter the Russian Army, he was retired with only half the pension of his rank. His nephew (my uncle and guardian) told me that the first lasting impression on his memory as a child of four was the glad excitement reigning in his parents' house on the day when Mr. Nicholas B. arrived home from his detention in Russia.

Every generation has its memories. The first memories of Mr. Nicholas B. might have been shaped by the events of the last partition of Poland,* and he lived long enough to suffer from the last armed rising in 1863,* an event which affected the future of all my generation and has coloured my earliest impressions. His brother, in whose house he had sheltered for some seventeen years his misanthropical timidity before the commonest problems of life, having died in the early fifties, Mr. Nicholas B. had to screw his courage up to the sticking-point and come to some decision as to the future. After a long and agonising hesitation he was persuaded at last to become the tenant of some fifteen hundred acres out of the estate of a friend in the neighbourhood. The terms of the lease were very advantageous, but the retired situation of the village and a plain, comfortable house in good repair were, I fancy, the greatest inducements. He lived there quietly for about ten years, seeing very few people and taking no part in the public life of the province, such as it could be under an arbitrary, bureaucratic tyranny. His character and his patriotism were above suspicion; but the organisers of the rising in their frequent journeys up and down the province scrupulously avoided coming near his house. It was generally felt that the repose of the old man's last years ought not to be disturbed. Even such intimates as my paternal grandfather, a comrade-in-arms during Napoleon's Moscow campaign and later on a fellow-officer in the Polish Army, refrained from visiting his crony as the date of the outbreak approached. My paternal grandfather's* two sons*and his only daughter*were all deeply involved in the revolutionary work; he himself was of that type of Polish squire whose only ideal of patriotic action was to "get into the saddle and drive them out." But even he agreed that "dear Nicholas must not be worried." All this considerate caution on the part of friends, both conspirators and others, did not prevent Mr. Nicholas B. being made to feel the misfortunes of that ill-omened year.

Less than forty-eight hours after the beginning of the rebellion in that part of the country, a squadron of scouting Cossacks* passed through the village and invaded the homestead. Most of them remained formed between the house and the stables, while several, dismounting, ransacked the various outbuildings. The officer in command, accompanied by two men, walked up to the front door. All the blinds on that side were down. The officer told the servant who received him that he wanted to see his master. He was answered that the master was away from home, which was perfectly true.

I follow here the tale as told afterwards by the servant to my grand-uncle's friends and relatives, and as I have heard it repeated.

On receiving this answer the Cossack officer, who had been standing in the porch, stepped into the house.

"Where is the master gone, then?"

"Our master went to J——"*(the government town some fifty miles off), "the day before yesterday."

"There are only two horses in the stables. Where are the others?"

"Our master always travels with his own horses" (meaning: not by post). "He will be away a week or more. He was pleased to mention to me that he had to attend to some business in the Civil Court."

While the servant was speaking the officer looked about the hall. There was a door facing him, a door to the right and a door to the left. The officer chose to enter the room on the left and ordered the blinds to be pulled up. It was Mr. Nicholas B.'s study with a couple of tall book-cases, some pictures on the walls, and so on. Besides the big centre table, with books and papers, there was a quite small writing-table with several drawers, standing between the door and the window in a good light; and at this table my grand-uncle usually sat either to read or write.

On pulling up the blind the servant was startled by the discovery that the whole male population of the village was massed in front, trampling down the flower-beds. There were also a few women amongst them. He was glad to observe the village priest (of the Orthodox Church) coming up the drive. The good man in his haste had tucked up his cassock as high as the top of his boots.

The officer had been looking at the backs of the books in the bookcases. Then he perched himself on the edge of the centre-table and remarked easily:

"Your master did not take you to town with him then."

"I am the head servant and he leaves me in charge of the house. It's a strong, young chap that travels with our master. If—God forbid—there was some accident on the road he would be of much more use than I."

Glancing through the window he saw the priest arguing vehemently in the thick of the crowd, which seemed subdued by his interference. Three or four men, however, were talking with the Cossacks at the door.

"And you don't think your master has gone to join the rebels, maybe—eh?" asked the officer.

"Our master would be too old for that, surely. He's well over seventy and he's getting feeble too. It's some years now since he's been on horseback and he can't walk much, either, now."

The officer sat there swinging his leg, very quiet and indifferent. By that time the peasants who had been talking with the Cossack troopers at the door had been permitted to get into the hall. One or two more left the crowd and followed them in. They were seven in all and amongst them the blacksmith, an ex-soldier. The servant appealed deferentially to the officer.

"Won't your honour be pleased to tell the people to go back to their homes? What do they want to push themselves into the house like this for? It's not proper for them to behave like this while our master's away, and I am responsible for everything here."

The officer only laughed a little, and after a while inquired:

"Have you any arms in the house?"

"Yes. We have. Some old things."

"Bring them all here, on to this table."

The servant made another attempt to obtain protection.

"Won't your honour tell these chaps . . . ?"

But the officer looked at him in silence in such a way that he gave it up at once and hurried off to call the pantry-boy to help him collect the arms. Meantime the officer walked slowly through all the rooms in the house, examining them attentively but touching nothing. The peasants in the hall fell back and took off their caps when he passed through. He said nothing whatever to them. When he came back to the study all the arms to be found in the house were lying on the table. There was a pair of big flint-lock holster pistols from Napoleonic times, two cavalry swords, one of the French the other of the Polish Army pattern, with a fowling-piece or two.

The officer, opening the window, flung out pistols, swords and guns, one after another, and his troopers ran to pick them up. The peasants in the hall, encouraged by his manner, had stolen after him into the study. He gave not the slightest sign of being conscious of their existence and, his business being apparently concluded, strode out of the house without a word. Directly he left, the peasants in the study put on their caps and began to smile at each other.

The Cossacks rode away, passing through the yards of the home farm straight into the fields. The priest, still arguing with the peasants, moved gradually down the drive and his earnest eloquence was drawing the silent mob after him, away from the house. This justice must be rendered to the parish priests of the Greek* Church that, strangers to the country as they were (being all drawn from the interior of Russia),* the majority of them used such influence as they had over their flocks in the cause of peace and humanity. True to the spirit of their calling, they tried to soothe the passions of the excited peasantry and opposed rapine and violence, whenever they could, with all their might. And this conduct they pursued against the express wishes of the authorities. Later on some of them were made to suffer for this disobedience by being removed abruptly to the far north or sent away to Siberian parishes.

The servant was anxious to get rid of the few peasants who had got into the house. What sort of conduct was that, he asked them, towards a man who was only a tenant, had been invariably good and considerate to the villagers for years, and only the other day had agreed to give up two meadows for the use of the village herd? He reminded them, too, of Mr. Nicholas B.'s devotion to the sick in the time of cholera. Every word of this was true and so far effective that the fellows began to scratch their heads and look irresolute. The speaker then pointed at the window, exclaiming: "Look! there's all your crowd going away quietly and you silly chaps had better go after them and pray God to forgive you your evil thoughts."

This appeal was an unlucky inspiration. In crowding clumsily to the window to see whether he was speaking the truth, the fellows overturned the little writing-table. As it fell over a chink of loose coin was heard. "There's money in that thing," cried the blacksmith. In a moment the top of the delicate piece of furniture was smashed and there lay exposed in a drawer eighty half-imperials. Gold coin was a rare

sight in Russia even at that time; it put the peasants be-
side themselves. "There must be more of that in the
house and we shall have it," yelled the ex-soldier blacksmith. "This is war time." The others were already
shouting out of the window urging the crowd to come
back and help. The priest, abandoned suddenly at the
gate, flung his arms up and hurried away so as not to
see what was going to happen.

In their search for money that bucolic mob smashed
everything in the house, ripping with knives, splitting
with hatchets, so that, as the servant said, there were no
two pieces of wood holding together left in the whole
house. They broke some very fine mirrors, all the
windows, and every piece of glass and china. They
threw the books and papers out on the lawn and set
fire to the heap for the mere fun of the thing apparently.
Absolutely the only one solitary thing which they left
whole was a small ivory crucifix, which remained hanging on the wall in the wrecked bedroom above a wild
heap of rags, broken mahogany and splintered boards
which had been Mr. Nicholas B.'s bedstead. Detect-
ing the servant in the act of stealing away with a japanned*tin box, they tore it from him, and because he
resisted they threw him out of the dining-room window.
The house was on one floor but raised well above the
ground, and the fall was so serious that the man remained lying stunned till the cook and a stable-boy
ventured forth at dusk from their hiding-places and
picked him up. By that time the mob had departed,
carrying off the tin box, which they supposed to be full
of paper money. Some distance from the house in the
middle of a field they broke it open. They found inside documents engrossed on parchment and the two
crosses of the Legion of Honour and For Valour.* At
the sight of these objects, which, the blacksmith ex-

plained, were marks of honour given only by the Tsar, they became extremely frightened at what they had done. They threw the whole lot away into a ditch and dispersed hastily.

On learning of this particular loss, Mr. Nicholas B. broke down completely. The mere sacking of his house did not seem to affect him much. While he was still in bed from the shock the two crosses were found and returned to him. It helped somewhat his slow convalescence, but the tin box and the parchments, though searched for in all the ditches around, never turned up again. He could not get over the loss of his Legion of Honour Patent, whose preamble, setting forth his services, he knew by heart to the very letter, and after this blow volunteered sometimes to recite, tears standing in his eyes the while. Its terms haunted him apparently during the last two years of his life to such an extent that he used to repeat them to himself. This is confirmed by the remark made more than once by his old servant to the more intimate friends: "What makes my heart heavy is to hear our master in his room at night walking up and down and praying aloud in the French language."

It must have been somewhat over a year afterwards that I saw Mr. Nicholas B., or, more correctly, that he saw me, for the last time. It was, as I have already said, at the time when my mother had a three-months' leave from exile, which she was spending in the house of her brother, and friends and relations were coming from far and near to do her honour. It is inconceivable that Mr. Nicholas B. should not have been of the number. The little child a few months old he had taken up in his arms on the day of his home-coming after years of war and exile was confessing her faith in national salvation by suffering exile in her turn. I do not know whether he was present on the very day of our departure. I have already admitted that for me he is more especially the man who in his youth had eaten roast dog in the depths of a gloomy forest of snow-loaded pines. My memory cannot place him in any remembered scene. A hooked nose, some sleek white hair, an unrelated evanescent impression of a meagre, slight, rigid figure militarily buttoned up to the throat, is all that now exists on earth of Mr. Nicholas B., only this vague shadow pursued by the memory of his grand-nephew, the last surviving human being, I suppose, of all those he had seen in the course of his taciturn life.

But I remember well the day of our departure back to exile. The elongated, *bizarre*, shabby travelling-carriage with four post-horses, standing before the long front of the house with its eight columns, four on each side of the broad flight of stairs. On the steps, groups of servants, a few relations, one or two friends from the nearest neighbourhood, a perfect silence, on all the faces an air of sober concentration; my grandmother all in black gazing stoically, my uncle giving his arm to my mother down to the carriage in which I had been placed already; at the top of the flight my little cousin in a short skirt of a tartan pattern with a deal of red in it, and like a small princess attended by the women of her own household: the head *gouvernante*, our dear, corpulent Francesca (who had been for thirty years in the service of the B. family), the former nurse, now outdoor attendant, a handsome peasant face wearing a compassionate expression, and the good, ugly Mlle. Durand, the governess, with her black eyebrows meeting over a short thick nose, and a complexion like pale brown paper. Of all the eyes turned towards the carriage, her good-natured eyes only were dropping

tears, and it was her sobbing voice alone that broke the
silence with an appeal to me: "*N'oublie pas ton français,
mon chéri.*"* In three months, simply by playing with
us, she had taught me not only to speak French but to
read it as well. She was indeed an excellent playmate.
In the distance, halfway down to the great gates, a light,
open trap, harnessed with three horses in Russian
fashion, stood drawn up on one side with the police
captain of the district sitting in it, the vizor of his flat
cap with a red band pulled down over his eyes.

It seems strange that he should have been there to
watch our going so carefully. Without wishing to treat
with levity the just timidities of Imperialists all the
world over, I may allow myself the reflection that a
woman, practically condemned by the doctors, and a
small boy not quite six years old could not be regarded
as seriously dangerous even for the largest of conceivable empires saddled with the most sacred of
responsibilities. And this good man, I believe, did not
think so either.

I learned afterwards why he was present on that
day. I don't remember any outward signs, but it
seems that, about a month before, my mother became
so unwell that there was a doubt whether she could be
made fit to travel in the time. In this uncertainty the
Governor-General in Kiev was petitioned to grant her
a fortnight's extension of stay in her brother's house.
No answer whatever was returned to this prayer, but
one day at dusk the police-captain of the district drove
up to the house and told my uncle's valet, who ran out
to meet him, that he wanted to speak with the master
in private, at once. Very much impressed (he thought
it was going to be an arrest) the servant, "more dead
than alive with fright," as he related afterwards,
smuggled him through the big drawing-room which was

dark (that room was not lighted every evening), on tiptoe, so as not to attract the attention of the ladies in the house, and led him by way of the orangery to my uncle's private apartments.

The policeman, without any preliminaries, thrust a paper into my uncle's hands.

"There. Pray read this. I have no business to show this paper to you. It is wrong of me. But I can't either eat or sleep with such a job hanging over me."

That police-captain, a native of Great Russia,* had been for many years serving in the district.

My uncle unfolded and read the document. It was a service order issued from the Governor-General's secretariat, dealing with the matter of the petition and directing the police-captain to disregard all remonstrances and explanations in regard to that illness either from medical men or others, "and if she has not left her brother's house"—it went on to say—"on the morning of the day specified on her permit, you are to despatch her at once under escort, direct" (underlined) "to the prison-hospital in Kiev, where she will be treated as her case demands."

"For God's sake, Mr. B., see that your sister goes away punctually on that day. Don't give me this work to do with a woman—and with one of your family, too. I simply cannot bear to think of it."

He was absolutely wringing his hands. My uncle looked at him in silence.

"Thank you for this warning. I assure you that even if she were dying she would be carried out to the carriage."

"Yes—indeed—and what difference would it make— travel to Kiev or back to her husband. For she would have to go—death or no death. And mind, Mr. B., I will be here on the day, not that I doubt your promise but because I must. I have got to. Duty. All the same, my trade is not fit for a dog since some of you Poles will persist in rebelling, and all of you have got to suffer for it."

This is the reason why he was there in an open three-horse trap pulled up between the house and the great gates. I regret not being able to give up his name to the scorn of all believers in the rights of conquest, as a reprehensibly sensitive guardian of Imperial greatness. On the other hand, I am in a position to state the name of the Governor-General who signed the order with the marginal note "to be carried out to the letter" in his own handwriting. The gentleman's name was Bezak.* A high dignitary, an energetic official, the idol for a time of the Russian Patriotic Press.

Each generation has its memories.

IV

It must not be supposed that in setting forth the memories of this half-hour between the moment my uncle left my room till we met again at dinner, I am losing sight of "Almayer's Folly." Having confessed that my first novel was begun in idleness—a holiday task—I think I have also given the impression that it was a much-delayed book. It was never dismissed from my mind, even when the hope of ever finishing it was very faint. Many things came in its way: daily duties, new impressions, old memories. It was not the outcome of a need—the famous need of self-expression which artists find in their search for motives. The necessity which impelled me was a hidden, obscure necessity, a completely masked and unaccountable phenomenon. Or perhaps some idle and frivolous magician (there must be magicians in London) had cast a spell over me through his parlour window as I explored the maze of streets east and west in solitary leisurely walks without chart and compass. Till I began to write that novel I had written nothing but letters, and not very many of these. I never made a note of a fact,* of an impression or of an anecdote in my life. The conception of a planned book was entirely outside my mental range when I sat down to write; the ambition of being an author had never turned up amongst these gracious imaginary existences one creates fondly for oneself at times in the stillness and immobility of a day-dream: yet it stands clear as the sun at noonday that from the moment I had done blackening over the first manuscript page of "Almayer's Folly" (it contained about two hundred words and this proportion of words to a page has remained with me through the fifteen years of my writing life), from the moment I had, in the simplicity of my heart and the amazing ignorance of my mind, written that page the die was cast. Never had Rubicon*been more blindly forded, without invocation to the gods, without fear of men.

That morning I got up from my breakfast, pushing the chair back, and rang the bell violently, or perhaps I should say resolutely, or perhaps I should say eagerly, I do not know. But manifestly it must have been a special ring of the bell, a common sound made impressive, like the ringing of a bell for the raising of the curtain upon a new scene. It was an unusual thing for me to do. Generally, I dawdled over my breakfast and I seldom took the trouble to ring the bell for the table to be cleared away; but on that morning for some reason hidden in the general mysteriousness of the event I did not dawdle. And yet I was not in a hurry. I pulled the cord casually, and while the faint tinkling somewhere down in the basement went on, I charged my pipe in the usual way and I looked for the matchbox with glances distraught indeed but exhibiting, I am ready to swear, no signs of a fine frenzy. I was composed enough to perceive after some considerable time the matchbox lying there on the mantelpiece right under my nose. And all this was beautifully and safely usual. Before I had thrown down the match my landlady's daughter appeared with her calm, pale face and an inquisitive look, in the doorway. Of late it was the landlady's daughter who answered my bell. I mention this little fact with pride, because it proves that during the thirty or forty days of my tenancy I had produced a favourable impression. For a fortnight past I had been spared the unattractive sight of the domestic slave. The girls in that Bessborough Gardens house were often changed, but whether short or long, fair or dark, they were always untidy and particularly bedraggled, as if in a sordid version of the fairy tale the ashbin cat had been changed into a maid.* I was infinitely sensible of the privilege of being waited on by my landlady's daughter. She was neat if anæmic.

"Will you please clear away all this at once?" I addressed her in convulsive accents, being at the same time engaged in getting my pipe to draw. This, I admit, was an unusual request. Generally on getting up from breakfast I would sit down in the window with a book and let them clear the table when they liked; but if you think that on that morning I was in the least impatient, you are mistaken. I remember that I was perfectly calm. As a matter of fact I was not at all certain that I wanted to write, or that I meant to write, or that I had anything to write about. No, I was not impatient. I lounged between the mantelpiece and the window, not even consciously waiting for the table to be cleared. It was ten to one that before my landlady's daughter was done I would pick up a book and sit down with it all the morning in a spirit of enjoyable indolence. I affirm it with assurance, and I don't even know now what were the books then lying about the room. Whatever they were they were not the works of great masters, where the secret of clear thought and exact expression can be found. Since the age of five I have been a great reader, as is not perhaps wonderful in a child who was never aware of learning to read. At ten years of age I had read much of Victor Hugo*and other romantics. I had read in Polish and in French,

history, voyages, novels; I knew "Gil Blas"*and "Don
Quixote" in abridged editions; I had read in early boyhood Polish poets and some French poets, but I cannot
say what I read on the evening before I began to write
myself. I believe it was a novel, and it is quite possible
that it was one of Anthony Trollope's novels. It is
very likely. My acquaintance with him was then very
recent. He is one of the English novelists whose works
I read for the first time in English. With men of
European reputation, with Dickens and Walter Scott
and Thackeray, it was otherwise. My first introduction
to English imaginative literature was "Nicholas
Nickleby."* It is extraordinary how well Mrs. Nickleby
could chatter disconnectedly in Polish and the sinister
Ralph rage in that language. As to the Crummles
family and the family of the learned Squeers, it seemed
as natural to them as their native speech. It was, I
have no doubt, an excellent translation. This must
have been in the year '70. But I really believe that I
am wrong. That book was not my first introduction to
English literature. My first acquaintance was (or
were) the "Two Gentlemen of Verona," and that in the
very MS. of my father's translation.* It was during our
exile in Russia, and it must have been less than a year
after my mother's death, because I remember myself in
the black blouse with a white border of my heavy
mourning. We were living together, quite alone, in a
small house on the outskirts of the town of T——.* That
afternoon, instead of going out to play in the large yard
which we shared with our landlord, I had lingered in
the room in which my father generally wrote. What
emboldened me to clamber into his chair I am sure I
don't know, but a couple of hours afterwards he discovered me kneeling in it with my elbows on the table
and my head held in both hands over the MS. of loose

pages. I was greatly confused, expecting to get into trouble. He stood in the doorway looking at me with some surprise, but the only thing he said after a moment of silence was:

"Read the page aloud."

Luckily the page lying before me was not over blotted with erasures and corrections, and my father's handwriting was otherwise extremely legible. When I got to the end he nodded and I flew out of doors thinking myself lucky to have escaped reproof for that piece of impulsive audacity. I have tried to discover since the reason of this mildness, and I imagine that all unknown to myself I had earned, in my father's mind, the right to some latitude in my relations with his writing-table. It was only a month before, or perhaps it was only a week before that I had read to him aloud from beginning to end, and to his perfect satisfaction, as he lay on his bed, not being very well at the time, the proofs of his translation of Victor Hugo's "Toilers of the Sea."* Such was my title to consideration, I believe, and also my first introduction to the sea in literature. If I do not remember where, how and when I learned to read, I am not likely to forget the process of being trained in the art of reading aloud. My poor father, an admirable reader himself, was the most exacting of masters. I reflect proudly that I must have read that page of "Two Gentlemen of Verona" tolerably well at the age of eight. The next time I met them was in a five shilling one-volume edition of the dramatic works of William Shakespeare, read in Falmouth,* at odd moments of the day, to the noisy accompaniment of caulkers' mallets driving oakum into the deck-seams of a ship in dry dock. We had run in, in a sinking condition and with the crew refusing duty after a month of weary battling with the gales of

the North Atlantic. Books are an integral part of
one's life and my Shakespearean associations are with
that first year of our bereavement, the last I spent with
my father in exile (he sent me away to Poland to my
mother's brother directly he could brace himself up for
the separation), and with the year of hard gales, the
year in which I came nearest to death at sea, first by
water and then by fire.

Those things I remember, but what I was reading the
day before my writing life began I have forgotten. I
have only a vague notion that it might have been one of
Trollope's political novels. And I remember, too, the
character of the day. It was an autumn day with an
opaline atmosphere, a veiled, semi-opaque, lustrous
day, with fiery points and flashes of red sunlight on the
roofs and windows opposite, while the trees of the square
with all their leaves gone were like tracings of indian ink
on a sheet of tissue paper. It was one of those London
days that have the charm of mysterious amenity, of
fascinating softness. The effect of opaline mist was
often repeated at Bessborough Gardens on account of
the nearness to the river.

There is no reason why I should remember that
effect more on that day than on any other day, except
that I stood for a long time looking out of the window
after the landlady's daughter was gone with her spoil of
cups and saucers. I heard her put the tray down in the
passage and finally shut the door; and still I remained
smoking with my back to the room. It is very clear
that I was in no haste to take the plunge into my writing life, if as plunge this first attempt may be described.
My whole being was steeped deep in the indolence of
a sailor away from the sea, the scene of never-ending
labour and of unceasing duty. For utter surrender to
indolence you cannot beat a sailor ashore when that

mood is on him, the mood of absolute irresponsibility tasted to the full. It seems to me that I thought of nothing whatever, but this is an impression which is hardly to be believed at this distance of years. What I am certain of is, that I was very far from thinking of writing a story, though it is possible and even likely that I was thinking of the man Almayer.*

I had seen him for the first time some four years before from the bridge of a steamer*moored to a rickety little wharf forty miles up, more or less, a Bornean river.* It was very early morning, and a slight mist, an opaline mist as in Bessborough Gardens only without the fiery flicks on roof and chimney-pot from the rays of the red London sun, promised to turn presently into a woolly fog. Barring a small dug-out canoe on the river, there was nothing moving within sight. I had just come up yawning from my cabin. The serang*and the Malay crew were overhauling the cargo chains and trying the winches; their voices sounded subdued on the deck below and their movements were languid. That tropical daybreak was chilly. The Malay quartermaster, coming up to get something from the lockers on the bridge, shivered visibly. The forests above and below and on the opposite bank looked black and dank; wet dripped from the rigging upon the tightly stretched deck awnings, and it was in the middle of a shuddering yawn that I caught sight of Almayer. He was moving across a patch of burnt grass, a blurred, shadowy shape with the blurred bulk of a house behind him, a low house of mats, bamboos and palm-leaves with a high-pitched roof of grass.

He stepped upon the jetty. He was clad simply in flapping pyjamas of cretonne pattern (enormous flowers with yellow petals on a disagreeable blue ground) and a thin cotton singlet with short sleeves. His arms, bare

to the elbow, were crossed on his chest. His black hair
looked as if it had not been cut for a very long time and
a curly wisp of it strayed across his forehead. I had
heard of him at Singapore; I had heard of him on board;
I had heard of him early in the morning and late at
night; I had heard of him at tiffin*and at dinner; I had
heard of him in a place called Pulo Laut* from a half-
caste gentleman there, who described himself as the
manager of a coal-mine; which sounded civilised and
progressive till you heard that the mine could not be
worked at present because it was haunted by some
particularly atrocious ghosts. I had heard of him in a
place called Dongola,* in the Island of Celebes, when the
Rajah of that little-known sea-port (you can get no
anchorage there in less than fifteen fathom, which is
extremely inconvenient) came on board in a friendly
way with only two attendants, and drank bottle after
bottle of soda-water on the after-skylight with my good
friend and commander Captain C——.* At least I
heard his name distinctly pronounced several times in
a lot of talk in Malay language. Oh, yes, I heard it
quite distinctly—Almayer, Almayer—and saw Captain
C—— smile while the fat, dingy Rajah laughed audibly.
To hear a Malay Rajah laugh outright is a rare experience, I can assure you. And I overheard more of
Almayer's name amongst our deck passengers (mostly
wandering traders of good repute) as they sat all over
the ship—each man fenced round with bundles and
boxes—on mats, on pillows, on quilts, on billets of wood,
conversing of Island affairs. Upon my word, I heard
the mutter of Almayer's name faintly at midnight,
while making my way aft from the bridge to look at the
patent taffrail-log*tinkling its quarter-miles in the great
silence of the sea. I don't mean to say that our passengers dreamed aloud of Almayer, but it is indubitable

that two of them at least, who could not sleep apparently and were trying to charm away the trouble of insomnia by a little whispered talk at that ghostly hour were referring in some way or other to Almayer. It was really impossible on board that ship to get away definitely from Almayer; and a very small pony tied up forward and whisking its tail inside the galley, to the great embarrassment of our Chinaman cook, was destined for Almayer. What he wanted with a pony goodness only knows, since I am perfectly certain he could not ride it; but here you have the man, ambitious, aiming at the grandiose, importing a pony, whereas in the whole settlement at which he used to shake daily his impotent fist, there was only one path that was practicable for a pony: a quarter of a mile at most, hedged in by hundreds of square leagues of virgin forest. But who knows? The importation of that Bali*pony might have been part of some deep scheme, of some diplomatic plan, of some hopeful intrigue. With Almayer one could never tell. He governed his conduct by considerations removed from the obvious, by incredible assumptions, which rendered his logic impenetrable to any reasonable person. I learned all this later. That morning, seeing the figure in pyjamas moving in the mist, I said to myself: "That's the man."

He came quite close to the ship's side and raised a harassed countenance, round and flat, with that curl of black hair over the forehead and a heavy, pained glance.

"Good morning."

"Good morning."

He looked hard at me: I was a new face, having just replaced the chief mate he was accustomed to see; and I think that this novelty inspired him, as things generally did, with deep-seated mistrust.

"Didn't expect you in till this evening," he remarked
suspiciously.

I don't know why he should have been aggrieved, but
he seemed to be. I took pains to explain to him that
having picked up the beacon at the mouth of the river
just before dark and the tide serving, Captain C——
was enabled to cross the bar*and there was nothing to
prevent him going up the river at night.

"Captain C—— knows this river like his own
pocket," I concluded discursively, trying to get on
terms.

"Better," said Almayer.

Leaning over the rail of the bridge I looked at
Almayer, who looked down at the wharf in aggrieved
thought. He shuffled his feet a little; he wore straw
slippers with thick soles. The morning fog had
thickened considerably. Everything round us dripped:
the derricks,* the rails, every single rope in the ship—as
if a fit of crying had come upon the universe.

Almayer again raised his head and, in the accents
of a man accustomed to the buffets of evil fortune,
asked hardly audibly: "I suppose you haven't got such
a thing as a pony on board?"

I told him almost in a whisper, for he attuned my
communications to his minor key, that we had such a
thing as a pony, and I hinted, as gently as I could,
that he was confoundedly in the way too. I was very
anxious to have him landed before I began to handle
the cargo. Almayer remained looking up at me for a
long while with incredulous and melancholy eyes as
though it were not a safe thing to believe my statement.
This pathetic mistrust in the favourable issue of any
sort of affair touched me deeply, and I added:

"He doesn't seem a bit the worse for the passage.
He's a nice pony, too."

Almayer was not to be cheered up; for all answer he cleared his throat and looked down again at his feet. I tried to close with him on another track.

"By Jove!" I said. "Aren't you afraid of catching pneumonia or bronchitis or something, walking about in a singlet in such a wet fog?"

He was not to be propitiated by a show of interest in his health. His answer was a sinister "No fear," as much as to say that even that way of escape from inclement fortune was closed to him.

"I just came down . . ." he mumbled after a while.

"Well, then, now you're here I will land that pony for you at once and you can lead him home. I really don't want him on deck. He's in the way."

Almayer seemed doubtful. I insisted:

"Why, I will just swing him out and land him on the wharf right in front of you. I'd much rather do it before the hatches are off. The little devil may jump down the hold or do some other deadly thing."

"There's a halter?" postulated Almayer.

"Yes, of course there's a halter." And without waiting any more I leaned over the bridge rail.

"Serang, land Tuan* Almayer's pony."

The cook hastened to shut the door of the galley and a moment later a great scuffle began on deck. The pony kicked with extreme energy, the kalashes* skipped out of the way, the serang issued many orders in a cracked voice. Suddenly the pony leaped upon the fore-hatch. His little hoofs thundered tremendously; he plunged and reared. He had tossed his mane and his forelock into a state of amazing wildness, he dilated his nostrils, bits of foam flecked his broad little chest, his eyes blazed. He was something under eleven hands; he was fierce, terrible, angry, warlike, he said ha! ha! distinctly, he raged and thumped—and sixteen able-bodied kalashes stood round him like disconcerted nurses round a spoilt and passionate child. He whisked his tail incessantly; he arched his pretty neck; he was perfectly delightful; he was charmingly naughty. There was not an atom of vice in that performance; no savage baring of teeth and laying back of ears. On the contrary, he pricked them forward in a comically aggressive manner. He was totally unmoral and lovable; I would have liked to give him bread, sugar, carrots. But life is a stern thing and the sense of duty the only safe guide. So I steeled my heart and from my elevated position on the bridge I ordered the men to fling themselves upon him in a body.

The elderly serang, emitting a strange inarticulate cry, gave the example. He was an excellent petty officer—very competent indeed, and a moderate opium smoker. The rest of them in one great rush smothered that pony. They hung on to his ears, to his mane, to his tail; they lay in piles across his back, seventeen in all. The carpenter, seizing the hook of the cargo-chain, flung himself on the top of them. A very satisfactory petty officer too, but he stuttered. Have you ever heard a light-yellow, lean, sad, earnest Chinaman stutter in pidgin-English? It's very weird indeed. He made the eighteenth. I could not see the pony at all; but from the swaying and heaving of that heap of men I knew that there was something alive inside.

From the wharf Almayer hailed in quavering tones: "Oh, I say!"

Where he stood he could not see what was going on on deck unless perhaps the tops of the men's heads; he could only hear the scuffle, the mighty thuds as if the ship were being knocked to pieces. I looked over: "What is it?"

"Don't let them break his legs," he entreated me plaintively.

"Oh, nonsense! He's all right now. He can't move. By that time the cargo-chain had been hooked to the broad canvas belt round the pony's body, the kalashes sprang off simultaneously in all directions, rolling over each other, and the worthy serang, making a dash behind the winch, turned the steam on.

"Steady!" I yelled, in great apprehension of seeing the animal snatched up to the very head of the derrick.

On the wharf Almayer shuffled his straw slippers uneasily. The rattle of the winch stopped, and in a tense, impressive silence that pony began to swing across the deck.

How limp he was! Directly he felt himself in the air he relaxed every muscle in a most wonderful manner. His four hoofs knocked together in a bunch, his head hung down, and his tail remained pendent in a nerveless and absolute immobility. He reminded me vividly of the pathetic little sheep which hangs on the collar of the Order of the Golden Fleece.* I had no idea that anything in the shape of a horse could be so limp as that, either living or dead. His wild mane hung down lumpily, a mere mass of inanimate horsehair; his aggressive ears had collapsed, but as he went swaying slowly across the front of the bridge I noticed an astute gleam in his dreamy, half-closed eye. A trustworthy quartermaster, his glance anxious and his mouth on the broad grin, was easing over the derrick watchfully. I superintended, greatly interested.

"So! That will do."

The derrick-head stopped. The kalashes lined the rail. The rope of the halter hung perpendicular and motionless like a bell-pull in front of Almayer. Everything was very still. I suggested amicably that he should catch hold of the rope and mind what he was about. He extended a provokingly casual and superior hand.

"Look out, then! Lower away!"

Almayer gathered in the rope intelligently enough, but when the pony's hoofs touched the wharf he gave way all at once to a most foolish optimism. Without pausing, without thinking, almost without looking, he disengaged the hook suddenly from the sling, and the cargo-chain, after hitting the pony's quarters, swung back against the ship's side with a noisy, rattling slap. I suppose I must have blinked. I know I missed something, because the next thing I saw was Almayer lying flat on his back on the jetty. He was alone.

Astonishment deprived me of speech long enough to give Almayer time to pick himself up in a leisurely and painful manner. The kalashes lining the rail had all their mouths open. The mist flew in the light breeze, and it had come over quite thick enough to hide the shore completely.

"How on earth did you manage to let him get away?" I asked scandalised.

Almayer looked into the smarting palm of his right hand, but did not answer my inquiry.

"Where do you think he will get to?" I cried. "Are there any fences anywhere in this fog? Can he bolt into the forest? What's to be done now?"

Almayer shrugged his shoulders.

"Some of my men are sure to be about. They will get hold of him sooner or later.

"Sooner or later! That's all very fine, but what about my canvas sling—he's carried it off. I want it now, at once, to land two Celebes cows."

Since Dongola we had on board a pair of the pretty little island cattle in addition to the pony. Tied up on the other side of the fore deck they had been whisking their tails into the other door of the galley. These cows were not for Almayer, however, they were invoiced to Abdullah bin Selim, his enemy. Almayer's disregard of my requirements was complete.

"If I were you I would try to find out where he's gone," I insisted. "Hadn't you better call your men together or something? He will throw himself down and cut his knees. He may even break a leg, you know."

But Almayer, plunged in abstracted thought, did not seem to want that pony any more. Amazed at this sudden indifference, I turned all hands out on shore to hunt for him on my own account, or, at any rate, to hunt for the canvas sling which he had round his body. The whole crew of the steamer, with the exception of firemen and engineers, rushed up the jetty past the thoughtful Almayer and vanished from my sight. The white fog swallowed them up; and again there was a deep silence that seemed to extend for miles up and down the stream. Still taciturn, Almayer started to climb on board, and I went down from the bridge to meet him on the after deck.

"Would you mind telling the captain that I want to see him very particularly?" he asked me in a low tone, letting his eyes stray all over the place.

"Very well. I will go and see."

With the door of his cabin wide open Captain C——, just back from the bath-room, big and broad-chested, was brushing his thick, damp, iron-grey hair with two large brushes.

"Mr. Almayer told me he wanted to see you very particularly, sir."

Saying these words I smiled. I don't know why I smiled except that it seemed absolutely impossible to mention Almayer's name without a smile of a sort. It had not to be necessarily a mirthful smile. Turning his head towards me Captain C—— smiled too, rather joylessly.

"The pony got away from him—eh?"

"Yes, sir. He did."

"Where is he?"

"Goodness only knows."

"No. I mean Almayer. Let him come along."

The captain's state-room opening straight on deck under the bridge, I had only to beckon from the doorway to Almayer, who had remained aft, with downcast eyes, on the very spot where I had left him. He strolled up moodily, shook hands, and at once asked permission to shut the cabin door.

"I have a pretty story to tell you," were the last words I heard. The bitterness of tone was remarkable.

I went away from the door, of course. For the moment I had no crew on board; only the Chinaman carpenter, with a canvas bag hung round his neck and a hammer in his hand, roamed about the empty decks knocking out the wedges of the hatches and dropping them into the bag conscientiously. Having nothing to do. I joined our two engineers at the door of the engine-room. It was near breakfast-time.

"He's turned up early, hasn't he?" commented the second engineer, and smiled indifferently. He was an abstemious man with a good digestion and a placid, reasonable view of life even when hungry.

"Yes," I said. "Shut up with the old man. Some very particular business."

"He will spin him a damned endless yarn," observed the chief engineer.

He smiled rather sourly. He was dyspeptic and suffered from gnawing hunger in the morning. The second smiled broadly, a smile that made two vertical folds on his shaven cheeks. And I smiled too, but I was not exactly amused. In that man, whose name apparently could not be uttered anywhere in the Malay Archipelago without a smile, there was nothing amusing whatever. That morning he breakfasted with us silently, looking mostly into his cup. I informed him that my men came upon his pony capering in the fog on the very brink of the eight-foot-deep well in which he kept his store of guttah.* The cover was off, with no one near by, and the whole of my crew just missed going heels over head into that beastly hole. Jurumudi Itam, our best quartermaster, deft at fine needlework, he who mended the ship's flags and sewed buttons on our coats, was disabled by a kick on the shoulder.

Both remorse and gratitude seemed foreign to Almayer's character. He mumbled:

"Do you mean that pirate fellow?"

"What pirate fellow? The man has been in the ship eleven years," I said indignantly.

"It's his looks," Almayer muttered for all apology.

The sun had eaten up the fog. From where we sat under the after awning we could see in the distance the pony tied up in front of Almayer's house, to a post of the verandah. We were silent for a long time. All at once Almayer, alluding evidently to the subject of his conversation in the captain's cabin, exclaimed anxiously across the table.

"I really don't know what I can do now!"

Captain C—— only raised his eyebrows at him, and got up from his chair. We dispersed to our duties, but Almayer, half-dressed as he was in his cretonne pyjamas and the thin cotton singlet, remained on board, lingering near the gangway as though he could not make up his mind whether to go home or stay with us for good. Our Chinamen boys gave him side glances as they went to and fro; and Ah Sing, our young chief steward, the handsomest and most sympathetic of Chinamen, catching my eye, nodded knowingly at his burly back. In the course of the morning I approached him for a moment.

"Well, Mr. Almayer," I addressed him easily, "you haven't started on your letters yet."

We had brought him his mail and he had held the bundle in his hand ever since we got up from breakfast. He glanced at it when I spoke and, for a moment, it looked as if he were on the point of opening his fingers and letting the whole lot fall overboard. I believe he was tempted to do so. I shall never forget that man afraid of his letters.

"Have you been long out from Europe?" he asked me.

"Not very. Not quite eight months," I told him. "I left a ship in Samarang with a hurt back and have been in the hospital in Singapore some weeks."*

He sighed.

"Trade is very bad here."

"Indeed!"

"Hopeless! . . . See these geese?"

With the hand holding the letters he pointed out to me what resembled a patch of snow creeping and swaying across the distant part of his compound. It disappeared behind some bushes.

"The only geese on the East Coast," Almayer informed me in a perfunctory mutter without a spark of faith, hope or pride. Thereupon, with the same absence of any sort of sustaining spirit, he declared his intention to select a fat bird and send him on board for us not later than next day.

I had heard of these largesses before. He conferred a goose as if it were a sort of Court decoration given only to the tried friends of the house. I had expected more pomp in the ceremony. The gift had surely its special quality, multiple and rare. From the only flock on the East Coast! He did not make half enough of it. That man did not understand his opportunities. However, I thanked him at some length.

"You see," he interrupted abruptly in a very peculiar tone, "the worst of this country is that one is not able to realise . . . it's impossible to realise . . ." His voice sank into a languid mutter. "And when one has very large interests . . . very important interests . . ." he finished faintly . . . "up the river."

We looked at each other. He astonished me by giving a start and making a very queer grimace.

"Well, I must be off," he burst out hurriedly. "So long!"

At the moment of stepping over the gangway he checked himself, though, to give me a mumbled invitation to dine at his house that evening with my captain, an invitation which I accepted. I don't think it could have been possible for me to refuse.

I like the worthy folk who will talk to you of the exercise of free will "at any rate for practical purposes." Free, is it? For practical purposes! Bosh! How could I have refused to dine with that man? I did not refuse simply because I could not refuse. Curiosity, a healthy desire for a change of cooking, common civility, the talk and the smiles of the previous twenty days, every condition of my existence at that moment and place made irresistibly for acceptance; and, crowning all that, there was the ignorance, the ignorance, I say, the fatal want of foreknowledge to counter-balance these imperative conditions of the problem. A refusal would have appeared perverse and insane. Nobody unless a surly lunatic would have refused. But if I had not got to know Almayer pretty well it is almost certain there would never have been a line of mine in print.

I accepted then—and I am paying yet the price of my sanity. The possessor of the only flock of geese on the East Coast is responsible for the existence of some fourteen volumes, so far. The number of geese he had called into being under adverse climatic conditions was considerably more than fourteen. The tale of volumes will never overtake the counting of heads, I am safe to say; but my ambitions point not exactly that way, and whatever the pangs the toil of writing has cost me I have always thought kindly of Almayer.

I wonder, had he known anything of it, what his attitude would have been? This is something not to be discovered in this world. But if we ever meet in the Elysian Fields*—where I cannot depict him to myself otherwise than attended in the distance by his flock of geese (birds sacred to Jupiter)—and he addresses me in the stillness of that passionless region, neither light nor darkness, neither sound nor silence, and heaving endlessly with billowy mists from the impalpable multitudes of the swarming dead, I think I know what answer to make.

I would say, after listening courteously to the unvibrating tone of his measured remonstrances, which should not disturb, of course, the solemn eternity of stillness in the least—I would say something like this:

"It is true, Almayer, that in the world below I have converted your name to my own uses. But that is a very small larceny. What's in a name, O Shade? If so much of your old mortal weakness clings to you yet

as to make you feel aggrieved (it was the note of your
earthly voice, Almayer), then, I entreat you, seek speech
without delay with our sublime fellow-Shade—with
him who, in his transient existence as a poet, commented
upon the smell of the rose. He will comfort you. You
came to me stripped of all prestige by men's queer
smiles and the disrespectful chatter of every vagrant
trader in the Islands. Your name was the common
property of the winds: it, as it were, floated naked over
the waters about the Equator. I wrapped round its
unhonoured form the royal mantle of the tropics and
have essayed to put into the hollow sound the very
anguish of paternity—feats which you did not demand
from me—but remember that all the toil and all the
pain were mine. In your earthly life you haunted me,
Almayer. Consider that this was taking a great liberty.
Since you were always complaining of being lost to the
world, you should remember that if I had not believed
enough in your existence to let you haunt my rooms in
Bessborough Gardens you would have been much more
lost. You affirm that had I been capable of looking at
you with a more perfect detachment and a greater
simplicity, I might have perceived better the inward
marvellousness which, you insist, attended your career
upon that tiny pin-point of light, hardly visible, far, far
below us, where both our graves lie. No doubt! But
reflect, O complaining Shade! that this was not so
much my fault as your crowning misfortune. I believed in you in the only way it was possible for me to
believe. It was not worthy of your merits? So be it.
But you were always an unlucky man, Almayer.
Nothing was ever quite worthy of you. What made
you so real to me was that you held this lofty theory
with some force of conviction and with an admirable
consistency."

It is with some such words translated into the proper shadowy expressions that I am prepared to placate Almayer in the Elysian Abode of Shades, since it has come to pass that having parted many years ago, we are never to meet again in this world.

V

In the career of the most unliterary of writers, in the sense that literary ambition had never entered the world of his imagination, the coming into existence of the first book is quite an inexplicable event.   In my own case I cannot trace it back to any mental or psychological cause which one could point out and hold to. The greatest of my gifts being a consummate capacity for doing nothing, I cannot even point to boredom as a rational stimulus for taking up a pen.   The pen at any rate was there, and there is nothing wonderful in that.   Everybody keeps a pen (the cold steel of our days) in his rooms in this enlightened age of penny stamps and halfpenny postcards.   In fact, this was the epoch when by means of postcard and pen Mr. Gladstone had made the reputation of a novel or two.* And I too had a pen rolling about somewhere—the seldom-used, the reluctantly-taken-up pen of a sailor ashore, the pen rugged with the dried ink of abandoned attempts, of answers delayed longer than decency permitted, of letters begun with infinite reluctance and put off suddenly till next day—till next week as likely as not!   The neglected, uncared-for pen, flung away at the slightest provocation, and under the stress of dire necessity hunted for without enthusiasm, in a perfunctory, grumpy worry, in the "Where the devil *is* the beastly thing gone to?" ungracious spirit.   Where indeed!   It might have been reposing behind the sofa for a day or so.   My landlady's anæmic daughter (as Ollendorff*would have expressed it), though com-·

90

mendably neat, had a lordly, careless manner of approaching her domestic duties. Or it might even be resting delicately poised on its point by the side of the table-leg, and when picked up show a gaping inefficient beak which would have discouraged any man of literary instincts. But not me! "Never mind. This will do."

O days without guile! If anybody had told me then that a devoted household, having a generally exaggerated idea of my talents and importance, would be put into a state of tremor and flurry by the fuss I would make because of a suspicion that somebody had touched my sacrosanct pen of authorship, I would have never deigned as much as the contemptuous smile of unbelief. There are imaginings too unlikely for any kind of notice, too wild for indulgence itself, too absurd for a smile. Perhaps, had that seer of the future been a friend, I should have been secretly saddened. "Alas!" I would have thought, looking at him with an unmoved face, "the poor fellow is going mad."

I would have been, without doubt, saddened; for in this world where the journalists read the signs of the sky, and the wind of heaven itself, blowing where it listeth, does so under the prophetical management of the Meteorological Office, but where the secret of human hearts cannot be captured either by prying or praying, it was infinitely more likely that the sanest of my friends should nurse the germ of incipient madness than that I should turn into a writer of tales.

To survey with wonder the changes of one's own self is a fascinating pursuit for idle hours. The field is so wide, the surprises so varied, the subject so full of unprofitable but curious hints as to the work of unseen forces, that one does not weary easily of it. I am not speaking here of megalomaniacs who rest uneasy under the crown of their unbounded conceit—who really never rest in this world, and when out of it go on fretting and fuming on the straitened circumstances of their last habitation, where all men must lie in obscure equality. Neither am I thinking of those ambitious minds who, always looking forward to some aim of aggrandisement, can spare no time for a detached, impersonal glance upon themselves.

And that's a pity. They are unlucky. These two kinds, together with the much larger band of the totally unimaginative, of those unfortunate beings in whose empty and unseeing gaze (as a great French writer*has put it) "the whole universe vanishes into blank nothingness," miss, perhaps, the true task of us men whose day is short on this earth, the abode of conflicting opinions. The ethical view of the universe involves us at last in so many cruel and absurd contradictions, where the last vestiges of faith, hope, charity, and even of reason itself, seem ready to perish, that I have come to suspect that the aim of creation cannot be ethical at all. I would fondly believe that its object is purely spectacular: a spectacle for awe, love, adoration, or hate, if you like, but in this view—and in this view alone—never for despair! Those visions, delicious or poignant, are a moral end in themselves. The rest is our affair—the laughter, the tears, the tenderness, the indignation, the high tranquillity of a steeled heart, the detached curiosity of a subtle mind—that's our affair! And the unwearied self-forgetful attention to every phase of the living universe reflected in our consciousness may be our appointed task on this earth. A task in which fate has perhaps engaged nothing of us except our conscience, gifted with a voice in order to bear true testimony to the visible wonder, the haunting terror, the infinite passion and the illimitable serenity; to the supreme law and the abiding mystery of the sublime spectacle.

*Chi lo sà?** It may be true. In this view there is room for every religion except for the inverted creed of impiety, the mask and cloak of arid despair; for every joy and every sorrow, for every fair dream, for every charitable hope. The great aim is to remain true to the emotions called out of the deep encircled by the firmament of stars, whose infinite numbers and awful distance may move us to laughter or tears (was it the Walrus or the Carpenter,* in the poem, who "wept to see such quantities of sand"?), or, again, to a properly steeled heart, may matter nothing at all.

The casual quotation, which had suggested itself out of a poem full of merit, leads me to remark that in the conception of a purely spectacular universe, where inspiration of every sort has a rational existence, the artist of every kind finds a natural place; and amongst them the poet as the seer *par excellence*. Even the writer of prose, who in his less noble and more toilsome task should be a man with the steeled heart, is worthy of a place, providing he looks on with undimmed eyes and keeps laughter out of his voice, let who will laugh or cry. Yes! Even he, the prose artist of fiction, which after all is but truth often dragged out of a well and clothed in the painted robe of imaged phrases—even he has his place amongst kings, demagogues, priests, charlatans, dukes, giraffes, Cabinet Ministers, Fabians, bricklayers, apostles, ants, scientists, Kaffirs,* soldiers, sailors, elephants, lawyers, dandies, microbes and constellations of a universe whose amazing spectacle is a moral end in itself.

Here I perceive (speaking without offence) the reader assuming a subtle expression, as if the cat were out of the bag. I take the novelist's freedom to observe the reader's mind formulating the exclamation, "That's it! The fellow talks *pro domo*."*

Indeed it was not the intention! When I shouldered the bag I was not aware of the cat inside. But, after all, why not? The fair courtyards of the House of Art are thronged by many humble retainers. And there is no retainer so devoted as he who is allowed to sit on the doorstep. The fellows who have got inside are apt to think too much of themselves. This last remark, I beg to state, is not malicious within the definition of the law of libel. It's fair comment on a matter of public interest. But never mind. *Pro domo.* So be it. For his house *tant que vous voudrez.** And yet in truth I was by no means anxious to justify my existence. The attempt would have been not only needless and absurd but almost inconceivable, in a purely spectacular universe, where no such disagreeable necessity can possibly arise. It is sufficient for me to say (and I am saying it at some length in these pages): *J'ai vécu.** I have existed, obscure amongst the wonders and terrors of my time, as the Abbé Sieyès,* the original utterer of the quoted words, had managed to exist through the violences, the crimes, and the enthusiasms of the French Revolution.* *J'ai vécu*, as I apprehend most of us manage to exist, missing all along the varied forms of destruction by a hair's-breadth, saving my body, that's clear, and perhaps my soul also, but not without some damage here and there to the fine edge of my conscience, that heirloom of the ages, of the race, of the group, of the family, colourable and plastic, fashioned by the words, the looks, the acts, and even by the silences and abstentions surrounding one's childhood; tinged in a complete scheme of delicate shades and crude colours by the inherited traditions, beliefs, or prejudices— unaccountable, despotic, persuasive, and often, in its texture, romantic.

And often romantic! . . . The matter in hand,

however, is to keep these reminiscences from turning into confessions, a form of literary activity discredited by Jean Jacques Rousseau*on account of the extreme thoroughness he brought to the work of justifying his own existence; for that such was his purpose is palpably, even grossly, visible to an unprejudiced eye. But then, you see, the man was not a writer of fiction. He was an artless moralist, as is clearly demonstrated by his anniversaries being celebrated with marked emphasis by the heirs of the French Revolution, which was not a political movement at all, but a great outburst of morality. He had no imagination, as the most casual perusal of "Émile"* will prove. He was no novelist, whose first virtue is the exact understanding of the limits traced by the reality of his time to the play of his invention. Inspiration comes from the earth, which has a past, a history, a future, not from the cold and immutable heaven. A writer of imaginative prose (even more than any other sort of artist) stands confessed in his works. His conscience, his deeper sense of things, lawful and unlawful, gives him his attitude before the world. Indeed, everyone who puts pen to paper for the reading of strangers (unless a moralist, who, generally speaking, has no conscience except the one he is at pains to produce for the use of others) can speak of nothing else. It is M. Anatole France,* the most eloquent and just of French prose writers, who says that we must recognise at last that, "failing the resolution to hold our peace, we can only talk of ourselves."*

This remark, if I remember rightly, was made in the course of a sparring match with the late Ferdinand Brunetière* over the principles and rules of literary criticism. As was fitting for a man to whom we owe the memorable saying, "The good critic is he who re-

lates the adventures of his soul amongst masterpieces,"
M. Anatole France maintained that there were no rules
and no principles. And that may be very true. Rules,
principles and standards die and vanish every day.
Perhaps they are all dead and vanished by this time.
These, if ever, are the brave free days of destroyed landmarks, while the ingenious minds are busy inventing
the forms of the new beacons which, it is consoling to
think, will be set up presently in the old places. But
what is interesting to a writer is the possession of an
inward certitude that literary criticism will never die,
for man (so variously defined) is, before everything
else, a critical animal. And, as long as distinguished
minds are ready to treat it in the spirit of high adventure, literary criticism shall appeal to us with all the
charm and wisdom of a well-told tale of personal experience.

For Englishmen especially, of all the races of the
earth, a task, any task, undertaken in an adventurous
spirit acquires the merit of romance. But the critics
as a rule exhibit but little of an adventurous spirit.
They take risks, of course—one can hardly live without
that. The daily bread is served out to us (however
sparingly) with a pinch of salt. Otherwise one would
get sick of the diet one prays for, and that would be
not only improper, but impious. From impiety of that
or any other kind—save us! An ideal of reserved
manner, adhered to from a sense of proprieties, from
shyness, perhaps, or caution, or simply from weariness,
induces, I suspect, some writers of criticism to conceal
the adventurous side of their calling, and then the
criticism becomes a mere "notice," as it were the
relation of a journey where nothing but the distances
and the geology of a new country should be set down;
the glimpses of strange beasts, the dangers of flood and

field, the hair's-breadth escapes, and the sufferings
(oh, the sufferings too! I have no doubt of the sufferings) of the traveller being carefully kept out; no shady
spot, no fruitful plant being ever mentioned either; so
that the whole performance looks like a mere feat of
agility on the part of a trained pen running in a desert.
A cruel spectacle—a most deplorable adventure.
"Life," in the words of an immortal thinker of, I should
say, bucolic origin, but whose perishable name is lost to
the worship of posterity—"life is not all beer and
skittles."* Neither is the writing of novels. It isn't
really. *Je vous donne ma parole d'honneur* that it—is—
not. Not *all*. I am thus emphatic because some years
ago, I remember, the daughter of a general. . .

Sudden revelations of the profane world must have
come now and then to hermits in their cells, to the
cloistered monks of Middle Ages, to lonely sages, men
of science, reformers; the revelations of the world's
superficial judgment, shocking to the souls concentrated upon their own bitter labour in the cause of
sanctity, or of knowledge, or of temperance, let us say,
or of art, if only the art of cracking jokes or playing the
flute. And thus this general's daughter came to me—or
I should say one of the general's daughters did. There
were three of these bachelor ladies, of nicely graduated
ages, who held a neighbouring farmhouse in a united
and more or less military occupation. The eldest
warred against the decay of manners in the village
children, and executed frontal attacks upon the village
mothers for the conquest of curtseys. It sounds futile,
but it was really a war for an idea. The second skir-
mished and scouted all over the country; and it was that
one who pushed a reconnaissance right to my very
table—I mean the one who wore stand-up collars. She
was really calling upon my wife in the soft spirit of

afternoon friendliness, but with her usual martial determination. She marched into my room swinging her stick . . . but no—I mustn't exaggerate. It is not my speciality. I am not a humoristic writer. In all soberness, then, all I am certain of is that she had a stick to swing.

No ditch or wall encompassed my abode. The window was open; the door too stood open to that best friend of my work, the warm, still sunshine of the wide fields. They lay around me infinitely helpful, but truth to say I had not known for weeks whether the sun shone upon the earth and whether the stars above still moved on their appointed courses. I was just then giving up some days of my allotted span to the last chapters of the novel "Nostromo,"* a tale of an imaginary (but true) seaboard, which is still mentioned now and again, and indeed kindly, sometimes in connection with the word "failure" and sometimes in conjunction with the word "astonishing." I have no opinion on this discrepancy. It's the sort of difference that can never be settled. All I know, is that, for twenty months, neglecting the common joys of life that fall to the lot of the humblest on this earth, I had, like the prophet of old,* "wrestled with the Lord" for my creation, for the headlands of the coast, for the darkness of the Placid Gulf, the light on the snows, the clouds on the sky, and for the breath of life that had to be blown into the shapes of men and women, of Latin and Saxon, of Jew and Gentile. These are, perhaps, strong words, but it is difficult to characterise otherwise the intimacy and the strain of a creative effort in which mind and will and conscience are engaged to the full, hour after hour, day after day, away from the world, and to the exclusion of all that makes life really lovable and gentle—something for which a material parallel can only be found in the

everlasting sombre stress of the westward winter passage round Cape Horn.* For that too is the wrestling of
men with the might of their Creator, in a great isolation
from the world, without the amenities and consolations
of life, a lonely struggle under a sense of over-matched
littleness, for no reward that could be adequate, but for
the mere winning of a longitude. Yet a certain longitude, once won, cannot be disputed. The sun and the
stars and the shape of your earth are the witnesses of
your gain; whereas a handful of pages, no matter how
much you have made them your own, are at best but an
obscure and questionable spoil. Here they are. "Failure"—"Astonishing": take your choice; or perhaps
both, or neither—a mere rustle and flutter of pieces of
paper settling down in the night, and undistinguishable,
like the snowflakes of a great drift destined to melt
away in sunshine.

"How do you do?"

It was the greeting of the general's daughter. I had
heard nothing—no rustle, no footsteps. I had felt only
a moment before a sort of premonition of evil; I had the
sense of an inauspicious presence—just that much
warning and no more; and then came the sound of the
voice and the jar as of a terrible fall from a great height
—a fall, let us say, from the highest of the clouds floating in gentle procession over the fields in the faint
westerly air of that July afternoon. I picked myself up
quickly, of course; in other words, I jumped up from my
chair stunned and dazed, every nerve quivering with the
pain of being uprooted out of one world and flung down
into another—perfectly civil.

"Oh! How do you do? Won't you sit down?"

That's what I said. This horrible but, I assure you,
perfectly true reminiscence tells you more than a whole
volume of confessions à la Jean Jacques Rousseau would

do. Observe! I didn't howl at her, or start upsetting furniture, or throw myself on the floor and kick, or allow myself to hint in any other way at the appalling magnitude of the disaster.   The whole world of Costaguana (the country, you may remember, of my seaboard tale), men, women, headlands, houses, mountains, town, *campo* (there was not a single brick, stone, or grain of sand of its soil I had not placed in position with my own hands); all the history, geography, politics, finance; the wealth of Charles Gould's silver-mine, and the splendour of the magnificent Capataz de Cargadores, whose name, cried out in the night (Dr. Monygham heard it pass over his head—in Linda Viola's voice), dominated even after death the dark gulf containing his conquests of treasure and love—all that had come down crashing about my ears.   I felt I could never pick up the pieces— and in that very moment I was saying, "Won't you sit down?"

The sea is strong medicine. Behold what the quarter-deck* training even in a merchant ship will do! This episode should give you a new view of the English and Scots seamen (a much-caricatured folk) who had the last say in the formation of my character.   One is nothing if not modest, but in this disaster I think I have done some honour to their simple teaching. "Won't you sit down?" Very fair; very fair indeed. She sat down. Her amused glance strayed all over the room. There were pages of MS. on the table and under the table, a batch of typed copy on a chair, single leaves had fluttered away into distant corners; there were there living pages, pages scored and wounded, dead pages that would be burnt at the end of the day—the litter cf a cruel battlefield, of a long, long and desperate fray. Long! I suppose I went to bed sometimes, and got up the same number of times. Yes, I suppose I slept, and ate the food put before me, and talked connectedly to my household on suitable occasions. But I had never been aware of the even flow of daily life, made easy and noiseless for me by a silent, watchful, tireless affection. Indeed, it seemed to me that I had been sitting at that table surrounded by the litter of a desperate fray for days and nights on end. It seemed so, because of the intense weariness of which that interruption had made me aware—the awful disenchantment of a mind realising suddenly the futility of an enormous task, joined to a bodily fatigue such as no ordinary amount of fairly heavy physical labour could ever account for. I have carried bags of wheat on my back, bent almost double under a ship's deck-beams, from six in the morning till six in the evening (with an hour and a half off for meals), so I ought to know.

And I love letters. I am jealous of their honour and concerned for the dignity and comeliness of their service. I was, most likely, the only writer that neat lady had ever caught in the exercise of his craft and, it distressed me not to be able to remember when it was that I dressed myself last, and how. No doubt that would be all right in essentials. The fortune of the house included a pair of grey-blue watchful eyes that would see to that. But I felt somehow as grimy as a Costaguana *lepero**after a day's fighting in the streets, rumpled all over and dishevelled down to my very heels. And I am afraid I blinked stupidly. All this was bad for the honour of letters and the dignity of their service. Seen indistinctly through the dust of my collapsed universe, the good lady glanced about the room with a slightly amused serenity. And she was smiling. What on earth was she smiling at? She remarked casually:

"I am afraid I interrupted you."

"Not at all."

She accepted the denial in perfect good faith. **And** it was strictly true. Interrupted—indeed! She had robbed me of at least twenty lives, each infinitely more poignant and real than her own, because informed with passion, possessed of convictions, involved in great affairs created out of my own substance for an anxiously meditated end.

She remained silent for a while, then said with a last glance all round at the litter of the fray:

"And you sit like this here writing your—your . . ."

"I—what? Oh, yes! I sit here all day."

"It must be perfectly delightful."

I suppose that, being no longer very young, I might have been on the verge of having a stroke; but she had left her dog in the porch, and my boy's dog, patrolling the field in front, had espied him from afar. He came on straight and swift like a cannon-ball, and the noise of the fight, which burst suddenly upon our ears, was more than enough to scare away a fit of apoplexy. We went out hastily and separated the gallant animals. Afterwards I told the lady where she would find my wife—just round the corner, under the trees. She nodded and went off with her dog, leaving me appalled before the death and devastation she had lightly made— and with the awfully instructive sound of the word "delightful" lingering in my ears.

Nevertheless, later on, I duly escorted her to the field gate. I wanted to be civil, of course (what are twenty lives in a mere novel that one should be rude to a lady on their account?), but mainly, to adopt the good sound Ollendorffian style, because I did not want the dog of the general's daughter to fight again (*encore*) with the faithful dog of my infant son (*mon petit garçon*). —Was I afraid that the dog of the general's daughter would be able to overcome (*vaincre*) the dog of my

child?—No, I was not afraid. . . . But away
with the Ollendorff method. However appropriate
and seemingly unavoidable when I touch upon anything
appertaining to the lady, it is most unsuitable to the
origin, character and history of the dog; for the dog was
the gift to the child from a man for whom words had
anything but an Ollendorffian value, a man almost
childlike in the impulsive movements of his untutored
genius, the most singleminded of verbal impressionists,
using his great gifts of straight feeling and right expression with a fine sincerity and a strong, if, perhaps,
not fully conscious conviction. His art did not obtain,
I fear, all the credit its unsophisticated inspiration
deserved. I am alluding to the late Stephen Crane,*the
author of "The Red Badge of Courage," a work of
imagination which found its short moment of celebrity
in the last decade of the departed century. Other
books followed. Not many. He had not the time. It
was an individual and complete talent, which obtained
but a grudging, somewhat supercilious recognition
from the world at large. For himself one hesitates to
regret his early death. Like one of the men in his
"Open Boat," one felt that he was of those whom fate
seldom allows to make a safe landing after much toil
and bitterness at the oar. I confess to an abiding
affection for that energetic, slight, fragile, intensely
living and transient figure. He liked me even before we
met on the strength of a page or two of my writing, and
after we had met I am glad to think he liked me still.
He used to point out to me with great earnestness, and
even with some severity, that "a boy *ought* to have a
dog." I suspect that he was shocked at my neglect of
parental duties. Ultimately it was he who provided
the dog. Shortly afterwards, one day, after playing
with the child on the rug for an hour or so with the most

intense absorption, he raised his head and declared firmly: "I shall teach your boy to ride." That was not to be. He was not given the time.

But here is the dog—an old dog now. Broad and low on his bandy paws, with a black head on a white body, and a ridiculous black spot at the other end of him, he provokes, when he walks abroad, smiles not altogether unkind. Grotesque and engaging in the whole of his appearance, his usual attitudes are meek, but his temperament discloses itself unexpectedly pugnacious in the presence of his kind. As he lies in the firelight, his head well up, and a fixed, far-away gaze directed at the shadows of the room, he achieves a striking nobility of pose in the calm consciousness of an unstained life. He has brought up one baby, and now, after seeing his first charge off to school, he is bringing up another with the same conscientious devotion but with a more deliberate gravity of manner, the sign of greater wisdom and riper experience, but also of rheumatism, I fear. From the morning bath to the evening ceremonies of the cot you attend, old friend, the little two-legged creature of your adoption, being yourself treated in the exercise of your duties with every possible regard, with infinite consideration, by every person in the house— even as I myself am treated; only you deserve it more. The general's daughter would tell you that it must be "perfectly delightful."

Aha! old dog. She never heard you yelp with acute pain (it's that poor left ear) the while, with incredible self-command, you preserve a rigid immobility for fear of overturning the little two-legged creature. She has never seen your resigned smile when the little two-legged creature, interrogated sternly, "What are you doing to the good dog?" answers with a wide, innocent stare: "Nothing. Only loving him, mamma dear!"

The general's daughter does not know the secret terms of self-imposed tasks, good dog, the pain that may lurk in the very rewards of rigid self-command. But we have lived together many years. We have grown older, too; and though our work is not quite done yet we may indulge now and then in a little introspection before the fire—meditate on the art of bringing up babies and on the perfect delight of writing tales where so many lives come and go at the cost of one which slips imperceptibly away.

VI

IN THE retrospect of a life which had, besides its preliminary stage of childhood and early youth, two distinct developments, and even two distinct elements, such as earth and water, for its successive scenes, a certain amount of naïveness is unavoidable. I am conscious of it in these pages. This remark is put forward in no apologetic spirit. As years go by and the number of pages grows steadily, the feeling grows upon one too that one can write only for friends. Then why should one put them to the necessity of protesting (as a friend would do) that no apology is necessary, or put, perchance, into their heads the doubt of one's discretion? So much as to the care due to those friends whom a word here, a line there, a fortunate page of just feeling in the right place, some happy simplicity, or even some lucky subtlety, has drawn from the great multitude of fellow-beings even as a fish is drawn from the depths of the sea. Fishing is notoriously (I am talking now of the deep sea) a matter of luck. As to one's enemies, those will take care of themselves.

There is a gentleman, for instance, who, metaphorically speaking, jumps upon me with both feet. This image has no grace, but it is exceedingly apt to the occasion—to the several occasions. I don't know precisely how long he had been indulging in that intermittent exercise, whose seasons are ruled by the custom of the publishing trade. Somebody pointed him out (in printed shape, of course) to my attention some time ago, and straightway I experienced a sort of reluctant

affection for that robust man.* He leaves not a shred of
my substance untrodden: for the writer's substance is
his writing; the rest of him is but a vain shadow, cherished or hated on uncritical grounds. Not a shred!
Yet the sentiment owned to is not a freak of affectation
or perversity. It has a deeper, and, I venture to think, a
more estimable origin than the caprice of emotional
lawlessness. It is, indeed, lawful in so much that it is
given (reluctantly) for a consideration, for several
considerations. There is that robustness, for instance,
so often the sign of good moral balance. That's a
consideration. It is not, indeed, pleasant to be stamped
upon, but the very thoroughness of the operation, im-
plying not only a careful reading, but some real insight
into work whose qualities and defects, whatever they
may be, are not so much on the surface, is something to
be thankful for in view of the fact that it may happen
to one's work to be condemned without being read at all.
This is the most fatuous adventure that can well
happen to a writer venturing his soul amongst criticisms. It can do one no harm, of course, but it is
disagreeable. It is disagreeable in the same way as
discovering a three-card-trick man amongst a decent
lot of folk in a third-class compartment. The open
impudence of the whole transaction, appealing in-
sidiously to the folly and credulity of mankind, the
brazen, shameless patter, proclaiming the fraud openly
while insisting on the fairness of the game, give one a
feeling of sickening disgust. The honest violence of a
plain man playing a fair game fairly—even if he means
to knock you over—may appear shocking, but it remains within the pale of decency. Damaging as it may
be, it is in no sense offensive. One may well feel some
regard for honesty, even if practised upon one's own
vile body. But it is very obvious that an enemy of that

sort will not be stayed by explanations or placated by apologies. Were I to advance the plea of youth in excuse of the naïveness to be found in these pages, he would be likely to say "Bosh!" in a column and a half of fierce print. Yet a writer is no older than his first published book, and, notwithstanding the vain appearances of decay which attend us in this transitory life, I stand here with the wreath of only fifteen short summers on my brow.

With the remark, then, that at such tender age, some naïveness of feeling and expression is excusable, I proceed to admit that, upon the whole, my previous state of existence was not a good equipment for a literary life. Perhaps I should not have used the word literary. That word pre-supposes an intimacy of acquaintance with letters, a turn of mind and a manner of feeling to which I dare lay no claim. I only love letters; but the love of letters does not make a literary man, any more than the love of the sea makes a seaman. And it is very possible too, that I love the letters in the same way a literary man may love the sea he looks at from the shore—a scene of great endeavour and of great achievements changing the face of the world, the great open way to all sorts of undiscovered countries. No, perhaps I had better say that the life at sea—and I don't mean a mere taste of it, but a good broad span of years, something that really counts as real service—is not, upon the whole, a good equipment for a writing life. God forbid, though, that I should be thought of as denying my masters of the quarter-deck. I am not capable of that sort of apostasy. I have confessed my attitude of piety towards their shades in three or four tales, and if any man on earth more than another needs to be true to himself as he hopes to be saved, it is certainly the writer of fiction.

What I meant to say, simply, is that the quarter-deck training does not prepare one sufficiently for the reception of literary criticism. Only that, and no more. But this defect is not without gravity. If it be permissible to twist, invert, adapt (and spoil) M. Anatole France's definition* of a good critic, then let us say that the good author is he who contemplates without marked joy or excessive sorrow the adventures of his soul amongst criticisms. Far be from me the intention to mislead an attentive public into the belief that there is no criticism at sea. That would be dishonest, and even impolite. Everything can be found at sea, according to the spirit of your quest—strife, peace, romance, naturalism of the most pronounced kind, ideals, boredom, disgust, inspiration—and every conceivable opportunity, including the opportunity to make a fool of yourself—exactly as in the pursuit of literature. But the quarter-deck criticism is somewhat different from literary criticism. This much they have in common, that before the one and the other the answering back, as a general rule, does not pay.

Yes, you find criticism at sea, and even appreciation—I tell you everything is to be found on salt water—criticism generally impromptu, and always *viva voce*,* which is the outward, obvious difference from the literary operation of that kind, with consequent freshness and vigour which may be lacking in the printed word. With appreciation, which comes at the end, when the critic and the criticised are about to part, it is otherwise. The sea appreciation of one's humble talents has the permanency of the written word, seldom the charm of variety, is .ormal in its phrasing. There the literary master has the superiority, though he, too, can in effect but say —and often says it in the very phrase—"I can highly recommend." Only usually he uses the word "We,"

there being some occult virtue in the first person plural,
which makes it specially fit for critical and royal
declarations. I have a small handful of these sea ap-
preciations, signed by various masters, yellowing slowly
in my writing-table's left-hand drawer, rustling under
my reverent touch, like a handful of dry leaves plucked
for a tender memento from the tree of knowledge.
Strange! It seems that it is for these few bits of paper,
headed by the names of a few ships and signed by the
names of a few Scots and English shipmasters, that I
have faced the astonished indignations, the mockeries
and the reproaches of a sort hard to bear for a boy of
fifteen; that I have been charged with the want of
patriotism, the want of sense, and the want of heart too;
that I went through agonies of self-conflict and shed
secret tears not a few, and had the beauties of the Furca
Pass spoiled for me, and have been called an "incorrigible Don Quixote," in allusion to the book-born
madness of the knight. For that spoil! They rustle,
those bits of paper—some dozen of them in all. In that
faint, ghostly sound there live the memories of twenty
years, the voices of rough men now no more, the strong
voice of the everlasting winds, and the whisper of a
mysterious spell, the murmur of the great sea, which
must have somehow reached my inland cradle and
entered my unconscious ear, like that formula of
Mohammedan faith the Mussulman father whispers into
the ear of his new-born infant, making him one of the
faithful almost with his first breath. I do not know
whether I have been a good seaman, but I know I have
been a very faithful one. And after all there is that
handful of "characters" from various ships to prove
that all these years have not been altogether a dream.
There they are, brief, and monotonous in tone, but as
suggestive bits of writing to me as any inspired page to

be found in literature. But then, you see, I have been called romantic. Well, that can't be helped. But stay. I seem to remember that I have been called a realist also. And as that charge too can be made out, let us try to live up to it, at whatever cost, for a change. With this end in view, I will confide to you coyly, and only because there is no one about to see my blushes by the light of the midnight lamp, that these suggestive bits of quarter-deck appreciation one and all contain the words "strictly sober."

Did I overhear a civil murmur, "That's very gratifying to be sure"? Well, yes, it is gratifying—thank you. It is at least as gratifying to be certified sober as to be certified romantic, though such certificates would not qualify one for the secretaryship of a temperance association or for the post of official troubadour to some lordly democratic institution such as the London County Council, for instance. The above prosaic reflection is put down here only in order to prove the general sobriety of my judgment in mundane affairs. I make a point of it because a couple of years ago, a certain short story*of mine being published in a French translation, a Parisian critic—I am almost certain it was M. Gustave Kahn,* in the *Gil-Blas*—giving me a short notice, summed up his rapid impression of the writer's quality in the words *un puissant rêveur.*° So be it! Who would cavil at the words of a friendly reader? Yet perhaps not such an unconditional dreamer as all that. I will make bold to say that neither at sea nor ashore have I ever lost the sense of responsibility. There is more than one sort of intoxication. Even before the most seductive reveries I have remained mindful of that sobriety of interior life, that asceticism of sentiment, in which alone the naked form of truth, such as one conceives it, such as one feels

it, can be rendered without shame. It is but a maudlin
and indecent verity that comes out through the strength
of wine. I have tried to be a sober worker all my life—
all my two lives. I did so from taste, no doubt, having
an instinctive horror of losing my sense of full self-
possession, but also from artistic conviction. Yet
there are so many pitfalls on each side of the true path
that, having gone some way, and feeling a little battered
and weary, as a middle-aged traveller will from the
mere daily difficulties of the march, I ask myself
whether I have kept always, always faithful to that
sobriety wherein there is power, and truth, and peace.

As to my sea-sobriety, that is quite properly certified
under the sign-manual of several trustworthy shipmasters of some standing in their time. I seem to hear
your polite murmur that "Surely this might have been
taken for granted." Well, no. It might not have
been. That august academical body of the Marine
Department of the Board of Trade takes nothing for
granted in the granting of its learned degrees. By its
regulations issued under the first Merchant Shipping
Act, the very word SOBER must be written, or a whole
sackful, a ton, a mountain of the most enthusiastic
appreciation will avail you nothing. The door of the
examination rooms shall remain closed to your tears
and entreaties. The most fanatical advocate of temperance could not be more pitilessly fierce in his rectitude
than the Marine Department of the Board of Trade.
As I have been face to face at various times with all the
examiners of the Port of London, in my generation,
there can be no doubt as to the force and the continuity
of my abstemiousness. Three of them were examiners
in seamanship, and it was my fate to be delivered into
the hands of each of them at proper intervals of sea
service. The first of all,* tall, spare, with a perfectly

white head and moustache, a quiet, kindly manner, and an air of benign intelligence, must, I am forced to conclude, have been unfavourably impressed by something in my appearance. His old thin hands loosely clasped resting on his crossed legs, he began by an elementary question in a mild voice, and went on, went on . . . It lasted for hours, for hours. Had I been a strange microbe with potentialities of deadly mischief to the Merchant Service I could not have been submitted to a more microscopic examination. Greatly reassured by his apparent benevolence, I had been at first very alert in my answers. But at length the feeling of my brain getting addled crept upon me. And still the passionless process went on, with a sense of untold ages having been spent already on mere preliminaries. Then I got frightened. I was not frightened of being plucked; that eventuality did not even present itself to my mind. It was something much more serious, and weird. "This ancient person," I said to myself, terrified, "is so near his grave that he must have lost all notion of time. He is considering this examination in terms of eternity. It is all very well for him. His race is run. But I may find myself coming out of this room into the world of men a stranger, friendless, forgotten by my very landlady, even were I able after this endless experience to remember the way to my hired home." This statement is not so much of a verbal exaggeration as may be supposed. Some very queer thoughts passed through my head while I was considering my answers; thoughts which had nothing to do with seamanship, nor yet with anything reasonable known to this earth. I verily believe that at times I was lightheaded in a sort of languid way. At last there fell a silence, and that, too, seemed to last for ages, while, bending over his desk, the examiner wrote out my pass-slip slowly with a noiseless pen.

He extended the scrap of paper to me without a word, inclined his white head gravely to my parting bow . . .

When I got out of the room I felt limply flat, like a squeezed lemon, and the doorkeeper in his glass cage, where I stopped to get my hat and tip him a shilling, said:

"Well! I thought you were never coming out."

"How long have I been in there?" I asked faintly.

He pulled out his watch.

"He kept you, sir, just under three hours. I don't think this ever happened with any of the gentlemen before."

It was only when I got out of the building that I began to walk on air. And the human animal being averse from change and timid before the unknown, I said to myself that I would not mind really being examined by the same man on a future occasion. But when the time of ordeal*came round again the doorkeeper let me into another room, with the now familiar paraphernalia of models of ships and tackle, a board for signals on the wall, a big long table covered with official forms, and having an unrigged mast fixed to the edge. The solitary tenant was unknown to me by sight, though not by reputation, which was simply execrable. Short and sturdy as far as I could judge, clad in an old, brown, morning suit, he sat leaning on his elbow, his hand shading his eyes, and half averted from the chair I was to occupy on the other side of the table. He was motionless, mysterious, remote, enigmatical, with something mournful too in the pose, like that statue of Giuliano (I think) de Medici*shading his face on the tomb by Michael Angelo, though, of course, he was far, far from being beautiful. He began by trying to make me talk nonsense. But I had been warned of that fiendish trait, and contradicted him with great assurance. After a while he left off. So far, good. But his immobility, the thick elbow on the table, the abrupt, unhappy voice, the shaded and averted face grew more and more impressive. He kept inscrutably silent for a moment, and then, placing me in a ship of a certain size at sea, under certain conditions of weather, season, locality, etc., etc.—all very clear and precise— ordered me to execute a certain manœuvre. Before I was half through with it he did some material damage to the ship. Directly I had grappled with the difficulty he caused another to present itself, and when that too was met he stuck another ship before me, creating a very dangerous situation. I felt slightly outraged by this ingenuity in piling up trouble upon a man.

"I wouldn't have got into that mess," I suggested mildly. "I could have seen that ship before."

He never stirred the least bit.

"No, you couldn't. The weather's thick."

"Oh! I didn't know," I apologised blankly. I suppose that after all I managed to stave off the smash with sufficient approach to verisimilitude, and the ghastly business went on. You must understand that the scheme of the test he was applying to me was, I gathered, a homeward passage—the sort of passage I would not wish to my bitterest enemy. That imaginary ship seemed to labour under a most comprehensive curse. It's no use enlarging on these never-ending misfortunes; suffice it to say that long before the end I would have welcomed with gratitude an opportunity to exchange into the *Flying Dutchman*.* Finally he shoved me into the North Sea (I suppose) and provided me with a lee-shore with outlying sandbanks—the Dutch coast presumably. Distance, eight miles. The evidence of such implacable animosity deprived me of speech for quite half a minute.

"Well," he said—for our pace had been very smart indeed till then.

"I will have to think a little, sir."

"Doesn't look as if there were much time to think," he muttered sardonically from under his hand.

"No, sir," I said with some warmth. "Not on board a ship I could see. But so many accidents have happened that I really can't remember what there's left for me to work with."

Still half averted, and with his eyes concealed, he made unexpectedly a grunting remark.

"You've done very well."

"Have I the two anchors at the bow, sir?" I asked. "Yes."

I prepared myself then, as a last hope for the ship, to let them both go in the most effectual manner, when his infernal system of testing resourcefulness came into play again.

"But there's only one cable. You've lost the other."

It was exasperating.

"Then I would back them, if I could, and tail the heaviest hawser on board on the end of the chain before letting go, and if she parted from that, which is quite likely, I would just do nothing. She would have to go."

"Nothing more to do, eh?"

"No, sir. I could do no more."

He gave a bitter half-laugh.

"You could always say your prayers."

He got up, stretched himself, and yawned slightly. It was a sallow, strong, unamiable face. He put me in a surly, bored fashion through the usual questions as to lights and signals, and I escaped from the room thankfully—passed! Forty minutes! And again I walked on air along Tower Hill, where so many good men had lost their heads, because, I suppose, they were not resourceful enough to save them. And in my heart of hearts I had no objection to meeting that examiner once more when the third and last ordeal became due in another year or so. I even hoped I should. I knew the worst of him now, and forty minutes is not an unreasonable time. Yes, I distinctly hoped . . .

But not a bit of it. When I presented myself to be examined for Master* the examiner* who received me was short, plump, with a round, soft face in grey, fluffy whiskers, and fresh, loquacious lips.

He commenced operations with an easy-going "Let's see. H'm. Suppose you tell me all you know of charter-parties."* He kept it up in that style all through, wandering off in the shape of comment into bits out of his own life, then pulling himself up short and returning to the business in hand. It was very interesting. "What's your idea of a jury-rudder*now?" he queried suddenly, at the end of an instructive anecdote bearing upon a point of stowage.

I warned him that I had no experience of a lost rudder at sea, and gave him two classical examples of makeshifts out of a text-book. In exchange he described to me a jury-rudder he had invented himself years before, when in command of a 3000-ton steamer. It was, I declare, the cleverest contrivance imaginable. "May be of use to you some day," he concluded. "You will go into steam presently. Everybody goes into steam."

There he was wrong. I never went into steam—not really.* If I only live long enough I shall become a bizarre relic of a dead barbarism, a sort of monstrous antiquity, the only seaman of the dark ages who had never gone into steam—not really.

Before the examination was over he imparted to me

a few interesting details of the transport service in the time of the Crimean War.*

"The use of wire rigging*became general about that time too," he observed. "I was a very young master then. That was before you were born."

"Yes, sir. I am of the year 1857."

"The Mutiny*year," he commented, as if to himself adding in a louder tone that his ship happened then to be in the Gulf of Bengal, employed under a Government charter.

Clearly the transport service had been the making of this examiner, who so unexpectedly had given me an insight into his existence, awakening in me the sense of the continuity of that sea-life into which I had stepped from outside; giving a touch of human intimacy to the machinery of official relations. I felt adopted. His experience was for me, too, as though he had been an ancestor.

Writing my long name (it has twelve letters) with laborious care on the slip of blue paper, he remarked:

"You are of Polish extraction."

"Born there, sir."

He laid down the pen and leaned back to look at me as it were for the first time.

"Not many of your nationality in our service, I should think. I never remember meeting one either before or after I left the sea. Don't remember ever hearing of one. An inland people, aren't you?"

I said yes—very much so. We were remote from the sea not only by situation, but also from a complete absence of indirect association, not being a commercial nation at all, but purely agricultural. He made then the quaint reflection that it was "a long way for me to come out to begin a sea-life"; as if sea-life were not precisely a life in which one goes a long way from home.

I told him, smiling, that no doubt I could have found a ship much nearer my native place, but I had thought to myself that if I was to be a seaman then I would be a British seaman* and no other. It was a matter of deliberate choice.

He nodded slightly at that; and as he kept on looking at me interrogatively, I enlarged a little, confessing that I had spent a little time on the way in the Mediterranean and in the West Indies. I did not want to present myself to the British Merchant Service in an altogether green state. It was no use telling him that my mysterious vocation was so strong that my very wild oats had to be sown at sea. It was the exact truth, but he would not have understood the somewhat exceptional psychology of my sea-going, I fear.

"I suppose you've never come across one of your countrymen at sea. Have you now?"

I admitted I never had. The examiner had given himself up to the spirit of gossiping idleness. For myself, I was in no haste to leave that room. Not in the least. The era of examinations was over. I would never again see that friendly man who was a professional ancestor, a sort of grandfather in the craft. Moreover, I had to wait till he dismissed me, and of that there was no sign. As he remained silent, looking at me, I added:

"But I have heard of one, some years ago. He seems to have been a boy serving his time on board a Liverpool ship, if I am not mistaken."

"What was his name?"*

I told him.

"How did you say that?" he asked, puckering up his eyes at the uncouth sound.

I repeated the name very distinctly.

"How do you spell it?"

I told him. He moved his head at the impracticable nature of that name, and observed:

"It's quite as long as your own—isn't it?"

There was no hurry. I had passed for Master, and I had all the rest of my life before me to make the best of it. That seemed a long time. I went leisurely through a small mental calculation, and said:

"Not quite. Shorter by two letters, sir."

"Is it?" The examiner pushed the signed blue slip across the table to me, and rose from his chair. Somehow this seemed a very abrupt ending of our relations, and I felt almost sorry to part from that excellent man, who was master of a ship before the whisper of the sea had reached my cradle. He offered me his hand and wished me well. He even made a few steps towards the door with me, and ended with good-natured advice.

"I don't know what may be your plans but you ought to go into steam. When a man has got his master's certificate it's the proper time. If I were you I would go into steam."

I thanked him, and shut the door behind me definitely on the era of examinations. But that time I did not walk on air, as on the first two occasions. I walked across the Hill of many beheadings with measured steps. It was a fact, I said to myself, that I was now a British master mariner beyond a doubt. It was not that I had an exaggerated sense of that very modest achievement, with which, however, luck, opportunity, or any extraneous influence could have had nothing to do. That fact, satisfactory and obscure in itself, had for me a certain ideal significance. It was an answer to certain outspoken scepticism, and even to some not very kind aspersions. I had vindicated myself from what had been cried upon as a stupid obstinacy or a fantastic caprice. I don't mean to say that a whole country had been convulsed by my desire to go to sea. But for a boy between fifteen and sixteen, sensitive enough, in all conscience, the commotion of his little world had seemed a very considerable thing indeed. So considerable that, absurdly enough, the echoes of it linger to this day. I catch myself in hours of solitude and retrospect meeting arguments and charges made thirty-five years ago by voices now for ever still; finding things to say that an assailed boy could not have found, simply because of the mysteriousness of his impulses to himself. I understood no more than the people who called upon me to explain myself. There was no precedent. I verily believe mine was the only case of a boy of my nationality and antecedents taking a, so to speak, standing jump out of his racial surroundings and associations. For you must understand that there was no idea of any sort of "career" in my call. Of Russia or Germany there could be no question. The nationality, the antecedents, made it impossible. The feeling against the Austrian service was not so strong, and I dare say there would have been no difficulty in finding my way into the Naval School at Pola.* It would have meant six months' extra grinding at German, perhaps, but I was not past the age of admission, and in other respects I was well qualified. This expedient to palliate my folly was thought of—but not by me. I must admit that in that respect my negative was accepted at once. That order of feeling was comprehensible enough to the most inimical of my critics. I was not called upon to offer explanations; the truth is that what I had in view was not a naval career, but the sea. There seemed no way open to it but through France. I had the language at any rate, and of all the countries in Europe it is with France that Poland has most connection. There were some facilities for having me a little looked after, at first. Letters were being written, answers were being received, arrangements were being made for my departure for Marseilles, where an excellent fellow called Solary,* got at in a roundabout fashion through various French channels, had promised good-naturedly to put *le jeune homme** in the way of getting a decent ship for his first start if he really wanted a taste of *ce métier de chien.**

I watched all these preparations gratefully, and kept my own counsel. But what I told the last of my examiners was perfectly true. Already the determined resolve, that "if a seaman, then an English seaman," was formulated in my head though, of course, in the Polish language. I did not know six words of English, and I was astute enough to understand that it was much better to say nothing of my purpose. As it was I was already looked upon as partly insane, at least by the more distant acquaintances. The principal thing was to get away. I put my trust in the good-natured Solary's very civil letter to my uncle, though I was shocked a little by the phrase about the *métier de chien.*

This Solary (Baptistin), when I beheld him in the flesh, turned out a quite young man, very good-looking, with a fine black, short beard, a fresh complexion, and soft, merry black eyes. He was as jovial and good-natured as any boy could desire. I was still asleep in my room in a modest hotel near the quays of the old port, after the fatigues of the journey *via* Vienna, Zurich, Lyons, when he burst in flinging the shutters open to the sun of Provence and chiding me boisterously for lying abed. How pleasantly he startled me by his noisy objurgations to be up and off instantly for a "three years' campaign in the South Seas." O magic words! "*Une campagne de trois ans dans les mers du sud*"—that is the French for a three years' deep-water voyage.

He gave me a delightful waking, and his friendliness was unwearied; but I fear he did not enter upon the quest for a ship for me in a very solemn spirit. He had been at sea himself, but had left off at the age of twenty-five, finding he could earn his living on shore in a much more agreeable manner. He was related to an incredible number of Marseilles well-to-do families of a certain class. One of his uncles was a ship-broker of good standing, with a large connection amongst English ships; other relatives of his dealt in ships' stores, owned sail-lofts, sold chains and anchors, were master-stevedores, caulkers, shipwrights. His grandfather (I think) was a dignitary of a kind, the Syndic of the Pilots. I made acquaintances amongst these people, but mainly amongst the pilots. The very first whole day I ever spent on salt water was by invitation, in a big half-decked pilot-boat, cruising under close reefs on the look-out, in misty, blowing weather, for the sails of ships and the smoke of steamers rising out there, beyond the slim and tall Planier* lighthouse cutting the line of the wind-swept horizon with a white perpendicular stroke. They were hospitable souls, these sturdy Provençal seamen. Under the general designation of *le petit ami de Baptistin** I was made the guest of the Corporation of Pilots, and had the freedom of their boats night or day. And many a day and a night too did I spend cruising with these rough, kindly men, under whose auspices my intimacy with the sea began. Many a time "the little friend of Baptistin" had the hooded cloak of the Mediterranean sailor thrown over him by their honest hands while dodging at night under the lee of Château d'If*on the watch for the lights of ships. Their sea-tanned faces, whiskered or shaved, lean or full, with the

intent wrinkled sea-eyes of the pilot-breed, and here
and there a thin gold loop at the lobe of a hairy ear,
bent over my sea-infancy. The first operation of seamanship I had an opportunity of observing was the
boarding of ships at sea, at all times, in all states of the
weather. They gave it to me to the full. And I have
been invited to sit in more than one tall, dark house of
the old town at their hospitable board, had the *bouillabaisse*ladled out into a thick plate by their high-voiced,
broad-browed wives, talked to their daughters—thick-
set girls, with pure profiles, glorious masses of black
hair arranged with complicated art, dark eyes, and
dazzlingly white teeth.

I had also other acquaintances of quite a different
sort. One of them, Madame Delestang,* an imperious,
handsome lady in a statuesque style, would carry me
off now and then on the front seat of her carriage to the
Prado, at the hour of fashionable airing. She belonged
to one of the old aristocratic families in the south. In
her haughty weariness she used to make me think of
Lady Dedlock in Dickens' "Bleak House," a work of
the master for which I have such an admiration, or
rather such an intense and unreasoning affection, dating
from the days of my childhood, that its very weaknesses are more precious to me than the strength of
other men's work. I have read it innumerable times,
both in Polish and in English; I have read it only the
other day, and, by a not very surprising inversion, the
Lady Dedlock of the book reminded me strongly of the
belle Madame Delestang.

Her husband (as I sat facing them both), with his
thin bony nose, and a perfectly bloodless, narrow
physiognomy clamped together as it were by short
formal side-whiskers, had nothing of Sir Leicester
Dedlock's "grand air" and courtly solemnity. He

belonged to the *haute bourgeoisie*°only, and was a banker, with whom a modest credit had been opened for my needs. He was such an ardent—no, such a frozen-up, mummified Royalist*that he used in current conversation turns of speech contemporary, I should say, with the good Henri Quatre;* and when talking of money matters reckoned not in francs, like the common, godless herd of post-Revolutionary Frenchmen, but in obsolete and forgotten *écus*—*écus* of all money units in the world!—as though Louis Quatorze* were still promenading in royal splendour the gardens of Versailles, and Monsieur de Colbert*busy with the direction of maritime affairs. You must admit that in a banker of the nineteenth century it was a quaint idiosyncrasy. Luckily in the counting-house (it occupied part of the ground floor of the Delestang town residence, in a silent, shady street) the accounts were kept in modern money so that I never had any difficulty in making my wants known to the grave, low-voiced, decorous, Legitimist (I suppose) clerks, sitting in the perpetual gloom of heavily-barred windows behind the sombre, ancient counters, beneath lofty ceilings with heavily-moulded cornices. I always felt on going out as though I had been in the temple of some very dignified but completely temporal religion. And it was generally on these occasions that under the great carriage gateway Lady Ded—I mean Madame Delestang, catching sight of my raised hat, would beckon me with an amiable imperiousness to the side of the carriage, and suggest with an air of amused nonchalance, "*Venez donc faire un tour avec nous,*"*to which the husband would add an encouraging "*C'est ça. Allons, montez, jeune homme.*"* He questioned me sometimes, significantly but with perfect tact and delicacy, as to the way I employed my time, and never failed to express the hope that I wrote regularly to my "honoured uncle." I made no secret of the way I employed my time, and I rather fancy that my artless tales of the pilots and so on entertained Madame Delestang, so far as that ineffable woman could be entertained by the prattle of a youngster very full of his new experience amongst strange men and strange sensations. She expressed no opinions, and talked to me very little; yet her portrait hangs in the gallery of my intimate memories, fixed there by a short and fleeting episode. One day, after putting me down at the corner of a street, she offered me her hand, and detained me by a slight pressure, for a moment. While the husband sat motionless and looking straight before him, she leaned forward in the carriage to say, with just a shade of warning in her leisurely tone: "*Il faut, cependant, faire attention à ne pas gâter sa vie.*"* I had never seen her face so close to mine before. She made my heart beat, and caused me to remaïn thoughtful for a whole evening. Certainly one must, after all, take care not to spoil one's life. But she did not know—nobody could know—how impossible that danger seemed to me.

VII

CAN the transports of first love be calmed, checked, turned to a cold suspicion of the future by a grave quotation from a work on Political Economy? I ask— is it conceivable? Is it possible? Would it be right? With my feet on the very shores of the sea and about to embrace my blue-eyed dream, what could a good-natured warning as to spoiling one's life mean to my youthful passion? It was the most unexpected and the last, too, of the many warnings I had received. It sounded to me very *bizarre*—and, uttered as it was in the very presence of my enchantress, like the voice of folly, the voice of ignorance. But I was not so callous or so stupid as not to recognise there also the voice of kindness. And then the vagueness of the warning—because what can be the meaning of the phrase: to spoil one's life?—arrested one's attention by its air of wise profundity. At any rate, as I have said before, the words of *la belle Madame Delestang* made me thoughtful for a whole evening. I tried to understand and tried in vain, not having any notion of life as an enterprise that could be mismanaged. But I left off being thoughtful shortly before midnight, at which hour, haunted by no ghosts of the past and by no visions of the future, I walked down the quay of the *Vieux Port* to join the pilot-boat of my friends. I knew where she would be waiting for her crew, in the little bit of a canal behind the Fort at the entrance of the harbour. The deserted quays looked very white and dry in the moonlight and as if frost-bound in the sharp air of that December*night.

A prowler or two slunk by noiselessly; a custom-house guard, soldier-like, a sword by his side, paced close under the bowsprits of the long row of ships moored bows on opposite the long, slightly curved, continuous flat wall of the tall houses that seemed to be one immense abandoned building with innumerable windows shuttered closely. Only here and there a small dingy *café* for sailors cast a yellow gleam on the bluish sheen of the flagstone. Passing by, one heard a deep murmur of voices inside—nothing more. How quiet everything was at the end of the quays on the last night on which I went out for a service cruise as a guest of the Marseilles pilots! Not a footstep, except my own, not a sigh, not a whispering echo of the usual revelry going on in the narrow, unspeakable lanes of the Old Town reached my ear—and suddenly, with a terrific jingling rattle of iron and glass, the omnibus of the Jolliette* on its last journey swung round the corner of the dead wall which faces across the paved road the charactertistic angular mass of the Fort St. Jean. Three horses trotted abreast with the clatter of hoofs on the granite setts, and the yellow, uproarious machine jolted violently behind them, fantastic, lighted up, perfectly empty and with the driver apparently asleep on his swaying perch above that amazing racket. I flattened myself against the wall and gasped. It was a stunning experience. Then after staggering on a few paces in the shadow of the Fort casting a darkness more intense than that of a clouded night upon the canal, I saw the tiny light of a lantern standing on the quay, and became aware of muffled figures making towards it from various directions—Pilots of the Third Company hastening to embark. Too sleepy to be talkative, they step on board in silence. But a few low grunts and an enormous yawn are heard. Somebody even ejaculates:

"*Ah! Coquin de sort!*"*and sighs wearily at his hard fate.

The *patron**of the Third Company (there were five companies of pilots at that time, I believe) is the brother-in-law of my friend Solary (Baptistin), a broad-shouldered, deep-chested man of forty, with a keen, frank glance which always seeks your eyes. He greets me by a low, hearty "*Hé, l'ami. Comment va?*"* With his clipped moustache and massive open face, energetic and at the same time placid in expression, he is a fine specimen of the southerner of the calm type. For there is such a type in which the volatile southern passion is transmuted into solid force. He is fair, but no one could mistake him for a man of the north even by the dim gleam of the lantern standing on the quay. He is worth a dozen of your ordinary Normans or Bretons, but then, in the whole immense sweep of the Mediterranean shores, you could not find half a dozen men of his stamp.

Standing by the tiller, he pulls out his watch from under a thick jacket and bends his head over it in the light cast into the boat. Time's up. His pleasant voice commands in a quiet undertone, "*Larguez.*"* A suddenly projected arm snatches the lantern off the quay—and, warped along by a line at first, then with the regular tug of four heavy sweeps in the bow, the big half-decked boat full of men glides out of the black, breathless shadow of the Fort. The open water of the *avant-port**glitters under the moon as if sown over with millions of sequins, and the long white breakwater shines like a thick bar of solid silver. With a quick rattle of blocks and one single silky swish, the sail is filled by a little breeze keen enough to have come straight down from the frozen moon, and the boat, after the clatter of the hauled-in sweeps, seems to stand at rest, surrounded by a mysterious whispering so faint and unearthly that it may be the rustling of the brilliant, over-powering moonrays breaking like a rainshower upon the hard, smooth, shadowless sea.

I may well remember that last night spent with the pilots of the Third Company. I have known the spell of moonlight since, on various seas and coasts —coasts of forests, of rocks, of sand dunes—but no magic so perfect in its revelation of unsuspected character, as though one were allowed to look upon the mystic nature of material things. For hours I suppose no word was spoken in that boat. The pilots seated in two rows facing each other dozed with their arms folded and their chins resting upon their breasts. They displayed a great variety of caps: cloth, wool, leather, earflaps, tassels, with a picturesque round *béret* or two pulled down over the brows; and one grandfather, with a shaved, bony face and a great beak of a nose, had a cloak with a hood which made him look in our midst like a cowled monk being carried off goodness knows where by that silent company of seamen—quiet enough to be dead.

My fingers itched for the tiller, and in due course my friend, the *patron*, surrendered it to me in the same spirit in which the family coachman lets a boy hold the reins on an easy bit of road. There was a great solitude around us; the islets ahead, Monte Cristo and the Château d'If in full light, seemed to float towards us— so steady, so imperceptible was the progress of our boat. "Keep her in the furrow of the moon," the *patron* directed me in a quiet murmur, sitting down ponderously in the stern-sheets and reaching for his pipe.

The pilot station in weather like this was only a mile or two to the westward of the islets; and presently, as we approached the spot, the boat we were going to relieve swam into our view suddenly, on her way home, cutting black and sinister into the wake of the moon under a sable wing, while to them our sail must have been a vision of white and dazzling radiance. Without altering the course a hair's-breadth, we slipped by each other within an oar's-length. A drawling sardonic hail came out of her. Instantly, as if by magic, our dozing pilots got on their feet in a body. An incredible babel of bantering shouts burst out, a jocular, passionate, voluble chatter, which lasted till the boats were stern to stern, theirs all bright now and with a shining sail to our eye, we turned all black to their vision, and drawing away from them under a sable wing. That extraordinary uproar died away almost as suddenly as it had begun; first one had enough of it and sat down, then another, then three or four together, and when all had left off with mutters and growling half-laughs the sound of hearty chuckling became audible, persistent, unnoticed. The cowled grandfather was very much entertained somewhere within his hood.

He had not joined in the shouting of jokes, neither had he moved the least bit. He had remained quietly in his place against the foot of the mast. I had been given to understand long before that he had the rating of a second-class able seaman (*matelot léger*) in the fleet which sailed from Toulon for the conquest of Algeria in the year of grace 1830. And, indeed, I had seen and examined one of the buttons of his old brown patched coat, the only brass button of the miscellaneous lot, flat and thin, with the words *Equipages de ligne**engraved on it. That sort of button, I believe, went out with the last of the French Bourbons. "I preserved it from the time of my Navy Service," he explained, nodding rapidly his frail, vulture-like head. It was not very likely that he had picked up that relic in the street. He

looked certainly old enough to have fought at Trafalgar
—or at any rate to have played his little part there as a
powder-monkey. Shortly after we had been introduced
he had informed me in a Franco-Provençal jargon,
mumbling tremulously with his toothless jaws, that
when he was a "shaver no higher than that" he had
seen the Emperor Napoleon returning from Elba. It
was at night, he narrated vaguely, without animation,
at a spot between Fréjus and Antibes in the open
country. A big fire had been lit at the side of the
cross-roads. The population from several villages had
collected there, old and young—down to the very
children in arms because the women had refused to
stay at home. Tall soldiers, wearing high, hairy caps,
stood in a circle facing the people silently, and their
stern eyes and big moustaches were enough to make
everybody keep at a distance. He, "being an im-
pudent little shaver," wriggled out of the crowd, creeping on his hands and knees as near as he dared to the
grenadiers' legs, and peeping through discovered standing perfectly still in the light of the fire "a little fat
fellow in a three-cornered hat, buttoned up in a long
straight coat, with a big pale face, inclined on one
shoulder, looking something like a priest. His hands
were clasped behind his back . . . It appears that
this was the Emperor," the Ancient commented with
a faint sigh. He was staring from the ground with all
his might, when "my poor father," who had been
searching for his boy frantically everywhere, pounced
upon him and hauled him away by the ear.

The tale seems an authentic recollection. He related it to me many times, using the very same words.
The grandfather honoured me by a special and somewhat embarrassing predilection. Extremes touch. He
was the oldest member by a long way in that Company,

and I was, if I may say so, its temporarily adopted
baby. He had been a pilot longer than any man in the
boat could remember; thirty—forty years. He did
not seem certain himself, but it could be found out, he
suggested, in the archives of the Pilot Office. He had
been pensioned off years before, but he went out from
force of habit; and, as my friend the *patron* of the Company once confided to me in a whisper, "the old chap
did no harm. He was not in the way." They treated
him with rough deference. One and another would
address some insignificant remark to him now and
again, but nobody really took any notice of what he had
to say. He had survived his strength, his usefulness,
his very wisdom. He wore long, green, worsted stock-
ings, pulled up above the knee over his trousers, a sort
of woollen nightcap on his hairless cranium, and wooden
clogs on his feet. Without his hooded cloak he looked
like a peasant. Half a dozen hands would be extended
to help him on board, but afterwards he was left pretty
much to his own thoughts. Of course he never did any
work, except, perhaps, to cast off some rope when
hailed: *"Hê, l'Ancien!* let go the halyards there, at
your hand"—or some such request of an easy kind.

No one took notice in any way of the chuckling within
the shadow of the hood. He kept it up for a long time
with intense enjoyment. Obviously he had preserved
intact the innocence of mind which is easily amused.
But when his hilarity had exhausted itself, he made a
professional remark in a self-assertive but quavering
voice:

"Can't expect much work on a night like this."

No one took it up. It was a mere truism. Nothing
under canvas could be expected to make a port on such
an idle night of dreamy splendour and spiritual stillness.
We would have to glide idly to and fro, keeping our

station within the appointed bearings, and, unless a
fresh breeze sprang up with the dawn, we would land
before sunrise on a small islet that, within two miles of
us, shone like a lump of frozen moonlight, to "break a
crust and take a pull at the wine bottle." I was familiar with the procedure. The stout boat emptied of her
crowd would nestle her buoyant, capable side against
the very rock—such is the perfectly smooth amenity of
the classic sea when in a gentle mood. The crust
broken, and the mouthful of wine swallowed—it was
literally no more than that with this abstemious race—
the pilots would pass the time stamping their feet on
the slabs of sea-salted stone and blowing into their
nipped fingers. One or two misanthropists would sit
apart perched on boulders like man-like sea-fowl of
solitary habits; the sociably disposed would gossip
scandalously in little gesticulating knots; and there
would be perpetually one or another of my hosts taking
aim at the empty horizon with the long, brass tube of
the telescope, a heavy, murderous-looking piece of
collective property, everlastingly changing hands with
brandishing and levelling movements. Then about
noon (it was a short turn of duty—the long turn lasted
twenty-four hours) another boatful of pilots would relieve us—and we should steer for the old Phœnician
port, dominated, watched over from the ridge of a dust-
grey arid hill by the red-and-white-striped pile of the
Notre Dame de la Garde.*

All this came to pass as I had foreseen in the fullness
of my very recent experience. But also something not
foreseen by me did happen, something which causes me
to remember my last outing with the pilots. It was on
this occasion that my hand touched, for the first time,
the side of an English ship.

No fresh breeze had come with the dawn, only the

steady little draught got a more keen edge on it as the
eastern sky became bright and glassy with a clean,
colourless light. It was while we were all ashore on the
islet that a steamer was picked up by the telescope, a
black speck like an insect posed on the hard edge of the
offing. She emerged rapidly to her water-line and came
on steadily, a slim hull with a long streak of smoke
slanting away from the rising sun. We embarked in a
hurry, and headed the boat out for our prey, but we
hardly moved three miles an hour.

She was a big, high-class cargo-steamer of a type that
is to be met on the sea no more, black hull, with low,
white superstructures, powerfully rigged with three
masts and a lot of yards on the fore; two hands at her
enormous wheel—steam steering-gear was not a matter
of course in these days—and with them on the bridge
three others, bulky in thick blue jackets, ruddy-faced,
muffled up, with peaked caps—I suppose all her officers.
There are ships I have met more than once and known
well by sight whose names I have forgotten; but the
name of that ship seen once so many years ago in the
clear flush of a cold pale sunrise I have not forgotten.
How could I—the first English ship on whose side I
ever laid my hand! The name—I read it letter by
letter on the bow—was *James Westoll*.* Not very romantic you will say. The name of a very considerable,
well-known and universally respected North-country
shipowner, I believe. James Westoll! What better
name could an honourable hard-working ship have?
To me the very grouping of the letters is alive with the
romantic feeling of her reality as I saw her floating
motionless, and borrowing an ideal grace from the austere purity of the light.

We were then very near her, and, on a sudden impulse, I volunteered to pull bow in the dinghy which

shoved off at once to put the pilot on board while our boat, fanned by the faint air which had attended us all through the night, went on gliding gently past the black glistening length of the ship. A few strokes brought us alongside, and it was then that, for the very first time in my life, I heard myself addressed in English—the speech of my secret choice, of my future, of long friendships, of the deepest affections, of hours of toil and hours of ease, and of solitary hours too, of books read, of thoughts pursued, of remembered emotions—of my very dreams! And if (after being thus fashioned by it in that part of me which cannot decay) I dare not claim it aloud as my own, then, at any rate the speech of my children. Thus small events grow memorable by the passage of time. As to the quality of the address itself I cannot say it was very striking. Too short for eloquence and devoid of all charm of tone, it consisted precisely of the three words "Look out there," growled out huskily above my head.

It proceeded from a big fat fellow—he had an obtrusive, hairy double chin) in a blue woollen shirt and roomy breeches pulled up very high, even to the level of his breast-bone, by a pair of braces quite exposed to public view. As where he stood there was no bulwark but only a rail and stanchions, I was able to take in at a glance the whole of his voluminous person from his feet to the high crown of his soft black hat, which sat like an absurd flanged cone on his big head. The grotesque and massive aspect of that deck hand (I suppose he was that—very likely the lamp-trimmer) surprised me very much. My course of reading, of dreaming and longing for the sea had not prepared me for a sea-brother of that sort. I never met again a figure in the least like his except in the illustrations to Mr. W. W. Jacobs'* most entertaining tales of barges and coasters; but the in-

spired talent of Mr. Jacobs for poking endless fun at
poor, innocent sailors in a prose which, however extravagant in its felicitous invention, is always artisti-
cally adjusted to observed truth, was not yet. Perhaps
Mr. Jacobs himself was not yet. I fancy that, at most,
if he had made his nurse laugh it was about all he had
achieved at that early date.

Therefore, I repeat, other disabilities apart, I could
not have been prepared for the sight of that husky old
porpoise. The object of his concise address was to call
my attention to a rope which he incontinently flung
down for me to catch. I caught it, though it was not
really necessary, the ship having no way on her by
that time. Then everything went on very swiftly. The
dinghy came with a slight bump against the steamer's
side, the pilot, grabbing the rope ladder, had scrambled
half-way up before I knew that our task of boarding
was done; the harsh, muffled clanging of the engine-room
telegraph struck my ear through the iron plate; my
companion in the dinghy was urging me to "shove off—
push hard"; and when I bore against the smooth flank
of the first English ship I ever touched in my life, I felt
it already throbbing under my open palm.

Her head swung a little to the west, pointing towards
the miniature lighthouse of the Jolliette breakwater,
far away there, hardly distinguishable against the land.
The dinghy danced a squashy, splashy jig in the wash
of the wake and turning in my seat I followed the
James Westoll with my eyes. Before she had gone in a
quarter of a mile she hoisted her flag as the harbour
regulations prescribe for arriving and departing ships.
I saw it suddenly flicker and stream out on the flagstaff.
The Red Ensign! In the pellucid, colourless atmosphere
bathing the drab and grey masses of that southern land,
the livid islets, the sea of pale glassy blue under the pale

glassy sky of that cold sunrise, it was as far as the eye could reach the only spot of ardent colour—flame-like, intense, and presently as minute as the tiny red spark the concentrated reflection of a great fire kindles in the clear heart of a globe of crystal. The Red Ensign—the symbolic, protecting warm bit of bunting flung wide upon the seas, and destined for so many years to be the only roof over my head.

THE END

EXPLANATORY NOTES

I am indebted in these notes to Ugo Mursia's edition of *The Mirror of the Sea* and *A Personal Record* (J. Conrad, *Opere varie*, Milan, 1982) and to Pierre and Yane Lefranc's notes to *The Mirror* in Sylvère Monod's Pléiade edition of Conrad's works (J. Conrad, *OEuvres*, vol. ii, Paris, 1985).

THE MIRROR OF THE SEA

Epigraph   From Chaucer's translation of Boethius' (*c.*480–524) *De Consolatione Philosophiae* (in the original: 'quoniam hoc me miraculum maxime perturbat'); the text mentions various miracles, but there is no reference to the sea.

Dedication *Mrs. Katherine Sanderson*: she was the mother of Edward Lancelot Sanderson (1867–1939), educationalist, who in 1893 was a passenger on board the *Torrens*, a clipper cruising between London and Adelaide, on which Conrad was first mate. Sanderson became one of Conrad's earliest English friends, and both he and his mother assisted him in correcting the manuscript of *Almayer's Folly*.

'Author's Note'

viii *for twenty years*: Conrad counts here the years 1874–94; in fact, he spent nearly half of them on shore, between voyages, looking for another berth, etc.

ix   *'In reading . . . behind the veil'*: the quotation is almost certainly apocryphal, but it expresses a sentiment found in many reviews of Conrad's autobiographical writings.

Text of The Mirror of the Sea

3 *'And shippes . . . a day or two'*: Geoffrey Chaucer (*c.*1340–1400), *The Canterbury Tales*, The Franklin's Tale, ll. 1160–1; critical editions have 'wowke' (week) instead of 'day'.

4 *The greatest number . . . the Scilly's light*: an allusion to his

voyage on the *Tilkhurst*, on which Conrad served as second mate. The clipper left Calcutta on 9 January and arrived at Dundee on 16 June 1886, thus after a passage of 158 days, but Conrad counts here only the days between the last and the first sight of land.

5 *Captain MacW——*: John McWhir, of County Down, master of the *Highland Forest*, an iron barque in which Conrad served as first mate on a single voyage, from Amsterdam to Semarang in Java, 18 Feb.–20 June 1887. The same name, with its spelling changed to 'MacWhirr', was given by Conrad to the much older hero of his *Typhoon*, the master of the *Nan-Shan*.

6 *sanctum sanctorum*: Latin, 'holy of holies'.

9 *Captain B——*: Edwin John Blake, the master of the *Tilkhurst*, on which Conrad served from 24 April 1885 to 20 June 1886, was in fact only 47.

I had just enough service for that: six years' service at sea was required to take the master's examination; Conrad has fulfilled this condition while serving on the *Tilkhurst*.

10 *Western Islands*: the Azores, an archipelago in the North Atlantic.

the Downs: roadstead in the English Channel off the east coast of Kent.

cross-bearings: the bearings of two or more points taken from a point of reference to chart the position of a ship.

11 *W. G. Grace*: William Gilbert Grace (1848–1915), the most famous cricketer of the time.

12 *rib*: one of the curved frame-timbers or ironworks of a ship, extending from the keel (i.e. the lowest longitudinal element of a ship's structure) to the top of the hull; planking is nailed to it.

13 *cat-heads*: beams projecting at each side of the bows (the rounded fore-end) of a ship, for handling the anchor.

14 *ring*: connects an anchor with its chain or cable; *stock*: a heavy crossbar; *shank*: the stem of an anchor, connecting the stock with the arms; *crown*: the part of the shank from which the arms extend; *flukes*: triangular plates of iron on the arms of an anchor; *palms*: the inner surfaces of flukes.

15 *Spithead*: strait of the English Channel between the Isle of Wight and the mainland.

17 *headgear*: rigging of the forepart of a vessel.

compressors: iron levers controlling the run of the cable.

18 *a man called B——*: Charles Born, a German, first mate on the *Otago*, the only ship Conrad commanded (Jan. 1888–Mar. 1889). He appears also in Conrad's 'The Secret Sharer' and *The Shadow-Line*. Born was only three years older than his captain.

19 *five-hundred-ton barque*: the *Otago* was a 346-ton iron barque.

21 *hand-spikes*: wooden bars, used as levers.

pawls: short bars preventing a windlass from recoiling.

her squared yards: to square the yards means to set the yards (spars slung at their centre from a mast and supporting a sail) at right-angles to the ship's keel.

23 *linear raters*: racing vessels of a certain class, defined by the relation of the ship's dimensions to the surface area of her sails.

26 *fore-and-aft*: longitudinal, i.e. not as traditionally axial, arrangement of sails on a vessel.

27 *rake*: the deviation of a vessel's masts from the perpendicular to the keel.

31 *Royal Academicians*: the Royal Academy of Arts, founded in 1768, with its headquarters in Burlington House, Piccadilly, London, has forty elected members, 'Royal Academicians'.

32 *Twentyman*: there was an apprentice of this name on board the *Highland Forest*, but that ship did not sail to Australia while Conrad served on it, nor does the description of the pompous master fit Captain McWhir.

35 *jib-boom*: a spar run out from the end of the bowsprit (a large spar protruding from the bow).

spanker: a fore-and-aft sail at the rear of the ship.

luff up: to turn closer to the direction of the wind.

truck: a wooden cap fixed at the head of the mainmast.

37 *royal yards*: spars holding the royal sail, above the topgallant and below the sky sail.

38 *The ship*: a reference to the *Loch Etive*, an iron clipper of 1,288 tons, built in 1877 in Glasgow by A. & J. Inglis. Conrad served on it, as third mate, from August 1880 to April 1881.

The masts of the *Loch Etive* were not unusually tall; and the ship's length and weight made it incapable of speeds achieved by the lighter and slimmer wooden vessels.

39 *Our captain*: William Stuart, of Peterhead (b. 1832); he commanded the *Tweed* 1863–77.

strong . . . breeze: Conrad uses the specialist terminology of his time to refer to a wind of 6 degrees on the Beaufort wind-force scale (*c*.25 knots).

poor P——: William Purdu of Glasgow, first officer on the *Loch Etive*.

40 *gale*: between 7 and 8 on the Beaufort scale (*c*.35 knots).

42 *The marvellous Tweed*: a clipper of 1,751 tons, built in Bombay in 1854.

sheer: the upward curvature of the ship's deck.

Indian famine of the 'seventies: between 1876 and 1878 about five million people died of hunger in Bombay, Madras, and Mysore.

44 *lee quarter*: or lee side, the side which is turned away from the wind (opposite to the weather side).

courses: sails attached to the lower yards of a ship.

46 *'Stevens on Stowage'*: R. W. Stevens, *On the Stowage of Ships and their Cargoes*, 1st edn. (Plymouth, 1858).

Coke on Littleton: *Coke upon Littleton* (1628), the first volume of *Institutes of the Lawes of England*, by Sir Edward Coke (1552–1634), comprising his commentaries to the legal writings of Sir Thomas Littleton (1422–81).

48 *by the head*: i.e. immersed a few inches deeper by her stem than by the stern.

Handelskade: now Oostelijke Handelskade, a street in central Amsterdam.

schuyts: small, flat-bottomed Dutch boats, used on canals and for coasting.

49 *chief mate*: of the *Highland Forest*, an iron barque of 1,040 tons, from Feb. to June 1887.

owners: Crane, Colvil and Company, of Glasgow.

café: Café Krasnapolsky, at Warmoesstraat.

50 *twenty-four*: in fact, he was 29.

demurrage: charge for detaining a contracted vessel longer than agreed.

52 *counter*: the curved part of a ship's stern.

fore and aft trim: balancing the vessel longitudinally.

53 *Samarang*: now Semarang, in Java; see note to p. 5, above.

54 *spanker-booms*: spars extending the bottom side of the spanker sail.

55 *a Far Eastern hospital*: in Singapore, where Conrad spent a few weeks in July and August 1887.

56 *in and out of the career*: a Gallicism: in or out of service.

57 *'Tempi passati!'*: Italian, 'Times gone by'.

59 *The Shipping Gazette*: *The Shipping and Mercantile Gazette and Lloyd's List*, or *The Shipping Gazette and Lloyd's Weekly Summary*.

60 *a Clyde-built barque*: again the *Highland Forest*, although she was in fact built in Leith.

knots per hour: a solecism (a knot means a maritime mile per hour), quite common but rather amusing in a text so concerned with the precision of specialist terminology.

slings: devices to hoist the yard.

62 *in fear and trembling*: St Paul, Philippians 2: 12: '. . . work out your own salvation with fear and trembling'.

63 *Such a one . . . New Zealand*: probably the *Waikato*, which in 1889, on the way from London to New Zealand, lost her propeller and drifted for 4,500 miles before being discovered and towed to Fremantle, near Perth in Western Australia.

69 *Damocles*: a courtier of Dionysius the Elder, tyrant (i.e. ruler) of Syracuse from 405 to 367 BC. When he extolled his sovereign's happiness, Dionysius invited him to a feast but seated beneath a naked sword, suspended from the ceiling by a single thread.

stranding . . . ship: this episode cannot be traced to Conrad's biography.

70 *I was elated . . . slightest hitch*: getting a sailing ship off the ground is a complex operation which, to make use of changing winds, tides, etc., involves the use of anchors, boats which change the position of the hull by pulling, etc.

bower: one of the two heavy anchors at the bows of a vessel;

stream: stream-anchor, used to moor a ship; *kedge*: a small anchor used in manœuvring a moored ship.

73 *its Portuguese discoverer*: Bartolomeu Dias discovered the Cape in 1488 and most probably gave that headland both the names mentioned by Conrad.

tout court: French, 'in short'.

Leeuwin: cape on the south-western coast of Western Australia, on the Indian Ocean.

74 *Port Elizabeth*: in South Africa, on the Indian Ocean.

East London: Oos-Londen, port in South Africa, on the Indian Ocean.

75 *barque*: the 346-ton barque *Otago*, Conrad's only seagoing command (Jan. 1888–Mar. 1889).

bulwarks: the raised woodwork along the sides of a vessel.

76 *Kerguelen Island*: known also as Desolation Island, a heavily glaciated main island of the Kerguelen Archipelago in the southern Indian Ocean.

77 *pampero*: irregular, cold wind blowing from the south and south-west in Argentina and Uruguay.

78 *The ship*: the *Duke of Sutherland*, a 1,047-ton clipper in which Conrad served as ordinary seaman from October 1878 to October 1879; she left Sydney on a homewards passage on 5 July 1879 and sailed the Horn in the middle of winter.

brought-to: turned towards the wind and with sails reduced.

79 *black squalls*: accompanied by clouds; *white squalls*: cloudless, and thus more unexpected.

80 *Trade Winds*: which 'blow trade', i.e. in a constant way.

83 *par excellence*: French, 'pre-eminently', 'typically'.

84 *Cape Farewell*: Kap Farvel, the southern tip of Greenland.

86 *mayhap*: perhaps, by chance (archaic).

87 *We*: a reference to Captain William Stuart of the *Loch Etive* and to the clipper's return to London in April 1881.

Cape Hatteras: on the coast of North Carolina.

88 *from fresh . . . to heavy*: growing from 7 to 9 on the Beaufort scale of wind force.

91 *bolt-ropes*: ropes sewn round the edge of the sail to prevent it from tearing.

St. Catherine's Point: the southernmost tip of the Isle of Wight.

93 *Great Banks*: shores of New Zealand.

sowing the wind and reaping the whirlwind: Hosea 8: 7: 'For they have sown the wind, and they shall reap the whirlwind.'

Finisterre: Land's End, the westernmost tip of Cornwall.

99 *Hohenzollern*: a German dynasty, established in the eleventh century, from which many European rulers descended, including a ruling house of Brandenburg-Prussia and the royal family of Romania.

Saxe-Coburg: correctly Saxe-Coburg-Gotha, an east-German dynasty, which in the nineteenth and twentieth centuries became one of the most prominently connected in Europe. Leopold I, the first king of Belgium, Albert, the husband of Queen Victoria, and Ferdinand, the first tsar of Bulgaria, were all members of this family.

'forties': 'the roaring forties', between latitudes 40° and 50° S.

Southern Ocean: southern parts of the Atlantic and Indian Oceans.

Agulhas: Cape Agulhas, the southernmost point of the African continent.

101 *The commander of the first Roman galley . . .*: the imagined story which follows does not quite tally with historical facts: the first Roman invaders (from Julius Caesar in 55 BC to Aulus Plautius in 43 AD) did not enter what is now England through the Thames estuary, but landed on the shore of Kent.

North Foreland: headland of northern Kent.

trireme: a type of ancient vessel, of Phoenician origin, with three banks of oars along almost the entire length of the hull.

102 *dyed*: they were, if anything, rather tattooed, like the Picts, who owed their Latin name (*picti*, 'painted') to that fact.

Isle of Thanet: the northern part of Kent, separated from the mainland by the River Stour. It was in those times inhabited by the Belgae, a Celtic tribe from the Continent.

103 *Shoeburyness*: in Essex, on the northern shore of the Thames estuary; an artillery range of the Royal Navy extends to the north-east.

the Nore: a sandbank and anchorage between Shoeburyness and Sheerness (on the shore of Kent). Much used by the

English fleet during the wars of the seventeenth and eighteenth centuries. In 1797 it was the site of a serious mutiny by the sailors. Until 1961 the Nore gave its name to the Royal Navy's command for the eastern area of England.

first time: in October 1879, on his return passage from Australia on board the *Duke of Sutherland*.

105 *Orfordness*: Orford Ness, a headland of Suffolk, at the northern end of the Thames estuary.

108 *I was the chief officer . . . ninety days' passage*: the following story has no precise equivalent in Conrad's biography.

111 *a certain river in the north*: the Tyne, and the port of Newcastle, which Conrad knew well from his voyages on board the *Skimmer of the Sea* (1878) and the *Palestine*.

113 *a crisis of national history*: on 8 Aug. 1588 at Tilbury Elizabeth I made her famous speech to the land forces of the kingdom, drawn up there to repulse the expected Spanish invasion (not knowing yet that the 'invincible Armada' had already been destroyed).

their creation: in 1886.

116 *tackle*: device consisting of a windlass, or a pulley-block, and a combination of ropes, used for hoisting wares.

120 *Hobart Town*: the capital of Tasmania.

second mate: H. J. Bastard, of Halifax; Conrad served with him on board the *Duke of Sutherland*.

some Australian port: Sydney.

122 *saveloys*: spicy cooked and dried sausages.

a violent death: the *Duke of Sutherland* was sunk by high seas while moored on the Timaru anchorage, at the eastern shore of New Zealand's South Island.

Mr. B——'s: A. G. Baker, of Norfolk, 37 at that time (Conrad was 21).

123 *The A.S.N. Company's*: The Australian Steam Navigation Company, specializing in cabotage.

127 *Mauritius*: the *Otago* loaded for Mauritius between 12 July and 7 Aug. 1888.

129 *load-line*: or load-water-line, or Plimsoll line, the line of flotation of a ship when fully loaded.

frigate side: the part of a ship's side broader on the level of the deck than below.

130 *mural crowns*: in ancient Rome, a crown was conferred upon the soldier who first scaled the wall of a besieged town.

11,000 miles: the approximate distance between London and Sydney, around the Cape of Good Hope.

exhibition: on board the *Cutty Sark*, now permanently moored at Greenwich.

131 *Fenchurch Street railway station*: in east London, close to the docks and to the offices of many shipping companies.

133 *river*: the Ganges.

hawse-pipes: cast-iron pipes fitted into hawse-holes (through which the anchor cables run) to protect the wood.

134 *ground-tackle*: all the gear used for anchoring or mooring a vessel.

135 *Odi et amo*: Latin, 'I hate and love', from *Carmina*, LXXXV, of the Roman lyrical poet Catullus (*c.*84–*c.*54 BC).

136 *'More fell than hunger, anguish, or the sea'*: *Othello*, V. ii. 365.

137 *wonder of the deep*: Ps. 107: 24: 'These see the works of the Lord, and his wonders in the deep.'

Danish brig: it has been impossible to establish the factual basis for this story.

139 *falls*: devices for lowering the boats.

140 *head-rails*: rails at the head of a ship.

scuppers: openings in a ship's side, on a level with her deck, to allow the water to run away.

146 *bowman*: the rower nearest to the bow.

149 *Salamis*: island in the Aegean Sea, at which in 480 BC the Greeks won a decisive naval battle against the Persians.

Actium: now Akra Nikólaos, a promontory in Western Greece, on the Ionian Sea, near which Octavian (later Augustus) defeated the fleets of Mark Antony and Cleopatra (31 BC).

Lepanto: or Návpaktos, in the Gulf of Patras (Greece), site of the victory of the allied Christian forces (mainly Spanish and Venetian) over the Turks in 1571.

Nile: the battle in the Abukir Bay, at the mouth of the Nile, when an English fleet under Nelson defeated the Napoleonic fleet in 1798.

Navarino: a harbour in the south-western Peloponnese, where in 1827 a combined British, French, and Russian fleet completely destroyed the Egyptian and Turkish naval forces.

151 *Happy he who, like Ulysses, has made an adventurous voyage*: the opening line of a famous sonnet by the French poet Joachim Du Bellay (1522–60), from his *Les Regrets*: 'Heureux qui, comme Ulysse, a fait un beau voyage'; see Introduction. Ulysses, or Odysseus, a mythical king of Ithaca (an island in the Ionian Archipelago at the western shores of Greece), is the hero of Homer's *Odyssey* (*c*.750 BC). Persecuted by the god Poseidon, whom he had offended, after the capture of Troy he spends nine years on dangerous wanderings before returning at last to his faithful wife Penelope and his kingdom.

Pan was dead: this story has its origin in the dialogue 'On the cessation of oracles' in the *Moralia* of the Greek historian and philosopher Plutarch (*c*.46–after 119). In Greek mythology Pan was the god of forests, herds, and shepherds; he later came to be regarded as a universal deity, pervading all nature. Plutarch tells of Tammuz, pilot of a ship sailing from Greece to Italy, hearing—in the vicinity of Paxos on the Ionian Sea, and thus not in the Gulf of Syrta, which is on the Libyan shore of the Mediterranean—a mysterious voice, which exhorted him to repeat the news that 'the great Pan is dead'. Plutarch says that since that time (about AD 30) the oracles (divine prophecies) stopped. The mysterious announcement was later interpreted as coinciding with the death of Christ.

153 *Majorca*: Conrad sailed on 15 Dec. 1874 from Marseilles as a passenger on board the *Mont-Blanc*, a barque going to Martinique. However, the ship would not need more than three days to reach Majorca and thus passed the Gulf of Lyons a week before Christmas.

galère: galley, a flat, seagoing vessel propelled by oars and sails; also metaphorically a place of hard toil and exploitation. Here a well-known quotation from the French playwright Molière (1622–73), *Les Fourberies de Scapin* (*The Knaveries of Scapin*), ii. 7: 'Que diable allait-il faire dans cette galère?'

uncle: Tadeusz Bobrowski (1829–94), Conrad's maternal uncle and guardian after the death of his father. He paid all Conrad's expenses at this time.

154 *Pillars of Hercules*: the rocks at the entrance to the Mediterranean, Gibraltar on the European and Mont Hacho (with the fortress of Ceuta) on the African shore.

strange shore: Martinique, a French island in the Caribbean sea.

Nausicaa: in the *Odyssey* the daughter of Alcinous, king of the Phaeacians, whom the shipwrecked Odysseus sighted playing ball with her maidens on the shore.

187—: 1875.

155 *Dead Sea fruit*: the mythical fruit, looking lovely but full of ashes within. See, for example, Byron's *Childe Harold*, iii. 34:

> Like to the apples on the Dead Sea shore,
> All ashes to the taste.

Don Quixote de la Mancha: the hero of the famous novel by the Spanish writer Miguel de Cervantes Saavedra (1547–1616), an embodiment of romantic idealism.

156 *middle turn of life's way*: an allusion to the opening line of Dante's *Divine Comedy*: 'Nel mezzo del camin di nostra vita.'

Cimmerian shore: in Greek mythology Cimmerians were the people inhabiting a dark and misty country on the western shores of the ocean, where the sun never shines.

Histoire des Treize: *The Thirteen* (1833–5), a novelistic trilogy by the great French writer Honoré de Balzac (1799–1850), in his series of 'scenes from Parisian life'.

de cape et d'épée: French, 'cloak and sword': full of adventure and fighting, a type of Spanish and later French comedies and novels.

She: nothing has been firmly established about the actual existence of this boat; neither her name (not found in any register), nor her type, nor the alleged origin provides a real clue.

Latin Lake: the Mediterranean.

157 *J. M. K. B.*: Captain John Young Mason Key Blunt, an American soldier of fortune.

158 *Américain, Catholique, et gentilhomme*: French, 'American, Catholic, and gentleman'; a curious replica of a dedication ('Pole, Catholic, nobleman') which the five-year-old Conrad wrote on his own photograph, given to his grandmother.

Mistral: Frédéric Mistral (1830–1914), Provençal poet, awarded the Nobel prize for Literature in 1904.

159 *Carlist*: the Carlists were supporters of Don Carlos de Borbón (1848–1909), Pretender to the Spanish throne. However, the story as told by Conrad does not tally with historical facts. He tries to fit it within his biography and in the years 1877–8, but Carlist activity effectively ended early in 1876. Therefore no attempt will be made to identify the real equivalents of the events mentioned in Conrad's tale. See also the Introduction.

Rey netto: Spanish, more correctly 'Rey neto', 'king without blemish'.

160 *Massilia*: the original Greek name of Marseilles.

Por el Rey!: Spanish, 'For the King!'

she: apparently the same person who served as the model for the heroine of Conrad's late novel *The Arrow of Gold* (1919). Nothing certain is known about her.

Guipuzcoa: Guipúzcoa, a small Basque province in Spain, on the Bay of Biscay.

161 *Gulf of Rosas*: on the Costa Brava, just south of the French–Spanish border.

162 *'Vous êtes bête . . . conséquence'*: French, 'You are silly, my dear, Anyhow, it has no importance.'

Dominic: Dominique Cervoni, a Corsican born in 1834, was first mate of the *Saint-Antoine*, a barque on which Conrad served from July 1876 to February 1877. It is impossible to say whether and how he was involved in Carlist affairs.

padrone: master, captain (in Corsican dialect).

163 *son of Laertes and Anticlea*: Ulysses (Odysseus).

one-eyed giant: in the *Odyssey* a Cyclops, who captured twelve of Odysseus' men and ate six of them before the hero managed to blind him.

guardacostas: coastguards.

164 *'Mais il est parfait, cet homme'*: French, 'But he is perfect, that man.'

caban: big, hooded cape (Corsican).

Cesar: César Cervoni, born in 1858, was an apprentice on board the *Saint-Antoine*; but he was not related to Dominique, and survived Conrad.

167 *mooring hawser*: a rope or cable, used for mooring.

charogne!: French, literally 'carcass'; 'cad', 'scoundrel'.

Canallia!: scoundrel (Corsican).

Mr. Mantalini: a character in Dickens's *Nicholas Nickleby* (1839); see ch. XXXIV.

168 *Par la Madonne!*: By the Madonna (Virgin Mary)! (Corsican).

This voyage: the following story, with all its topographical and nautical details, cannot consistently be fitted within the real geography of the area.

171 '*Chi va piano va sano*': who goes slowly, goes surely (Italian proverb).

172 *bournuss*: burnous, a cloak with a hood, worn by Arabs.

wing-and-wing: sailing wing-and-wing means sailing before the wind, with the foresail hauled over one side and the mainsail over the other, as though with stretched wings.

Cape San Sebastian: 55 miles north-east of Barcelona.

173 *gabelou*: French, derogatory term for a customs officer.

The Cape: unclear which.

175 *signorino*: Italian, a polite form of addressing a young man.

176 '*Il faut la tuer*': French, 'She has to be killed.'

177 *halyards*: ropes used for raising and lowering the foresail.

water-butt: a large open cask to receive rainwater.

178 *Cape Creux*: about 10 miles from the French border.

'*Prenez la barre, monsieur*': French, 'Take the tiller, sir.'

181 *Traditore!*: traitor (Corsican).

183 *The legendary wanderer*: again Ulysses, to whom the 'legendary soothsayer' Tiresias predicts such a journey in book 11 of the *Odyssey*.

'*A fellow . . . the touchhole*': quotation from *The Letters and Papers of Sir Thomas Byam Martin* [1773–1854], 3 vols., ed. Sir R. V. Hamilton (The Navy Records Society, vols. 12, 19, 24), vol. i [London], 1903, p. 66; *touchhole*: a hole in the breech of a firearm, though which the charge is ignited.

185 *Nelson . . . our nation*': as above, pp. 73 and 65.

two kings and a queen: in fact, three kings (George III, George IV, and William IV), and Queen Victoria.

186 'Anchor, Hardy—anchor!': Nelson's last order, given to Captain Thomas M. Hardy, his flag officer.

Lord Hood: Admiral Samuel Viscount Hood, of Whitley (1724–1816), a distinguished naval commander.

Admiral Keith: George Keith Elphinstone, Viscount Keith (1746–1823), directed several successful naval operations.

Earl St. Vincent: Admiral John Jervis, earl of Saint Vincent (1735–1823), naval officer and politician; Conrad alludes to his decision to dispatch Nelson to Tenerife in 1797.

187 Sir Hyde Parker: (1739–1807); he commanded the British Baltic fleet in the battle of Copenhagen (2 Apr. 1801) against the Danish navy; Nelson ignored his order to withdraw and won.

'a most happy way . . . his command': Martin, iii [London], 1901, pp. 307–8. (See note to p. 183.)

band of brothers: see Shakespeare, Henry V, IV. iii. 60, 'we band of brothers'.

'without hearing . . . his subordinates': Martin, iii. 308. It is not a precise quotation, as Martin writes not about 'subordinates' but about 'all who showed themselves zealous in the execution of their duties'.

188 'We are . . . with Nelson': Martin, iii. 308. Again not quoted precisely: Stopford wrote about 'full recompense', not 'reward'. Sir Robert Stopford (1768–1847) commanded the Spencer in spring 1805 during Nelson's pursuit of the French fleet under Admiral Pierre de Villeneuve.

189 memorandum: of 9 Oct. 1805, with formation orders for the battle of Trafalgar twelve days later.

steerage way: a motion of the vessel sufficient to steer it (i.e. for the helm to have effect). During the battle of Trafalgar the prevailing wind was westerly, shifting north.

First of June: in 1794, a naval engagement at open sea about 430 miles west of Ushant Island (Île d'Ouessant, at the western tip of Brittany) between the British fleet under Earl Howe and the French under Louis Villaret de Joyeuse. The British won a technical victory, but the French realized their goal of protecting a big American convoy of grain ships.

191 Teneriffe expedition: in July 1797; wounded by a grapeshot in his right elbow, Nelson had his arm amputated.

Faro: the southernmost city of Portugal, at the base of Cabo de Santa Maria; *Spartel*: a cape in Tangier, Morocco, at the south-west entrance to the Strait of Gibraltar. The line Conrad mentions encloses both the Gulf of Cádiz and the Strait of Gibraltar. Conrad sailed through this area five times, on board the *Mont-Blanc* and the *Saint-Antoine*, during the years 1874–7.

to bear up: to put the helm up so as to set the ship in the direction of the wind.

192 *Twenty Years' War*: traditional, and imprecise, name given to England's war with first revolutionary and then Napoleonic France (1793–1815).

193 *'Le temps . . . est un galant homme'*: Time is a gentleman. The 'distinguished Frenchman' was Jules Mazarin (1602–61), in fact Italian by origin and naturalized in France only in 1639. An outstanding politician, he was a cardinal (although not a priest) and the first minister of France.

two fleets: French and Spanish.

Goliath: ship leading the British squadron.

Guerrier: ship leading the French squadron; she was quickly dismasted.

194 *Captain Blackwood*: Sir Henry Blackwood (1770–1832) commanded the *Euryalus* at the battle of Trafalgar.

A PERSONAL RECORD

A Personal Record was initially published, in both serial and book form, with the title *Some Reminiscences*, which became the subtitle in the third edition, in 1916. The new title removes a suggestion of looseness and accidentality, and introduces the new sense of a summing-up.

'Author's Note'

iii *The question of language*: by the time Conrad wrote *A Personal Record*, and even more by the time he added this Note, it had become generally known that his native language was Polish. See Introduction.

these comments . . . vanity: in fact, not all these comments were flattering.

Sir Hugh Clifford: Sir Hugh Charles Clifford (1866–1941), British civil servant (working mostly in the Far East) and writer on Malaya. He befriended Conrad in 1899; however they met for the first time only after the publication of Clifford's (unsigned) article 'Mr Conrad at home and abroad' in the *Singapore Free Press* (1 Sept. 1898).

iv *Mr. Cunninghame Graham*: Robert Bontine Cunninghame Graham (1852–1936), Scottish aristocrat, writer, traveller, champion of the oppressed, member of Parliament (1886–92), supporter of the Labour Party. He wrote to Conrad expressing his enthusiasm for 'An Outpost of Progress', first published in *Cosmopolis* in June and July 1897, and became one of Conrad's closest friends.

Malay sketches: *Studies in Brown Humanity* (London, 1898), which Conrad happened to have reviewed in the *Academy* (23 Apr. 1898), reprinted in his *Notes on Life and Letters*.

Frank Swettenham: Sir Frank Swettenham (1850–1946), British colonial official and specialist in the Malay language.

a study: 'The Genius of Mr Joseph Conrad', *North American Review* (June 1904).

vii *'the son of a Revolutionist'*: see John Galsworthy, 'Joseph Conrad: A Disquisition', *Fortnightly Review*, (1 Apr. 1908).

Polish risings of 1831 and 1863: there were insurrections in the Russian-governed part of the country (in 1795, Poland was partitioned between Russia, Prussia, and Austria) on 29 Nov. 1830 and 22 Jan. 1863. Conrad's concept of the 'revolutionary' is here a very narrow one, and doubtless influenced by the recent Russian 'October' Revolution of 1917. He is right when he says that both Polish uprisings were wars of national liberation and not internal conflicts; he is wrong in suggesting that the insurgents did not want to change the existing socio-political order: most of them were democrats and republicans, who opposed Russian autocratic and monarchic rule.

no more revolutionary than the others: not quite true. Apollo Korzeniowski (1820–69), poet, translator, and political publicist and organizer, sided with the more radically democratic and egalitarian (especially with regard to the peasantry) groups; that, of course, implied a programme to change not only the political but also the socio-economic system.

viii *funeral*: 26 May 1869 in Cracow.

surrender: the story of Apollo Korzeniowski's burning of his manuscripts is not supported by evidence.

ix *for preservation*: indeed, many of Korzeniowski's manuscripts, and his letters to several friends, have been preserved in the Jagiellonian Library in Cracow. The 'most intimate friend' is Stefan Buszczyński (1821–92), an eminent liberal-democratic political writer.

Alfred de Vigny: (1797–1863); French Romantic poet, dramatist, and novelist, who extolled the ideals of honour and fidelity.

for some men . . . to the world: S. Buszczyński's booklet *Mało znany poeta* (Cracow, 1870) is the main reference.

National Committee: more precisely 'Committee of the Movement', which became the kernel of the later underground National Government. It was formed on 17 Oct. 1861. Its objectives were organizational and political, not simply 'moral'.

x *Warsaw house*: at Nowy Świat, no. 45.

not yet thirty: Conrad's mother, Ewa, née Bobrowska (1831–65), was 30 at the time; his confusion about her age may have had its source in the memoirs of his uncle Tadeusz (see following note).

her death: 18 Apr. 1865, of tuberculosis, while in exile in Chernikhov in north-east Ukraine. Her brother whom she visited (in summer 1863) was Tadeusz Bobrowski (1829–94), Conrad's future guardian and benefactor. His memoirs were published in 1900 (see note to p. 29, below).

'A Familiar Preface'

xi *friendly pressure*: of Ford Madox Ford (1873–1939), novelist, critic, editor, and memoirist, Conrad's close friend between 1898 and 1909, with whom he collaborated on two novels (*The Inheritors*, 1901, and *Romance*, 1903). Ford was the founder and editor of the *English Review*, in which *A Personal Record* was originally serialized.

xii *Emperor*: Marcus Aurelius (121–80), Roman emperor (after 161) and Stoic philosopher, author of the famous *Meditations*.

'Let all thy words . . . heroic truth': not a quotation, but a faithful rendering of an idea expressed in Book III. 12 of the *Meditations*.

xiii *'Imitation of Christ'*: *De imitatione christi* (I. viii. 2), a medieval and Christian counterpart of Marcus Aurelius's *Meditations*, written about 1425 most probably by a German monk Thomas a Kempis (1379?–1471).

thirty-six: the implication is that before 1893 Conrad, who had begun writing *Almayer's Folly* in 1889, did not think about publishing his novel.

xv *sécheresse du cœur*: dryness (coldness) of the heart.

xix *'Il y a toujours la manière'*: There is always the manner.

xx *seriatim*: Latin, 'one after another'.

Text of A Personal Record

3 *a town*: Rouen in northern France, on the Seine; although it lies 75 miles inland, it is a major deep-water port.

Flaubert: Gustave Flaubert (1821–80), the great French novelist, whose artistic scrupulousness made him both a legend and an example to follow. He lived for most of his life on a family estate at Croisset near Rouen.

Adowa: the 2,097-ton passenger steamer on which Conrad served as second mate from 29 Nov. 1893 to 17 Jan. 1894.

4 *Mr. Kipling*: an allusion to 'The Song of the Banjo', in the volume *The Seven Seas* (1896).

5 *Bovary*: husband of the heroine of Flaubert's famous novel *Madame Bovary* (1856). Her father's name was Rouault, not Renault.

Lucia di Lammermoor: an opera (1835) by Gaetano Donizetti (1797–1848), based on Walter Scott's novel *The Bride of Lammermoor* (1819); the reference is to ch. XV of *Madame Bovary*.

6 *It flourished no longer than roses live*: echo of a well-known line in 'Consolations à du Perrier sur la mort de sa fille' by the French poet François de Malherbe (1555–1628).

7 *Captain Froud*: Albert George Froud, secretary of the Ship-masters' Society, had his office at 60 Fenchurch St.

9 *Pimlico*: a residential district in south-west London; Conrad lived there, at Bessborough Gardens, between May 1889 and May 1890.

Pantai: river on the banks of which most of the action of *Almayer's Folly* takes place; it corresponds to the River Berau in eastern Borneo, known to Conrad from his voyages on board the *Vidar*, a 204-ton steamer (Aug. 1887–Jan. 1888).

10 *Belgravia*: an elegant district in south-west London, neighbouring Pimlico, which Conrad treats here as a part of Belgravia.

12 *petit bourgeois*: lower middle-class (French).

14 *Congo*: Conrad went to the Belgian Congo in June 1890 to work, on a river steamer, for a Belgian commercial company, Société Anonyme Belge pour le Commerce du Haut-Congo. After five months he resigned, disgusted with the ruthless exploitation of the natives he witnessed, and ill with dysentery and tropical fever. The incident described occurred apparently at the end of October. Léopoldville and Kinshasa, which now together form the city of Kinshasa, capital of Zaïre, were at that time two distinct settlements. The 'awkward turn' was Pointe de Kalina (Kalina Point), now in the centre of Kinshasa, so named after a young Austrian, an officer in the Belgian service, drowned there in December 1883.

Boma: now in Zaïre, 50 miles up-river from the Congo estuary, was at that time the capital of the 'Congo Free State', later the Belgian Congo.

Champel: Champel-les-Bains, on the outskirts of Geneva, where Conrad underwent water therapy in May and June 1891.

15 *Novalis*: pseudonym of the German Romantic writer Friedrich von Hardenberg (1772–1801); this sentence from his *Fragmente* serves also as the epigraph of Conrad's *Lord Jim*.

Cambridge man: William Henry Jacques (1869–93); in 1892/3 he sailed with Conrad on board the *Torrens* from London to Adelaide and back, and died on shore in England.

Torrens: a passenger clipper on board which Conrad served as first mate during two voyages to Australia, from November 1891 to July 1893.

Gibbon's History: *The History of the Decline and Fall of the Roman Empire* (1776–88), by Edward Gibbon (1737–94), a classic work which covers more than thirteen centuries up to the fall of Constantinople in 1453.

dog-watch: one of the two short or half-watches, from 4 to 6 or from 6 to 8 p.m.

19 *Ukraine*: the part of the Ukraine where Conrad's family lived had belonged to the Polish Commonwealth until 1793. In the following reminiscence Conrad telescopes his two visits to his home country: one from February to April 1890, before his stay in the Congo, and the other in August and September 1893.

Gladstone bag: a light travelling bag, named after William Ewart Gladstone (1809–98), the eminent British statesman and Prime Minister.

Koffertäger: porter.

20 *railway station*: Kalinówka (Kalinovka), on the line between Koziatyń (Kazatin) and Winnica.

country house: Kazimierówka, the family estate of Conrad's uncle Tadeusz Bobrowski, near Lipowiec (Lipovec).

factotum: a man-of-all-work.

uncle: Tadeusz Bobrowski (1829–94), Conrad's uncle and guardian, with whom he regularly corresponded and who supported him financially until 1886.

23 *in the year*: in fact, in summer 1863, when Ewa Korzeniowska was allowed to leave Chernigiv in north-eastern Ukraine for three months and travel about 120 miles to her family in Nowochwastów, south-west of Kiev.

permission: in fact, Ewa Korzeniowska had not 'followed' her husband, but had also been sentenced to exile.

eldest brother: Stanisław Bobrowski (1827–59), officer in the hussars of the Tsar's Guard.

24 *Moscow school of journalists*: led by Mikhail Katkov (1818–87), editor of *Moskovskie Viedomosti* and *Russki Viestnik* and a chauvinistic reactionary.

27 *chibouk*: long pipe smoked by the Turks.

28 *Oratow*: in Polish Oratów, the Bobrowskis' family estate in the province of Kiev.

Nicolas B.: Mikołaj Bobrowski (1792–1864), brother of Conrad's grandfather.

aunt: Teofila Bobrowska (1833–51).

34 *father's*: Józef Bobrowski (1790–1850).

man: Apollo Korzeniowski, Conrad's father, whom Ewa Bobrowska met in 1847, nine years before their marriage.

29 *Polish womanhood*: the whole fragment about Conrad's mother and aunt is partly a translation and partly a summary of a fragment in Tadeusz Bobrowski's memoirs (*Pamiętniki*, Lwów 1900, vol. ii, ch. 1). See Introduction.

31 *en suite*: French 'leading from one to another'.

sixty-two: this places the action in 1891.

Officier d'Ordonnance: aide-de camp, an officer who assists a senior commander in the field.

Marshal Marmont: Auguste-Frédéric-Louis Viesse de Marmont (1774–1852), Marshal of France and one of Napoleon's most distinguished commanders.

Congress of Vienna: convened from September 1814 to June 1815 by the allies victorious over Napoleon, it established spheres of influence in Europe and sanctioned the partition of Poland.

de visu: Latin, 'from sight'.

32 *Legion of Honour*: Légion d'honneur, a French order of distinction and reward, instituted by Napoleon in 1802.

Virtuti Militari: 'for military virtue', the highest Polish military decoration, established in 1792.

32 *Man of St. Helena*: after the defeat at Waterloo (18 June 1815) and his surrender to the British government, Napoleon was exiled to the island of St Helena, in the South Atlantic.

Russian campaign: of 1812, begun on a great scale and ending with disaster.

34 *grandmother*: Teofila Bobrowska (?–1875).

la vache enragée: literally 'furious cow'; to eat it means, in French, to suffer misery.

salt junk: salt meat used on long sea voyages, compared to rope.

trepang: a marine animal, considered a luxury by Chinese gourmets.

35 *Pro patria!*: For the sake of his native land! (Latin).

36 *hidalgo*: a gentleman by birth (Spanish); the reference is to the story of Don Quixote de la Mancha, the hero of Miguel de Cervantes' (1547–1616) famous novel.

37 *Louis-Philippe*: (1773–1850); he accepted the French crown in 1830 after the July rebellion against Charles X, and abdicated in 1848 in view of spreading popular discontent with his rule. He lived in exile in England.

1873: Conrad lived at that time in Cracow, where he did not attend school but took regular exams.

39 *tutor*: Adam Pulman (1846–after 1881); he studied medicine in Cracow 1868–75.

Mavis: a small (763 tons) steamer on which Conrad, probably as an unofficial apprentice, travelled in spring 1878 from Marseilles to Lowestoft.

42 *Mr. T. B.*: Tadeusz Bobrowski.

43 *certain reasons*: as a teenager, Conrad suffered from nervous attacks which made school attendance difficult.

pour prendre congé: French, 'to take leave'.

44 *master*: Conrad passed his examination for ordinary Master of the British merchant marine on 10 Nov. 1886, and so more than thirteen years later.

45 *true vocation*: in fact, Pulman never studied philosophy; his medical studies lasted seven years.

A day: between 21 Nov. 1885 and 8 Jan. 1886; Conrad was then second officer on the coal clipper the *Tilkhurst*.

obscure little town: Pulman practised medicine in Sambor, a town south-east of Przemyśl; it is not known when he died.

46 *Friedland*: town in East Prussia, site of a major victory on 14 June 1807 of Napoleon's army over the Russians.

Bar-le-Duc: in the Meuse department in north-eastern France. In January and February 1814 Napoleon's army, retreating towards Paris, fought several battles in this area.

47 *Leipzig*: from 16 to 19 Oct. 1813 the site of a major battle, called the 'battle of the nations' and a decisive defeat for Napoleon, whose army of 185,000 men fought 320,000 allied Austrian, Prussian, Russian, and Swedish troops.

48 *Poniatowski*: Prince Józef Poniatowski (1763–1813), Marshal of France, commanded the Polish troops covering Napoleon's retreat and was killed in the battle.

49 *Hundred Days*: between Napoleon's escape from Elba on 20 Mar. 1815 and his abdication, after the defeat at Waterloo, on 22 June 1815.

relative: Piotr Pilchowski (1771–1862), uncle of Tadeusz Bobrowski's mother.

mother: Katarzyna, born Błażowska.

a man: Leon Staniszewski; the whole story is repeated after T. Bobrowski's memoirs (i. 1).

53 *public school*: in Lubar in Volhynia; it was run by the Dominicans, not the Benedictines, and was neither the only nor the most prestigious one of its kind in this province. Conrad departs here from his uncle's text.

Alexander I: (1777–1825); tsar of Russia 1801–25.

Grand Duke Constantine: Konstantin Pavlovich (1779–1831), younger brother of Alexander I, virtual ruler of the Congress Kingdom of Poland 1815–30.

54 *Nicholas*: (1796–1855); tsar of Russia (as Nicholas I) 1825–55).

not serfs: Polish peasants, although attached to land and subject to the tenure system, were not personally the property of landowners.

1831: in fact, 29 Nov. 1830.

56 *Paris*: the allied armies of Napoleon's opponents entered Paris on 31 March 1814.

last partition of Poland: between Russia, Prussia, and Austria, in 1795.

1863: the insurrection, immediately provoked by a military conscription, broke up on 22 Jan.

57 *paternal grandfather's*: Teodor Korzeniowski (?–1863).

two sons: Robert, killed in the 1863 uprising, and Hilary, who died in exile in 1878.

daughter: Conrad's aunt, whose name remains unknown; she was exiled with her husband for taking part in the 1863 uprising.

Cossacks: light cavalry in the Russian army.

58 *J——*: Jitomir, in Polish Żytomierz, in Ukrainian Zhytomir.

61 *Greek*: Russian Orthodox is meant here.

interior of Russia: in 1839 the tsarist government forcibly abolished the Ukrainian Catholic Church; priests who did not convert to Russian Orthodoxy were expelled and others brought in to replace them.

62 *japanned*: varnished or lacquered in Japanese fashion.

For Valour: i.e. Virtuti Militari; see note to p. 32, above.

65 *'N'oublie pas . . . mon chéri'*: Do not forget your French, my darling.

66 *Great Russia*: i.e. Russia proper, as distinct from Little Russia, the Ukraine.

67 *Bezak*: Alexandr Bezak (1800–68); Conrad repeats the story as reported by Bobrowski, ii. 11.

68 *note of a fact*: this is contradicted by the existence of Conrad's *Congo Diary*, kept in 1890.

69 *Rubicon*: a small river which separated ancient Italy from the province of Cisalpine Gaul. When Julius Caesar, with the words 'the die is cast', crossed it with his legions in 49 BC, he committed himself to a civil war against the Roman Senate.

70 *maid*: Cinderella (literally a little girl of cinders, or ashes).

Victor Hugo: (1802–85); French Romantic poet, novelist (*The Hunchback of Notre Dame*, 1831; *Les Misérables*, 1862, etc.), and dramatist, immensely popular in his time.

71 *'Gil Blas'*: a famous novel of adventure by the French novelist and dramatist Alain-René Le Sage (1668–1747), published in 1715.

'*Nicholas Nickleby*': a novel by Charles Dickens, published in 1839.

translation: never published; the manuscript is also unknown. At the same time Apollo Korzeniowski translated *A Comedy of Errors* and published it in 1866.

T——: Tchernikhov; in Polish Czernihów, in Ukrainian Chernigiv.

72 '*Toilers of the Sea*': Hugo's novel of sea adventures (1866). Korzeniowski's translation has been lost.

in Falmouth: while second mate on board a 427-ton barque, the *Palestine*, immortalized by Conrad in his '*Youth*', from January to September 1882.

oakum: loose fibre, obtained by untwisting old rope.

74 *Almayer*: the hero of Conrad's first novel, *Almayer's Folly* (1895), who also figures in his second, *An Outcast of the Islands* (1896). His prototype was Charles William Olmeijer, a Eurasian Dutchman living in Borneo; but in reality the two had little in common apart from the sound of their names.

steamer: the *Vidar*, a coastal steamer of 204 tons; Conrad served on it as first mate from August 1887 to January 1888, cruising between Singapore and small ports on the shores of Celebes and Borneo.

river: Berau, called also Pantai; the wharf was in Tanjung Redeb (or Tanjungredep).

serang: a native boatswain.

75 *tiffin*: midday meal.

Pulo Laut: Pulau Laut, an island off the south-east shore of Borneo.

Dongola: Donggala, a port in western Celebes.

Captain C——: James Craig (1846–1929), master of the *Vidar*.

taffrail-log: a log mounted on the taffrail (a rail around the stern of a ship), consisting of a rotator, log line, and recording device.

76 *Bali*: an island in Indonesia, east of Java.

77 *bar*: sand or gravel bank on the bed of the river.

derricks: contrivances for hoisting heavy objects.

78 *Tuan*: sir or lord, a form of politeness to superiors in Malay.

kalashes: native East Indian sailors.

80 *Order of the Golden Fleece*: an order of knighthood instituted in 1429 by Philip the Good, Duke of Burgundy; its badge is a golden sheepskin with head and feet attached.

84 *guttah*: gutta-percha, leathery material obtained from the latex of certain trees in Malaysia; used for insulation and in chewing-gum.

85 *some weeks*: Conrad left his ship, the *Highland Forest*, in Semarang (Java) on 1 July, arrived in Singapore five days later, and spent a few weeks in hospital in July and August.

East Coast: of Borneo.

87 *Elysian Fields*: in Greek mythology, the land of happiness after death.

90 *In fact . . . novel or two*: an oblique allusion to the postal reform of 1870, carried out during Gladstone's first premiership. It introduced halfpenny postcards.

Ollendorff: the founder of a method of teaching langauges, popular in the nineteenth century.

92 *French writer*: Anatole France, in *Le Mannequin d'osier* (1897); not an exact quote. See note to p. 95, below.

93 *Chi lo sà?*: Italian, 'Who knows?'

Walrus or the Carpenter: in the well-known verse from *Through the Looking-Glass* (1871) by Lewis Carroll (1832–98), 'The Walrus and the Carpenter / Were walking close at hand / They wept like anything to see / Such quantities of sand'.

Fabians: members of the Fabian Society, an association of intellectuals sympathetic to socialism, founded in 1884.

Kaffirs: South African blacks of the Bantu race.

pro domo: short for *pro domo sua* (Latin), 'for his house', i.e. in his interest.

94 *tant que vous voudrez*: French, 'as much as you want'.

J'ai vécu: I remained alive.

Abbé Sieyès: Emmanuel-Joseph Sieyès (1748–1836), French priest, constitutional theorist, and political pamphleteer.

French Revolution: of 1789; directed initially against the monarchy and aristocracy, it led to much bloody infighting between its original enthusiasts.

95 *Jean Jacques Rousseau*: (1712–78); Swiss-born French thinker, enormously influential through his educational, moral, and political ideas. His self-justifying *Confessions* were published posthumously in 1788.

Émile: Rousseau's famous educational romance (1762), describing the bringing-up of the hero Émile, according to the so-called principles of nature.

Anatole France: pen-name of Jacques Anatole François Thibault (1844–1924), French novelist and essayist, known for his ironical wit.

'failing . . . of ourselves': France, *La Vie littéraire*, vol. ii, p. 177. France repeats this formula in the preface to the third volume, answering Brunetière's article published in the *Revue des deux mondes* in January 1891.

Brunetière: (1849–1906); influential French literary critic.

97 *skittles*: ninepins, a kind of bowling game.

Je vous donne ma parole d'honneur': French, 'I give you my word of honour'.

98 *'Nostromo'*: Conrad finished this novel, which indeed cost him a great effort, in August 1904.

prophet of old: not a 'prophet', but Jacob, who wrestled all night with a man whose identity as God was revealed at daybreak (Genesis 32: 24–30).

99 *round Cape Horn*: such passage runs against the prevailing winds and currents. Conrad sailed around the Horn in summer (i.e. Antarctic winter) 1879, but going eastwards.

100 *quarterdeck*: that part of the upper deck of a vessel which extends between the stern and aftermast, used by the ship's officers.

101 *Costaguana lepero*: Costaguana is the fictitious South American country where the action of Conrad's *Nostromo* takes place; *lepero* is a Mexican proletarian.

103 *Stephen Crane*: (1871–1900); a talented American novelist and short-story writer, who lived in England for the last three

years of his life; he was a friend of Conrad's. 'The Open Boat' (1898) is one of his best stories.

107 *robust man*: most probably Robert Lynd (1879–1949); see Introduction.

109 *definition*: France's famous definition of a good critic, formulated in his Preface to the first volume of *La Vie littéraire* (1888), was one who 'tells the adventures of his soul among masterpieces'.

viva voce: orally, in one's own voice.

111 *short story*: 'Karain', published in *Mercure de France* in November and December 1906.

Gustave Kahn: (1859–1936); French symbolist poet, critic, and editor. He mentioned Conrad in his review of a French translation of George Moore's *Esther Waters*, 'Un réaliste anglais: George Moore', 24 Feb. 1907.

Gil-Blas: French daily newspaper (1879–1914), to which many prominent intellectuals contributed.

un puissant rêveur: a powerful dreamer; Kahn used the expression 'un puissant visionnaire', a powerful visionary.

112 *first of all*: Captain James Rankin, who examined Conrad for second mate, 28 May 1880.

114 *ordeal*: his examination for first mate. Conrad failed the first time, on 17 Nov. 1884, but passed at his second attempt on 3 Dec. 1884. His examiner was Captain P. Thompson.

Giuliano . . . de Medici: in fact, it is the statue of Lorenzo de' Medici (d. 1519), duke of Urbino, represented as Thinker; Michelangelo's famous tomb is in the Medici chapel of the church of San Lorenzo in Florence.

115 *Flying Dutchman*: a legendary spectral ship, doomed never to return to port.

117 *Master*: Conrad failed at his first attempt on 28 July 1886 and was successful the second time, 11 Nov. 1886.

examiner: probably Peter Thompson (1836–1918).

charter-parties: the deeds made between owners and merchants for hiring ships and cargo delivery.

jury-rudder: a makeshift rudder put up in place of one lost or broken.

not really: most of Conrad's sea service was on sailing vessels, but he was also first officer on the steamer *Vidar* and second on the *Adowa*, his last ship.

118 *Crimean War*: between Russia and Turkey and its allies (England, France, and Sardinia), 1854–6.

wire rigging: wires (instead of ropes) employed to support the masts and to manipulate yards and sails.

Mutiny: the 'Sepoy Mutiny', 1857–8, against British rule in India, begun by Indian troops in the service of the British India Company; it caused the transfer of government over India from the Company to the Crown.

119 *British seaman*: biographical evidence does not support Conrad's claim.

name: Komorowski.

121 *Pola*: now Pula, a port in Croatia (Yugoslavia), from 1866 to 1918 the main harbour and naval arsenal of the Austro-Hungarian navy. In reality, Conrad could not have 'found his way' there because until 1886 he remained a Russian subject.

122 *Solary*: Baptistin Solary, friend of Wiktor Chodźko, a Pole who was supposed to look after the young Conrad in Marseilles; he took care of him during his stay in France.

le jeune homme: the young man.

ce métier de chien: this dog's occupation.

123 *Planier*: an islet 10 miles south-west of Marseilles.

le petit ami de Baptistin: Baptistin's little friend.

Château d'If: a rocky islet, with a castle, at the entrance to the port of Marseilles.

124 *bouillabaisse*: traditional Provençal seafood soup.

Madame Delestang: wife of Jean-Baptiste Delestang, a cousin of Solary's and the owner of a shipping firm.

125 *haute bourgeoisie*: upper middle class.

Royalist: support of the restoration of the monarchy in France; legitimist.

Henri Quatre: Henri IV (1553–1610), king of France 1589–1610, the first of the Bourbon dynasty; he brought the country peace and prosperity after its religious wars.

Louis Quatorze: Louis XIV (1638–1715), king of France 1643–1715, her greatest autocratic monarch.

Monsieur de Colbert: Jean-Baptiste Colbert (1619–83), minister of finance to Louis XIV and a great administrator who modernized the French navy.

'Venez donc . . . nous': Then come for a ride with us.

'C'est ça . . . jeune homme': That's it. Come on, climb up, young man.

126 *'Il faut . . . sa vie'*: Nevertheless, one should take care not to waste one's life.

127 *Vieux Port*: the oldest part of Marseilles, its port from the seventh century BC to the middle of the nineteenth century.

December: probably in 1875.

128 *Joliette*: the modern port of Marseilles.

129 *Coquin de sort!*: a southern French oath.

patron: chief.

'Hé, l'ami. Comment va?': Hey, friend. How goes it?

'Larguez': Let go.

avant-port: outer harbour.

131 *Equipages de ligne*: naval crews.

134 *Notre Dame de la Garde*: a basilica, built in the mid nineteenth century in Roman-Byzantine style on the top of a steep hill.

135 *James Westoll*: the *James Mason*, a steamer which entered Marseilles on 10 Dec. 1875, seems the only plausible real model for the ship of Conrad's reminiscence.

136 *Jacobs*: William Wymark Jacobs (1863–1943), a popular English short-story writer.

THE WORLD'S CLASSICS

A Select List

The Portrait of a Lady
Edited by Nicola Bradbury
With an introduction by Graham Greene

Roderick Hudson
With an introduction by Tony Tanner

The Spoils of Poynton
Edited by Bernard Richards

Washington Square
Edited by Mark Le Fanu

What Maisie Knew
Edited by Douglas Jefferson

The Wings of the Dove
Edited by Peter Brooks

RUDYARD KIPLING: The Day's Work
Edited by Thomas Pinney

The Jungle Book (in two volumes)
Edited by W. W. Robson

Kim
Edited by Alan Sandison

Life's Handicap
Edited by A. O. J. Cockshut

The Man Who Would be King and Other Stories
Edited by Louis L. Cornell

Plain Tales From the Hills
Edited by Andrew Rutherford

Stalky & Co.
Edited by Isobel Quigly

WALTER PATER: Marius the Epicurean
Edited by Ian Small

Dr. Wortle's School
Edited by John Halperin

The Duke's Children
Edited by Hermione Lee

The Eustace Diamonds
Edited by W. J. McCormack

Framley Parsonage
Edited by P. D. Edwards

He Knew he was Right
Edited by John Sutherland

Is He Popenjoy?
Edited by John Sutherland

The Kelly's and the O'Kelly's
Edited by W. J. McCormack
With an introduction by William Trevor

The Last Chronicle of Barset
Edited by Stephen Gill

Orley Farm
Edited by David Skilton

Phineas Finn
Edited by Jacques Berthoud

Phineas Redux
Edited by John C. Whale
Introduction by F. S. L. Lyons

The Prime Minister
Edited by Jennifer Uglow
With an introduction by John McCormick

The Small House at Allington
Edited by James R. Kincaid

The Warden
Edited by David Skilton

The Way We Live Now
Edited by John Sutherland

VILLIERS DE L'ISLE-ADAM: Cruel Tales
Translated by Robert Baldick
Edited by A. W. Raitt

VIRGIL: The Aeneid
Translated by C. Day Lewis
Edited by Jasper Griffin

The Eclogues and The Georgics
Translated by C. Day Lewis
Edited by R. O. A. M. Lyne

HORACE WALPOLE: The Castle of Otranto
Edited by W. S. Lewis

IZAAK WALTON and CHARLES COTTON:
The Compleat Angler
Edited by John Buxton
With an introduction by John Buchan

A complete list of Oxford Paperbacks, including The World's Classics, Twentieth-Century Classics, OPUS, Past Masters, Oxford Authors, Oxford Shakespeare, and Oxford Paperback Reference, is available in the UK from the General Publicity Department (JH), Oxford University Press, Walton Street, Oxford OX2 6DP.

In the USA, complete lists are available from the Paperbacks Marketing Manager, Oxford University Press, 200 Madison Avenue, New York, NY 10016.

Oxford Paperbacks are available from all good bookshops. In case of difficulty, customers in the UK can order direct from Oxford University Press Bookshop, Freepost, 116 High Street, Oxford, OX1 4BR, enclosing full payment. Please add 10 per cent of published price for postage and packing.

2919